DEPTHS
OF
DESTINY

THE MAXWELL CHRONICLES

DEPTHS OF DESTINY

MICHAEL PHILLIPS

MOODY PRESS

CHICAGO

ISBN: 0-8024-6319-3

1 3 5 7 9 10 8 6 4 2

Printed in the United States of America

Dedicated to

The future evangelists and leaders and wall-builders of the next generation of God's people, the Joshuas and Nehemiahs who will take the land and build the walls up around its cities . . .

Those seeking full evangelism, a complete rather than partial message of life, to spread to those to whom the Father sends them, who will take the gospel unto all the world in preparation for the coming of the King,

and to
George Yacoubian,

in whose office and around whose "seat of learning" Depths of Destiny *first took form and substance.*

Books by Michael Phillips

Building Respect, Responsibility, and Spiritual Values
  in Your Child
Getting More Done in Less Time
George MacDonald, Scotland's Beloved Storyteller

The Maxwell Chronicles
  Pinnacles of Power
  Depths of Destiny

The Journals of Corrie Belle Hollister (with Judith Pella)
  My Father's World
  Daughter of Grace
  On the Trail of the Truth
  A Place in the Sun
  Sea to Shining Sea
  Into the Long Dark Night

The Russians (with Judith Pella)
  The Crown and the Crucible
  A House Divided
  Travail and Triumph

The Stonewycke Trilogy and Legacy (with Judith Pella)
  The Heather Hills of Stonewycke
  Flight from Stonewycke
  The Lady of Stonewycke
  Stranger at Stonewycke
  Shadows over Stonewycke
  Treasure of Stonewycke

The Highland Collection (with Judith Pella)
  Jamie MacLeod: Highland Lass
  Robbie Taggart: Highland Sailor

About the Author

MICHAEL PHILLIPS is one of today's prolific and versatile Christian authors. As an editor (chiefly of the works of George MacDonald), he has produced some thirty titles. As a co-author (with Judith Pella), his Stonewycke, Highland, Russians, and Corrie Belle Hollister historical series number seventeen books. In addition, Phillips has written twelve books on his own, and as a publisher has produced still another score of titles. His books, with total sales of more than three million, have won a number of awards, have appeared on numerous best seller lists, have been chosen upon repeated occasions as book club selections, and have been translated into several foreign languages.

Phillips, 45, was raised in northern California, and educated at Humboldt State University. President of One Way, Ltd., which operates a publishing company as well as retail bookstores, Phillips has been active in all phases of the Christian bookselling and publishing industry for more than twenty years. He and his wife, Judy, make their home in Eureka, California, with their three sons, Patrick, Gregory, and Robin.

CENTRAL EUROPE

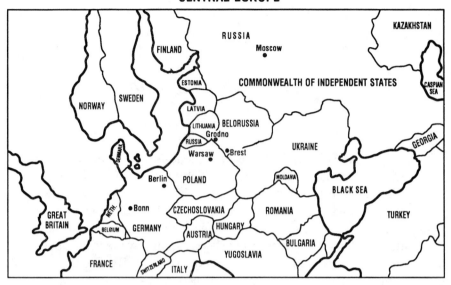

DETAILS OF ESCAPE ROUTE

Cast of Characters

Jackson Maxwell—reporter for *Christian World Magazine*
Jacob Michaels—head of Evangelize the World (ETW)
Hamilton Jaeger—president of Evangelical Unity Unlimited (EU)
Robert Means—Michaels's friend and associate in ETW
Sondra DeQue—press secretary and spokeswoman for ETW
Elizabeth Michaels—Jacob's wife

At the Conference

Anthony Powers—organizer of Berlin Conference on Evangelism in the post-Cold War era, head of Students Committed to World Evangelism (SCWE)
Owen Bradford—speaker at conference, founder of OBU University and Deeper Life Training Center
Sandra Black—co-founder Countdown Ministries
Carson Mitchell—speaker at conference, head of Sonburst Ministries, noted author
Bob MacPatrick—speaker at conference, Christian media giant, author, and fund-raiser
Trevor McVey—conference panelist, Pilgrim Institute
Dieder Palacki—outspoken Polish Christian leader, fiery speaker at conference

In the West

Heinrich and Marla Folenweiter—Jackson's West German friends, farmers
Gentz Raedenburg—German Lutheran church official, speaker at conference
Klaus Drexler—German politician, head of SDP party in German Bundestag, allied with Desyatovsky

9

Hans Kolter—chancellor of Germany, head of CDU party

Gerhardt Woeniger—leader of minority CSDU part in German Bundestag

Dmitri Rostovchev—originator of *Das Christliche Netzwerk*

In the East

Udo Bietmann—East German Christian leader of small group of dedicated believers

Andrassy Papovich Galanov—KGB spy and persecutor of Christians in pre-Gorbachev Russia and satellite countries, assistant to KGB chief

Leonid Bolotnikov—head of KGB in pre-Gorbachev Russia, currently attached to military in Russian republic

Bludayev Desyatovsky—Russian Defense Minister in new regime, secretly allied with Drexler

Dan Davidson—American spy in Russia, code named "Blue Doc"

Yaschak—unscrupulous Russian bureaucrat

Marta Pavlovna Repninka—filing assistant for Desyatovsky in Moscow

Yuri Pavlovich Repninka—factory worker in Kiev, brother of Marta

The world is not saved en masse. It is one by one we enter life in the first birth, and one by one through which we pass through the kingdom's doors in the second. No programs of mass evangelism can widen those narrow gates or shove crowds of humanity through them more quickly. Soul by single soul does the brotherhood of God's family expand its number.

—Depths of Destiny

All authority in heaven and on earth has
been given to me. Therefore go and make
disciples of men in all nations, baptizing
them in the name of the Father and of
the Son and of the Holy Spirit, and
teaching them to obey all the commands
I have given you. And surely I am with
you always, to the very end of time.
—Matthew 28:18-20

PROLOGUE

Secrets Behind the Curtain
1984

1

With uncanny precision the black Mercedes roared through the eerie night.

The narrow, half-paved back roads through the Brandenburger Wald southeast of the city scarcely widened in some spots beyond the breadth of the vehicle itself. But the man at the wheel had driven this route before. Though more than sixteen hundred kilometers separated him from his home, he still considered Poland and the DDR his turf. Galanov knew all the escape routes like the back of his hand.

He had been tracking the moves of the network for two weeks now—from eastern Poland, across the border near Eisenhuttenstadt, and finally here—to the moment of final showdown. He knew they considered their present charge an important one. No old woman wanting to see loved ones in the West, no idealistic student hoping for a so-called better life. This time they had a big fish in tow. The biggest! Their own leader—the man who had set up *Das Christliche Netzwerk* years ago in the early Brezhnev days. And he, Galanov, stood ready to drop the net over his arch rival who had evaded the rest of the KGB for more than fifteen years!

For this confrontation his superior had sent him west three weeks ago with his own personal vendetta against the Christian leader hanging in the balance.

"You get him, Galanov, do you hear me?" he could still hear the furious voice shouting across the cornfield. "I want him! Don't show your face again if you return empty-handed!"

A quick glance back revealed Leonid Bolotnikov, the top agent of the empire, pistol in hand, standing over the dead peasant's body, fist lifted in rage, as the three men they'd trailed half the night disappeared into the surrounding wood.

Minutes later the revving of an automobile engine sounded

through the trees. They had been outmaneuvered. A night of pursuit lost! Even as the escape vehicle sped away and the sound faded into the distance, in his ears echoed further angry shouts from his director. "After him! Don't let him get to Berlin, or you'll rot in Siberia!"

The kingpin of the underground network—the man they called *Der Prophet*—had eluded them, for the present.

Within an hour of the failed capture, a car bearing Galanov careened recklessly southwest toward Minsk. He had crossed into Poland early the next afternoon, and reestablished contacts in Warsaw that night. It had taken several days to sniff out the cooled trail of *Das Netzwerk*'s moves. But once he had picked up the unmistakable clues of their presence, everything confirmed that indeed his quarry was close to his grasp. He had smelled the urgency in their movements immediately. After questioning his own operatives, he knew that only hours ahead of him they were passing *Der Prophet* from hand to hand along the very underground circuit that the fugitive himself had established.

And steadily Galanov drew closer.

This time no hole in the system would allow the man to escape. He would ensnare him! No screwups! Tonight destiny would shine its face upon him. He would deliver the hated and troublesome apostle into the hand of his chief. No one would get out—especially not the so-called *Prophet*. Galanov would kill if he had to. But he would not let the man into the West.

His headlamps danced about, sending luminescent beams into the thick clumps of pines bordering the way on each side. Like menacing eyes probing the blackness, with every bend and twist of the road they sought their prey with fiendish divination

Behind the wheel, his foot nearly to the floor, sat the latter-day Saul who considered himself guardian of the reputation of the Committee of State Security, otherwise known as the KGB. Even as the lights of his car glared into the night, his own eyes glistened with the evil fire of their dark intent. If only he could do what the KGB chief himself had failed at! Promotion would be his. Perhaps a position in the Kremlin—maybe as Bolotnikov's top assistant or some other high post in Chairman Chernenko's government.

It won't be long now, he thought as the automobile raced along.

No other noise sounded for miles. The night remained empty and black. Respectable people had taken to their beds hours ago. In this region so close to the border nothing but trouble could come to one caught abroad after midnight.

2

In another part of the same district of Brandenburg, two darkly clad individuals hastened along. They had left Fürstenwalde by foot, walking some three kilometers to a solitary barn far removed from any human abode in the middle of one of the collective's expansive wheat fields.

The man in front puffed from the effort, for they strode with long and quickly paced steps. He baked bread and rolls and sweets for the village by day, and in truth carried a few kilograms more than was good for him. By night he did the network's business and did it bravely in spite of the exertion—and the hazards.

Behind him followed a tall, strongly built man of some forty-five years, though darkness rendered certainty of age difficult. Herr Brotbacker had heard of *Der Prophet* and had even picked up vague rumors that hard times had befallen the Russian patriarch. A plan was said to be in place to get him out, but as to specifics no one in any of the neighboring fellowships knew anything. He had no idea that the man he now led across the grainfields to Brother Herman's old deserted barn was none other than he who had smuggled behind the Curtain the very Bible the baker so treasured, stashed in his small apartment under the bed where his wife now slept.

Neither man had spoken since leaving the lights of town.

Finding their way inside the structure of the barn, now decaying from disuse under East Germany's communal farming system, the German bread-maker assisted his silent Russian brother aboard an aging wooden wagon, already hitched to a sturdy plow horse. Still without sound of human voice to disturb the sleeping night, he

17

walked across the packed dirt floor and opened the large door, kept well oiled and thus without so much as a creak in spite of its age. Farmer Herman, already waiting atop the wagon with leather reins in hand, clicked his tongue, urging his faithful equine collaborator into motion. The baker closed the door behind them. As the clomping footfall of the horse and the groan of the wagon's wheels faded across the field, he began the walk back to town. He would be able to catch about two hours' sleep before the morning ovens and loaves demanded his attention. Now the mysterious traveler bounced slowly along in the hands of the farmer, who would pass him on at the next rendezvous point to someone neither Brotbacker nor Herman had ever met.

Thus did *Das Christliche Netzwerk* operate. No one knew much. Words remained as few as possible. A look, a brief smile, the scantest of necessary instructions, perhaps a parting nod. Carrying on the work remained the vital imperative—preserving the chain, keeping strong its links, protecting God's people. The less each knew of what his brothers and sisters of the underground did, the safer for all. The last decade and a half had brought welcome change and eased restrictions since the days of Khrushchev and Brezhnev. But lives still could be lost. Shootings occurred at the wall with continued regularity. Caution remained a matter of life and death.

Two and a half hours later, the lone pilgrim, a stranger in the hands of his brothers, weary now from night after night of intermittent and tedious travel, having slept but fitfully in the back of the wagon before being passed along again several times from one silent accomplice to the next, approached a small clearing in the wood where two dirt roads intersected.

A faint flicker of light shone through the darkness, then disappeared. It was the sign by which the man who had the sojourner in tow—neither baker nor farmer this time, but in fact a converted local Communist official attached to the constabulary—knew that his leg of the clandestine itinerary had come to an end. He had never seen the face behind the brief flash of light, nor would he—for the protection of all. At this juncture came the final hand-off, and vulnerability mounted the closer they came to the border.

"Come with me—quickly." From behind the tiny penlight, a hand reached across through the night to clutch that of the nomadic evangelist, who noticed that two persons had come to meet him. The second, slighter of build and shorter of stature, stood a little behind the man who had spoken. The man's daughter, fifteen and already active in the network's activities for years, had begged to accompany him.

The official turned to retrace his steps to his own home, while the man of God continued with the other and his daughter. He heard but a few words more and did not hesitate in his return through the trees. They were on their own now. *God be with them,* he silently breathed.

"Make haste," whispered the voice to the refugee. "We must get you to the safehouse in the city before dawn."

With that, the three hurried the pace of their steps, father and daughter leading the man for whose escape already so many had risked so much.

3

An hour and twenty minutes later, father, daughter, and prophet exited the cover of trees through which their path had taken them. The first gray hints of dawn made the horizon faintly visible in the east, though the protection of darkness still covered them.

They were close now!

Safety lay but twenty minutes further. The contact who would guide them to the city probably already crouched in wait someplace on the opposite side of the large field they had just entered.

In the distance the sound of a car's engine came into hearing.

Indistinct at first, gradually it loudened. The leader of the trio stopped briefly, listened, then quickened his pace. The automobile bore in their direction—and fast. It probably meant nothing. They must make every second count nonetheless. If nothing else, the approaching car signaled that the end of their cloak of night came nearer every second.

The huge car rounded a curve, and suddenly headlights blazed above them in the air.

The small band broke into full flight across the barren pastureland. No hope of cover lay anywhere. At the far end, a solitary figure had risen from a hollow and now stood helpless, watching in mute agony as the most feared of all nightmares played itself out before him. Silently he prayed, tears rising in his eyes.

The three fugitives sprinted courageously, measuring half the distance to him. But it was too late. Their persecutor had spotted them, and the enormous Mercedes rumbled over the flat dirt, bouncing high over the ruts with the wild fearlessness of an army tank, spotlighting the fleeing forms ahead of it in naked exposure of their helplessness.

Another ten seconds—the chase took no longer. The revving engine screamed by them, then sputtered into silence as the machine skidded a half-circular arc in front of the tiny company. It cut them off, sending a choking cloud of gritty dust all about, momentarily dimming the headlamps. Even before the Mercedes came to its final stop, its door flew open and the driver burst out onto the turf, automatic pistol brandished, eyes aglow in the intoxication of at long last outwitting the Christians he despised.

A silence, pregnant with supressed passions, followed. Only the laboring lungs of the three renegades broke the stillness of the dusty air. They stood as still as statues while their adversary inspected them from head to toe.

Slowly, a cunning smile spread over his face.

"So, Rostovchev," he said at length, speaking in Russian, "it *is* you they call *Der Prophet*. I suspected as much."

"We meet again, Comrade Galanov," replied the tallest of the three. He did not return the smile, yet his tone hinted nowhere of hatred. It was the first time the East German and his daughter had heard the voice of the man they had been attempting to lead to safety.

"Under less than pleasant circumstances for you, I must say," replied the agent, punctuating his words with a wave of his gun. The smile, still on his face, gave evidence that he enjoyed this moment of his triumph.

"Danger comes with walking as a Christian."

"Bah! And foolishness along with it!" The smile vanished.

"In the eyes of the world, I suppose, it must look that way."

"Always preaching, eh, Dmitri?" rejoined the other sarcastically. "Well, no matter," he added. "It would seem I have you checkmated at last. My chief will be pleased to see you again."

"I doubt Leonid Bolotnikov is capable of feeling pleasure," replied the one called Rostovchev. "Hatred too thoroughly consumes him. Though no doubt seeing me dead would give him an evil kind of satisfaction."

"I am sure it will."

"And you as well?"

"Let's just say that I shall provide it for him."

A momentary pause followed.

"Tell me, Andrassy," said Rostovchev, "when did you take up the KGB's cause again? I understood you had gone to work for the British."

A huge laugh bellowed from Galanov's throat. It revealed glistening white teeth in a face that under any other circumstances would have been considered well sculpted. But the traitorous glare of his eyes undid the attraction. Even the most cursory of glances confirmed this man as one to stay away from. On his head shone a thick crop of healthy, red-orange hair, rumpled and unkempt from his frenzied night behind the wheel.

"The British!" he repeated, still laughing. "Morons every one! Ja, ja, Comrade Prophet, they think I work for them, because I turn over something insignificant every couple of months. Fools—they're the easiest of all to double-deal in this game!"

"So you're still a KGB man at heart."

"I am a Russian."

"Can't say I'm surprised."

"Bolotnikov pays better than the British too," said Galanov, chuckling again.

"You really ought to give our side a try, Andrassy."

"You're as Russian as I."

"I meant our Christian side," he said, staring deeply into the agent's eyes with a heart full of compassion.

The other hesitated a moment, returning the stare, then seemed to shake himself free from its spell. "Bah!" he snapped.

"You just might find that there's more to what we believe than—"

21

"None of your sermons!" snapped the KGB agent.

"It's about life, Andrassy. Nothing but death results from the tangled game you play."

"Shut up, Rostovchev!"

"It's you I'm concerned for, Andrassy. I only wanted to say—"

"Enough of this ridiculous drivel!" interrupted Galanov again. "Death will result, just as you say—yours!"

"Whether I live or die is in His hands."

"We've wasted enough time pretending as friends!" retorted Galanov with disdain. "You know how it works, Rostovchev. Into the car, and your two spying friends with you. It'll be the firing squad for you, the gulag for them!"

"Please. These two are innocent of any crime. They are Germans. Let them go."

Again Galanov laughed. "Let them go free—so they can continue helping our enemies escape into West Berlin!"

"Christians are not your enemy," said the evangelist sadly.

"What kind of fool do you take me for? Bolotnikov would shoot me if I returned to tell him a wave of compassion had come over me and I had let the kingpin of *Das Netzwerk* go free. Now come, all three of you—into the car!"

Dmitri Rostovchev slowly began to make his way forward in the glare of the headlights. As he did, the East German who had remained silent thus far spoke hurriedly to his daughter, hoping the KGB agent would have difficulty hearing their soft voices.

"Geh, Tochter!" he said. "Schnell—mit dem Prophet. Ein Mann wartet dahinten im Feld. Lauf, Tochter!"

The girl hesitated. "Nein, Papa—du musst auch mit," she replied in a pleading voice.

"Ich folge," he answered. "It is still dark enough. In a few paces you will be out of sight. Run to the man waiting on the other side of the field!"

Suddenly he lurched forward in front of the prophet. Before the surprised man of God knew what was happening, he found himself shoved with strong arms into the darkness, away from the two beams of the Mercedes.

"Geh, Tochter!" he cried. "Take him and run!"

Without further hesitation, the girl obeyed, gripping the hand of Rostovchev and yanking him after her.

"Stop!" cried Galanov, hardly aware of what had happened until it was too late. His eyes had grown accustomed to the visibility provided by the lights of his car. All at once he realized he could see only the ridiculous German standing there. Dmitri and the girl had disappeared!

He advanced in a rage, crying out for them to stop. "Don't make me shoot, Rostovchev!" he shouted. "You only make it harder on your—"

But further words did not come from his lips. With unexpected swiftness the German sprang forward with a powerful lunge and threw himself upon the KGB agent, knocking him to the ground.

Momentarily stunned by the assault, Galanov crawled to his knees, then sought his gun in the dirt. The next instant a punishing kick from the German's boot sent the pistol across the ground. Galanov screamed in pain, cursing with vehement anger.

The German bolted after his daughter and the prophet.

"Stop, Rostovchev!" cried Galanov behind them, as he sought his feet and scanned about frantically for his gun. "You can't get across the border, not now! I'll alert the guards. Come back or I'll kill you all!"

Still the three ran, though separated, toward the contact they had seen earlier.

Seconds went by. Only the muffled thudding of feet broke the silence.

Suddenly explosions of gunfire rang through the morning air. More shouts from the enraged Galanov, whose footsteps now pursued the fleeing Christians.

Sharp reports from the automatic pistol continued to ring out in rapid-fire succession. A cry. The sound of a fall. Running footsteps. More shots.

All at once the gunfire stopped. Stillness descended over the field, but only briefly. Without warning, the engine of the Mercedes turned over, then revved to full throttle. The next instant it tore across the field in the direction Galanov had last seen his foes heading.

Lying motionless on his belly in the grass, the German who had imperiled his own life for his brother heard the car rumble past about thirty feet to his right. Slowly he rose to his feet.

But he did not walk far. In the gathering light of pre-dawn

he could make out a form lying ahead of him.

The Mercedes rampaged into the distance its driver maniacally flying after what turned out to be a stray cow at the far border of the pasture. By the time he discovered his fatal error and spun the huge car around, not a single sign of life met his eyes. The man he had come west to capture already lay hiding in a culvert, safely in the hands of the waiting emissary.

And in another corner of the field, hidden by grass tall enough to keep him out of sight, a German father knelt over the body of his only daugther, weeping bitter tears of anguish and grief.

But even in his season of severest earthly trial, the words of his whispered prayers of agony rose heavenward not only for his daughter or for his wife or for himself. They had all chosen the perilous road where faith had to be put on the line daily, knowing that in this region of the world, martyrdom was no mere ancient myth from the days of early Christendom but a present reality. They knew the sacrifces that could be exacted from them.

"O God, O God!" he whispered from depths of the spirit known but to a holy few. "God, my Father, forgive the man they call Galanov for his great sin against Your name and Your people. Put forgiveness and compassion in my heart toward—"

His words broke off. Convulsive moans of silent lament shook his manly frame. He lay his head upon the girl's chest, still warm from the life so recently extinguished and wept the tears of a father giving over his only child into the hands of the Father of them both.

PART 1

Assignment: Berlin

4

Readying for takeoff never lost its thrill.

The airport stimulated one's senses—businessmen with brief-cases, broadcast messages, foreign tongues, uniformed pilots, and three-piece suits lending an air of sophistication, everyone wide-eyed with the anticipation of travel—the place reeked with the sensation that important goings-on were in the wind. Every overheard call at the bank of pay phones gave snatches of world-significant conversation. Being in the midst of it elevated your perceptions, drawing you subliminally into the fancy that you too were part of it all—an intrinsic element in some daring, unspoken plot, an enterprise upon which the fate of the world hinged.

It was all make-believe, of course. Yet the very ambiance of the place contradicted reason, telling you that maybe it *was* true—and *you* possessed the key, the clue all those other people were looking for.

And the final level of intoxication arrived the moment you had stowed your bags securely above and below and had eased into your seat, glanced out the window, and sighed with satisfaction. You had eluded them all and had made it safely to the plane. You could relax until time for phase two of the operation at the other end.

Jackson Maxwell exhaled deeply with contentment. He supposed that if he had to fly every week or two his enthusiasm would quickly wear thin from the fatiguing pattern. But it remained uncommon enough that he could savor it fully every time. Especially a rare international flight.

It never failed to inject him with the exhilaration of walking into the middle of adventure. Maybe he was only an unknown writer for an obscure Christian publication. Yet his pulse quickened, his imagination soared. Faraway places, intrigue, mystery, romance. He was John Wayne, Indiana Jones, or James Bond in disguise. Who could tell what might be awaiting him once they touched down in Tangier or Monaco or Istanbul, and he stepped onto the tarmac to discover—

"We'll be in the air soon now," the voice beside him interrupted his fanciful reverie.

Pulling his daydreaming gaze away from the window and back to the plane, Jackson turned toward his father. "Yeah." He nodded with a smile. "Hard to believe we'll be across the Atlantic in less than twelve hours."

"I'm glad you talked me into coming," said Jacob.

"Entirely selfish." Jackson laughed. "As much as I've itched to see what Germany's like after reunification, the thought of attending the convention alone didn't exactly rivet my senses. Besides, seeing sights by yourself is no fun."

"I hope I won't disappoint you."

"No chance. We'll have a great time."

"Anyway, thanks for not giving up on me so easily. Now I'm happy about my decision to come."

"Even though you have to speak?" asked Jackson.

"That was part of Tony's invitation."

"You could have attended as a spectator, just like me."

"It's only one session. And I suppose I have to accept the fact that I am still Jacob Michaels, however much I may have changed inside."

"Made any more progress on your speech?"

Jacob shrugged. "Not much." He thought for a moment.

"I have to tell you," he went on, "I'm feeling a little gun-shy about standing up in front of such a big gathering of Christian leaders."

"You mean embarrassment over what happened?" asked Jackson.

"I'm not sure it's exactly embarrassment. I think I've dealt with that end of it. I've been publicly open enough to shatter my pride."

"Presumption then?"

"I imagine that's part of it. Who am I, after all—chief of sinners, in Paul's words—to be so pompous as to give my views on such an important topic, one about which I'm only now discovering how little I know?"

"But that's not the root of discomfort either, is it?"

"I do feel presumptuous," replied Jacob. "But on a deeper level it has more to do with the kind of person I'm becoming."

"The less-public image?"

"Exactly! I haven't spoken once since—you know, since everything broke last year. After all those years in the spotlight, now I find myself becoming a quiet and private man within my heart and mind, where I live."

"Can you convey that?"

"You know these gatherings—there's so much hoopla and so many people with their own agendas that the personal messages aren't the ones anybody pays much attention to."

"You're not just some guy off the street. They'll listen to what you have to say."

"I never listened when I was on the other side of the fence!" Jacob laughed ironically. "I sponsored enough of these things myself—I ought to know what the prevailing mentality is."

"Maybe you have a point," agreed Jackson.

"They want to be roused. That's why they come—for motivation, a shot in the arm—so they can go home with a feeling of being able to conquer the world for Christ. Quiet reflection and reevaluation—they're just not part of the scenario. I'm sure everyone will expect a standard ETW oration on evangelism a la the old Jacob Michaels. They'll think I've slipped a cog or two once I start speaking. I wonder if anyone will really hear what I'm trying to say."

"What *are* you going to say?"

"Ah," replied Jacob with a knowing grin, "I can't divulge that—even to my own son. You'll have to wait and hear it along with everyone else!" Immediately, however, his face turned serious again. "To tell you the truth," he went on, "I have no idea."

"No idea? I thought you told me last week that you had the speech roughed out."

"I've had a half-dozen outlines on paper." Jacob sighed. "And so far every one of them has ended up in the trash can."

"That bad?"

"Actually, I think the process is good—not for getting a speech written, but for me personally. I began to write a speech on evangelism. But the more I thought about it, the more I found myself reevaluating the views I've held all my life. It's been a learning and growing experience. And yet I'm nowhere near any solid conclusions. As I read the Scriptures and pray, all the old is being stripped away, but as yet there's no new to replace it. I'm praying that while we're in Berlin the Lord will show me how it fits together."

"If your views and ideas are changing and you're pessimistic about anyone listening, why did you accept the invitation?"

"I don't know." Jacob sighed. "Probably because you were covering the conference. And Bob thought it would be good for me, stimulating me even further in the things I've been wrestling with."

"That does sound like Bob." Jackson chuckled.

" 'You might as well jump into the middle of it,' he said, 'if you're serious about finding the deeper purposes of evangelism.' His reasoning made sense. So here I am en route to the conference but still trying to figure out what evangelism *is*."

"And scheduled to speak on the last night to top it off!"

"That's the perplexing part," said Jacob. "Why me? Why now? Yet—if someone does hear what I say, even if it's only one man or woman, and if he or she acts on something I say about true gospel-evangelism, the impact could be enormous for the cause of Christ. You know what it says about the day of small beginnings. So I have to hope that this quandary will be just that—a small beginning from which something good will grow in the end."

The sound of the captain's voice over the plane's intercom broke off their conversation. It was followed by the first movements of the 747 as it backed away from the gate, then began making its way across acres of pavement toward the runway. As they proceeded, the German-accented voice of the stewardess gave seat belt, oxygen mask, and other information procedures.

Within ten minutes the deafening jet engines were lifting the plane at a steep angle into the sky above Chicago's O'Hare. The next minute the 747 began its bank eastward over Lake Michigan.

5

By the time Jackson Maxwell and Jacob Michaels resumed their conversation, Lufthansa flight 431 for Frankfurt had approached its cruising altitude of 37,000 feet. They loosened their seat belts and sipped the coffee they had just been served.

The father and son had only known one another some two years, and intimately even less than that. Raised as the adopted son of an Illinois farm couple in the southern part of the state, Jackson had been writing for several years for *Christian World Magazine* and its sister newspaper, the *National Profile.* In the process of routinely researching the expanding global ministry of Evangelize the World, Inc., he had uncovered information that had changed the life of ETW's head, renowned evangelist Jacob Michaels, not the least of which was the astonishing revelation that Jackson was in fact his own son.

Thus, at thirty-two and fifty-five, Jackson Maxwell and Jacob Michaels had discovered in each other the father and son neither had known he had. And now in the trying crucible of the public spotlight, they were attempting to forge a relationship of growth, friendship, love, and mutual respect. In the process the faith of both men was deepening, and renewal and fresh life breathed throughout the entire fabric of ETW and the Michaels family.

They had made as yet no public announcement of their relationship. Maxwell had written up the story for *Christian World,* and the friendship that had sprung up between the journalist and the "new" Jacob Michaels was no secret. But that was as far as it went outside the immediate confines of the Michaels and Maxwell families and the handful of intimate friends who had been deeply involved in the events of the previous year.

Their invitations to attend the Berlin conference had come separately. Michaels himself had participated in more conventions and symposiums and panel discussions on evangelism than he could remember. His reputation as one of the most well-known evangelists of the last twenty years insured that his voice carried loud and far whenever the Great Commission of Mark 16:15 was the topic. Even though he had canceled all scheduled appearances for more than a year and stepped completely out of the limelight, most of the Christian evangelical community still thought of his name as synonomous with worldwide soul-winning endeavors where the salvation of thousands was the result.

Now that the financial scandal disclosed by Jackson's investigation had begun to fade, many found themselves wondering when Jacob Michaels would resume his former position of prominence. Unlike other Christian leaders rocked by tarnishing stains on their reputations, Michaels's long-term respectability did not seem to have been destroyed by the disclosure. If anything, because of the straightforward integrity with which he had handled them, in some circles he was held in just as high repute as before. If not perfect, he was at least seen as honest. And his behavior had won him a certain admiration. The request to address the conference in Berlin as one of its featured speakers was the result of the renewed interest in the man many said had seen as many mass conversions to the Lord as any evangelist alive.

I hope they know what they're getting themselves into, mused Michaels after hanging up the phone with Powers. *I don't think he or anyone else realizes how much I've changed. I'm not sure I know myself how much.*

Jackson had not even been aware of the *Berlin Conference on Evangelism in the Post Cold War Era* until his editor, Bob McClanahan, had asked him to attend on behalf of the *World.* Having itched for an opportunity to return to Germany after spending time there briefly during his years at Wheaton College, Jackson leaped at the chance. A few days later he learned of Jacob's invitation and immediately undertook to talk his father into going with him.

6

"Listen to this," said Jackson, who had been perusing the latest issue of *Time,* which he'd nabbed from the magazine bin on his way into the cabin. "We picked some time to go to Europe!"

"What's going on?" asked Jacob.

"The same thing that's been going on for the last three or four years—change. Everything is turning upside-down. Listen to this article by Lance Talbote. It's called 'Europe in the Throes of Silent Revolution.'

"The result of people and nations squeezing closer, pushing against one another, is either conflict or unity. The world has seen more than enough of the former—now suddenly the latter appears to be flowering.

"With the remarkable events of the 1980s, culminating in the toppling of the Berlin Wall in 1989, the reunification of Germany in 1990, and the dismantling of the Warsaw Pact and Soviet Union in 1991, a new revolution in Europe began. It was unlike any that had preceded it, unlike any the world has seen before. Not only was this new European revolution nearly bloodless, it was a revolution of unity rather than disparity—a revolution that said, 'We lay down hostilities and join *with* you,' rather than, 'We are taking up arms to fight against you.'

"Indeed, with the end of the Cold War, the first truly global revolution began. A revolution of peace is shaking the very foundations of the world. And with the new political alignments, new spiritual awakenings are alive as well, offering charity and perhaps even cosmic focus to this new age of harmony."

Jackson put down the magazine and grew pensive.

"Something wrong?" Jacob asked.

"No. I just found that last sentence triggering my thoughts, which then went sailing off in a million directions. It ties in to everything I've been reading and thinking about for the last several months—trying to figure out where Christians fit in to all this new world order stuff."

"You mean what he said about the new spiritual climate?"

"Right—the current attitude that says, 'Isn't everything wonderful?' and the claims of world peace and the end of the Cold War. It's natural that the New Age people would see it as heralding not just a new political age, but a new age of enlightenment and peace and harmony and brotherhood—you know, all the cosmic unity of mankind stuff. Talbote as good as spells it out."

"You sound skeptical," said Jacob.

"My brain's been turning all this over for months. The end times, a new world order, preparing for new days ahead, peace, the collapse of Communism—it *is* a new world we're suddenly faced with. What is to be a Christian's response? All the old lines of demarcation are gone. The entire course of social and political direction is changing. The possibilities are limitless.

"And in the middle of it is a spiritual factor too. God is shaking up everything. It's a unique time in the history of the world. And the biggest question of all is, What does God have in mind for His children? What is our destiny as God's people? The answer is obviously multi-faceted. Whatever that destiny is, both for Christians and for the world at large, it has depths and factors that will not always be easy to see at first glance."

"So what do you think our spiritual destiny is?"

"Jesus Himself said that everyone would be saying, 'Peace here, peace there,' prior to the devastation that would come to the world before His return. That makes me suspicious of too much peace breaking out all over the world."

"You're not saying peace is a bad thing?"

"Of course not. I'm excited about Germany's reunification and can't wait to see what used to be the eastern sector. I'm as delighted with the end of the Cold War as anyone. But we can't place too much stock in it. People are still people, after all, and you know what Jeremiah said about the heart of man. Political shake-ups in Moscow and Berlin, realignments of national allegiances, and the tearing down of a few miles of concrete wall—none of that's going to alter the intrinsic sinfulness at the core of man's being."

"I hadn't thought of it like that."

"It's worth praising the Lord that we're no longer on the brink of nuclear holocaust and that the leaders of the world's most powerful nations are trying to forge friendships. All I'm saying is that what Scripture says about who rules the world remains as true now as it was in the days of Noah. We're still going to face famine and economic hardship and disasters in the newly 'freed' countries of Eastern Europe. Earthquakes, nuclear accidents—everything, just like always, and probably some new problems to boot. Well, that's exactly what Talbote emphasizes later in the article:

> "Revolution has indeed come to Europe—without bombs or tanks or guns, but no less revolutionary in its remaking and reorganizing impact upon peoples and nations who find themselves suddenly thrust into a new era. The Europe of the mid 1990s is no mere five or ten years changed from the Europe of the 1980s, but rather altered by centuries. Between 1980 and 2000 will yawn a gulf, not of two decades but of a millennium.
>
> "But where is this revolution leading? What will this priceless but uncertain and tenuous commodity called 'freedom' bring? In 1865 the bewildered blacks and dispossessed whites of the South wondered where the liberation was for them during the painful carpetbagging years of reconstruction. Is something of the same order in store for the newly freed people of the Soviet Commonwealth and Eastern Europe? What does it mean for the people of Poland and Hungary and Czechoslovakia and Russia, whose recent harvests are poor and whose economies remain in shambles? What does it mean for the wealthy of former West Germany and the now potentially wealthy of former East Germany who want their full slice of the affluent German pie?
>
> "Who will provide the aid to rebuild, to reconstruct this new 'South' and to lead its former 'slaves' into the freedom and prosperity of this new post Cold War era? Even now, major aid packages are being considered in Bonn and Washington and London. How far should the Western nations go financially?
>
> "Such are the questions asked after every war—be it hot or cold—and they form an intrinsic part of the revolutionary equation."

"He's put his finger on it," remarked Jacob. "Where's the money going to come from to finance the new age of peace? Let's face it, the United States is broke."

"Some congressman with presidential ambitions will probably draft a new world order Marshall Plan." Jackson laughed.

"We don't have the capital or industrial health to pull it off as we did in the 40s."

"But you can bet the rest of the world will expect us to pour billions of dollars we don't have into the reconstruction of Eastern Europe. So where will it come from? I can hardly see Japan pouring billions into the rebuilding of Russia—a natural enemy for thousands of years. And I doubt Germany will be the pot of gold everyone expects either."

"It's the most economically healthy of the Western nations right now."

"Yes, and I think that will cause more problems in the long run than it solves."

"How so?"

"Because the have-nots of Eastern Europe—after they realize how quickly the U.S. bank is going to run dry—will turn to whoever else has the fattest bank account. By their perception that will be Germany. The expectation is that if you've got nothing, you have a right to what the haves possess."

"That's one of the hallmarks of the new age," agreed Jacob. "Everyone has a right to a handout, a free ride."

"The minute the wall came down, East Germany wanted in on West Germany's wealth. And in that particular case, it was OK. West Germany wanted to share. But the rest of the Eastern Bloc wants in on it too. Now that a few years have passed, the reality is that the rebuilding process has been more costly than anticipated and has taken a great deal of money out of West German hands."

"And then you add the problem of immigration," Jacob added. "I was reading about it the other day—foreigners streaming into the cities of West Germany. Jews from Russia, gypsies from Romania begging on the streets, almost a hundred thousand Vietnamese. Apparently there is a massive movement into Germany from Asia, and especially westward across once closed borders. West Germans fear that the immigrants are taking homes and jobs and lowering their unusually high standard of living."

"You're more up to speed on what's going on than you let on!" Jackson laughed.

"I only read that one article," rejoined Jacob. "And I suppose I put all of it under the heading of growing pains in the changing times."

"Perhaps. But I think there are more serious issues in the European consciousness occurring than meet the eye—especially in Germany. That's one reason I'm excited to be going—to see it all firsthand. I have a feeling all this change is going to rub some rough edges raw and bring about responses no one anticipates. In fact, I can see room for the wrong kind of world leader to capitalize on the new range of forces, new fears."

"What are you implying—the rise of another autocrat, a dictator?"

"No, probably not. Whatever comes, it won't be like anything we've seen before. But even though the Cold War has ended, greed and the lust for power haven't. I can envision highly fertile ground for a New Age, smiling, 'peace-loving' world leader who is yet a wolf in sheep's clothing. It's just the kind of thing the Bible foretells, and it seems to me Talbote opens the door for it in his article."

Jackson again picked up the *Time* and read aloud:

> "The balance of power, the very basis of power, is shifting. From military to economics, from old alliances left over from the Second World War and modified by the Cold War, suddenly everything is new. The United States seems to be in a cycle of decline. Germany and Japan represent the new global powerhouses. And the entire fabric of Eastern Europe and Russia is being remade from the inside out.
>
> "Out of this will emerge new leaders and new powers. The soil is too fertile and the climate too ripe to expect anything less. It's a cultural, social, political, and perhaps even spiritual rebirthing of Europe. Yet not even the most astute historian or politician or sociologist can predict who the baby's parents are or what it will look like or what it will grow up to be.

"See what I mean?" said Jackson. "There are many possibilities for the unknown. And when you factor in the spiritual dimension, which of course none of the world's analysts see, it becomes even more dynamic.

> "In many respects, former East Germany lies at the very heart of this silent birthing revolution, bridging the gap between the wealth of the West and the crying needs of the East. In East Germany, with Berlin at its center, do all the forces for revolution converge. And it is to Germany that many look for answers, simply because it is *there,* situated at the crucial vortex of all these forces, the Mason-Dixon line of the 1990s.
>
> "The unrest of revolution is clearly visible throughout Germany,

especially as one walks the streets of Berlin. It is an unrest distinctive from that of 1916 St. Petersburg, but rather due to the uncertainty of what comes next.

"German Chancellor Kolter and his coalition in the Bundestag represent the political focal point. The rest of the former Iron Curtian nations look hopefully to the German parliament for compassion and generosity at the specially reconvened session on the 18th of this month to decide upon aid to the East. Meanwhile Russian leader Boris Yeltsin must wonder where the future direction of power lies for the Soviet Commonwealth.

"We are heading right into the heart of it, aren't we!" exclaimed Jackson, putting down the magazine.

"I'll say," replied Jacob. "No better place to have this convention."

"Berlin sits right at the crossroads."

"The opportunities for evangelism in the midst of this new climate must be exciting," said Jacob.

"But I'm not certain that the Christian groups and leaders who are pushing for this great evangelistic thrust know what's being birthed either," Jackson continued. "I doubt that the methods they've used in the past are necessarily going to result in revival erupting everywhere. I don't think it's going to be that easy. These are unique and momentous times, perhaps the prelude to Jesus' return. I think evangelism is going to have to be new, too. That's my two cents worth."

"That's more than two cents worth!" Jacob laughed. "That's a couple hundred dollars at least. My son, the opinionated journalist!"

"A writer can't help himself. He's always full of ideas, you know—sometimes more than is good for him! That's one thing I'm determined to do when I get older and wiser, like you: learn to keep my mouth shut!"

"I'm glad we talked about this. It helps me feel a little better prepared for this next week. As I said earlier, most of my time's been spent thinking about aspects of my own faith that I've been trying to put into perspective, rather than evaluating the world scene. Actually, during the past year when the face of Europe has been changing, I've been in another world altogether. I have to admit

I feel out of touch."

"A week in Berlin will cure that!" said Jackson. "If you want to feel the pulse of the new world order, what better place to go than to its very heart?"

7

August 3, 2:18 A.M.
Outside Kiev

As the plane bearing the evangelist and his son flew away from the setting sun, several thousand miles away where night had already descended, a man in black and carrying only a set of heavyweight metal-cutters, approached an unlit portion of a chain-link fence. He had walked to the back of the factory through a dense wood, not the way he came to work every morning on the road to the front gate. But his present assignment was far different from what he was paid to do after punching in every morning and going to his assembly station at the plant.

He would be paid for tonight, of course. And handsomely! So well that he had scarcely thought twice before accepting the offer. Even in newly democratic Ukraine, pay was still miserable, and there was never enough for anything extra. This one hour's work would get his wife a refrigerator and his two children new shoes. Marta was supposed to be handsomely compensated too, and he would do anything for her. If he was lucky, there might even be something left over for him. But his personal reward would come later, after they had . . .

Actually, the man who had hired him hadn't exactly said what would come afterward. But the strong suggestion that he could find himself *foreman* of the entire assembly section one day was enough. With the three thousand rubles they were paying him, he was willing to take his chances. He was a member of the fledgling union himself, and he wished neither it nor any of his fellow workers harm. But this was an opportunity he couldn't pass up. And the man had assured him that it would be to everyone's advantage in the end.

Pavlovich knelt in the moist grass at the end of the wood, pulled out the heavy wire cutters, and began snipping through the links of the fence. There was enough light to see by, but it was still dark enough to keep him hidden. The complex security systems in his country were not intended to keep people *out,* but rather to keep them in. The only guard on duty tonight was well inside the compound and on the other side anyway. Pavlovich knew him well enough, and knew that he was probably asleep by now, with half a glass of vodka on his desk.

He was through the fence in ten minutes. He would hardly have needed to run to the back door of the factory, but he did so nevertheless. The man had given him a key. Pavlovich hadn't asked where he'd stolen it. It didn't matter.

Once inside, he did have to be careful. Sound traveled and echoed about the bare floors and machinery in the tomblike quiet— enough that even a half-drunk guard might hear.

The work would take him probably an hour. Several tiny explosive charges had to be set, some papers pilfered from two or three files, a handful of dirt mixed into the oil of one of the large hydraulic lifts, and finally one of the supporting guy wires for the overhead crane sawn three-quarters through. This last could not help making some noise, but he would go slowly and watch himself.

They hadn't told him the precise purpose behind the sabotage of the auto factory, but none of his nighttime activities would destroy the plant. It was designed to make the management look bad, was all they would tell him. The records he'd stolen, along with other evidence they would take care of themselves, would point the finger for the damage and shutdown straight at the managers, who were none too popular right now. Pavlovich was perfectly willing to go along and do his part. Especially for three thousand rubles!

Ever since the first day they'd heard the word *perestroika,* there'd been talk about how much better it was going to be. Well, that had been six or eight years ago. Gorbachev hadn't made it any better, neither had Yeltsin, neither had their new right to vote, neither had the group of Americans who had come to the plant five months ago to help modernize it and set up the union. Now they had a union, but still nothing had changed. Conditions remained terrible and pay low, and Pavlovich had waited long enough. He'd heard enough about change. Now it was time he did something to help it along.

He set the last of the charges, then went to work with the tiny diamond-bladed hacksaw they had given him to cut through the guy wire. It was tedious work, but the special saw made little noise and one by one the individual steel wires began to snap. He would have to cut through about fifty of the seventy-five or so that combined to hold up one corner of the crane. When they notified him, he would add an extra 2,300 kilograms to the load. Since loading the crane was his job, that wouldn't prove too difficult. He would make sure there was no one in danger underneath, then give the signal to the crane operator above. He would raise the hoist, and a few seconds later the wire would give way and the load come crashing to the ground.

That, along with the other things, would cause pandemonium. The plant would have to shut down temporarily. The union would call an investigation. The managers would be implicated and thrown out. The union would install its own people, Pavlovich among them, in the management positions. Repairs and modernizations would be made, pay increased, hours shortened, and the change that had been talked about for so long would finally begin.

Pavlovich knew that several of his colleagues were influential union leaders, one was even on the state committee. What he did not know was that the subversion of which he was a part was not the mere localized mischief of one automobile factory as it had been represented to him by the man who had approached him last month. How could a man of Pavlovich's limited education and intelligence fathom the widesweeping breadth of a conspiracy intended to domino from several such factories into a sweeping, nationwide worker revolt throughout the Motherland?

8

August 3, 1:35 A.M.
Bonn

That night, unknown either to the American travelers or the factory saboteur, in another part of Europe to the west, a man waited on a darkened street corner. In spite of the summer warmth, he was wrapped tightly in an overcoat, and a wide-brimmed hat was pulled well down over his forehead. By all appearances, he did not want his face seen.

In a few minutes a large white automobile pulled alongside him. The door opened, he stepped quickly inside, and the auto pulled forward, turning into an underground parking garage below one of the many dozens of buildings once in governmental use but now with an uncertain future after reunification. The long process of removing the inhabitants to the new capital of Berlin was well underway, but it would not be completed for several years.

It was late. No other cars were about. It wheeled inside the garage. The automatic gate closed behind them. The driver pulled to the far wall, then shut off the engine.

"You were not followed?" said the driver of the car in a deep, resonant voice without turning around.

"Nein, Herr Bundesminister."

"Are you available to perform certain services for me?" asked the driver. The commanding strength of his voice made it sound as though nothing but an affirmative response would be tolerated.

"I am at your disposal, as is my custom."

"The usual fee?"

"Information is negotiable. If there are those you wish removed, yes, the usual forty thousand D-marks per."

"You have new equipment?"

"Always."

"You sound rather cocky, Herr Claymore." The pale, deep set eyes of the man in front squinted slightly, and he was tempted to turn around and pierce them straight into those of his lackey. But with calm determination he restrained the urge, letting only the

42

imperceptible movement of his thick, dark eyebrows indicate his displeasure. In this business, although you had to be careful, you had to use whomever was available. And as much as he hated him, the fellow whose only known label was the nickname for Bonnie Prince Charlie's famous two-handed broadsword was the best he'd ever been able to find. He didn't know what the man looked like, and he didn't ever want to know. Things like this were best kept that way.

"I make sure of myself," replied Claymore, as full of annoyance at the self-important politician as the latter was of condescension toward him. "Nothing I do can ever be traced. What is it you want this time?"

"Information first. Perhaps other things later. I want you working solely for me for the next two weeks. I will pay you a retainer on top of the other fees. You need to be ready to move at a moment's notice. Is your Russian visa current?"

"I can travel anywhere from England to Japan without difficulty—yes, all is current."

"It may require carrying weapons across the Soviet border."

"That is no problem. I have done so many times."

"The next two weeks are critical. There is no telling where I may need to send you."

"Give me instructions in the usual way. You can depend on the result."

"First of all, a man you have watched for me before, the head of the CSDU. Keep an eye on him, his wife too. An update is all I need. I must reel him in soon, and if there are new affiliations, relationships, idiosyncrasies, to add to my dossier on him, I want to know. He is too straight for any dirt. But one never knows what one may turn up. Make sure you check out his wife carefully. I've heard a rumor or two."

"How long?"

"Two or three days. Time is short."

"And then?"

"Then I don't know. It depends on other things. But be ready to catch a quick flight east."

The next moment the engine of the car revved to life. It pulled cautiously out of the garage, then eased into the adjoining street. The driver did not stop for several blocks. When he did, it was along a dark stretch of the avenue where the streetlight was out. He continued to stare straight ahead until he heard the back door of the car slam. Immediately he accelerated.

Neither man had seen the other's face.

9

August 2, 8:17 P.M.
Over northern Canada

"The sun's turning that orange and red of sunset," said Jackson, glancing out the plane's window, "and we've only been in the air two hours."

"It's only—what—six-thirty or so Chicago time," replied Jacob, looking at his watch. "Where are we, anyway?"

"The plains of northern Quebec. We won't be over the Atlantic for a long time yet."

"It'll be a short night, flying away from the sun."

"Do you ever get any sleep on flights like this?" asked Jackson.

"I never do," laughed Jacob. "Just the time you drift off, they wake you for breakfast. It's around three in the morning your time, and they expect you to be up and at it for the next day!"

"It's a good thing we'll have a week to unwind and get our systems back to normal before the conference."

"Visit with your friends and see the sights, right?"

"You bet! It isn't often I get my way paid to Europe. I want to make the most of it."

"But especially see your friends?"

"Yeah. That's going to be special. I didn't want to cut it short. That's why I wanted the extra week. I love that old farm of theirs!"

"Maybe when we're there I can focus on my speech."

"What do you mean? I'm liable to put you to work!"

44

"I don't know anything about farm work."

"That's no prerequisite. I didn't know anything either. But maybe you're right. There is a certain peacefulness about their place."

"I'll tell you, I could use some help. You have to realize how many changes I've gone through since the last time I took to the podium. It may not seem such a significant thing to anyone else, but I'm going through more internal debate over this one hour-long talk than I have over any other sermon I've delivered in my life. I tell you, Jackson—everything's changed for me. Do you understand—upside down!"

Jackson nodded.

"Of course you do!" Jacob laughed. "You're the one who started the whole thing and who has lived through it with me. If anyone understands, it's you!"

"I hope I do," replied Jackson. "But I'm not inside your skin, so I can't grasp it completely."

"There's so much going on inside this brain of mine that sometimes I think my head's going to explode. I feel as though I've been asleep all these years, and now all of a sudden I'm coming awake. Everything's new! My brain is tumbling in a hundred directions. Don't you see the irony of it? Me—*the* evangelist of Christendom—suddenly reexamining the very precepts I have given my life to! Why, if people knew the kinds of things I was asking the Lord, they'd have me ridden out of town on a rail."

"You've been facing your own weakness, trying to deepen your walk with God, and live what you preach—there's nothing wrong with that," objected Jackson. "That's why people respect you and are still anxious to hear from you—because you came clean and humbly admitted you were a weak, fallible human being like everyone else. Sure, you're not sitting at the pinnacle of power anymore. But that's by your own choice. People admire that humility."

"The changes go deeper than that, Jackson."

"I don't understand you. Surely you don't mean—"

"No, I'm not questioning the foundations of faith itself."

"Then what are you getting at?"

"It's not the foundations but how we as a body of God's people communicate that faith to the world—that's what's been troubling me."

"Evangelism?"

"Exactly! How do we transmit the truth to the world? That's the most important question in all of history. It's the question of the ages—how is God's life communicated, passed on, spread—to individuals, to nations, from father to son, mother to daughter, friend to friend? How does it widen to encompass the whole globe? How are His followers to take the life Jesus brought and give it to the world? You said it earlier—what is our destiny as God's people, in the midst of a new world order, in the midst of a world refocusing *its* destiny? What is the role of evangelism?"

"Matthew twenty-eight, nineteen and twenty."

"And Mark sixteen, fifteen. The Great Commission. How do we fulfill it? How do we obey Jesus' words? I've given my life to preaching. Salvation prayers—I've seen multiple thousands bow their heads and pray them. One columnist several years ago called me the 'convert king of Christianity.' I hate the very thought of such a label now! But be that as it may, I have been head of a worldwide organization. And yet here I am on my way to a conference on how to spread the gospel in the Eastern Bloc countries, and I think I know less of what the Great Commission means and how those two Scripture passages fit together than at any former time of my life. I'm in a hopeless dilemma, Jackson. It's almost—it seems like heresy, the kinds of things I find myself thinking."

"Pretty strong word. Aren't you exaggerating?"

"Maybe." Jacob sighed. "It's just that I've never heard anyone else say anything like the things I'm wondering about. I've never heard it preached. I've never read it. I tell you, I'm questioning the very basis for much of what evangelicals do—and it scares me. What if it isn't the Lord guiding my thoughts and prayers at all? What if I'm going off the deep end?"

"I doubt God will let you go that far." Jackson chuckled. "He's got too much invested in you."

Jacob let out a long breath, then looked away for a moment. "I hope you're right," he said at length. "It's all so new—asking God for insight, and then trying to put together all that comes to me as a result, reading Scriptures and seeing huge new vaults of possibilities exploding out of them that go against traditionally held viewpoints that I always took for granted because—well, because that's what everybody said was true. I tell you, if I have anything

46

coherent to say at that conference beyond sixty or ninety minutes of my own questions, that will be a miracle in itself."

"I honestly believe that God *will* give you what you are to say," said Jackson seriously. "And when the time comes, I think you will be able to speak with strength and authority."

Jacob nodded thoughtfully, assessing his son's words. But before he had a chance to reply, they were interrupted by a stewardess in the aisle next to them.

"Would you care for some dinner, gentlemen?" she asked.

10

"Did you get to Berlin when you were here before?" asked Jacob as they ate their German meal.

"Once," replied Jackson, "but only briefly. I took a bus through the eastern sector and stayed there overnight."

"Did you see East Berlin?"

Jackson laughed. "Yeah, but it was an experience I'd just as soon forget."

"How so? What happened?"

Jackson laughed again. "I'll tell you about it another time. It's a long story. But you've spoken in Europe a number of times. Surely all this isn't new to you."

Jacob sighed. "Yes, I've been there. I've *been* to all the places—London, Paris, Rome, Hamburg, and Berlin too. But only as the man in the spotlight, the evangelist—everything official and first-class, nice hotels, limousines, the finest of everything. They kept me shielded from real life. But what am I saying? *I* kept myself shielded! I was never interested. I never cared about real, flesh-and-blood individuals, only the thousands I so glibly referred to. I never walked the streets, went to little villages, explored fields and paths and riverbanks, tried to converse with strangers. It's obvious that you know the people and what they're like better than I do. Now I see—as in so many areas!—that I had it all backward."

"You'll have your chance this time."

"I am so glad we're going to be a little early. I can't wait to see your friends' farm in Wessendorf."

"I tell you, I might put you to work!" kidded Jackson.

"Great!" rejoined Jacob. "A little honest labor might do me some good."

"When I asked them if we could spend a few days before going on to Berlin, I said we were available to help with any projects Heinrich needed a couple extra men for."

"What did he say?"

"He said he could no doubt keep us busy. It's just him and Marla, and with the harvest due any time, I'm sure there's more than they can keep up with. You ever hoisted hay or driven a tractor?"

"Me? Are you kidding?"

"I thought maybe when you were young—"

"You have no idea how complete a novice I am, Jackson. That's why this is such a thrill to me—to get down off my high horse and actually *do* something for a change."

"It's hard work."

"It won't hurt me a bit. I'd be proud to show up at that conference with blisters on my hands."

"And manure on your shoes?"

"That might be a little harder to explain!"

Both men laughed.

"You know, that reminds me," Jacob said. "Bob gave me something just before we left. Things were so hectic getting to the airport that I forgot to mention it."

He reached into the vest pocket of his coat and pulled out an envelope.

"Speaking of grass-roots people," he went on, "just wait till you see this!"

Opening the envelope, he pulled out two sheets of paper, very thin and yellowed, which had clearly been folded and refolded many times. "Believe it or not, this came to Bob more than fifteen years ago—from East Germany. What was *then* East Germany, I should say. I never saw it, but he held onto it and even corre-

48

sponded with the fellow, and sort of kept in touch all these years. Bob thought that now might be the time for me to fulfill this man's request at last, or at least see if I might contact him, now that Germany's united and there are no more travel or religious restrictions."

He handed the letter to Jackson, who took it carefully and began to read the German script, though the letter had been penned in English.

"It's addressed to you," he said, looking up. "Why didn't you see it when it first came?"

"Oh, Jackson, Jackson." Michaels sighed. "You need to understand how things used to be. I was out of touch with the 'little' goings-on. Thousands and thousands of letters poured into ETW every month, and I suppose most of them were addressed to me. Not only did I consider myself too important to be bothered with them, but it wouldn't have been possible for me to see everything. That was Bob's job, and he responded in my stead. Frankly, I'm glad now that it was him replying to all those people instead of me. He had something to give them that I didn't."

"He didn't answer *all* the mail?"

"Oh no. We had a pretty large section that handled the routine requests and many of the phone calls. But when it got really personal, Bob took it. I was oblivious to everything, but he's told me in the last year that he developed his own ministry out of it, within the huge walls of ETW. Anyway—this particular letter was one he believed was important, and as I said he corresponded with this Mr. Bietmann for years."

Jackson continued to read the letter before him:

Dear Jacob Michaels,

Please forgive my boldness for writing to you in this way but we are so isolated here that sometimes we feel a desperate longing to reach out to our Christian brothers and sisters in the West. Communication is so scanty that we often do not know if you are aware we are here.

Because of censorship restrictions, I am watched in particular by the authorities, I am sending this letter by way of my West German friend Franz Schmidt. I pray that it finds its way to you.

We are a small number of believers in the Deutsche Democratische Republik, what you call East Germany, in a town not many

49

kilometers southeast of Berlin, Kehrigkburg. Oppression here is not nearly as severe as it is for our brothers and sisters in Russia. They must take care never to gather in too large a group at once for fear of arousing suspicion. We in the DDR are not what you call an "underground" fellowship, for technically worship here is allowed. Yet persecution still comes to us, in different ways. Our children are harrassed at school and denied educational privileges. I myself have been imprisoned three times, though the beatings have not been severe. Yet for the sake of my wife and seven-year-old daughter, Herga, I must take care. Some have been sent to Russia and never heard from again, and the KGB is active, even here, in trying to root out "subversive" leaders who teach contrary to the doctrines of the Kremlin.

I am not a pastor, as such, though often I lead our times of Bible study and prayer. I am a farmer. My father owned a large farm before and during the war. But as you know, all the land was confiscated and now I work on one of the state collective grain processing factories.

My reason for taking pen in hand to write to the American Christian leader Jacob Michaels is to ask you specifically if you would consider praying to ask our Lord if He might send you to visit us, to speak words of encouragement and teaching among isolated believers such as we. My friend and brother Herr Schmidt, I am certain, could arrange such a visit, though you would have to travel incognito in the DDR to keep from bringing danger to yourself. Likewise, we could not expose our people to the potential recriminations of meeting in a large group with a well-known Christian as yourself.

I know you have visited many European cities and that huge gatherings result from your presence. I am hopeful, however, that you may feel led to consider this different form of ministry. I realize, even as I make such a bold request, the risk it would involve for you. Nevertheless, as the apostle Paul spoke, with God all things are possible.

I am very appreciative of your time and prayerful consideration. We in our fellowship will pray for you, brother Jacob, and ask that you please pray also for us.

> I am your humble servant in
> the Lord Jesus Christ,
>
> Udo Bietmann
> Kehrigkburg, DDR
> 27 October 1976

A handwritten note from Schmidt followed at the bottom of the page with instructions on how a reply could be made through him.

"And you never responded?" asked Jackson when he had completed it and handed it back to his father.

"Bob said he sent me a memo about the request, but I never replied. I don't remember—which doesn't surprise me," he added with a forlorn sigh. "Now I don't know how much Jaeger kept from me—or what I just plain ignored. In any case, Bob did what he could, established a correspondence, and says he's been praying for Bietmann for years, though he hasn't heard from him for about the last five."

The two fell silent.

"Anyway," Jacob resumed, "here we are going to Berlin, and now I can't think of anything I'd rather do than meet with a small group of believers—people who have paid a price for their faith—like this." He gestured a hand toward the letter. "Frankly, this seems more interesting to me than the conference."

"I'm game," said Jackson. "But do you think we could find him? You don't even have his address."

"Bietmann himself said it," answered Jacob, "don't you remember? With God all things are possible!"

PART 2

Déjà Vu

11

The sky in Bonn was gray, the air chilly and dank.

This was no place from which to run a government, thought the black-suited official as he strode quickly along Goerres Strasse, then bounded up the steps two at a time into the building next to the Bundeshaus that had for years and until very recently been his parliamentary home.

An aberration in the history of Germany's self-rule, that's all it had been. Notwithstanding Beethoven's birthplace and the Kurfurstliches Schloss and the Poppelsdorfer Schloss, and its 2,000-year history, in his estimation this was a city without character, without culture, given a status it did not deserve to house the nongovernment of the postwar period.

Thank the heavens it had ended two years ago. The Bonn tenure would one day be a mere asterisk in the history books of Germany's proud Reichs—preceding the Fourth, which he fully believed would be the proudest and mightiest of all.

Hitler had been an uneducated and egotistical incompetent, he reflected. One utterly ill-equipped to carry forth the grand ideas embodied within his brilliant creed. But not a fool. His convictions were daring. They had simply been made public several generations before their time. The Nazis and storm troopers—they were all idiots who couldn't see the limitations of militarism to achieve their ends.

Such would not be Klaus Drexler's mistake.

When his time came—and it would come, very soon!—he would take Der Fuhrer's vision to new global heights never conceived of by Himmler, Goring, or any of the other imbecilic goons with which Hitler surrounded himself. And he would do so *without*

55

so much as a single bullet being fired. He would do so without a military at all! His destiny, the cosmic alignment of forces upon him, could not fail to bring it about.

This was a new age! A time in which xenophobic fervor had to be combined with the spiritual values of the age and fueled by economic and political clout, given brawn and cohesiveness, not with tanks and weapons and missiles but with the power of Das Geld and the knowledge of how to use it! A new age whose time, thanks to Herr Gorbachev, was now at hand!

With purposeful direction he strode down the deserted hall to the office he still maintained in the former and still provisional capital. Not many were here by 6:00 A.M. these days. Now that the important offices were being removed to Berlin, these once-active corridors had all the life of a drowsy, bureaucratic, record-keeping basement.

But he would not have to return to Bonn many more times. Berlin had beckoned to him all his life. How eagerly he had yearned to get out of this hole—forever! Now that reunification had come and the Bundestag moved, he would shut down the last of his offices here at the first available opportunity.

Given the delicacy of some of his activities, however, and the secretive nature of a number of important associations, he found it convenient to yet conduct certain discreet business from this location. It was more private. Fewer prying eyes. Individuals such as Claymore he had to see as far from Berlin as possible. That's why he had flown in last night. And now he would get a few final things in order before the summit in Moscow. He would play the loyal leader of his contingent of Bundestag members, supportive and enthusiastic of the Chancellor's negotiations over aid.

But the real history to be made in Moscow a few hours from now would likely be seen by no one. He and the Defense Minister of that troubled conglomeration of new republics would finalize their timetable for action. They had been waiting years, and now suddenly events were lining up perfectly. The summit could not have provided a more perfect cover.

He opened a drawer and took out a file, glanced through it hastily, then tossed it into his briefcase. He sat down, made two phone calls, then glanced at his watch. Six twenty-three. He had to catch the plane in an hour and a half. He would be in Moscow three hours after that for the meetings.

He rose, then cast one last look about the small office. With any luck, this might be the last he saw of this place. Within days, a week or two at most, his plans would not have to be hidden any longer.

12

He was onto something. That much he was sure of.

What it was, he didn't know. But it was big—bigger than any of the old Cold War games. Russia and the U.S. may be friends now, but the world was still full of self-seeking men out to gain their own ends. And as long as politics was about power, there would be plenty of work to keep spies like him busy.

He eased out into traffic and settled in three or four cars behind the huge, black limousine.

Trouble was, he thought, now he was trying to get out of the game. How ironic that in the very process of getting out of the country for good, he should stumble upon this! He'd probably uncover the whole scheme and have no place to go with it. He had no friends, no allies, no havens anymore. He was in danger even here in Moscow.

Yet he had to play out his hand. He'd been a KGB man too long to be able to stuff his curiosity when everything in him said something was happening. It was almost a reflex. You developed a sixth sense in the spy business, and you could just tell—your gut told you so.

That was the feeling he had right now about that limousine in front of him. If only he'd had time to plant a bug underneath! Somehow or another he had to find out what this clandestine meeting between Desyatovsky and the German official was about! He could tell from the looks on their faces at the press conference that it had to do with more than the German and French aid package to the new Commonwealth of Soviet States. A critical vote was scheduled in the German Bundestag the week of the seventeenth at a special session, and this little mini-summit of leaders had ostensibly firmed everything up for the aid package to sail through. At least Kolter had promised to keep his coalition intact.

But something else was in the wind. Whether it had to do directly with the vote, he didn't know. It might not even be linked to the aid debate at all. Somehow he sensed something of greater import.

He'd known Bludayev Desyatovsky too long not to be able to see that he was nervous, wiping his forehead more often than could be accounted for by the mild summer's day. They'd worked together for the same government for two decades. He'd even had to spy on him a time or two. So he knew Bludayev's mind was not on the aid agreement. And the German! Too smooth—too polished. He had never trusted Klaus Drexler, and seeing him now—all smiles but clearly hiding something—did nothing to alleviate that reaction. All eyes had been on Yeltsin and Kolter and French President Santierre—the star centerpieces of a mutually trusting, new European community.

But not Galanov's. His eyes had remained riveted on the two underlings, the Soviet Defense Minister and the German minority Bundesminister. And he had wasted no time in sprinting to his own car the moment the press conference had broken up. He would follow to see what might develop.

Who could tell? Perhaps he could parlay whatever information he gained into free passage west, or to a post in the new government without the baggage he was currently carrying as a result of his previous position.

No, come to think of it, he didn't want to stay—even if he could get out of this hot water. Everything had changed. Everything was upside down, and his present predicament only typified what so many of his occupation now faced. He could have no future here. His life was in danger. In the West he would be safer than he could ever be if he remained in his native Motherland. Some of his old colleagues had found ways to mainstream into the new Russian society. But he wasn't sure he wanted to chance it. An open pipeline existed to China, he knew, where many from the old Communist Guard and KGB were winding up.

But that wasn't for him. He knew it would be just like the Nazis in Argentina after the Second World War—talk about the old times, always with the idealistic notion of a resumption of power. Not that there wasn't an enormous contingent left throughout what had so recently been the Soviet Union—the fifth column, silently awaiting events until the dream of 1917 could once again assert itself.

It could happen, he thought. The Gorbachev and Yeltsin eras represented but the blink of an eye in Russian history. It was no sure bet that all this democratic stuff would even stick in a nation where autocracy had been the ruling force for more than ten centuries.

But he wasn't going to stick around to find out which way the future went. It would be too dangerous. None of that was for him anymore. He had to get out. He had to find a place where he could start a new life.

The danger was real. In the topsy-turvy world of international espionage, the good guys had become the bad guys, and vice versa. Suddenly his own people were after him. Having been a higher-up in the KGB made you a criminal in the new order. How had Bolotnikov managed to ingratiate himself with the new regime? he wondered. But now was no time to untangle that mystery. He had to worry about his own skin first. Desyatovsky was already after him, and he had probably seen him at the press conference besides. Whatever he might discover, he'd have to watch his step. If it was information he could use to blackmail the Defense Minister, it still might not save him. He'd have to find out what was going on first, and decide how to use the information later. And he'd have to stay out of sight. Desyatovsky would know he was snooping around if he left so much as one trace of his footsteps.

A few days, that was all he could spare. He'd already sent word through some of his old contacts in Poland and Germany that he needed to get out and would need transport and new identity papers. When those came through, he'd have to get out of Russia for good, whether he'd unraveled this new mysterious twist or not.

But first, if at all possible, he'd dearly love to find out what

59

was going on in that limo up ahead. After that, when his papers came, he'd resume his personal life, and get out of the danger that was stalking *him*.

13

August 3
Folenweiter farm, Wessendorf, Germany

Marla Folenweiter and her eleven-year-old daughter and nine-year-old son were standing to greet Jackson and Jacob the moment they cleared customs. Jackson, who had not seen Marla for twelve years, embraced the German woman with an enthusiastic shout of greeting, fumbling with his rusty German as he introduced Jacob.

"It has been too long, Jackson," Marla said.

"I know. I have longed to see you also. Is Heinrich well?"

"Well, and anxious to see you. Come, let's get your bags and be on our way. We have a long drive ahead of us."

The two Americans dozed along the way, trying to catch up on their lost night. But when they arrived at the farm in Wessendorf, Jackson woke to the sight and smell of a place that he had long loved and remembered.

"I can hardly believe I'm here again," he said that evening after supper. "Even though I have dreamed of another visit, I honestly didn't know if I'd see the two of you again."

"Has it changed, Jackson?" asked Marla.

"Nothing. It could have been yesterday. Nothing, I should say, except the two of you. We have all put on a few years and a few pounds."

They all laughed.

"I've never heard you speak German," said Jacob, in English, to Jackson. "I can't understand a word you are saying!"

"Well, get used to it. I'll be your translator for a few days."

"Ask them what it's like after reunification," said Jacob.

Jackson relayed Jacob's question. Heinrich was the first to reply, glancing back and forth between his two visitors, but speaking primarily to Jackson.

"It isn't as easy as everyone thought it would be," he began. "There was a tendency toward a great idealism at first. We had all yearned for East and West to be reunited someday—everyone—on both sides of the wall. Many never thought it would happen, but we hoped and prayed for it. We were a divided country, and we could not help feeling it deep inside our very marrow."

"So you must be excited that it has actually happened," said Jackson.

"Excitement was what we felt at first," replied Marla, "but the reality is proving difficult."

"How do you mean—financially, emotionally?"

The two Germans glanced at one another. It was clearly not the first time they had thought about such things.

"Finances certainly are a big part of it," replied Heinrich. "You have to understand how good we've had it here. Our generation—those of us born during and after the war—is too young to clearly remember the deprivation and devastation of the 40's and early 50's. We received the fruit of the so-called 'economic miracle' of the Adenauer era. The Cold War may have been a time of tension and nuclear danger for most of the world. But for West Germany it was a time of unprecedented affluence."

"I noticed that the last time I was here," said Jackson. "It seemed as though everybody was well off, the cities were clean and new. There appeared to be little want."

"There wasn't," added Marla. "But most Germans take that for granted. Our young people are taught in school that it is all the result of our hard work and diligence. The American money that was poured in to rebuild our country is scarcely mentioned."

"But *you* are aware of where the aid has come from," said Jackson, puzzled. "Why isn't everyone?"

Marla smiled. "When you become a Christian, many of your perceptions change," she replied. "And then, of course, we have a good friend who is an American. And knowing him keeps our view of the United States more balanced than that of most of our countrymen."

Now it was Jackson's turn to smile. "Well, I'm glad I can be of some benefit." He laughed. "But are you really in such a minority in how you view the United States?"

"Oh, yes," rejoined Marla. "There is a huge resentment toward the United States in our country. Perhaps people do know that America is largely responsible for our postwar success and prosperity, so they feel guilty somehow, and that guilt expresses itself as resentment."

"Humility, you know, Jackson," put in Heinrich, "is not a natural German trait. We are a self-absorbed people."

"But why are *you* saying such things? You are Germans too."

"Naturally. Marla said it—when you give your life to the Lord, your attitudes change. You see yourself differently, you see life differently. We realize that we too suffer from German pride and even a tendency to look down our noses at other peoples, other nations. But at least we are seeing those things within ourselves and can work toward a more humble attitude. Unfortunately, most of our countrymen do not know the Lord and therefore see no reason that they shouldn't consider themselves the most skilled and intelligent people in the world."

"What does all this have to do with reactions to reunification?" asked Jackson, after he had relayed the gist of the conversation to Jacob.

"Hmm, that's a complicated question," said Heinrich seriously. "Newspapers and magazines have been full of editorials and articles about it for the last two years, representing every side of the spectrum. In fact, my opinion is probably not representative of most Germans. What I have to say isn't particularly kind to my countrymen."

"I consider myself warned."

"Of course we wanted reunification. But once the borders were opened and East Germans began coming here, we realized that though those people spoke our language and shared our blood, they had ceased to be 'Germans.' They had grown fat, lazy, and listless. Under Communism they had forgotten how to work. Now they wanted a hand-out. They came to our cities, and they bought our goods and our cars and our clothes. They wanted our jobs, but when they got them they didn't know how to apply themselves."

"Surely you didn't begrudge their desire to be free from the

Communist oppression?"

"No, certainly not. We truly wanted to help. One side of us felt great compassion for what they had endured. But you see, the pride I spoke of earlier now turned against our own brothers and sisters in the East. 'We pulled ourselves up by the bootstraps; let them do the same.' What is irrational is the fact that we *didn't* pull ourselves up at all. We had American and British help. When we are in the same position of being able to help, we don't like it. Suddenly there aren't enough jobs. Inflation is rising. There is a high cost to reunification, and it's going to come out of *our* pockets.

"Clearly, Jackson," Heinrich concluded, "I'm greatly over-simplifying what I say. But all these threads have been floating about in the German psyche these last couple of years. They're complex emotions, and that's why we've had a difficult time adjusting to the changes."

"There are other factors too," put in Marla, "that don't tie in with reunification directly, but they do affect the changing face of Europe as a whole."

"How do you mean?"

"Well, not only have we enjoyed affluence all this time, but there has also been a stability and predictability in Germany that has been secure. We have been, in a sense, an isolated nation. No one could come in from the east. Our government restricted immigration from other parts of the world. We kept our jobs and our money pretty much to ourselves. You cross the border into France or Italy, and within a mile you see poverty the likes of which you have to search very hard to find in Germany."

"And now?"

"The breakup of the Communist bloc has changed all that. Suddenly our borders are literally being run down by millions of people from all over the world. No longer are we securely situated at the farthest edge of freedom, but we are right in the middle of a whirlpool of change. Suddenly Europe's roads lead to Germany. Everyone wants to come here because Germany is where the jobs and money and opportunities are."

"And Germans don't like it?"

"It's threatening," answered Heinrich. "Our prosperous world is crumbling. I should say, we have the *perception* that it is falling apart. Suddenly Turks and Poles and Africans and Arabs want jobs here. They are getting welfare money from our government. They are diluting the labor force."

"Not to mention the added burden caused by East Germany's needs," said Jackson.

"Exactly. It's all mixed in together. Suddenly throughout Germany there are poor and homeless and beggars wandering about."

"Berlin's the worst," said Marla. "We were there four months ago, and I could hardly believe it. I was frightened just to go out on the streets. Berlin, I should say, and Köln. It's become a spooky city, too."

"Great!" Jackson laughed ironically. "Right where we're headed."

"Berlin has become the cosmopolitan city of Europe. Everything focuses there. What used to be the last outpost of the free world, even behind the Iron Curtain, has now become the very epicenter. East meets West, old meets new, Democracy meets Communism, rich meets poor, Cold War meets post–Cold War—it's all on the streets of Berlin."

Jackson turned to Jacob and took a minute or two to relate what Marla and Heinrich had just said.

"And here we are on our way to a conference on evangelism, right in the middle of the tinderbox," Jacob exclaimed.

"Yes, where do Christians fit into this scene?" Jackson added.

"For us, the questions have as much to do with being German as being Christian," said Marla. "We see so many things differently from any of our friends and family. There is a mind-set in Germany that just can't seem to grasp this new outlook we have."

Involuntarily, Jackson let out a yawn. Marla laughed. "It is time we were *all* in bed," she said. "We have to be up early for the cows. You two need to sleep off your jet lag."

"You save the cows for me!" said Jackson. "The only way I'll feel like I've had a vacation is if I can help with some of your work."

"We'll see," laughed Heinrich.

They all rose and left the Stube.

"Gute Nacht, Jackson," said Marla as Jackson and Jacob headed up the tall flight of stairs in the huge old farmhouse.

"Gute Nacht," returned Jackson. "Thank you for everything."

PART 3

Evangelism and Intrigue

14

"Claymore?"

"That's right—who is it?"

"It's your employer."

"Why are you calling me? I thought you said—"

"Shut up. Time is running short. I have to know if you've found out anything on Woeniger."

"Nothing new—on *him*."

"What do you mean?"

"Your lead turned out to be a live one."

"His wife?"

"She's some lady." Claymore's gravelly chuckle could be heard on the other end of the phone.

"What do you have?"

"Enough to make him do anything you want."

"Good. Send me the file on her—you have pictures?"

"You pay for the best, you get the best."

Now it was the politician's turn to laugh.

"Well, send me all of it—usual name and postbox in Berlin. You got it?"

"You want me to keep working on the husband?"

"Yes, keep digging. I'll be seeing him soon. Anything on the Russian?"

"No. I'll have to go to Moscow to get to the real dirt."

"That may have to wait. I want you close by for now. I'll be in touch."

Drexler hung up the phone, thought for a minute, then quickly punched in another number. He had no need to look it up. He had known it quite well from memory for several years now.

"It's me," he said in decent but accented Russian when the voice on the other end answered. "Any more developments since I was there?"

"Not much can change in two days."

"You thought we were being followed?"

"Ja, a troublesome ex-KGB fellow. He is trying to bring me down. But I have people on him. He will be eliminated before many days."

"We cannot afford the slightest leak!"

"Not to worry, my friend. He knows nothing. He can find out nothing."

"All your other connections—everything is in readiness?"

"Not to worry, not to worry. All is ready. In a matter of days, the unions throughout the country will be shouting for change, the railways will be crippled, financial centers in chaos, and the military firmly behind me. I have good people working very hard, even at this moment."

"It is almost time. The vote comes in less than two weeks. That may provide my moment. Will you be ready?"

"I can move within forty-eight hours' notice."

"Just make sure your people are ready."

Bludayev Desyatovsky put down the phone.

That was the trouble with Germans, they worried too much. An anxious, fretful people, he thought, always neverous, always on edge. And they could not give anyone but a German credit for doing anything right. A pompous, egocentric race. But alas, they were his western neighbors, like them or not. History had shown that one had either to work with them or against them, and he hoped he was making the right decision for the future of *his* people to choose the former.

Bah! The fair-eyed one had only better cover his *own* responsibilities for this thing! More could go wrong on his end than here. One little lapse, one vote taken for granted that went to the Chancellor, one slip-up with the fellow of the other party, whose support he had to woo, against the aid package—one slip, and he himself would be out in the cold, making his bold move and then left hanging by his own rope!

Nyet! My teutonic friend, he thought, *it is not I you need worry about, but yourself.*

He rose and strode about the room in mounting disgust at the phone call. He would have to take steps to gain complete control of the reins himself once the initial phase was completed. He didn't want to be forever at the mercy of that man. He didn't trust him.

But for the present, he was stuck with him.

15

August 8, 4:15 P.M.
Berlin

"Jacob Michaels!" boomed a rousing and enthusiastic voice across the lobby.

Jackson looked up to see a man striding toward them with a huge grin to match his exuberant greeting, hand outstretched.

He and his father had driven into Berlin only an hour before. They had just walked into the lobby of the Worldwide Hotel from the parking basement and had scarcely glanced around long enough to locate the check-in desk when the familiar voice assailed them.

They hardly had time to turn and focus before the boisterous hand of Anthony Powers landed with a friendly slap across the upper half of Jacob's back. "It is wonderful to see you again!" he said.

Recovering himself, Jacob shook his hand warmly. "So, Tony," he said, "how is the conference shaping up?"

"Couldn't be better! Especially since you decided to join us. I'm delighted, and so is everyone else—and looking forward eagerly to what you have to say."

Jacob threw Jackson a quick glance, with one eyebrow lifted, as if to say, "I'm glad *he's* so confident!"

"And this is your—" Powers went on, turning toward Jackson.

69

"My friend and associate, Jackson Maxwell," put in Jacob quickly. "Jackson," he added, "meet Anthony Powers of SCWE and organizer of this conference."

"Ah yes, Mr. Maxwell!" said Powers as the two shook hands. "I know you by reputation—*Christian World,* isn't it?"

Jackson nodded.

"You're the one, as I understand it, who latched onto the investigation of Jacob here, and was responsible for—"

Suddenly he realized the hot water he'd stumbled into and faltered. If it were possible for a man of Powers's confidence to be flustered, now was such a moment.

He was relieved when Jacob rescued him with a hearty laugh.

"You're exactly right, Tony," he said. "Jackson was indeed the one who brought me down from my high horse. And you have no idea how thankful I am!"

"And the two of you are—friends?" said an astonished Powers, recovering himself.

"The best!" assented Jacob. "Why, if it weren't for Jackson being so intent on the truth and his importunity in confronting me and making me face it, uncomfortable though it might have been at the time, why, Tony, I'd still be—well, I shudder to think what I would still be."

"Wrote a book about it, didn't you?" asked Powers.

"No," replied Jackson, "just an article for my magazine."

"I still find it incredible," said Powers, "that—well, you must see my point—that two men would be friends after—after the one is responsible for what you might call destroying the career and reputation of the other. It's not something you see very often."

"Maybe we should see it more often, at least among Christians," said Michaels seriously. "I tell you, Tony, I was dead two years ago—spiritually and morally, and even intellectually. This young man—well, I owe him my life. His investigation woke me up. And you expect me to hold that against him? Sure, my pride was dealt a momentary blow. But it was short-lived. And now, for the first time in my life, I am growing—really growing!—as a Christian and as a man. For the first time in my life, maybe I *do* have something to say."

"Well, that's wonderful, I must say!" exclaimed Powers expansively. "Then I'm doubly glad you have both come. It's going to be a powerful conference!"

"You have much to be grateful to Jackson for as well, Tony," Michaels went on. "Had it not been for his uncovering Hamilton's scheme when he did, *you'd* have been in a fix yourself."

A cloud passed across Powers's face, as if the memory of being taken in was not a pleasant one. But it lasted only an instant and was replaced by a breezy expression of non-worry, which showed how quickly he was able to put such things behind him.

"Yes, well—come, both of you, there are some people I want you to meet!"

A small crowd had already begun to gather around them once the presence of Jacob Michaels became known. He shook several hands, as Powers attempted to lead them away, while Jackson tagged along at the back of the growing throng.

Anthony Powers, president of the worldwide student mission organization, Students Committed to World Evangelism (SCWE), was one of the most well-known leaders in American evangelical circles. Charismatic, tall, lean, handsome, and incurably confident and outspoken, he had taken the organization vastly past the bounds of college and university campuses where it had begun some twenty years before. SCWE now boasted a publications arm, for which Powers had himself written several best-sellers, and a vast communications network stretching throughout the world. Reaching the lost on every continent and in every nation had long been the goal and vision of SCWE, and in recent years they had undertaken grandiose new methods to proclaim the gospel to every creature. Obtaining support and backing from dozens of other Christian groups, Powers had been seeking in recent years to launch a state-of-the-art communications satellite into orbit, committed exclusively to Christian use, preprogrammed with twenty-four-hour-a-day earthbound transmissions in every known language, with power to continue such uninterrupted broadcasts well into the twenty-first century. With the collapse of the Berlin Wall and disintegration of the USSR, Powers had turned his attention to this conference in Berlin, his own brainchild, which he hoped would be the equivalent of Laussane and Evangelism 2000 and every other such conference all wrapped into one, and provide a major new impetus for evangelical groups to impact what had once been the closed Eastern Bloc of Europe. Never before had such a mighty gather-

71

ing of Christian leaders been assembled in one place for a single purpose before, and Anthony Powers was at the apex of his sanguine being in pulling it all together. His hopes were boundless for what would result from the week of meetings.

By the time Jackson and Jacob reached their room an hour and a half later, both were nearly exhausted and fell across their beds with mingled sighs and groans. Powers had kept up nonstop conversation and instructions since they had arrived.

"Well, he's got everyone here, I'll say that much for him," said Jacob as he stretched out with a relaxing sigh.

"With you as his star centerpiece," quipped Jackson.

"Knock it off," kidded his father. "I'm just one in Tony's cast of thousands."

"Come on! You saw his eyes when we walked in. Your presence gives Powers's whole effort major-league credibility. You're one of the featured draws; you must know that."

"He's got Carson Mitchell, Sandra Black. I hear Palacki's going to be here from Poland—he's a huge factor, especially now—plus representatives from South America, Africa, Indochina. I'm just a small cog."

"One of many, I'll grant you that—but a key cog."

"Have you seen the workshop and seminar and lecture schedule? Why it reads like a Who's Who of Protestantism! And besides that, several high-ranking Catholics are going to speak too, including a couple of archbishops. There are nuns and priests, and Anglicans, Lutherans, liberals, Pentecostals, fundamentalists, Raedenburg, political leaders from East and West—the most remarkable mix I've ever seen. It is going to be an amazing week—I see why Tony is beside himself with excitement!"

"All that may be true, but I still contend that Powers is plenty happy about your presence."

"I'm not going to debate the point, but somehow I think most people lost interest in Jacob Michaels a year ago."

"I don't agree," said Jackson. "I think you are more highly respected now than you ever used to be. Your coming clean and stepping out of the spotlight may have jolted a few people at the time. But as your new priorities come to the fore, people are curious. They want to know what the 'new Jacob Michaels' is all about. I think you're going to find that you have just as much impact as before, though perhaps in different ways."

"Impact is not something I'm seeking," said Jacob thoughtfully. "*I* want to learn how to live before I tell the rest of the world what they ought to be doing."

"Nevertheless, you can't avoid who you are, and therefore you *are* going to have an impact."

"I suppose you're right. But as I told you on the plane, I'm not sure that the kinds of things I've been thinking fit in too well with what Tony has in mind for this conference."

16

August 9, 8:45 A.M.
Berlin

The following morning, the large conference hall of the convention center across the street from the Worldwide Hotel on Leitzenburger Strasse was filled to capacity when Anthony Powers strode to the podium confidently, his face bright with smiles, one hand gesturing in greeting to the crowd as it applauded.

"Thank you—thank you!" he said into the microphone, one hand still raised as he looked around, nodding and smiling, at the audience before him. "Thank you, and welcome. Welcome, all of you!"

As the noise subsided, Powers launched into his opening remarks.

"I cannot tell you how happy I am that you all have come," he began. "So—especially to those of you unable to attend last evening's opening informalities—I extend to you the warmest of welcomes! I am as confident as I have ever been of anything that God is going to do many remarkable and amazing things among us this week. I trust none of you will depart regretting the time and expense involved in attending this conference. I truly believe we stand in one of the great watersheds of human existence, with perhaps the single greatest opportunity for fulfilling the Great Commission in history before us. And we, ladies and gentlemen, *we* stand at the very threshold. We have the ability to carry out Christ's command to go unto all the world in a more massive way than any group of Christians has before. That is, of course, why we are all here. We all share the vision of a world in which the gospel has been preached throughout every one of its distant corners. Suddenly we find ourselves facing a scenario where it is at last possible!"

Powers paused, took a breath, then settled into the flow of his introductory remarks.

"On behalf of the organizing committee and myself," he said, "let me officially welcome you, and hereby open the Berlin Conference on Evangelism in the post–Cold War era. You are some twelve hundred, and thus clearly this is *not* the largest gathering of Christians ever to take place. It is, however, I have no doubt, the most prestigious and auspicious. Each one of you has been invited here because you represent a cross-section of leadership spanning the entire spectrum of Christendom. Each one of you represents tens, hundreds, and even thousands of men and women back home. Some thirty-three languages are represented in this hall this morning, from one hundred and six nations. And when you return home, transmitting the principles you have gleaned here, a wave of evangelistic fervor will be unleashed to affect literally millions of God's people.

"Men and women, my brothers and sisters—can you grasp the enormity of our potential impact? We who are gathered together at this moment are the very leaders of Christendom itself! With the doors to Eastern Europe and Russia open before us, vast throngs will soon be entering the kingdom as a result of *our* efforts. You will send people into the East! You will print books and Bibles! You will raise money to purchase materials! You will take books and pamphlets and tracts by the millions into regions where the gospel has never before been heard! No longer will you smuggle them in by ones and twos, hidden in suitcases. Now you will take Testaments and materials in by the very truckload!

"The technology is available to us. We have the resources to accomplish what no other generation of Christians has done. You who listen to me at this moment possess the facilities and man-power and resources to turn the world upside down! And working together, in harmony and unity, I have no doubt that we can, and we will, fulfill Christ's Great Commission before the year 2000!"

As he paused, his words were interrupted by enthusiastic applause, with here and there an "Amen!" shouted throughout the auditorium. As Jackson listened from his seat about halfway toward the rear of the hall, it was clear why Anthony Powers had risen to such a position of prominence in evangelical circles and why he had been successful in drawing together such an array of Christian leaders. The man was indeed dynamic and his words electrifying.

And in spite of Powers's grand utterances, Jackson detected no trace of arrogance or pomposity. There was nothing like what had made him so uncomfortable two years earlier listening to his father. This was a sincere man, Jackson thought, a good man, a man alive with vision and purpose—intelligent, hard-working, above reproach. Jackson found within him far different responses from those which had so discomforted him at the former Michaels crusades. *These people are sincere,* he thought, *dedicating their very lives to the furthering of the gospel.* The looks on their faces, the fire burning from their eyes, exuded commitment and depth. This was no gathering of shallow religiosity, but exactly what Powers had said—a group unlike any other ever assembled.

Though nearly all of those present could be said to be "important" individuals in their own right in the spheres of influence they represented, they sat spellbound by Powers's charismatic enthusiasm.

". . . hope and pray that *this* conference will be unlike any other you have attended," Powers was saying as Jackson once more focused his attention upon him. "Practicality has been the goal of the organizers as they put together the week's events for you. Not only will there be inspirational addresses from such men as Carson Mitchell, Erick Mills, and Jacob Michaels, there will be a host of workshops and seminars and discussions on every conceivable facet of evangelism in today's world. Finances are of vital concern to all of us, and several authorities will address fund-raising and how we can most efficiently use the resources we have at our disposal. Literature is, of course, a fundamental part of any outreach program, so we will be offering assistance on all phases of it—from the actual obtaining and operation of printing equipment to the printing of Bibles, books, pamphlets, and tracts in many of the Slavic, Serbian, Croatian, and Russian languages and their multitude of dialects. We will deal with the set-up and operation of actual missionary excursions into the countries behind the former Iron Curtain. Many of you have already been to those areas, and we hope to hear of your experiences and insights during the discussion times. It is important that we learn from one another, and encourage and help one another. Radio and television, political factors, where and how the state churches—both Protestant and Orthodox—fit into the scheme, and how we must vary our approach to reach what we might call 'State Christians.' All these issues will be treated in some depth. I personally am enthusiastic about the future of satellite ministry and eagerly anticipate the day when a Christian satellite will orbit the earth, bombarding every corner of it continuously with the reading of Scripture and salvation messages. There are *so* many unprecedented opportunities before us!

"One of the priorities that the organizers have sought to emphasize is a dialog between many various segments of Christendom. Most of you know that my background and point of view is solidly evangelical. But from the beginning I realized that I had to offer far more than just my *own* particular slant on evangelism. Therefore, we have drawn upon a wide diversity of perspectives so that you have the opportunity to mix and interact with contrast, even disparity. Our desire is to find strategies whereby we may work together as God's *united* body, rather than continuing to move in our own separate directions. So take advantage of ideas that may be new to you. You may be surprised from what corner an idea may come that will ignite your vision to new heights."

Powers paused, smiled broadly, then went on. "In short, nothing has been omitted. When you leave here a little more than a week from now, you should be equipped to carry home specific strategies with which you can immediately begin working with men and women under your charge to fulfill what I believe is our joint destiny—carrying the good news throughout the earth."

He stopped momentarily, then added, "So, consult your programs and begin planning your time to maximum effect. After lunch, at one-thirty, we will be privileged to hear some challenging remarks from Mr. Victor Schultz. Then our first workshops and small-group seminars will kick off at three o'clock."

Jackson and Jacob rose together. At the opposite side of the hall, Jacob saw a man he recognized as Gentz Raedenburg, a renowned figure in both German religious and political circles, with high connections in Bonn and a solid reputation among evangelicals as well, Raedenburg offered a curious contrast to the speech Jacob had just heard. The German leader did not seem to fit in with the beam-the-gospel-via-satellite-into-the-jungle mentality. *Perhaps,* Jacob reflected, *Tony might indeed have pulled together a wider spectrum than I had given him credit for.*

Seeing Raedenburg caused Jacob to reflect further how the new politics of Europe fit into evangelism. *Or does it?* he wondered. *To what extent does evangelism intersect with one's political worldview? Does the so-called new world order signal a new approach to evangelism as well?*

Filling his bin of unanswered questions to overflowing, Jacob filed out of the hall with the rest of the throng, absorbed, reflective, unconscious of those around him. It was one of the few times in his life that he had sat with the audience of such a large gathering, and many and diverse were the thoughts stirring within him.

He was thus unusually quiet as he shuffled out at Jackson's side, hardly noticing the stares and comments directed toward him by attendees when they recognized his face. A number of well-wishers approached with handshakes and greetings, and Jacob responded with a friendly but preoccupied detachment.

17

August 6, 11:49 A.M.

Moscow

The Defense Minister had had dealings with the former head of the KGB before. But never on anything approaching an intimate basis. They had merely been comrades in the regime.

But now events necessitated a closer alliance. Desyatovsky frankly didn't know if Bolotnikov was a man he could trust. But he had to find out. He was going to need men of his unique abilities who would be loyal to him. He had plenty of them already. But now he believed it was time to bring the old KGB chief into the inner circle. He had to know, when it all came down, which side Bolotnikov was going to land on. In the meantime, he could use his help.

"Ah, Comrade Bolotnikov," said the Defense Minister as the ex-KGB chief entered his office. "How are you finding your new— uh, position in the government?"

"Not without its adjustments," replied Bolotnikov guardedly.

"Nothing insurmountable, I hope?"

"Not at all, Comrade Defense Minister."

Leonid Bolotnikov had made a career of studying both allies and adversaries, reading them, and discerning motives and objectives. Without a cunning perceptiveness that came as second nature to him, he would not have risen to the KGB's top position. Nor would he have been one of the few to slide into the post-Soviet Union Government nearly unscathed by his past reputation. Most of his former associates had not been so fortunate.

At fifty-six, he was still a powerful man, six-foot-three, hair still mostly black, with bulging strength throughout his arms and shoulders and upper body. He had joined the Soviet military at eighteen. During the Hungarian uprising in 1956 he had distinguished himself, and after that his career moved into the fast track. By 1968 and the Czechoslovakian invasion, he had become a division commander and in 1982 was appointed commander of the Warsaw Pact Forces, one of the youngest men ever to hold the position, though in light of the Kremlin's propensity for filling their positions of power with octogenarians, the distinction was empty of significance. Shortly thereafter he had been elevated to full membership in the Politburo, an advancement made possible by his occasional mentor, the late Defense Minister Dmitri Ustinov, one of Desyatovsky's predecessors. Ustinov had always considered Bolotnikov one of the Motherland's future leaders, and thus when the chairmanship of the KGB became available in 1984, he recommended his protege for the post.

Desyatovsky had first encountered him during their mutual years in the Politburo, but this was their first private meeting. He had never been exactly clear on how Bolotnikov had managed in the critical years of the late 80s when so many of the KGB's henchmen suddenly found themselves out in the cold. As top man, however, he probably had files that could bring down anyone he wanted. *He probably had enough dirt on both Gorbachev and Yeltsein,* thought Desyatovsky, *to write his own ticket during the disintegration and changeover.*

As Bolotnikov sat in his superior's office, the wheels of his mind were not idle. Everyone in Russia had a motive these days, and he wondered what was Desyatovsky's. He would wait—and listen—and watch for events to develop.

"You used to have an associate," Desyatovsky continued, "one of your assistants, I believe, who is proving a bit troublesome to me."

Bolotnikov smiled. "I know precisely who you mean," he replied. "I have heard reports that he has been trying to get out of the country."

"That may be. But he remains here—and has been tailing me."

"And you think, perhaps, I may be able to help?"

"He used to be one of the KGB's best men."

"But he and I have been out of touch since—you must realize, of course, how greatly things have changed. I found my way again into the military, under the auspices of the Russian republic, whereas the man you speak of has been, shall we say, less fortunate." Bolotnikov was feeling his way through the conversation gingerly, until he knew what Desyatovsky's game was.

"I understand," said the Defense Minister. "I am aware of his dilemma, that he is being sought even now by the police in connection with his past crimes with the KGB—meaning, of course, no disrespect to you."

"None taken."

"But as yet, he has not been found, nor has he been successful in getting out of Russia. To my knowledge he is still in Moscow itself."

"So I have heard," assented Bolotnikov.

"And as long as he remains at large, he threatens certain plans and negotiations of mine that are highly delicate in nature."

"You think he is trying to undermine these—these *plans,* as you call them?"

"Of that there can be no doubt."

"Then he must be stopped."

"Precisely."

"I begin to see your point, Comrade Defense Minister. And he is being sought, you say, by the police?"

"To no effect! If I may be so bold, times have just—"

Desyatovsky paused, eyeing Bolotnikov carefully.

"May I speak frankly, Comrade Bolotnikov?" he asked at length.

"Please," replied Bolotnikov, nodding his head in assent.

"What I was going to say," Desyatovsky went on, "is that times have changed. The police today are—I hope you will forgive me for being so blunt—little more than low-level office workers from the old days. Your KGB was, I must say, considerably more effective with this sort of thing. You and your men knew how to handle problems quickly and efficiently—*if* you understand me."

Desyatovsky was probing, feeling the man out to see where he stood. And Bolotnikov knew it. A thin hint of a smile cracked his lips. Perhaps he had musjudged the Defense Minister. It sounded as if the two might actually get along rather nicely.

"I believe I do," smiled Bolotnikov. "I will take your words as a compliment."

"I do not think they know the man has two residences. Even my limited intelligence knows that much."

"They are tracking him?"

"Ja, and finding nothing but cold trails."

"Why do you not put them onto the right path?"

"Don't you understand? I cannot get involved personally. Matters are too—sensitive right now. Which is exactly why I asked you to see me. Do you think—that is, do you still have contacts, as it were, whom you might call upon, men of resource and skill?"

"I could perhaps see what might be done." Bolotnikov's tone was again guarded and distant.

"You sound reticent to help me."

"Times are sensitive for us all, Comrade Defense Minister. One must walk warily in the new order. You cannot be unaware that I myself, as former head of the KGB, face certain perils if I were to stumble in the wrong direction."

"I understand perfectly. Yes, you are right—tenuous times. One must walk with caution, choosing his allegiances and friendships with care."

A long silence followed. The words remained heavily suspended in the air, both men clearly reflecting on their import relative to the present conversation. If an alliance were to form between them, it would not be based on trusting natures but on the fact that each saw in the other a way to gain his own objectives.

"Tell me, Comrade Bolotnikov," said Desyatovsky after several long moments, "what do you think of the new order?"

"Your question is a broad and complex one, Comrade Defense Minister."

"Admittedly. Do you have the courage to answer?"

Bolotnikov squinted imperceptibly, then smiled. It was a bold challenge—one he could not resist. He would see what Desyatovsky had to say.

"Times have changed," he replied at length. "No one can deny that. Not even I. Yet sometimes one cannot help but wonder if the change has been positive for the Motherland—or negative."

They were just the words Desyatovsky had been hoping to hear. Apparently he had not misjudged this man.

"Do I gather from your words that you are *dissatisfied* with the course events are taking?"

It was a bolder challenge yet.

"*Dissatisfied?* It is a strong word, Comrade Defense Minister."

"Indeed. But I stick with my choice of phrase. What is your answer?"

It was Bolotnikov's turn to weigh his options one final time. But it did not take him long.

"Let me answer you then with a partial answer. I will say that, yes, perhaps I am, as you say, dissatisfied."

It was all Desyatovsky needed. In the elusiveness of Russian double-talk, he knew what Bolotnikov meant.

"Then, perhaps you might be interested in *why* I must see that your former associate is stopped?"

"Indeed I would—most intrigued!"

"Would you care for a glass of vodka first? It is a rather lengthy story."

18

August 9
Berlin

For the rest of the conference's first full day, Jackson and Jacob split up to attend separate activities.

Jackson decided to attend the workshop on "Tracts, Tapes, and Books: Winning Souls with the Giveaway," co-led by Sydney Feldmen of the American Tract Society and Jack McGovern of Word of God Publishers, whereas Jacob opted for a talk by Father Erick Mills, Episcopalian bishop from the Philadelphia diocese, on his well-known program for the homeless.

The first thirty minutes of Mills's talk was devoted to the recounting of his program in Philadelphia. The remaining time was spent making interpolations from his experience to the current situation in Eastern European cities.

"We have sent both individuals and teams," he was saying, "into all the major cities of the Eastern Bloc. We had begun to do so even before the crumbling of the wall, but of course accelerated our efforts the instant the doors fell open to us.

"The streets of Warsaw, Prague, Budapest, Krakow, and Bucarest have been suddenly filled with that most Western of blights—the homeless.

"Herein, my friends, lies our greatest challenge, the greatest opportunity for evangelism of our era. These are hungry people—we must feed them. They are thirsty—we must take them drink. They have no shelter—we must provide them places to go. They are cold—we must wrap blankets around their shivering frames. They live in despair—we must show them we care.

"The key is people—men and women with Christian hearts of compassion and charity—who are willing to lay down their comfortable lives of affluence and ease and go to the places where the need is desperate. People who—"

As Jacob listened, he glanced around at the others in the room. Some were taking notes. One or two held pocket tape recorders. Nearly all sat spellbound. *It is no wonder,* he thought, *that Father Mills had been so successful on the East Coast setting up such programs as he is now describing.* When the talk was over, several persons went forward to ask questions, while the rest filed out. Jacob spoke to no one, left the room, and met Jackson in the lobby. They had agreed to go to the afternoon meeting together.

"How was it?" asked Jacob.

"Oh, halfway as I expected," answered Jackson. "Here is *the* best approach to evangelism that *everybody* ought to adopt."

"Which was?"

"Witness, salvation tracts, and music. Books geared toward pressing people to invite the Lord into their life—that kind of thing. And the need to get zillions of things printed up in all the Eastern languages for instant giveaway and distribution."

Jacob laughed lightly. "That's just the opposite of what I heard!"

"What was *your* workshop like?"

"Actually, pretty interesting," replied Jacob as they began walking to the next session. "What struck me though was who was there as much as what was said."

"How so?"

"For one thing, the room wasn't even half full—twenty-five, maybe thirty people was all. And I mean this guy is big-time in some circles—he's been written up in *Newsweek*—a major figure on the East Coast. Yet here he is, and it's as if no one knew it. I didn't see a single person I knew, and no one seemed to even recognize me either."

"Your feelings weren't hurt?"

"No—good grief!" exclaimed Jacob. "Why would you even ask that? What I meant was, there didn't seem to be any 'evangelicals' there. You know what I mean, your fundamentalist, conservative crowd. Father Mills presented a standard liberal package— social evangelism. But it wouldn't surprise me a bit if the only people there listening to him were the ones who already believed along similar lines. Neither would it surprise me if everyone at your tracts and giveaway workshop was already involved in the things they espoused, right?"

"The crowd seemed pretty much in tune with their direction all right," said Jackson. "And the faces I recognized were mostly from the ministries you'd expect."

"See what I mean?" rejoined Jacob. "People don't mix it up. For this thing to work there needs to be cross-pollination of ideas and methods and personalities. The people who should have been at Father Mills's lecture were probably all hearing lectures on things they're already doing. And those people who *were* there listening to him could have used a dose of McGovern's enthusiasm about handing out literature along with food and blankets."

19

The final workshop hour of the first day was billed simply as "Ideas That Work." It featured five diverse organization personalities, each of whom would spend five minutes sharing a single idea or technique that he or she had found particularly fruitful. The remainder of the hour had been reserved for questions from the floor. Anticipating a large turnout because of the names represented, the largest meeting room other than the auditorium had been reserved, and as Jackson had noted, there were probably three to four hundred in attendance.

The moderator of the symposium stood and briefly introduced

the five speakers. He then turned the floor over to Captain Ted Craddick of the Salvation Army.

"One of the first principles of evangelism, it has always seemed to me," began the Captain, dressed in the familiar navy blue with red trim of the Salvation Army, "is that you've got to get people's attention. If they don't listen to you, then there's not much you can tell them. You can preach at people till you're blue in the face, but if they're not interested, they're either going to walk on by if you're on a street corner, or they're going to go to sleep if you're in a church or a meeting hall. You've got to get them interested—rule one of evangelism!

"So, how do you do that?"

The man's easy, self-effacing style put everyone at ease. There were a few chuckles and shiftings around as he continued.

"There's nothing that works quite so well as giving them something. I suppose it's a bit like the shrewd grandfather who always has a lollipop handy when his young granddaughter comes around. I don't mean to imply that we can buy people's salvation with a gift. I'm just saying that nothing quite perks people's ears up and opens their hearts like giving them something.

"And speaking of perking people's ears up—I don't suppose it'll come as any surprise to any of you that the thing I'm talking about that we in the Salvation Army like to give away is *music.* That's our gift to folks, and we've been singing and playing and making music all around the world for more than a century. It's an idea that works!"

As Craddick took his seat spontaneous applause burst out. His message had been so simple and brief and so refreshing in contrast to some of the more ponderous and cerebral presentations thus far, that his humble style and gravelly voice sent a breeze of fresh air through the room.

After another brief introduction, Sister Jeanne Marie came forward in the customary black habit of her order, representing the Sisters of Jesus' Hands and Feet. Her skin was nearly as dark as her garb. She had flown in from Kisangani in Zaire only two days before.

"Our work in the heart of Africa," she began, "might at first seem quite different from what many of you have been accustomed to in your various fields of endeavor, and quite different from what might seem to be required in the countries of Europe formerly under the Communist yoke. It is my hope, however, that parallels exist that you will all find beneficial."

She paused, glanced down briefly at the sheet of paper on the podium before her, scanned the audience, and then went on in the heavily accented English of the tongues of native Africans.

"The needs of people in the Third World are basic. Starvation and disease are rampant. The epidemic of AIDS on my own continent of Africa is out of control and spreading like uncontained wildfire. Sanitation, illiteracy—so many problems!

"In the midst of all this, the church offers a stabilizing solidity, a solace, a calm in the midst of the world's pain and anguish. The physical presence of a church in a community gives the hope that somewhere there are people who might care and might help.

"Everywhere the need cries out to us. It is not I or other workers like me who bring life. It is the *church* that brings life. It is the church that has for countless generations been the source of ministry and service and love, the source of hope. We servants of the church may be the hands and feet, but it is the church that gives us the place to function, the place to administer the healing touch of the Saviour.

"My humble message, therefore, is this: The church and its institutions must be taken to those regions of the world where there is great need. Workers, food, blankets, medicine, literature, and equipment—all those things must be provided as well. But without the church, they exist in a vacuum and are unable to bring change to nations and cultures. Whatever else is done for the countries of the Communist world, the one thing we must do is take the church to them. I do not propose to you an *idea* of evangelism that works, but rather that the church itself works."

Sister Jeanne Marie walked back to her seat, amid scattered applause from the audience.

In contrast to Sister Jeanne's composed and quiet demeanor, the next speaker fairly bounded out of her chair and to the podium with visible animation and a sparkling smile of excitement. Every word of her delivery exuded the exhilaration she felt about her ministry.

Sandra Black, one of several co-founders of Countdown Ministries, was without a doubt the best-known personality on the stage, and in fact was one of the major drawing cards of the entire conference. The worldwide efforts of Countdown were well-known throughout fundamentalist circles whose focus was largely end-times oriented. An active magazine and publishing arm kept Mrs. Black and her colleagues visible in the public eye of evangelicalism.

"I am so happy to be here!" she began enthusiastically. "The Lord is so good to have brought us all together. I've already been blessed abundantly today, listening to inspiring speakers and feasting on rich fellowship of the saints. Praise the Lord, I can hardly believe it's just the first day of the conference!

"We at Countdown Ministries are involved in many things I would like to tell you about. I really loved what our brother from the Salvation Army said a few minutes ago about the need to give something away to get people's attention. Well, that's exactly what we're trying to do. What we're giving is the Word of God, in little chunks of teaching, through tracts and pamphlets.

"That's why I present this as our 'idea that works'; giving away the gospel and printed messages of Christian teaching by the millions! Our goal is to print and distribute one million of each of our five top-selling tracts and pamphlets, in *each* of the major Eastern European languages—Russian, Polish, Czech, Bulgarian, Romanian, Hungarian, Serbo-Croatian—as well as a hundred thousand in as many of the minor languages, such as Slovene, Ukrainian, Slovak, Armenian, Lithuanian, Serbian, Estonian, and Latvian, as possible. The job is so enormous that we are trying to raise two million dollars to accomplish the task. And if any of you listening can help by sponsoring a certain portion of this translation and printing effort, I know the Lord would bless you abundantly and reward many times over the generosity of your donations.

"I just returned from Russia myself, where I led a small team in 'spying out the land' for possibilities for future ministry, making contacts, and assessing need. We're sending people in to visit and share in the Spirit and fellowship with small gatherings of believers. What would have been illegal two years ago is no longer prohibited, and we believe we must act without delay.

"Well, praise the Lord, and I sincerely do hope you'll pray about being part of this fabulous outreach with us. People are being saved literally every day, but we need funds to continue spreading the gospel as we hope to do. God bless you all!"

The moderator stood as the bubbly Mrs. Black returned to her seat. He glanced quickly at his watch, and then made the next introduction of Herb Randon.

Mr. Randon represented Global Vision Missions, and his remarks reflected an approach to evangelism more traditional than any that had preceded him. "Strange to say," he began, "especially at an evangelism conference where reaching out with the gospel into foreign lands is the topic of discussion, but I feel somewhat out of step. It would appear that our methods and efforts are in a distinct minority—even rather old hat and boring alongside some of the newer and flashier techniques being proposed here.

"Yet I think there remains a great deal that this entire conference can glean from the experiences and history of the missionary agency—not only *ours* but all missions groups. Traditionally, organizations such as ours recruit 'missionaries,' not short-term 'teams.' Missionaries who will devote the rest of their lives to living with native peoples all over the world. We offer no holiday excursions, only lifetime commitments. We send people not to stand on street corners and preach, but to *live* with and among the people with whom they will involve themselves.

"Now my idea that works involves people back home. It personalizes missions. Let's face it, how many of you would dig into your wallets or purses and give me twenty dollars right now if I said to you, 'Global Vision needs money'? But if your next-door neighbor or close friend came to you and said, 'I've decided to go to the mission field. I'm going to be living in a village in South America where there is no running water and the nearest town is three hundred miles away. We hope to help curb an epidemic of malaria among the young children there. We'll be working with a medical team, as well as helping to translate the gospels of Mark and John into the native dialect. Do you suppose you might help support us with ten dollars a month?'—Now how many of you would turn such a request down? I imagine most of you would say, 'Please, let me give fifty a month!'

"It is my firm belief that evangelism that works involves a much wider range and broader base of people than merely those on the front lines. I would hope, therefore, that you would seek to find ways to apply this principle to your specific ministries. Thank you."

"Thank you, Herb," the moderator said. "We certainly are

getting a diverse set of workable and time-tested ideas. And now, for our final speaker this afternoon, it gives me great pleasure to introduce a personal friend whose work I know and support enthusiastically, Mr. Brad Kimball, co-founder and President of Vets With A Mission."

The athletic-looking Kimball stepped up to the microphone with a broad smile. "Many of you probably haven't heard of us, so I'll just tell you briefly about how we began, and that will lead into what we do—which is my idea that works. Vets With A Mission began about five years ago when two of us who were Marines in Vietnam got to reminiscing about the war. We found within ourselves a great burden for that tiny land in Southeast Asia that we had helped blow apart. We talked and prayed at length. And out of that time of prayer came the first trip the two of us took back to Vietnam, twenty-some years after we had been there.

"What we noticed was the decrepit condition of their buildings. It was abysmal. Shacks posing as hospitals. Walls falling apart, dirt floors, no sanitation, no running water. I suppose that was what we noticed because we were both in the building trade.

"Suddenly the idea came to us: *Hey, what would happen if we brought a bunch of guys in here and, say, built a new wing on that hospital there? Built it good—with real wood and a cement floor!*

"We looked at each other and said "Why not! Why couldn't we do that?'

"We went back home, and it wasn't long before we'd raised ten thousand dollars.

"Bob and I arranged to fly back to Vietnam. The rest of the guys agreed to pay our way there and back so we'd have the whole ten thousand to use for the hospital. So Bob and I flew to Saigon and boldly went to see the administrator of the little thing they called a hospital and told him what we wanted to do. He was full of questions—Why? Who are you? What will it cost us? Understand—the mentality is Communist, East suspicious of West, that kind of thing. They were very closed, very bound to tradition. The government bureaucracy controls everything. You couldn't even walk up to a starving beggar on the street and give him a loaf of bread without having to go through three months of red tape to OK the transaction.

"Anyway, this guy was nervous, so he went to his superior, and he went to his, and before we knew it, Bob and I were sitting before this official inquisition of stern-faced men throwing question after question at us. And we kept saying the same thing: We were here a while back, we saw this hospital's need, we went home, we raised some money, and we'd like to bring a small team of men here to build a new wing.

" 'But *why*?' they insisted. 'Look,' we said candidly, 'we make no apologies about being Christians. And we want to do this because we are Christians. But we recognize the customs of your land. We recognize that Christianity is not accepted here. We have no intention of trying to proselytize.'

"Well, I could go on for hours telling you about the process we went through. It was really something! But in the end, because they were in such desperate need, and because they couldn't turn away such an obviously beneficial thing, they consented to let us build the wing."

Kimball stopped momentarily, glancing away and trying to calm himself with a deep breath or two. The recollection had brought moisture to his own eyes, and it was a moment or two before he could go on.

"Sorry," he said. "It just chokes me up whenever I realize all that God has done over there."

Another short pause. "I'm sorry to take so long going into all this," he said, glancing apologetically back toward his friend who had introduced him.

"I'll try to wrap it up quickly. The long and short of it is this, and here's the *idea* that I want to present: When your motive is to help, to do good, and when you're up front and open about what you will and won't do, even the most intransigent of people and regimes and bureaucracies will respect your motives."

Kimball turned and walked back to his seat.

20

The moderator again took the podium. "Well, I'm sure we would all agree that we have been presented with a great deal of food for thought! We have heard five distinct ideas: using music, solidifying the institution of the church, passing out literature, helping those who support our work to feel personally involved, and finding ways to work with existing officialdom even where the gospel message may not be welcome.

"Now in the approximately twenty minutes we have left, I would like to open the floor for questions."

Several hands immediately shot into the air. He recognized a portly gentleman sitting about a third of the way back. The man stood.

"Pastor Harold McFadden," he said in a thick bayou drawl, "from Shreveport, Louisiana. I just wanted to mention the powerful impact that occurs when you put together two of these ideas we've been hearing about. When we've got a big revival or tent meeting planned, we print up thousands of flyers inviting folks to come hear the powerful preaching of the Word and get themselves saved. Then we do just what young Mrs. Black there said—we get our folks out there in the streets passing them things out by the dozens and hundreds. Of course, they've got a salvation message right there too, just in case the conviction of God falls on them before the service. But I like the word she used—*saturate* folks with the Word! And that's what we do with our flyers. We just saturate 'em everywhere all around Shreveport.

"But you see, what we're doing is inviting all them folks to *church*, and that's where the idea the good Catholic sister talked about comes in. You don't just try to get 'em saved on the street corner, you got to get 'em into the church where you can build the Word of God into their lives."

As he spoke, Sister Jeanne Marie bristled perceptibly at having her convictions about the solemn, centuries-old stability of the Church of Rome compared to a Pentecostal tent meeting revival in the Bible Belt.

"—and we get in the music too!" McFadden was saying in a

good-natured and jovial boast. "We always try to get one of the most popular singing groups for our revival meetings so we can tell the young people there's going to be plenty of entertainment. We put on a regular show, and folks have learned that when the Lakeside Assembly says, 'Y'all come,' they oughta not miss it!

"So what I reckon I'm getting at is to say a big *Amen!* to these ideas. They work all right! 'Cause Lakeside's now the fourth fastest growing Assembly church in the state, and there's no doubt in my mind it's on account of just these things!"

With an unsuccessful attempt to hide his pomposity, McFadden resumed his seat. Without waiting to be recognized, a second man stood several rows behind him and launched into his own mini-discourse.

"With all due respect," he said, "I feel I must take exception. I don't think that's what Sister Jeanne had in mind when she spoke of the institutions of the church at all. I've been working in the inner city of Chicago for twelve years, and I can tell you from personal experience that what those people need is not a tract inviting them to some flashy revival service with a country rock group. No, what those people need, plain and simple, is help. *Basic* help. They're struggling to survive, just like the people of Eastern Europe.

"We're out on the streets of Chicago with food vans and leaflets telling drug users about the danger of AIDS rather than about what sinners they are. And I make no apology for counseling young people about safe sex or handing out clean needles to drug addicts. To me that's evangelism. That's where Jesus was—out among the people."

He sat down, face red from the obvious emotion he felt.

He had unleashed a potential torrent of response. At least fifteen hands shot immediately into the air, and nearly as many voices began to speak at once. The moderator raised his hands and called for quiet.

"Please," he said. "We can't turn this into a free-for-all. Now, let's see—you there, the lady in the blue sweater," he said, pointing toward the rear of the room.

"To call handing out IV needles to drug users evangelism as taught by Jesus is ridiculous. To even hint at a parallel is—is beyond my comprehension. We're here to discuss *evangelism*, not what we think might be good. Evangelism means preaching the gospel and calling people to repentance. The test of evangelism is whether people are being saved, *not* whether the AIDS rate is reduced!"

"Then what do you make of Jesus Himself—He was always among the poorest and socially outcast," argued the man who had just spoken, turning around to face the woman. "If He were alive today I have no doubt He'd be right there with the AIDS victims."

"*If* He were alive?" called out another. "He *is* alive, by the power of the Holy Spirit!"

"Amen to that, brother!"

"I've heard all the do-good liberalism I can stand," called out another voice with a Southern accent. "All we need to do is get out there and preach the old-time gospel and plead the blood of Jesus."

"Wait just a minute," interjected the lady in blue. "I want to ask you one more thing," she said to the AIDS man. "If you think our mission should be to the downtrodden, what do you make of Jesus' saying that we would always have the poor with us, but that our first call is to love God and *then* our neighbor?"

"He made clear that without love to our neighbor, there can be no love for God. The one validates the other. All this pious talk of calling people to a religious experience while you ignore their suffering sounds a lot like the Pharisees that Jesus condemned."

"No one is advocating ignoring their—"

"Please, please, ladies and gentlemen!" called out the moderator over the microphone. "You simply must direct your comments to each other or to the speakers in a more orderly fashion. You will have ample opportunity as the week progresses to air these different viewpoints, I'm sure. Now, is there anyone we haven't already heard from? Yes—go ahead." He pointed to a young man in the row where Jackson and Jacob were listening to the heated interchange with great interest.

"I would like to ask a question of both Sister Jeanne Marie and Mrs. Black. How do the two of you, obviously representing different perspectives along the religious spectrum, balance your two philosophies of evangelism—passing out salvation literature versus ministering to the basic needs of life among Third World native peoples? As I listened to you, Sister, I did not hear much of an urgency to confront people with their need of repentance and salvation. But likewise Mrs. Black, I did not hear you speak to any role the church plays in what you are doing."

He sat down. The audience, quieted now by the first legitimate question posed of the speakers, waited. Sandra Black spoke first.

"Your question points out the beauty of First Corinthians twelve," she said with enthusiasm. "Body life is about diversity. When Paul spoke of the many functions of the body, he said that hands are not eyes and feet are not ears. That is why so many varied ministries are here—not that any one or two of us can accomplish the whole task of winning the world for Jesus, but that working together, as different parts of Christ's body, we do different things and draw the world to Him.

"A ministry such as ours puts energies into salvation literature, yet we recognize the vital role of local ministries and churches who must shepherd and disciple the converts after we are gone."

"Would you include the Catholic church in that statement?" the man, still on his feet, asked simply and without motive.

"I—uh, I hadn't really considered the specifics of that process."

"Sister Jeanne," the persistent questioner went on, "how would you respond to my original question of balancing such divergence?"

"Might I inquire as to *your* point of view?" the nun asked. "What church do you represent?"

"No church, as such," he replied. "I am Oscar Guinsmann, director of The Retreat in England."

"You are a Protestant evangelical?"

"We dislike labels, but if you had to pin one on us, that would probably be accurate," replied Guinsmann. "Our ministry is one of encouraging dialogue with the intellectual community and of speaking out on contemporary world issues from a Christian perspective."

"I do not much care for labels either, Mr. Guinsmann," said Sister Jeanne with an engaging smile. "But my reason for asking was to make a point. It will come as no surprise to you that we in the Catholic church have not been as eager to stress a personal salvation experience as have you Protestants, and especially what I believe you call fundamental evangelicals. It goes all the way back to the sixteenth century and Luther and Calvin and the historic splits that occurred then and which have endured more or less ever since.

"All this is to say that we view evangelism and the Christian life much differently than you do. To us, evangelism is getting out into the world as Jesus did and taking His life to the people around us. It is not trying to coerce them into making some decision, as you call it, but to share life with them. That is why the church—with its sacred rites of baptism and Communion and the mass and confession—in all these ways the life of Christ is deepened in us. We see such corporate practices as being more solidifying and strengthening in an individual's life than leaving him with only an ethereal experience to fall back on.

"For Catholics, therefore, Mr. Guinsmann, it is very difficult to find a 'balance,' as you say, between such divergence. I think I would simply agree with you. You are right—we do *not* feel an urgency to confront people with their need for repentance and salvation. The urgency we feel is to serve them and involve them with the church, wherein they will be able to discover their own means of working out what salvation means."

Jacob looked at Jackson beside him and smiled as if to say, "We landed in the middle of a lively one, didn't we!"

Meanwhile, another hand from the floor was being recognized.

"I would like to ask Mr. Randon what immediate plans Global Vision has in the Iron Curtain countries?"

The missions representative responded briefly. "Of course we are evaluating the possibilities and intensifying our recruitment procedures for that part of the world. But we have not yet finalized the locations where we hope to establish new works."

"And Vets With a Mission?" the same man asked. "What are your plans?"

"To be honest with you," replied Brad Kimball, "we do not anticipate setting up any kind of work in Eastern Europe. The vision the Lord gave us was specifically for Southeast Asia, and unless He prompts otherwise, we plan to continue in that region only. We are here primarily to share some of the things He has shown us, as well as glean ideas from the rest of you."

Many hands were still in the air, but the moderator ended the session. "I'm sorry," he said, "but our hour is up. This has been a stimulating time, and I know many of you still have questions and comments. I encourage you to seek out these and other speakers, as well as each other, so that this dialogue and healthy exchange can continue. Thank you all for coming. You are excused."

21

August 10, 1:20 P.M.
Chicago

An unseasonably cool spell had treated Midwesterners in general and Chicagoans specifically to four days of 60- and 70-degree weather, with accompanying offshore breezes blowing inland.

The front had been driven down from Canada. An overnight thunderstorm and drenching rains had given way to a more normal day in mid-August of 91 degrees with nearly the same level of humidity, and air conditioners throughout the city were blowing near peak capacity.

In his small office, where the air conditioner worked only well enough to keep it around 80 degrees, Robert Means sat with one foot propped on his desk, the phone cradled against his right ear, and a look of concern on his face.

At fifty-four, Means had been with ETW some twenty-five years, most of it spent ignominiously behind the scenes handling the requests and correspondence deemed too unimportant to involve what would have been called "the brass" of the organization. The years out of public view, however, had deepened the fiber of his spiritual being to such an extent that now almost overnight he had become something of a mentor to literally dozens of men and women who had for years walked past him in the hall without so much as a nod. With the internal shake-up that had occurred a year before in the wake of the humbling revelations of ETW's head, the entire organization had embarked upon a new and untried course.

In that process, if any single individual could be said to embody the new "soul" of the life that now seemed to flourish in the Luxor Towers, that man was Robert Means.

Evangelize the World, begun by the elder Michaels brothers, Jacob's father and uncle, was an organization far different from a short two years before. Jacob's decision to vastly scale back the stretch of ETW's activities, curtail speaking and writing commitments, suspend publication of books, and re-prioritize every aspect of financial spending and accountability had met with a wide range of responses. Some thought he had slipped a few mental cogs and promptly left ETW for other Christian organizations. Others found their own attitudes challenged to new depths by Jacob's example.

During the months of change, Jacob had arranged to meet individually with every member from every corner of the three floors occupied by ETW, explaining to each what he envisioned for the future, though, as he was always sure to say, there were a host of unknowns for which he was relying on the Spirit of God for guidance. Then he prayed with each one, telling him (or her) that if he chose to remain with ETW, there would be a place for him, but making sure he understood that henceforth things would be a great deal different and that servanthood would come before personal rewards or gain.

When the dust had settled several months later, ETW's staff had been trimmed by about 35 percent—comprising those who did not feel they could remain under the new arrangement. The vast reduction in payroll was augmented by a consolidation of many former operations and departments to such an extent that one entire floor of suites in the Luxor was no longer necessary.

The cutbacks, along with the sale of certain holdings of real estate, were sufficient to offset for a time the reduction in revenues that inevitably followed Jacob's videotaped message and Jackson's article. They were thus able to keep ETW functioning until God made clear His course for the future.

Over the span of the next six months, the atmosphere around ETW began to shift. There was a greater emphasis on people and their needs, both inside and outside the organization. People talked to one another. There were laughter and smiles, a caring that went beyond a mere "Good morning" and "How are you?" Whereas before Jacob Michaels had scarcely been seen, now he was all over the building, that is, when he wasn't out in the community hammering nails for a building project in the inner city or raising money on behalf of one of a dozen charitable groups. Among his employees it was a standard weekly question that made the rounds, "Well—what is Mr. Michaels involved in *this* week?"

They meant no disparagement by it, however. The esteem in which his people held him in fact rose with every new activity he got himself into. And at root, most everyone knew the change had something to do with Robert Means, the man they had so long ignored down in the "Correspondence" section.

Therefore, as time went on, Means's involvement began to grow as more and more people sought him out. Those who did discovered that the change they observed in the head of ETW had come from nothing more remarkable than the simple, practical application of vital biblical principles of faith. What had begun with Means and Michaels and two or three others gathering twice weekly for lunch, had now grown to more than sixty, whose hunger was not merely for that which supplied the body with nourishment. In the midst of one of the country's largest Christian organizations, none had realized what an impoverishment of spirit had existed.

Thankfully, that was changing. Dozens of others were now experiencing the revitalization of their spiritual pilgrimage, along with Jacob, and great was the joy within the breast of Robert Means to see coming to life the very realities for which he had prayed so long.

The telephone conversation had been a lengthy one, punctuated with occasional nods, words of acknowledgment, with here and there a question. At length he withdrew his foot from his desk and sat forward in his chair.

"Yes—I understand," he said. "Yes, we'll be sure to do that. I'll try to get together with them today if we can arrange it."

Again silence filled the office as he listened another moment.

"Right—give him my regards too." A laugh followed.

"Well, you certainly have the right! It's your nickel, you know— I know you're busy . . . good, I'm glad. Blessings to you!"

He hung up the phone and let out a long sigh. But the next instant he picked it up again and dialed a local number. The conversation was brief. When it was over, he dialed a three-digit ETW extention.

"Sondra," he said, "it's Bob. Could you come over to my office in an hour? We need to pray."

Fifty-five minutes later the door to Means's office opened with a knock. A tall, well-dressed woman walked in.

"Elizabeth," said Means rising with a smile to go along with his extended hand. "How are you?"

"Well, Bob," she replied, sitting in the seat he offered. "He must have called you immediately after hanging up with me!"

"A man that hungry for prayer from home must either be lonely for his wife, or else in a real quandary," replied Means. "In either case, we ought not to delay."

"I'm glad you called. I know God hears but there is something that seems to have a bit more force when you pray with someone."

"As the Bible teaches, where two or three are gathered. By the way, how's Diana doing?"

"Having the time of her life. I just got a letter from her yesterday."

"It's—what? Remind me what she's doing down there."

"It's a music camp the Baptist missionaries put on in Haiti every summer, that is, when there isn't too much unrest. She's trying to put together a children's choir of native youngsters."

"How much longer does it last?"

"She'll be home in two weeks, and from the sound of it, our daughter may never be the same."

"Rubbing shoulders with the hurting world usually changes us—ah, I think I hear Sondra coming now." Means rose and walked toward the door just in time to greet Sondra DeQue, the last member of their assembled trio.

"Sondra, how have you been?" asked Mrs. Michaels. "I haven't seen you for a couple weeks."

"I was out for a few days with a summer flu bug," answered Sondra. "I missed both last week's studies."

"Sondra, Jacob called just before I rang you," Bob said.

"Is something wrong?" asked Sondra, concerned.

"Not especially. Just a sense he has of discomfort. He said that after the past year here and all the changes he's been through, it's like suddenly being thrown back into the middle of the old ways of looking at things. Is that what he told you, Elizabeth?"

Jacob's wife nodded. "He said he's uncomfortable. He knows he's been given a tremendous opportunity there, but he doesn't know what to do with it, how to get through to people he doesn't think can see except in the traditional ways they always have."

"I suppose any time you get that many Christians together, especially leaders," Bob went on, "you're bound to have differences and conflicts. Anyway, he specifically asked us to pray for him, you included, Sondra, and I think we ought to do just that."

They fell silent. Bob moved to a chair between the two women, then took each of their hands in the two of his as Sondra and Mrs. Michaels completed the circle.

"Our Father," prayed Bob after a minute or two of silence. "We do lift our brother and friend and husband and leader up to You in this moment. As we have prayed for this opportunity facing him, we do so again. Be near him, Lord—guide him, speak to him, lead him, give him *Your* impressions and thoughts."

"Reveal to him the words You would have him speak," said Sondra.

"Fill him with compassion, heavenly Father," prayed Elizabeth, "for his fellow leaders in Berlin, the other men and women who, like him, must answer for Your people. Give Jacob eyes and ears and a heart to understand what needs to be said and the priorities that You would have him stress. Let him not lose his newfound convictions. Let him not flinch in standing strong. Let him be a light to those at the conference. May they see a difference in him, a new vibrancy of life."

"In the name of our Lord Jesus," said Bob, "even over this great distance, we stand on the promises of God to do battle on our behalf. We confidently take authority over the principalities and powers of the enemy, and in Jesus' name renounce all such disruptive influences that would work on Jacob's mind and heart."

The three continued to pray, both silently and aloud, for another fifteen minutes or so. At length Sondra looked, first at Elizabeth then toward Bob, and asked, "Did he say anything about how Jackson is doing?"

Bob smiled. "You know Jackson!" he said. "He's already got two cassette tapes and half a notebook filled with material for ten articles."

"Is he enjoying the conference?"

"Jacob didn't say—exactly. But again, if I know Jackson, the organizational platitudes always so evident at such gatherings are probably driving him crazy by now."

"That's Jackson!" Elizabeth laughed.

"I'm sure he'll find a way to bring some excitement to the rigor of a boring schedule of meetings."

"He usually does," agreed Bob.

"Maybe he'll do the tour of Berlin's museums," suggested Sondra.

"And drag Jacob along!"

All three laughed at the picture of Jackson and Jacob trying to find a European adventure trudging through the somber halls of a dusty, old museum.

PART 4

Danger in High Places

22

Gerhardt Woeniger had been around long enough to see the handwriting on the wall. He knew the winners and losers, and what came of playing on the wrong side of political fences—fences strewn with more barbs than the slashing thick wires that used to be strung along the wall in the middle of this city.

He was also enough of a historian to know it had always been so. *Loyalties and alliances are fleeting commodities on the European political landscape,* he thought as he made his way purposefully down the hall. Funny, he mused, only a few brief years earlier these buildings were little more than empty shells. Now a new home for the Bundestag was being constructed a short distance away, and here he was on the way to the Chancellor's temporary office—the Chancellor of a united Germany!

Yes, such was the speed with which things could change. One must be on one's toes, always sniffing the winds of fortune, guarding one's flank. Loyalty—a fleeting commodity indeed. You didn't have to know much German history to be painfully aware of that fact. Gerhardt had worked too hard to let pet loyalties keep him from doing what might have to be done to insure his own survival. These were times when people got shoved out into the cold for indecisiveness. Russia and Poland were full of yesterday's leaders who had become today's unemployed and imprisoned. It could happen in Germany too, and he had no intention of being one of the casualties. He would not get left behind. Sure, he owed Kolter his life, not to mention his family's. But he'd repaid that debt in full many times over. He'd been a loyal soldier all these years, delivering him the votes needed. But realities were realities, and in this game—

105

His thoughts were interrupted by his arrival at the outer lobby of the Chancellor's chambers.

"Guten Morgen, Herr Woeniger," the receptionist greeted him crisply. "Wie geht es Ihnen heute?"

"Sehr gut, Frau Wildig, danke," he replied.

"The Chancellor is just finishing up with the Finance Minister," she told him. "Please take a seat. It won't be but a minute or two, I'm sure."

Woeniger nodded and complied. As he glanced around at the Chancellor's new, lavishly appointed quarters, he could not help reflecting on everything that had occurred recently. Who could have foreseen it happening so suddenly? Men like him had come up through the civil service ranks in the 50s and 60s, taking for granted that West and East would never meet again, in spite of the lip service paid to the goal of reunification periodically by Bonn throughout the Cold War. Nobody really *believed* it would happen.

Yes, he had seen a great deal. What a shambles Germany had been after the war. Even as a boy he remembered the rubble, the bombed out shells of buildings and cathedrals and apartment houses, the desolation, the quiet, the old ladies silently weeping over the Fatherland.

But then had come the economic miracle. Gerhardt had first entered the political arena under the miracle's author himself, Economics Minister Ludwig Erhard. Never before had there been anything like the turnaround and growth of the Bundesrepublik Deutschland during the era of Chancellor Adenauer. The huge reservoir of skilled laborers had been tapped, throughout the country men, women, and children rolled up their sleeves with hard work and determination, industry rebounded in the valleys of the Ruhr and the Rhine, efficiency was high, unemployment low, competition, new industrial centers, a vital agricultural system, vast improvements in roads, airports, cities, modernizations sweeping through all corners of the land—what achievements had been accomplished during that period! He was proud to have been part of it. The gross national product had tripled in the decade of the 50s. They had shown the world what the German people were made of. Why they had made the BRD the third strongest industrial country in the world!

Yes, it had been a miracle, and not merely an economic one—it was a miracle of will and determination and work—the progress of a people unlike any other on earth. He was proud of his heritage—proud to be a German. They could be beaten down but never defeated. They would always rise, look up, and move forward with purpose and will.

He reflected on his own career. He had first been elected to the Bundestag in 1967 as part of the minority move of neo-Socialists rising out of the turmoil of the 60s. Though the CSDU part had never attracted a wide following, over the following decades it had usually garnered between 50 and 60 seats. This 10-12 percent of the vote was well in excess of the 5 percent minimum share required for a party to maintain the seats of its MPs, and he had been reelected to his seat every four years since. Through the intricacies of the parliamentary system, fate had from time to time placed upon the CSDU a pivotal role in the BRD's affairs. His own predecessors had been instrumental in putting together the coalition in 1969 that had brought the SPD's Willie Brandt to power. And ever since, though it was usually the second or third smallest part in the Bundestag, the CSDU nearly always found itself in the midst of coalition battles, holding the swing votes that were able to determine whether the CSDU or the RDP received the majority.

Woeniger himself had risen to head the CSDU's contingent in the lower house of the Federal Assembly in 1983, a position he had occupied ever since. Because the CSDU would always be a small party, barring a miracle he could never hope to become Chancellor himself. But he enjoyed the power afforded him by the Brandts, the Schmidts, the Scheels, and the Kolters. His name wasn't in the international limelight like theirs. But they knew he wielded the reins of a critical cluster of votes that could make or break them. Without his support, their coalitions would collapse.

Gerhardt Woeniger was a king-maker. He knew it, and he rather enjoyed the status, albeit an invisible status it was for the most part. His name came before the public every four years and whenever there began to be talk of a no-confidence initiative bandied about by some aggressive newshound. But the rest of the time, outside the periphery of Bonn itself, his face had remained unknown.

The thought brought a smile to his face. There was one who *did* know his face, however—the very man he now sat waiting to see. The old adage was certainly true: It wasn't how many people you knew, but *who* you knew that made the difference. If power and influence was the game—and who could deny it?—then he was one of the game's winners. For here he sat about to be stroked and cajolled by one of the world's most important men.

Hans Kolter *needed* him, needed his votes, needed his support. He—Gerhardt Woeniger—was the man the Chancellor turned to in order to push through his legislative programs! Power—yes, he had to admit, he liked possessing such influence.

When he stopped to reflect on the ironies of their personal histories, however, it galled him with a certain acrid bitterness that Hans should be Chancellor and not him. Hans was a good enough fellow but shallow and full of the kind of bluster and aplomb that the public ate up. He wasn't nearly the man of half the MPs in the Bundestag, including Gerhardt, if honesty forced him to admit it. But fate had thrust Hans upward, and the toppling of the wall less than a mile from here in 1989 had sealed his destiny in future history books forever. The reunification of the BRD and the DDR in 1990 had, of course, been the coup upon which his reputation would rest, and he had risen steadily on the wave of the world's adulation ever since, rivaling Reagan, Gorbachev, Bush, Thatcher, and Yeltsin as one of the globe's major players.

But still, Woeniger could not help thinking Kolter was not as big a man inside as the largesse of his outer frame would indicate. A hero created by the times, but not a hero who made events march to the drum of his determination and vision. A second-rate hero, he thought—perhaps not a hero at all in the true historic sense of the word.

Yet, there he sat—Chancellor of a united Germany. Who could deny that he had played his cards skillfully? And if Woeniger were just a bit jealous, who could deny him the luxury? Why shouldn't a politician of his substance and depth envy the good fortune of one who sat at the apex? His own time might come yet—if he played *his* cards right!

Again his reflections were cut short, this time by Frau Wildig's voice.

23

"Ah, Gerhardt," the Chancellor greeted him cordially. "Thank you for coming over so promptly."

"Your request is my duty, Herr Chancellor," Woeniger replied.

"Please, please, " Kolter said, indicating a seat near his, "not so formal, Gerhardt. We have been through too much over the years to reduce our friendship to platitudes."

"I am sorry, sir."

"No need for apologies," the Chancellor went on. "It is only that, though we represent different constituencies and occasionally must debate across the aisle from one another, we respect one another and have seen too much together to let that stand in the way of our friendship. Wouldn't you agree?"

"Of course," replied Woeniger.

The Chancellor stood and walked to the large window behind his desk. Woeniger remained silent.

"I still am caught up in sheer amazement at times," Kolter said after a moment or two, "when I realize what has happened in these last two or three years. Incredible times, Gerhardt—truly incredible! Can you believe it? We're looking out on a united, free Berlin—a *free* Berlin! Look at it out there—building and construction, cars and buses and trucks, and tourists. Why, the city's bursting with life and activity—from the Alexander Platz to the Kurfusten-damm, east, west—throughout the whole city. Life, energy, vigor, vitality. You can see it in how the people move along the sidewalk down there—"

As he spoke, still with his back to Woeniger, the Chancellor pointed with animation through the window.

"—even they walk with purpose and exuberance and bounce! It's a spirit of zest. I love our people, don't you, Gerhardt? There's no race like them. I have no doubt they will make of the former eastern sector a powerful and invigorating tribute to the German spirit, just as we did here in the 50s."

He turned from the window, but with a look of reflection still on his face. "So many changes—and in such a short time," he sighed. "Almost from the instant of our friend Mr. Gorbachev's ascension to power, the dominoes began to fall—in reverse order from what the Americans used to fear! Momentous events, new freedoms in Russia, elections, the waves of public demands in the east, the toppling of the wall, the crumbling of the Soviet Union. Where is it leading? What will be next? Where does the future lie—and in whose hands?"

A long silence followed, during which the Chancellor made his way back toward Woeniger, at length settling into a chair opposite him.

"It lies in *our* hands, Gerhardt," he said seriously, once he was seated. "Perhaps as at few other times before, individual men have decisions before them that can truly alter the course of history. I believe that you and I are in such a position—Hans Kolter and Gerhardt Woeniger, two old friends and politicians thrust side by side into the very center of world affairs—"

As he listened, Woeniger kept a cautious ear tuned to the political realities underlying Kolter's blandishments. Spreading the butter on a bit thick was the usual preparatory exercise for making a request. He would wait before allowing himself to feel *too* elevated in stature by the Chancellor's words.

"—ripe with opportunities," Kolter was saying, "like no other time in Germany's history. Hitler was a maniacal idiot. He set the Fatherland back half a century or more. But now we have again reached the acme where we can step full into our calling as one of the great nations in the history of the world. New demands now fall upon us, Gerhardt, as part of this heavy responsibility. Demands of leadership. New relationships have to be forged throughout the world community. What is the direction of the EEC, and who will now be involved? With the breakup of the Soviet Union into its constituent republics, how will those multifaceted relationships and alliances fit into both the world picture and the European picture?

"Leadership, Gerhardt—leadership! That is the key to the future. There is indeed what Mr. Bush has termed a 'new world order.' No one denies that. But who will provide the leadership to take this new world into the twenty-first century?

"No doubt you see what I'm driving at? The leadership will come from *us,* that's where! From Germany, from Berlin, from the Chancellery and Bundestag—from this very office, Gerhardt. This is the focal point of the future, of the new world order. *This* is the center of it all!"

He stopped and drew in a deep breath, clearly impassioned by what he was saying.

"The Bundesrepublik was a forceful entity, certainly. And similarly, the DDR was the leader of the Eastern Bloc in every way. But now, a united Germany possesses a might beyond what any of our predecessors ever dreamed possible. With the Soviet Union effectively out of the picture, Germany has become the major player in Europe. Three nations control the course of events now, Gerhardt—the United States, Japan, and ourselves. It's awesome, almost frightening in a way when you think of it. Yet Japan is so small—how long will it be able to sustain its present economic boom? It has nowhere to grow, no manpower resources to tap beyond its own. And eventually the energy of this burst of creative and industrial spike will begin to wane. It is inevitable that it cannot keep pace forever.

"Do you see what I mean, Gerhardt? We are in the driver's seat. Even the U.S. is in a slow, protracted decline. We owe it a great deal, and it is in the interest of world stability that the U.S. and the North Atlantic alliance remain strong. But initiative still belongs to us. We must steward this leadership trust with care. We must guard and protect the world's resources—natural, financial, and the resources of man's energy and vision—as well.

"All this brings me to the reason I asked to see you today, Gerhardt. I need to speak with you about the upcoming situation next week, to make sure I may still count on the support of your people in the CSDU. Do things still look good, Gerhardt?"

"As good as they could look at this preliminary juncture," replied Woeniger noncommittally.

"Not so preliminary," rejoined Kolter, with a hint of exasperation in his tone, though he quickly masked it. "A decision is scheduled next week," he went on. "This vote on aid to the Russian republics is critical, Gerhardt. It could well set the course for the very survival of those young struggling nations. And it will set an example of assistance for the rest of the world to follow. I need to be sure that your people are fully on board with me. The opposition is going to fight me on it tooth and nail. Klaus is determined to oppose me no matter what the cause. I think he'd oppose me even if inside he favored a bill, just to spite me. He's going to have the other minorities with him on this one, I think, and," he added, throwing Woeniger a sly grin, "he's probably already been doing his best to woo you too!"

"There are no secrets in this city," replied Woeniger, returning the smile. Both men knew more than they were willing to admit openly.

"In any case," the Chancellor went on, "you and I have always maintained an understanding. You've never let me down in the past. You've been the staunchest ally a man in my position could ask for, and I want you to know that I'm grateful."

"Thank you, sir."

"So you see how important this particular vote is, Gerhardt. It's vital, not only for the republics, but for me as well—for my prestige both at home and abroad. So important that I felt it justified my calling the Bundestag back in for a special session. I make no secret of it to you, my friend, that you are the one holding my coalition together. That's why I said earlier, it's the two of us—Kolter *and* Woeniger—who jointly hold the power to steer events in the right direction. That is why—"

He was interrupted by the sound of his secretary's voice through the intercom on his desk.

"Entschuldigung, Herr Chancellor," she said. "I am terribly sorry to interrupt. But Herr Raedenburg has telephoned, and I know you do not like to miss his calls."

"He's on the phone now?" asked Kolter.

"Yes, sir."

"Thank you, Helga. I will speak briefly to him," replied the Chancellor, rising and moving toward his desk. He picked up the receiver. "Gentz," he said smiling. "How are you? . . . Yes. Today? . . . I see . . . Of course I do want to see you when you are in town . . . I understand. Conferences tend to squeeze your schedule dry—just like politics!"

He listened another moment or two. "I see," he said at length, ". . . Yes . . . That sounds good. Set something up with Helga, and I will look forward to seeing you."

He set down the receiver and rejoined Woeniger. "Do you know Gentz Raedenburg?" he asked as he resumed his seat.

"Only by reputation," replied Woeniger. "We've never met."

"A fine man!" said Kolter. "He and I go back years. As committed to his beliefs as anyone I know—in town for a religious convention."

Woeniger nodded in acknowledgment but said nothing.

"Getting back to the point I was making," the Chancellor went on, "you and I hold the cards to make sure the right thing gets done for these people. They're anticipating a rugged winter, as you know, and their economic problems are still severe. They need our help, and I'm committed to leading the world community forward in providing it."

He rose abruptly, signaling that the interview was drawing to an end.

"So can I count on you, Gerhardt?" he said, extending his hand for a closing handshake.

"You have always been able to, Herr Chancellor," replied Woeniger rising to his feet also. He shook Kolter's hand, then exited the expansive office the way he had come.

24

Gerhardt Woeniger left the provisional Chancellery building with a gnawing feeling somewhere in the region of his stomach that Reichschancellor Hans Kolter had been subtly toying with him.

It was probably not even intentional. As he had become more at home with the power he wielded, Hans had taken up certain condescending mannerisms that were no doubt inevitable consequences of his steadily enlarging ego. *He displays the consummate German arrogance,* thought Woeniger. But he didn't like its being directed at him.

All that smooth talk about their sharing power together—bah! Kolter didn't believe a word of that nonsense any more than he did. They never saw one another unless a close vote was pending, and then Hans always poured on the syrup.

He didn't appreciate being taken for granted. He'd been in that position for years, and he'd had enough. Hans knew he'd bring in the CSDU's votes on his side—he always did! He *had* to. like it or not, he owed Hans Kolter. Even his condescending and pompous overconfidence could never alter that fact. Hans Kolter had him in the palm of his hand.

Sometimes Gerhardt almost wished it had turned out differently. Not that he would ever stop being grateful for his family's safety. If only the circumstances of that fateful day hadn't come to hinge quite so universally on the man whose office he had just left.

Nine and a half years ago. Frankfurt airport. He and his wife and two youngest daughters, then twelve and fifteen, were on their way to Barcelona for the Christmas holidays.

The bomb had gone off behind them, some fifty feet away—a distance that saved their lives.

He awoke in a small room. One leg was numb. Blood covered his light blue slacks. He felt no pain.

At the other end of the room one of the terrorists was talking on a phone in broken German. As Woeniger tried to eavesdrop on the conversation, all he could make out was the single name, "Kolter." Could it really be the new Chancellor calling to talk directly to the terrorists? he wondered. It would be unprecedented—a daring ploy!

The man barked out some orders to his subordinates, who then ran from the room. A moment later he hung up the phone and left the room himself, leaving only one young boy watching them—*with* his submachine gun slung menacingly around his neck and gripped tightly with both hands. But when the door opened again, he left, and the hostages were alone.

His wife and daughters were safe. He had been wounded in the leg, but without permanent damage. Needless to say, there was no holiday that year.

Everyone held hostage in both rooms credited Hans Kolter with their very lives. In a daring and risky move, the Chancellor had instantly promised full compliance with the terrorists' demands—the plane with safe passage, the money, the release from German prison of their comrades. The inmates were already being transferred to a bus, he said, the plane was taxiing to the end of the runway even as he spoke. His only condition, Kolter had insisted, was that they act immediately—without delay. If they were not airborne within fifteen minutes, his order would be withdrawn.

The plan was full of risks. But Kolter had pulled it off in one of the brilliant strokes of his early tenure as Chancellor. By seizing the aggressive posture, he had thrown the leader of the terrorists into confusion just long enough for him to make a hasty decision.

What the terrorists did not know and which few around the world ever knew, since for security reasons details were never revealed to the international press, was that the German State Police had been hatching a plan to thwart a terrorist threat of this kind on German soil. A Boeing 707 had been innocently sitting in a distant hangar of the Frankfurt airport, painted in the blue and white stripes of the Lufthansa log. But in its cockpit, cleverly disguised so that it would have taken an expert to detect, was an advanced computer guidance system whose technology had been donated for the experimental aircraft by NASA in Houston. At any time up to a distance of a thousand miles the plane's onboard flight controls could be overridden and the plane directed to any of a dozen locations, where authorities would be waiting in great numbers, well away from possible civilian casualties, to receive the terrorists again.

The unsuspecting pilot had taken off from Frankfurt, landed outside Munich to collect the prisoners, and taken off again, only to find after setting his course for El Kairouan that he was no longer in control of the 707. Thirty minutes later they found the plane setting down for an unplanned landing on a remote strip south of Nurnberg. Their high hopes unraveling before their eyes, the bewildered terrorists had gone out in a blaze of ignominious glory, bursting out of the plane firing wildly. Only the young boy had been taken alive.

As Gerhardt relived the incident while he walked to his car, he had no doubt that at least some of the hostages would have been killed had it not been for Kolter's bravado. Terrorists valued life so little that sending a spray of gunfire into a crowd of people meant no more than a child sending the spray from the end of a hose into his playmates on a hot summer's day.

Yes, he probably did owe Hans his life. But the Chancellor had never let him forget it. His references were subtle, to be sure. But one way or another, whenever a critical vote was called for, he knew just where to apply a bit of pressure. It might be asking about his wife, or a question about one of the girls, with a tone and glance that let Gerhardt know what he *really* meant—that he remembered too. Men of his kind had their way of getting their psychological clutches into you and never letting go, tying you to them in a twisted patrimonial kind of bondage. It was not an easy pressure to free oneself from—somehow worse than parental expectations. Hans Kolter was a master of such pressure, like any successful politician.

How many times did he have to repay Kolter for his family's well-being? But he was tiring of feeling indebted to a man whom he knew looked down on him!

Gerhardt had not remained head of the CSDU all these years by being anyone's fool. He resented being treated like a neophyte after all he had done to keep the Kolter coalition intact all these years. He'd been a good soldier. He'd delivered the votes innumerable times. Wasn't it about time he received something in exchange?

But going against Chancellor Hans Kolter could be a dangerous game. If he misstepped at this stage of his life, his career in politics would be over in an instant. Kolter was not the kind of man you wanted for an enemy, especially as high as his stock was presently riding in the world market. If he made a switch, he had to be sure to choose the right side!

That was why the clandestine appointment he had later this evening was so vital. The futures of many people were riding on the outcome.

25

In a seedier part of Berlin than where Gerhardt Woeniger waited for the time to pass, checking his watch and peeking outside to the street below every several minutes, another man hastened along a half-lit deserted sidewalk carrying a small parcel under his arm.

In truth, though the street-watcher knew nothing of the existence of the street-walker, the latter knew a great deal about the former. The nervous politician, in fact, was the very reason Claymore had come to Berlin, having flown in only two hours before, and Woeniger was the subject of the confidential packet he now held in his grip. He was on his way to a rendezvous with the same man, in fact, whom Woeniger would see before the night was out.

He had instructions to walk to the Brandenburg Gate in the center of Berlin, in that which had formerly been the Eastern sector, then to make his way south along Grotewohlstr., then east on Behrenstr. through the maze of tall, stone-block buildings now housing a few makeshift offices of the new joint German government, right along Friedrichstr. until he came to the region of his own hotel. A car would pull alongside him somewhere on his route, he was told, and he would get in. If the car did not come, he should return to the hotel and wait.

No car came. And after thirty minutes he arrived back at the hotel from which he had recently taken a taxi to the Brandenburgertor. He passed through the lobby without glancing at the desk clerk, then took the stairs two at a time to the second floor. The threadbare carpet on the stairs and corridors was barely enough to keep his steps from broadcasting his presence throughout the building. Inserting his key into the lock, he opened the door of his room and walked inside. The accommodations were far from deluxe. He flipped on the 40-watt overhead light and sat down, irritated at the wasted time he had just spent walking the streets.

Two minutes later the phone in the room rang. He let it go two or three times before finally lurching to his feet, walking to the small desk where it sat, and picking up the receiver. He held it to his ear, but did not say a word other than "Ja."

"I see you made it to Berlin on schedule," the caller said.

"A schedule that could have included an hour's nap," snapped Claymore, "if you hadn't sent me out on that wild goose chase! Why did you tell me to go to the Gate if you had no intentions—"

"Relax, Claymore," said Drexler, with a deep-throated chuckle. "It was for your own good."

"*My* good! I don't need that kind of exercise. Why didn't you meet me out there?"

"I have my reasons. I was watching you."

"Watching me? If you didn't trust me, then you—"

"Relax—relax! I had to make sure you weren't being watched or followed. The stakes are high in this game, and I'm not about to take any chances. Do you have the dossier on my colleague of the Bundestag?"

"I have it," barked the undercover investigator and killer.

"His wife—the photographs?"

"It's all here."

"Good. Leave it outside the door."

"Outside the door! Are you crazy?"

"It won't be there more than ten seconds. I'm close."

"And the money?"

"I'll leave it. I'll rap on the door, you wait fifteen seconds, then open it."

"How do I know it'll be enough?"

"If it isn't, you can put me on the top of your hit list. But I think you'll find it sufficient. Besides, I'm not through with you yet."

"What next?"

"You remember I mentioned Moscow?"

"I remember."

"I want you to go there."

"To do what?"

"Just call me on my private number, let me know how I can reach you. I'll get in touch with you."

"Will it be surveillance or a hit?"

"It might be both. Be ready for anything."

26

It was not his first meeting with Klaus Drexler by any means, though certainly the most important. And never had he seen the man under quite such unusual circumstances.

Nobody exactly called Drexler the second most powerful man in Germany. He was actually on about the same political level as Woeniger himself, an MP and leader of his party. Drexler hadn't even been in the Bundestag a full three terms yet and had only been head of his party for one. In a sense, some people still regarded him as a newcomer to the national scene, and he was completely unknown outside the borders of Germany. But those who thus underestimated him had not looked into his eyes. A fire burned there that spoke of larger things than one could see on the surface. Woeniger had seen it. Once he had, he would never underestimate Klaus Drexler again. He knew that despite appearances and his own parliamentary seniority, Klaus Drexler was a man in the path of destiny. When Drexler's time came, he wanted to be sure that he was on the right side of the fence.

It had been Drexler who had contacted *him* and set up the late-night interview in his office. He had sent a car for him, whose driver said nothing as they threaded their way through the silent streets of Berlin. Now he found himself, not without a slight sense of trepidation, climbing the stairs to the second floor where Drexler's office was located.

All evening Woeniger had tried to prepare by telling himself that he had nothing to feel nervous about, that *he* was the more experienced of the two. Yet try as he would, he could not quite succeed in removing the sense of intimidation that insisted on rising within him. Now he walked down the long, silent corridor, painfully aware of the echo of his footfall, stopped before the large closed door, took a deep breath, and lifted his closed hand. The knock was more tentative than he intended but sufficient. A commanding voice from within answered. He opened the door slowly.

"Gerhardt," said his host warmly in greeting, walking toward him with outstretched hand, "so good of you to come! I am most appreciative—sit down, please!"

Woeniger thanked him.

"Coffee?"

Woeniger nodded and watched as the other man poured out two cups from a wet bar at one side of the office. Drexler stood 6′, perhaps 6′1″. His height was not extraordinary—Kolter was 6′3″ and of much larger girth. But the man before him possessed what he would call "stature." He carried himself with absolute confidence in every inch of his being. A thick crop of light brown hair came down to just above his ears, neatly parted slightly off-center, dry and full and clean, not a hair out of place, and only the beginning hints of gray just above the sideburns. His healthy supply of thatch came sufficiently low so that the forehead under it did not have much room to reveal itself, though the lines that could be seen were expressive and showed no traces yet of the troughs of worry. Below them, thick eyebrows—darker than the hair above—moved about in curious expressiveness, highlighting the eyes they seemed almost to surround. High cheekbones framed the eyes below and rested calmly above sculptured, indented cheeks, which flowed downward without a trace of jowel-fat into a sturdy chin, slightly squared, and bony, solid jaw. The impression was of handsome strength. The lips were as full as a man's ought to be but no more, prone to the protruding German exaggeration of vowel shapes, with movements and twists about them that seemed to vary with every distinct word. The voice from deep in the throat was a smooth baritone, not deep nor even particularly loud, yet resonant and commanding, reminding the listener of a Meistersinger holding an abundance of sound in check, a thoroughbred in rein. The timbre, though subdued, confirmed great repositories of sinewy dynamism behind it. An unmistakable magnitude of power existed below the surface that was apparent without the pretense of volume a lesser man might have used to mask his insecurity. The overall effect would have been pleasing to a Hollywood studio, for a more classic replica of the hardy, well-proportioned, exquisitely crafted Teuton would have been difficult to find.

The eyes, however, were the most prominent feature, recessed into deep-set caverns of skillful expressiveness. Out of their depths shown two orbs of pale blue light, so full of the dance of fiery life that the unsuspecting observer found himself caught in the mesmerizing, hypnotic web of the man's penetrating and probing gaze.

Gerhardt Woeniger knew the effect of those eyes, however, and thus avoided their direct onslaught as they now zeroed in on him. He let his own gaze find temporary rest on the mouth, the forehead, or even to flit momentarily about the room. He knew the eyes were seeking his, but he resisted the impulse to let them lock onto his own.

A silence followed while Drexler took a seat adjacent to Woeniger, and both men took several tentative sips from their cups. Drexler seemed to be pondering the best way to begin. His forehead and black eyebrows creased in thought. At last he looked up.

"Gerhardt," he said, "I want to confide in you."

Woeniger listened attentively, cautious but intrigued.

"As you know," he went on, "I am opposed to our esteemed Chancellor on the matter of aid to the Soviet republics. I have my reasons, and this is not the time to detail them now. You no doubt are familiar with all sides of the issue, and I know you have been carefully considering it as well."

Woeniger nodded in the affirmative.

"However, it is not specifically with regard to the matter of the upcoming vote that I want to speak with you, but of much larger concerns. This particular vote will come and go, alliances will form on each side, you and I and Hans and the other party leaders will coax and cajole our people, and in the end some arrangement will be made between the various parties and all the members of the Bundestag, and the matter will be decided. Perhaps Hans will win the vote and get the aid package he is requesting, perhaps I will be able to prevent it.

"But bigger issues are at stake—in the long run, I mean, Gerhardt. It is a new world, a new age. I believe that over the next few years, international alliances and friendships will be fluid. Times of great change are coming, and I for one want to be ready for them, for the sake of my constituency, and for the sake of the German people. That's why I thought that it would be useful for you and I to have an understanding, so that our mutual leadership— might I even be so bold as to say our mutual 'friendship,' Gerhardt—can be instrumental in helping to guide the Germany of the future in a direction that is the best for our people, our economy, and our rightful status and position in this new world order. Do you hear what I am saying, Gerhardt?"

"Yes, sir, I believe I do," replied Woeniger. "I too am a firm believer in a strong future for our country."

"Not merely strong," Drexler went on, an orange glow almost visible in the midst of the blue of his eyes, the orange of hot embers, of coals fanning themselves to life, "but in a position in the world order to maximize that strength. We of the German nation are a people of strength and fortitude and power and determination and skill—everyone knows that. German technology, German ideas, German education, German engineering, German theology, German literature—these have existed in the forefront of the world's progress since the ancient days of our progenitors, the Celts. This is a people, a land, a nation of great might and individuality. Wouldn't you agree?"

"Of course."

"But it has been unrecognized, unfulfilled, always taking a backseat to inferior peoples—the Italians in the fourteenth century, the Portuguese in the fifteenth, the Spaniards in the sixteenth, the French in the seventeenth, the Dutch in the eighteenth, the British in the nineteenth, and the Americans and the Russians in the twentieth. The Russians! Can you imagine *us* taking a backseat to such an imbecilic backward culture? It's hard to conceive how such a thing could have come about. Yet—"

He paused with a sigh and a thoughtful expression of pain.

"—our *own* recent history has been unkind to us, as we all know only too well," he went on.

Another pause.

"But I believe a new era is coming, a new age of opportunity, where power and progress will be measured not by military might but along other lines, where the strength of a people's belief will count more than the firepower of their arsenals, where economics will direct more courses of action than armies. And where a people of vigor and energy will be required to exercise the leadership in this new order. Belief, Gerhardt! Belief in the higher values of the cosmic design, belief in man's ability to harmonize himself with the creation and with his fellows of the global creation. Belief— *and* leadership. Those are the two keys that will unlock the future, that will pave the way for what the Americans call the new world order. And both, I humbly believe, must come from outside the traditional power bases of the past, East *and* West.

"It *is* a new era. New dawns rise daily all about us. New interpretations of old beliefs must pave the way. New centers of world leadership must rise to take dominion over the affairs of man.

"So—where do you and I fit in? I confide in you, Gerhardt, because I have long been observing you, and it is my conviction that you are a man of vision, a man who shares my optimistic and bold outlook. And it is men such as yourself with whom I want to ally myself in the days and years ahead. I am not asking for your support on this particular vote next week, though you can see already that the lines of the future are beginnning to be drawn over such issues. As I said, I am looking much further ahead. The panorama is larger. I am seeking men I can trust, men who share a vision of Germany's future, a future of leadership in the community of global nations.

"By my assessment, *you* are such a man—a man of integrity and loyalty, and of belief in the new order, of vision, of leadership. Do I mistake you, or do these thoughts strike a chord deep within you? Do I not gauge you correctly, that you are dissatisfied with the status quo? Do you not also want to look ahead to a new time? Tell me, Gerhardt, how do you feel about the future?"

Woeniger could not help being bewitched by Drexler's inflating grandiloquence. Especially, coming as it did on the heels of what Gerhardt had interpreted as one more in a long string of nettling condescensions on the part of their beloved Chancellor. It felt good, naturally, to be appreciated for a change, to be recognized for what you were, to be spoken to with respect as a leader, as a man who counted for something in the scheme of things. Who wouldn't, given Woeniger's position and his reaction to his interview earlier in the day with Kolter—who wouldn't feel gratified by Drexler's flattery?

As Drexler sat back in his chair and waited, gazing upon his colleague with the penetrating expression of inquiry, a humble look of expectancy, he gave every impression of desiring intently to know what the other thought, almost as if he, Drexler, were the neophyte, and his guest were the seasoned mentor, the man of the world whose experience and insights he must have, or perish.

In actual fact, Drexler knew prescisely what was going through

Woeniger's brain. Had he not been so skilled at hiding it, the corners of his mouth might have revealed the hint of a crafty smile. He knew Gerhardt Woeniger, because he knew *men*—knew their strengths and weaknesses and foibles and frustrations and tender spots, knew their secret dreams and ambitions, knew their pettinesses and secret hurts and anxieties. But more than knowing him in general, he knew Woeniger well enough in particular also to know what he was doing by the flow of his conversation and his questions. He had chosen his words like a master surgeon selecting a scalpel, and he knew exactly where to slice. Woeniger had been set up, and Drexler had him right where he wanted him!

Klaus Drexler had been harboring many secret designs and aspirations for years. But things took time, and he knew he had to move slowly. He had to cross each hurdle one at a time, methodically putting the building blocks of the future in place. He would need people; he had always known that. And thus, as he had risen slowly through the ranks of the BRD's political hierarchy, he had kept his eye peeled for those whom he might gradually begin to enlist and win over—not especially to his way of thinking (that could come later)—but to his person. Make friends of them, that was the first order of business. Win their trust. Then slowly, slowly—other elements would fall into line.

Long and slow. No asinine Beer Hall Putsch tactics like his fool of a predecessor! An ignoramus who thought he was qualified to lead an empire! No, his strategy was much more subtle and cleverly designed.

And he *had* brought them along. Many were now in his camp, many even from the opposing parties. They might not vote for him on the issue of Soviet aid. But he was garnering IOUs, developing a bevy of influential leaders throughout the country who trusted him, and, he thought, *would* trust him when push came to shove.

He had been watching Gerhardt Woeniger for years and had had him spied on twice now. He had what he needed if Woeniger proved obstinate. But he didn't think he'd need to bring in the ugly details he had uncovered about his wife. That file probably would never have to see the light of day. Woeniger had enough weak spots and character flaws that he'd be able to twist his pysche up in so many knots that he wouldn't know whether he was coming or going. But he had intentionally refrained from direct overtures for a long time. Woeniger, as head of the CSDU and one whom Kolter trusted to keep his coalition intact, was a relatively big fish, and he had to tread carefully. Alienating either Woeniger or the Chancellor prematurely could set him back a good while.

But the time seemed right now. He had seen Woeniger squirming under the pressure lately. The mole he'd planted within the inner circle of Woeniger's staff eight years ago confirmed that his titular boss was annoyed with the Chancellor, and every once in a while could be heard commenting about what Kolter might think if "I went my own way and voted independently for a change!" He would apply no pressure, just feel Woeniger out, open a dialogue, massage his somewhat delicate and bruised ego.

A relationship, that was all he wanted for now. He would gently knead it into place, so that when the time was right—well, he wouldn't even reflect on that just now!

Thus he had requested this meeting in his office, late enough to protect both their reputations from prematurely prying eyes.

Still he waited, gently trying to draw out the confidence of his guest with his eyes of sincerity and guilelessness.

"I appreciate your generous words," Woeniger replied after a minute's reflection. "And yes, I *do* share your optimism for the future and Germany's role in it. Of course, I too desire to be part of that leadership."

"You shall, Gerhardt," put in Drexler enthusiastically. "I am confident of it. It is men such as yourself whom I see as the leaders of the future, men who have served this land of ours for years, who know its people, which is one of the reasons I find myself personally drawn to you and want to ally myself with you. I want to follow in the footsteps of your leadership in the years ahead."

"I—I trust I will—uh, be worthy of your kindness," faltered Woeniger, not prepared for the turn things had taken. "But of course it is you," he went on, "who control a far larger block of votes in the Bundestag than I could ever hope to. My leadership is paltry beside—"

"Paltry indeed!" interrupted Drexler. "The relative size of our parties is immaterial, Gerhardt. I'm talking about leadership. Your party is made up of independent thinkers, of free spirits. It will never command large numbers. But it's that independent spirit of leadership I am talking about. You are an independent man, deter-

125

mined to stand for what you believe in. All these years you have continued to stand firm on the principles of the CSDU, knowing that you are in a minority. Dedication! You are a man for the future, a man whose leadership will be recognized one day by the people of this nation. I would stake the future of my *own* career on it. And as you do come into this leadership, Gerhardt, I want to be there with you. I want to help you achieve your dreams for this nation. I want to put all the power of my own position behind you. I believe in you, Gerhardt, and I see a bright future for us when we have the opportunity to work together—*closely* together in the leadership of the future."

"I would like to think you are right."

"Of course I am right. The age of light and destiny is approaching, drawing us into its evolutionary vortex. Peace has come to the globe, and out of recent events a new age, a new dawn for mankind, is about to emerge. Mankind's harmony with itself, with nature, with the consciousness of the universe will bring the long history of human development to its apex. I tell you, Gerhardt, the leaders who pave the way will come from a new generation of leaders raised up throughout the earth, men and women who perceive this purpose and harmony, and who recognize our destiny to take history to the crowning summit of its fulfillment. It is my conviction that we can reconstruct society along the lines of ideals only dreamed of by utopian star-gazers of the past. With the dismantling of old barriers of hostility and the end of death-producing military alliances, these goals of a global society based on principles of the god-consciousness that has all this time lain dormant within man, can be achieved. Toward this has man's long history been pointing. To this great cause I have committed myself, to enlighten this nation, and hopefully in time other nations of the world, so that we might provide a searchlight of hope to all peoples of the globe, helping to lead them out of the bondage and limited ways of thinking of the past, and into the new era of peace and brotherhood and unity that is at hand. And men like you and me are the leaders who must seize the initiative when the time comes."

He paused, still eyeing his quarry with cunning observation.

"So tell me, Gerhardt," he went on after a moment, "what are your perceptions about the future and where the German nation is heading? How do you visualize your role as one of its leaders and spokesmen? I vitally want to know how you view these things I am speaking of. Because, as I said, I am committed to working with you in any way I am able."

Having laid his foundation well, Drexler now sat back and listened, seeking appropriate opportunities to further charm and inveigle the gullible Woeniger. By the time the older man left to be driven by Drexler's car to his home, he had been altogether seduced and could hardly have been more thoroughly or willingly ensnared into the latter's camp.

27

The spacious office was quiet. Even the janitors had long since gone home, and only a security man or two sat downstairs in front of television monitors. The building slept.

Slowly Drexler rose from his chair and walked across the room to the darkened window. He stood for ten minutes, gazing out. Even at 2:00 A.M. Berlin was alive with lights stretching as far as he could see in every direction. Truly this was the heart of the old Prussian kingdom, the domain of the Hohenzollerns—mighty, historic, proud.

The city at the heart of the Fatherland—and more! The city at the heart of Europe, at the heart of the world. There was no place on earth like Berlin. And he stood in its very epicenter! His city—his country! How had they even imagined they would have run a government from that plebian little outpost of Bonn? If anything gave clear signal that the hour of his destiny was approaching, the reunification and change of theater was it. He could never have done it from Bonn. That had been a makeshift apparatus at best. But now here he stood overlooking the center of empire, from which a new global power base would emerge. The crumbling of the wall, the vote to unite, the disintegration of the Soviet Union, and now here he stood surveying the heart of Belin—it was all too much to have dreamed of happening so rapidly. Suddenly it was within his grasp and falling into place piece by piece with every passing day.

Klaus Drexler was a man who knew how things worked. America was so full of its own do-good complex that it would throw money at any defeated adversary. The Americans had rebuilt both Germany and Japan after the Second World War, while watching their and Britain's own industries slowly sink down the toilet. Now their old enemies were rich and healthy beyond compare, dictating the entire world's industrial momentum, while America sank further and further into bankruptcy from the incurred debt.

The double irony was that neither Japan nor Germany gave an ounce of credit to the United States for their present dominance, nor seemed to realize that they would have been on the scrap heap of the world's nations had it not been for the Marshall Plan. He smiled at the thought. His own short-sighted countrymen—especially the rising new affluent generation—actually resented the United States, feeling more favorably inclined toward their eastern neighbors, even though it had been the Soviet Union who had ripped apart their nation and killed hundreds of thousands of German citizens. How foolish his own people could be! Yet that would work to his advantage in the end.

Then too, it was pitifully ironic that even seeing how its generosity had backfired with Germany and Japan, building up newly industrialized powerhouses to threaten its *own* industry, the U.S. continued to dish out billions in aid all over the world, propping up failing dictatorships, providing money for arms and military technology that would one day be used to kill the very Americans and allies who had supplied it. The foolish Americans seemed bent on giving, giving, giving, until the day they would discover their country bankrupt!

Even though the aid had been to his own nation's benefit and had provided the foundation for his plans, Drexler could not help but consider the Americans saps. That they should have perpetrated such a policy might have been magnanimous and even, all other things being equal, a good thing to do. But to continue doing so to the demise of their own system was nothing short of foolhardy. Within fifty years there had been a complete reversal. The haves gave to the have-nots until the haves no longer had and were at the mercy of those who fifty years earlier had been ploughing through the ashes and rubble of their destroyed cities. Was it some latent form of guilt that kept the Americans throwing money at their vanquished foes?

He had no doubt that they would do the same thing in Eastern Europe and the Soviet republics, now that they had "won" the Cold War. For fifty years they had spent billions of taxpayer dollars to keep the Soviet Union down, but the moment it collapsed, the aid talk began to surface. He was certain that they would spend the next fifty years pouring money into Eastern Europe; whether it was in cash or other forms hardly mattered. Grain credits, loan guarantees, subsidies on anything and everything, food assistance programs—the net result was the same.

Such a scenario, in fact, was what he was banking on as the cornerstone of his scheme.

The nerve center of global power and economic might was in for a titanic shift. The history of the Cold War provided the forerunning example of what he was sure would come next. As Marshall Plan aid had created the economic powerhouses of the Cold War years out of the rubble of defeat, so too would the *next* economic power center emerge from this new defeat—Warsaw, Budapest, Bucharest, Belgrade, Prague, Moscow, Kiev, and newly renamed St. Petersburg. Out of defeat would grow capitalistic muscle. American aid would succeed in turning Eastern Europe and Russia upside down as it had Japan and Germany. With democracy and capitalism in full swing in all these capitals, with the foundation of American dollars and technology, and the massive manpower pool available, Poland and Hungary and Czechoslovakia and Romania and Russia would within a generation or two be as bright and prosperous as was Germany today—wealthy, new, rebuilt, productive, dynamic, healthy, and bursting with efficient energy, zero unemployment, multiplying GNP—to the even *further* detriment of the West, who would succeed in bankrupting itself all the more in effecting this latest in post-hostilities reversal.

There was the factor of national energy as well—currently so visible among Asians. Similarly, the new industrialized countries of Europe and the Soviet republics would be highly motivated. All over Eastern Europe a vitality of energy was waiting to explode, just as Germany's productivity had in the last forty years. It was in the Celtic and Slavic bloodlines—something in the native character or psyche, pent up all this time under the demotivation of Communism, was now ready to burst out. True, maybe it would never match the superior ethic and determination of the Teutonic bloodline, but he had no doubt that the Slavic temperament was ready to set its corner of the world on fire too.

As industry was even then moving in massive realignments to Korea and Taiwan and China because of the energy of their people, so too would the world's industry gradually shift toward Eastern Europe. There resided eager manpower, hungry not for exorbitant pay and excessive benefits like American workers, but simply hungry to work for the satisfaction of at last being part of a free market economy.

The future would occur in the former Communist bloc and Warsaw Pact countries. With the resources and manpower available, and the money and technology that would be thrown at them by the West, the fulcrum of the future of the world lay somewhere between Warsaw, Budapest, and Prague—heavily influenced, if *he* had anything to do with it, by Berlin!

And Germany, if she played her cards right, could be the power base to direct this shift in the world balance of strength, *if* she didn't bankrupt herself. That was why he opposed his own Chancellor's joint aid package with the French and British and Americans to the Soviet Union's newly independent republics. For Germany to reject it would cause some international flak, but the United States would, after slapping Kolter's hand, pick up the slack, and their hesitancy would eventually be forgotten. The aid would come. The republics and their Eastern European counterparts would get all the money they needed, and eventually they would forget where it came from. Likely enough, thirty years from now they would all hate the United States anyway, while laughing all the way to the bank! Meanwhile, Russia's leaders would be loved and adored, everyone forgetting that *they* were the ones who had squeezed the world dry for fifty years. How short was the common man's historical memory!

That was the key—let America and whoever else wanted to pick up the tab for Eastern Europe's reconstruction. Germany herself had to remain healthy fiancially, not give her surplus away, and stay ahead of the curve of events, reserving true clout for herself *within* the borders of the Fatherland, keeping her hands tightly around banks, financial institutions, and the centers of industry.

There were always boundaries and borders in the world, in Drexler's view, and they were always fluid and changing. With the Iron Curtain suddenly gone, where would the next alliances be? Where would the next lines be drawn? For centuries the struggle had been essentially between East and West, so graphically illustrated by the Berlin Wall.

He looked down at the city. He imagined he could just see the course where the 45-kilometer no-man's land had snaked its way cruelly through the center of Berlin.

Now it was gone. Only 200 meters of the wall remained, fenced off as a monument. Outside it a large slab lay on the ground for tourists to hack at.

And the new global destiny would be based on a huge power block that sat right in the middle, neither East nor West, but at the very crossroads between east, west, north, and south—a convergent Eurasian alliance, a newborn twenty-first century community of peoples!

The Iron Curtain was gone. The new demaracation would extend straight down from The Hague to Zurich.

In this very city.

By the year 2030, he predicted the whole world would be run from Berlin. London, Paris, Rome, New York, and Washington would be power-and-influence ghost towns. In the very triumph of the capitalism they so ardently fought for, they would ultimately be buried.

They had given away the store. And they had given it to him!

After some time he turned from the window, returned to his desk, and sat down. Notwithstanding the hour, there was work to be done.

He opened a drawer and pulled out several private files. The next week would be critical. He had to keep all the major players moving and coordinated. He flipped through the folders—

Besides Woeniger, there were several lower-level bureaucrats in the Bundestag and Ministries whose roles could not be ignored—Otto Greim of the FDP, Weisskopf, and others. And then there was Claymore—he was a loose cannon who had been invaluable thus far, but if he went off at the wrong place or the wrong time—

well, you sometimes just could never tell about those kinds of people. The Russian and all the constituent players on his side, the fellow he'd mentioned precipitating a worker revolt in a handful of auto factories, the former KGB man who was loose in the streets trying to unravel the whole thing . . .

He exhaled deeply. There was still plenty that could go wrong!

A moment's pause more was all it took before his efficient and confident brain shook the melancholy thought away. He grabbed up a blank sheet of paper, then a pencil, and began jotting down notes of everything to be taken care of tomorrow morning.

PART 5

Disunity, Twentieth-Century Style

28

August 12, 6:15 A.M.
Berlin

An unseasonably crisp chill swept through the air.

Of course it was 6:15 in the morning, and Berlin was situated only a hundred miles south of the Baltic. It was hardly surprising that it should be nippy.

Jacob Michaels breathed in deeply. It wasn't exactly fresh country air, but it felt good nevertheless. He hadn't come out for the fresh air anyway. He had spent a fitful night, tossing and turning, his mind full of contradictory questions. It seemed that every week he spent trying to *live* his faith in a down-to-earth and real way only presented him with new and perplexing quandaries. The whole struggle was intensified by the sense that he was alone in the kinds of questions he was attempting to sort through. And being at this conference on evangelism wasn't clarifying matters any further!

Last evening's video replay in the Bavarian Room had triggered the night's round of mental gymnastics. He shouldn't have gone. Jackson had had the good sense to retire to their room for a snack, some Bible reading, and the news on TV. But he had decided to go watch the thing.

There had been Bob MacPatrick, darling of evangelicals the world over, on a wide-screen monitor, making his impassioned plea for donations for Russian and Eastern bloc evangelism. He had sung, had brought in dozens of big-name guests, had conducted interviews and shown film clips. The whole thing more resembled a Jerry Lewis telethon than a religious show. The series, called "Help Save the World 2000," which had run on his syndicated television program several months back, had been so wildly successful—raising a staggering $23 million for the printing and distribution of gospel literature in a dozen Slavic dialects—that the conference organizers had decided to run it again nightly in the hotel. The decision was no doubt prompted by the fact that MacPatrick was due to fly into Berlin any day and would later in the week personally present Christian leaders from the Eastern bloc nations checks for financial assistance for their ministries.

That was Jacob's quandary: Who wouldn't be all for taking the gospel wherever possible by whatever means possible? Who could deny MacPatrick's worldwide impact? That was the whole point of this conference, to take advantage of changing world conditions to rush through the doors of opportunity in the East. As MacPatrick had said on his show, "We can't tell how long this tremendous opportunity will last, so we must do all we can immediately to send literature and radio and television messages everywhere in an all-out blitz of the gospel message."

Yet something struck a disquieting nerve in his spirit. It had been gnawing at him ever since their arrival. There was a subtle spirit of self-promotion in the whole thing. Most of the speakers thus far used every opportunity to plug their own vision and program and books and tapes and products. All in the name of spreading the gospel, of course, but there was such a sense of "My way is best so all the rest of you ought to jump in and support what *I* am doing."

MacPatrick had raised plenty of money, to be sure. But a good deal of it would go into his own organization to purchase new equipment and to further his own publishing and broadcasting empire. Not to mention the ever-important "administrative" expenses with which Jacob was all too familiar. He knew how the system worked. How much of the $23,000,000 would *actually* result in hands-on evangelism? Ten percent, 20 percent—as much as 30 percent?

All was ostensibly for the purpose of spreading the Word. So why did Jacob sense men's and women's egos vying for places of preeminence? They reminded him of himself three years ago. Maybe that was the rub—he knew what drove them. He saw the same looks in their eyes. He could detect the faint tones and gestures and glimpses of self-importance in the midst of the spiritual-sounding jargon. He knew—because he had been there.

Over and over MacPatrick's voice replayed itself in his memory: "Send us your money, help us save the world by the year 2000!"

Help us *save the world,* thought Jacob. As if God had nothing to do with it. The messages thus far had stressed political changes and windows of opportunity and how much money it would take and who can make the pitch that will bring in the dough.

All the key players at the conference—at least most of those from the evangelical side of the spectrum, such as Powers, Black, and Bradford—sang the same tune. Money, money, money—testaments—literature—tracts! It was the gospel blimp all over again. Who was talking about prayer, about God's doing *His* work among men? To listen to the biggest names of evangelicalism, nobody could come to God without them. Those on the other side of the continuum, those speaking about people's needs, weren't being heard. He recalled the Mills workshop. And *they* weren't talking about God's role in their programs either.

He had been caught in the same trap for most of his life. His organization and ministry was dedicated to evangelism—to Evangelizing the World. He had spent a lifetime doing exactly what these men were doing now—promoting world evangelism through books, radio, television, tapes, and raising money. Now suddenly, after Jackson's entry into his life, and after realizing what a hypocrite he had been, it seemed shallow, devoid of gutsy contact with people.

Arm's length evangelism. "Come on, everyone, send us your money. It's clean and tidy. You won't have to do any down-and-dirty evangelism yourself. You can let your money evangelize the world for you. Give your nice, fat check to your church or your favorite missions organization or TV preacher and then you won't have to actually go out in your own neighborhood and find some hungry soul to feed. You don't have to actually share your faith with anyone. Send your money, and let the professionals do it for you."

Jacob laughed sardonically. He was getting too sarcastic for his own good. Just once, he would like to explain what he now knew he believed to someone one-on-one rather than to hundreds or thousands! He wondered if any of the other men on his mind had personally led anyone to the Lord, just two people alone together, and then stuck by their side for five years to get them solidly grounded and walking with God. He never had. It seemed ironic.

By this time he had walked about a mile from the hotel, past the huge and modern Europa-Center and beyond on the Kurfürsten-damm, to Breitscheid Platz and Kaiser-Wilhelm-Gedachniskirche. He and Jackson had already taken the time to tour the war memorial at the bombed-out cathedral, and had spent some time praying inside the new church next to it. But this morning he was hardly conscious of the colossal metropolis waking up all around him.

The city was truly one of the world's major conglomerations of people, industry, business, and politics. Here in the western sector, there was evidence of prosperity, yet signs of moral decline and seediness were everywhere mingled with the newness of the streets and buildings. Eccentrics of every size, shape, color, and inclination lined the streets. Refugee families wandered about. Minstrels sought hand-outs whether they possessed talent or not. Millionaire businessmen on their way to offices stepped over homeless beggars on the sidewalks.

Pervading the entire city was a whole series of flashpoints, where opposites met. Democracy and Communism had intersected and for thirty years exchanged angry words in Berlin. Now that the wall was gone, the volatility was still present, though not as visible. The hardworking, stoic German temperament had suddenly encountered a mass infusion of foreigners. The promise of Western prosperity meeting needs of the East seemed too much to hope for.

Everywhere was contrast, and underneath it were the stress fractures of a society suddenly finding itself squarely atop the fault line of a major political cataclysm. To the east only a mile or two away, the huge need for economic rebuilding had already strained the West's equilibrium. Money had come from Bonn to build up this new capital of the united nation. More was promised from other Western nations. But would it be enough to accomplish the job without rupturing the economy West Germany had preserved for so long? Would the fall of the wall bring harmony in the long run, or had the fault line been running beneath it too long to be healed? Were earthquakes of the spirit and psyche and economy destined to be part of Germany's future forever? What would be the new characteristic of *realpolitik* at the end of the twentieth century?

Jacob's mind strayed from the conference as he took in the sights and the ambiance of the city itself. What would a world with Berlin as its hub be like in ten years? he wondered. A city in chaos, it almost struck him. Change—contrast. Ex-Communists, it was said, were fleeing here from all the Eastern Bloc countries, hoping in this mad, turbulent melting pot of millions to find corners to hide in to escape the new wave of democratic intolerance. Meanwhile, swastikas and anti-Jewish slogans could be seen on billboards and walls, painted with spray can haste. Every half-block or so sat a news kiosk selling candy and gum and newspapers and magazines displaying nudity and pornography unimaginable in the States. People walked by in clusters of tens and hundreds, impersonal looks of unconcern on their faces—painted leather jackets decorated with chains, brushing against thousand-mark suits, little children walking by displays of magazine covers of nude men and women, shouts and horns, trucks and buses—and everyone continuing with the business of his or her own private world.

Truly, Jacob thought, *Berlin is a microcosm of the changing face of the world at this moment of climax. How do you bring the gospel to a place like this? Why would they even want to listen? Would that man lying on the sidewalk or that skinhead with the earring dangling from his ear or that man with the briefcase walking with such brisk, orderly tempo—would any of them pay attention to a Polish or German translation of Carson Mitchell's new pamphlet on the end times?*

Maybe so. Who could tell? But somehow pouring in planes and truckloads of literature seemed a bit removed from the streets where these people lived.

How could the American evangelical style exercise an impact in the midst of such variant forces and trends?

Jacob wondered what it was like in Russia, Poland, and Romania. Would people respond to tracts and books distributed blitzkrieg style, as the evangelical faction of the conference seemed to advocate? Perhaps beam-it-over-the-airwaves evangelism *was* the method Jesus would use in this day and age. Perhaps Jacob's doubts had more to do with his own personal attempt to redefine his faith in a meaningful way than with an intrinsic weakness in what was being put forward at the conference. Yet it seemed there ought to be a more personal element in it somewhere. Yet Father Mills's or Sister Jeanne Marie's approach of helping people without ever mentioning the Lord's power to change life hardly seemed to be complete evangelism either.

Lord, he prayed silently as he walked, *show me how to fit all these questions together. I do not want to be critical of my brothers and their efforts—where is the balance? I don't know what to think anymore.*

Jacob's thoughts fell to Jackson and the past year. With Jackson he had learned to see many things in a new light. He had learned to pray, learned to ask questions, learned to read the Scriptures in a new, practical way. He and Bob Means and Jackson had met weekly. Never had Jacob grown so much.

What had begun as a "scandal" with Jackson's investigation into ETW, Jacob now viewed as the best thing that had ever happened to him. What a son! A young man who said what he thought, down-to-earth and unassuming, with ideas and thoughts and convictions—and a no-nonsense head on his shoulders.

He was drawing near the hotel. The long walk may not have solved anything, but he'd had a chance to air some thoughts and voice some prayers, and he felt refreshed.

As he returned along Kurfurstendammstrasse, a woman walked toward him, a thin baby in her arms, holding out her hands begging for money. He kept moving, not understanding a word she said. *Probably not a German,* he thought. Turkish, Arab—the city was *full* of beggars! On every corner they abounded—in the midst of German wealth and abundance.

Suddenly his feet stopped. The face of the woman he had just seen filled the eyes of his mind. A face of desperation and loneliness, of hunger, with sunken eyes—hollow, empty.

And the baby. It couldn't have been six months old. Quiet, probably too hungry and ill-nourished to make much fuss at being out in the street so early on a cold morning. Wrapped in one scant blanket that Elizabeth wouldn't have called a rag at home.

O God! he cried inside as his heart stung him. *How could I be so callous, so unseeing, so unfeeling—walking by just as the Pharisee did! God, forgive me!*

Quickly he spun around, fishing out his wallet as he retraced his steps. He had—what?—twenty or thirty German marks was all. He had been using his credit card for just about everything.

Sure, they'd warned them about the beggars at the opening of the conference, telling them it was all a ploy. You had to steel your emotions against feeling sorry for them, against the forlorn looks and hungry faces—and especially against the little children they used the way blind organ grinders used to use monkeys.

Jacob didn't care what they said. What did all that matter? This was flesh-and-blood life. That baby wasn't faking the hollow look of hunger!

In only a moment or two he was back to where the sad-looking woman stood. He walked straight to her then handed her the wadded-up money with a half-smile. He did not put it in the cloth cap at her feet, but took her one free hand, pressed the money into it, then held it a moment as her fingers clutched around the bills and coins. He looked into her eyes and, knowing she could not understand a word he was saying, said, "I am so sorry I walked by you before. Take this from the heart of love. I wish I could give you more. And, dear young lady, Jesus your Saviour loves you and your baby, and I will pray for you that He will take care of you. I will pray for you every day!"

She returned his gaze, tears filling her eyes. She had not grasped the meaning of his words but had certainly grasped the intent of his heart.

With one last squeeze of her hand, Jacob released her, leaned down and gently kissed her child, then smiled at the mother again, and walked toward his hotel, his eyes already clouded with tears.

"Lord Jesus," he sighed, full of emotion, "what would You have done for that poor, dear, lovely, lost young woman? How would You have ministered life to her?"

Suddenly as he walked along the now crowded street, he felt almost a physical sensation such as that recorded in Acts 9:18, as if something were falling from his eyes. Suddenly he saw everything around him through intensified eyes of—what could he call it?—compassion, eyes of sympathy, of love. The beggars and skinheads and street vendors and musicians singing in foreign tongues and the drunks still lying asleep—suddenly everywhere he saw desperate lostness! As he looked into face after face, his heart swelled with currents never before felt of love for his fellow humans. Out of every eye that met his came the gaze of souls, though they knew it not, speaking the language of the universal brotherhood of mankind. In that incredible moment of intensified internal vision, every man, every woman, every child he passed was personally and uniquely his brother, his sister, a part of God's creation.

He could not stop the tears welling up in his eyes. He wanted to run up to everyone he saw, and embrace him or her, and say, "I love you—come, let me tell you about our Father!" The bonds of brotherhood tugged at his heart. All the human faces around him were divinely reflecting the God who made them. Yet they did not know. How he longed to tell them!

Lord, he continued to pray, *show me what to do. How would You reach them, Lord Jesus? Would You give them money, clothes, food? Would You speak words of life to them? O, Lord, what are we to do to reach a crying, dying, hopeless, hungry world in our day?"*

Still praying, with eyes wet with emotion, he reached the door of the Worldwide Hotel.

29

August 12, 8:22 A.M.
Berlin

Hoping to make a hasty passage through the lobby and up to the room unseen, Jacob hurried past the main desk to the elevators. He pushed the up button, waited about thirty seconds, then heard the doors begin to open.

"Why, Jacob!" said a voice from inside the elevator. "I certainly didn't expect to see you so soon after arriving in Berlin!"

Jacob grimaced inwardly, sucked in a quick breath of air to steady himself, and looked up to answer the unexpected salutation. He would have known the voice anywhere. It was Hamilton Jaeger.

"Why Hamilton—" faltered Jacob. "I suppose the feeling is mutual. Neither did I know you were going to be here." Quickly he fumbled for his handkerchief.

He extended his hand as Jaeger exited the elevator. It was the first time they had seen one another since the previous summer. "I could hardly miss a gathering of this importance, now could I, Jacob?" Jaeger went on, smiling as if the two were old friends. "I'm President of EU now, and as committed to evangelism and unity within the Body of Christ as we are, it was felt that my presence here was essential."

"I see," replied Jacob without much enthusiasm.

"You look—out of sorts—is everything all right?"

"Yes, of course," replied Jacob, wiping his eyes. "Sinuses, you know," he added, disgusted with himself for explaining away his tears.

Neither man made any allusion to their long history together, nor to the events of the previous year which had forced Jaeger from his position as number two man at ETW. When Jackson Maxwell's investigation had uncovered indiscretions and ethical violations, Michaels and Jaeger had borne the brunt of the charges with vastly different dispositions. Michaels had humbly accepted responsibility and made a clean breast of it. Jaeger, on the other hand, had arrogantly threatened and blustered and accused, until the disclosure of events left him no option but to quietly resign. He had never been one to take defeat graciously and had not done so then.

Within months of the scandal, Jaeger had landed on his feet in Atlanta, among the leadership of a new organization by the name of Evangelical Unity, Unltd., whose avowed purpose was to assist in the unification of leadership of a broad spectrum of evangelical Christianity. In the past year, they had built up a rather sizable financial organization, which had enabled EU to send discipling teams out to churches and ministries across the country, helping to align many smaller and independent groups into a somewhat homogeneous and parallel organizational structure, as envisioned by the founders of EU.

Jacob Michaels had intentionally avoided all news of his former colleague. The memory of Jaeger's deception was too painful, heightened by his own shallow gullibility that had made it all possible. He had wanted to climb to spiritual health, both personally and for ETW, without the distraction of wondering what Jaeger was up to. He had known nothing about Jaeger's appointment as EU's new president. But he was not surprised. He had told Jackson several times that nothing would keep Hamilton down.

On his part, however, Hamilton Jaeger had kept very close tabs on his former boss. An irrational jealous streak, no doubt always dormant, had surfaced since being humiliated and, in his view, thrown out of ETW on the word of a ridiculous green reporter. In his heart of hearts he had vowed vengeance on both Michaels and that cub writer Maxwell. Though as time had passed he moderated the bitterness of his anger and opted instead to gain his revenge by becoming on his own what he could never have hoped to be under Jacob Michaels. All those years working side by side, Jaeger had gained a great deal of knowledge and experience. Unfortunately the deepest and best things in the soul and character of Jacob Michaels had never rubbed off. Jaeger had come out from under Jacob's wing assuming himself capable of anything and everything, without any inkling of the vast differences in the intrinsic fibers of their beings.

Jaeger was a skilled manipulator and a genius with finance. Even Jacob would give him that much. He had used that ability and his background and experience in the Michaels organization to move quickly and decisively to the top of the newly founded Evangelical Unity, Unltd., and had in a very short time given it a powerful financial base from which he was beginning to feel comfortable and confident about his own personal prospects as a recognized Christian leader.

In fact, as he now laid eyes on Jacob for the first time since his own rapid rise in Atlanta, he realized what a fool he had been to be jealous of this man. He should be grateful both to him and Maxwell for precipitating the crisis that led to the change. Suddenly Jacob looked small, weak, and unsure of himself. Now who was on top? Who was in command of an organization on the move and in a position to influence Christian direction in the 1990s?

Yes, he had had people keeping close watch on Jacob all year, and at first he had not even believed the reports, thinking they had followed the wrong man. They were crazy things he heard: days spent with plumbers and carpenters, weekend retreats to a cabin with some low-level staffer by the name of Means, long walks in Chicago's worst slums—all kinds of ridiculous activities that seemed to have nothing to do with ETW. And then there was all that business about canceled appearances, canceled book contracts, selling off existing tape and book stock at 75 percent discounts, the huge giveaways. What was it all about? he had wondered. It was a good thing he had dumped his share of Luxor Towers stock. Jacob was liable to take the whole place down the drain! From the reports, he would have concluded that Jacob was going off the deep end. But now taking one look at him, suddenly it made sense. With Jacob's reputation and public image tarnished, there was nothing left but the shell of a man who never had had any substance. For the first time Hamilton saw Jacob for what he had always been. How could he have looked up to him for so long? *He* should have been running ETW all the time! Jacob had nothing left but a sinking ship, one of the great many in a long string of so-called ministries that eventually fizzled and died from lack of leadership. With Jaeger no longer pulling the strings behind the scenes, Jacob had let ETW fade into ineffectiveness and soon-to-be oblivion. What a fool he had been to relinquish the power he had had in his grasp, all for the sake of what that ridiculous reporter called the *truth*!

Jaeger was glad that chapter in his life was over. Jacob was a loser. He should have seen it sooner. The tables were turned now. He was on the way up, Jacob on the way down. They would see who had held the winning hand all along!

"Yes," Jaeger went on after the momentary appraisal of his former boss and colleague, in which all this passed quickly through his inflated consciousness, "the promotion came four months ago. We're making some fairly major plans that may involve a number of the men and ministries represented here. Unity and all that. But then of course, you aren't interested in unity within the Body of Christ, are you, Jacob? So I don't suppose my activities would interest you." He smiled with a condescending air.

"As you perceive unity, Hamilton, I'm sure you're right. Your plans would probably not interest me much."

"Yes, well, we must all pursue the Lord's work as we are led," said Jaeger expansively. "You, I hear, are—uh, scaling back ETW quite drastically, Jacob. Getting out of the evangelism business, are you?"

"Trying to, Hamilton. I am seriously trying to."

"You ought to be careful, Jacob," counseled Jaeger, warming up to playing the leadership role. "Evangelism is our primary calling as Christians and men of God. You mustn't allow yourself to get too liberal on such a biblical issue as the Great Commission."

"Now, I suppose you're right, Hamilton," replied Jacob with a half-smile at how completely Jaeger had missed his meaning. "I'll try to watch my step."

"Well, I hope you find whatever it is you're searching for before you let everything we worked so hard for go down the tubes, Jacob. But in the meantime—"

He glanced down hurriedly at his watch.

"Listen, it's been great seeing you, but I've got breakfast scheduled with Bradford, Powers, Mitchell, and MacPatrick, so I've got to run."

"MacPatrick is here already?"

"Just flew in late last night."

"Hmm—"

"Great days ahead for the cause of Christ in this part of the world," Jaeger went on, "and back home too. Lots of things in the works."

"You never were one to let the grass grow under your feet, were you, Hamilton?" said Jacob with a smile.

"Ha, ha!" laughed Jaeger. "From you, Jacob, I'll take that as a compliment. Say, why don't you join us? You're still considered one of the major players in some circles. I'm sure none of the other men would mind."

"Thanks just the same, Hamilton, but no. Give the others my regards."

"Have it your way. But you know what they say, Jacob, if you keep letting opportunities pass you by, pretty soon they'll quit knocking on your door."

"I suppose that's a chance I'll have to take," replied Jacob, wondering who the *they* were that Jaeger had heard such a statement from. "I wish God's best for you, Hamilton, I truly do— *God's* best."

"Thanks, Jacob. Same to you—of course."

Jacob returned to the elevator, this time making it up to the sixth floor without further interruption.

30

As Jacob walked into the room, Jackson was coming out of the bathroom with his cordless electric razor whirring over his cheeks.

"Nice walk?" he asked.

Jacob sighed. "Yeah," he said thoughtfully. "It's quite a city, Jackson. Boy, the Lord really is working me over."

"How so?"

"Lots of questions. Nothing new. Wondering what Jesus would do in certain situations. Hey, you'll never guess who I saw downstairs just now."

"Who?"

"Our old friend Hamilton Jaeger."

"Oh, no!" groaned Jackson.

"In the flesh."

"I suppose I shouldn't be surprised. Look at this." Jackson handed Jacob a sheet of paper. "It's some of the last-minute schedule changes." Jackson went on. "Look at this afternoon."

Jacob scanned quickly down the page. "Hmm," grunted Jacob with a half-laugh, half despairing sigh, "I suppose it's to be expected: 'Mega Fund-Raising for Major Ministries in the 1990s: An unscheduled workshop on dramatic new fund-raising strategies for ministries committed to major evangelistic efforts in our changing world. Led by EU President Hamilton Jaeger.' "

"Are you going to go?" asked Jackson.

"Are you kidding!" rejoined Jacob. "It would send me into so many sins of spiritual attitude that I'd be six months getting back on track. No, I see no sense in opening myself up to the enemy. Let Hamilton have his day. The Lord's purposes won't be thwarted."

"But what if he takes other good men down with him the way he almost did you?"

"That's their responsibility, not mine. If they think money and fund-raising are necessary to tell the world about Jesus, then maybe they and Hamilton deserve each other. I've got my hands full keeping myself where I'm supposed to be. Right now, I've got to find what the Lord wants *me* to do, and then try to do it, as Bob always tells us to pray, remember?"

"I was just going to go down to the buffet and see about some breakfast. Want to join me?"

"You really love that stiff, sour bread, don't you?" Jacob laughed.

"Yeah. Never get tired of it. But they've had a pretty adequate spread here, even for your American palate, haven't they?"

"Sure, it's been fine—you go on ahead. I need some more time to sort out my morning. See if you can find me some fruit, will you—banana, grapefruit—anything."

"Sure," replied Jackson, then left the room.

Jacob walked across the room and gazed out at the city of Berlin. For several long minutes he stood there, thoughts straying in many directions. At length he drew in a long sigh and exhaled as he turned away. He stooped down, untied his shoes, took them off, then knelt on the carpet beside his bed, and bowed his head to the floor.

31

August 12, 9:30 A.M.
Berlin

The morning's general session featured Owen Bradford speaking on "Anointed Gifts and Offices as the Empowering Behind Evangelism." The topic as well as Bradford's style and reputation would all seem to have lent themselves toward a smaller workshop format. He was distantly separated from a good many of the conferees in his ultra-conservative, Southern Baptist, charismatic approach. Not only was there scant representation from the left wing and more liberal elements at the session, but even a good many mainline evangelicals had their own reservations about Bradford, though reluctantly accepting him as one of their own. As a result the conference hall was less than half full. Anthony Powers winced inwardly at the paltry turnout, yet it could not be helped. Bradford was a big name among a certain contingent of fundamentalism, and he had to have him for the prestige his name had added to advance publicity. But Bradford had only agreed to come as a general session speaker, and the topic was one he had insisted upon. Thus, Powers found his conference tainted early by this tacit boycott of one of the major morning addresses.

Bradford was president and founder of OBU, the university which bore his name, and the adjacent Deeper Life Training Center which sponsored both weeklong and weekend seminars, conferences, retreats, and crusades. Among his faithful the enthusiasm was frenetic. He was quoted and read and video-taped throughout the country, his followers reluctant to take a step or think a religious thought without consulting some resource to find out what "Brother Bradford" had to say about it. The emphasis of his teaching was healing and prophecy, the "twin miracles of the anointing," as he called them. He was something of a self-proclaimed authority on recognizing God's anointing and training oneself to be effective in one's particular calling. Out of his ministry had grown a publishing company, mostly distributing Bradford's own books and pamphlets, but also publishing the words of fellow evangelists and authors and miracle workers who had allied themselves with the Bradford complex in Alabama. Several television broadcasts and highly publicized revivals and prophetic conferences kept the entire coterie ever before the public eye.

Bradford's speech was, as anyone familiar with him would have anticipated, high on miraculous outpourings, low on personal accountability of obedience, and long on personal experience from Bradford's vast repository of firsthand episodes. The events of his own life were to him the *summum bonum* of reality whereby truth was verified.

Jackson and Jacob attended together, but afterward split up for separate workshops.

Father and son met for lunch to talk about their mornings.

"I heard an interesting talk by a fellow named Larry Richels," said Jackson.

"What on?"

"He's with Bethany College of Outreach," replied Jackson,

"and he talked about what they do. It's a pretty unique place, and I liked the sound of it. They balance missionary vision with hard work and discipleship and responsibility. If I were going to the mission field, that's where I'd start for schooling, training, and on-site experience. They cover all the bases, and with a quality and professionalism that I like."

"I've heard of them. A small school, isn't it—up north some-where?"

Jackson nodded as he finished a bite of his cheese-covered rye.

"Community is a big part of what Richels talked about too," Jackson went on, "and that has always appealed to me. In their case, it seems to work. They've been on the same plot of ground for fifty years, and the community aspect—everybody living and working together—adds a depth and stability to the missions pro-gram. What did you do this morning?"

"I was planning to go to Dieder Palacki's talk."

"The Polish leader?"

"That's right. He was going to give a couple of small group sessions before his general address later in the week. But Tony Powers came in and announced that the Palacki talk had been cancelled. So we all had to choose something else. I went to listen to Loren Cunningham."

"Good?"

"Oh sure. Cunningham's a great guy. But the interesting thing was that as I was getting up to go, Tony pulled me aside and whis-pered that things weren't going too well with Palacki. Apparently he is making some unsettling noises about the way the conference is shaping up."

"Hmm," said Jackson, "that's surprising. I thought Palacki and his longtime work with the underground church would be one of the highlights."

"It was supposed to be—at least by Tony's perception. His pres-ence here was the great unifying thread—the underground church of the East at last meeting the free church of the West, hands across the wall and all that. Palacki's highly thought of, so naturally his being disgruntled would disturb Tony."

"Have you ever met him?"

"Who—Palacki? No, only by reputation."

"I don't know much about him."

"For years he was imprisoned for his Christian preaching and teaching. I think he was behind bars for about fifteen years—beaten, tortured, solitary confinement, the whole nine yards. But even there he kept up his preaching. By the time he was finally released he was recognized as one of the leaders of the underground church movement. He traveled all over—Bulgaria, Poland, Russia, Hungary, Romania—encouraging little pockets of believers, even managing to get a manuscript smuggled out of Poland and to Scotland, where it was published."

"Oh yeah, I remember," said Jackson, "several years back. What was it called?"

"*Tortured but Undaunted: Faith in Action Behind the Iron Curtain*," replied Jacob.

"And then he got out and went on tour in the West, drumming up support and raising money to help. I remember that—mid-80s."

"I don't know if *tour* is what you'd call it." Jacob laughed. "He traveled around the United States, speaking in churches and wherever he could, trying to raise enough support to get Bibles home to his people who had so little."

"How successful was he?"

"I didn't follow it too closely," said Jacob. "I don't think he raised that much money, and from a few things I heard, he was a little cynical about it. A crusty, outspoken guy—not that I'd deny him the right to say anything he wanted. Fifteen years in prison—he's got more guts than I've ever had for *my* faith, that's for sure!"

"Is he still in the States?" asked Jackson.

"Oh no, he went back to Poland several years ago. Matter of fact, I hadn't heard of him again until this conference. He dropped out of sight for a while, though I assume he's kept active in the East all this time."

They continued their discussion as they left the restaurant and walked back across the street to the hotel. As they entered the lobby, Jacob grabbed Jackson's arm and whispered, "There he is." He motioned across the floor. "With Powers again."

"He doesn't look particularly pleased," said Jackson.

"Apparently nothing has changed since this morning."

"Powers seems trying to placate him."

"It's obvious he's not happy."

"Which is hard to figure. Didn't you tell me he was scheduled to get a good-sized donation from MacPatrick's TV fund-raiser?"

"I heard a rumor to that effect," said Jacob.

"When is Palacki supposed to speak?"

"Next to last night."

They had crossed the lobby, during which time Powers and Palacki had disappeared into an elevator, and were now walking down the corridor toward several of the workshop rooms.

"And when did you say is Jaeger's workshop on fund-raising?"

"Later this afternoon," replied Jacob.

"You still not going?"

"Are you kidding!"

"I just thought—you know, just for interest's sake," said Jackson.

"I wouldn't go for a hundred bucks—not even for a thousand!"

32

August 12, 1:00 P.M.
Berlin

They walked into the immense general meeting hall, already filling up.

At five minutes till one, several of the big names of the conference walked onto the platform and took seats along the back of it. The hall gradually quieted, and Anthony Powers at length took the microphone. The Polish leader Dieder Palacki was noticeably missing from the entourage, conspicuous in that he had become one of the most talked about speakers present. The newest guest had come in next to Powers, full of smiles and self-satisfied ebullience, clearly accustomed to and fully enjoying being the center of attention.

"Before we get underway," Powers began enthusiastically, "I

would like to introduce the latest arrival of our speakers, a man whom I know will require no introduction—Mr. Bob MacPatrick!"

A great ovation went through the hall as MacPatrick stood, beaming and waving to the gathering of Christian leaders, among whom his name was one of the most preeminent in all of Christendom. It would be difficult to imagine a more overweening expression of confidence, though it went unnoticed by nine out of ten of those watching. Flushed with a sense of his own renown, MacPatrick continued to wave and gesture and smile to the approving crowd, inflating more fully every second the clapping continued. He did not seem to be readying himself to teach on the truths contained in the final four words of the fifteenth chapter of Proverbs.

"Bob will, as you already know," Powers went on as the clapping subsided, "be addressing us and doing some hands-on furtherance of the gospel on Friday evening, when he and Dieder Palacki will share this podium together. As leading representatives of Christ's church on earth, they will symbolically bring East and West together, as it were, in a demonstration of the unity that binds all of us together as one. But tonight I wanted to introduce him to you and welcome him to the Berlin Conference on Evangelism."

Powers shook MacPatrick's hand vigorously, then turned back to the microphone as his marquee headliner resumed his seat.

"And now," Powers went on, "it gives me further pleasure to introduce the General Director for Budgetary Planning of the Lutheran Church in Germany, a man highly respected both among the political and church leaders of his country and, I would have to say, by the Christian community worldwide—Mr. Gentz Raedenburg."

Raedenburg shook Powers's hand and stood quietly behind the podium amid scattered and moderate applause. The welcome, though sincere, was certainly not like that afforded MacPatrick. Raedenburg, however, hardly seemed to notice, but stood serenely waiting, almost appearing reticent to begin. When at last he did speak, his voice was soft and methodical, though anything but timid. The power and impact of his carriage did not come from volume of voice, public praise, or self-approval, but rather from a reservoir of bearing and dynamism that dwelt somewhere altogether deeper inside his being.

"I so earnestly appreciate this opportunity to be with you," Raedenburg began. "This gathering is, as you all know, unusual in itself. But that uniqueness is further heightened by the variety of backgrounds and viewpoints represented here. Thus I consider it a singular honor to be asked to address you, for it is not often that conservative American evangelicals and 'liberal' German church officials interact.

"Frankly, I do not consider myself a liberal. Neither do I consider myself primarily a 'church official,' though I do serve in such a capacity. I am first of all a Christian and, I pray, a seeker and obeyer of truth. Yet I am not so naive as to be unaware of the labels that have traditionally floated about among us, and German liberalism has been an anathema to fundamentalists in England and the United States for two centuries. Yet I hope you will afford me sufficient trust to discover that I do not fit such a mold."

His voice contained not a hint of his native German accent, but reflected flawless English, striking an intriguing balance between the American and British versions.

"I would like to talk to you about several areas of concern to me," he went on. "As I see from your schedule, two workshops already have touched on an urgent issue with regard to evangelism at the urban and national level. In the United States, among evangelicals at least, there has been an emphasis on personal evangelism. But from where I stand, as a German, involved in the German church and even involved to some degree with the politics and leadership of this country—from that vantage point I would say that we are a *nation* in deep, deep need.

"I do not think I am speaking in too strong of terms—we are approaching spiritual bankruptcy. We need an infusion of *life!* It is not that we are without our spiritual roots. The very Reformation began within our borders. But by the very blessings that came with our postwar economic miracle *Wirtschaftswunder,* has come also a certain sense of invulnerability, that we can do anything we set our minds and hands to, a sense that we need nobody and nothing except ourselves to succeed. Not even God.

"So here we are now, with prosperity untold, with our country united again. Yet we are dying, spiritually suffocating in our affluence. We need more than a mere tearing down of the wall to heal the enmity that has grown in our hearts. What we desperate-

154

ly need is a reunification of the spirit, not merely of political entities.

"And do not all the nations we represent, in fact, stand in need of the same thing? You who have come from the United States could reflect similarly upon the spiritual roots of your nation and how liberality and New Age humanistic thinking have undermined those roots. We need a reunification of the spirit; you need a revitalization of your first love. In both of our countries, the national fervor of faith no longer exists and could spell our collective demise.

"Now as we attempt to spread the gospel, there are unique cultural and historical factors that we must take into account. The way you tell a lost American or Scot or Frenchman, for instance, will differ from the approach you would use with a German or Russian or Arab. And from certain things I've heard this week, it appears to me that there's a one-dimensionalism to the strategies many of you are talking about—as if what has worked for you in the past will automatically work in the countries of Eastern Europe. I consider that a grievous error.

"Let me give you an example. Notwithstanding all the spiritual vibrancy and activity in the United States, an ungodliness still pervades your society as a whole. In terms of your evangelization efforts, that may be good. By and large, the people in your country *know* there is a spiritual vacuum. I have in fact heard all three of your most recent presidents speak of such things. That may not mean that Americans *want* spiritual revival in their lives, but at least there is a degree to which such words communicate truth.

"In Germany, however, such talk is never heard. Nobody talks of spiritual need because no one is aware of the morass of unbelief that is killing our country. If I went out to people on the street and asked them if they were Christians, probably six out of ten would look at me as if I had spoken nonsense. The question would be meaningless. Of course they're Christians—isn't everybody?

"You see, our two countries have both lost our spiritual vitality—our loss of the Reformation efficacy of Luther, your loss of the foundation stones of your nation's spiritual beginnings—in different ways. Your modern leaders have simply thrown out spirituality by outlawing it in the name of equality. Now prayer in your schools is against the law, whereas abortion is legal. We in Germany, on the other hand, have taken a different tack. We have institutionalized the Christian faith. We have done the very opposite from you. Religion and prayer and the articles of the creeds are taught to our young people in school. Religion is a subject taught just like arithmetic. Confirmation in the church at fourteen is no more than a graduation ceremony. You *withhold* spiritual teaching, we *give* it—in just a sufficient dosage as to inoculate our people and make them immune to the life and power of it.

"Now you may look at me and say, 'But you are in a position of responsibility and prestige. Why do you not tell your country's leaders these things?'

"Yes, I am on intimate terms with my nation's leaders from all the parties. Chancellor Hans Kolter is a close personal friend. In fact, I am meeting with him this week. And when I speak of spiritual matters, Hans is an open and willing listener. But to him the words may as well be from another politician. The church is just one more faction of the government. Christian Socialists, Christian Democrats—we blindly mingle the very word *Christian* with our politics.

"Hans is likely to ask me what I think of a crucial vote coming to the Bundestag next week on economic aid to the Commonwealth of the former Soviet Union. There are undercurrents of dissatisfaction with the Chancellor's policies, and I know Hans is concerned whether he will be able to carry the day and see the package approved. But he will be asking me, not because he wants to discover what might be God's mind on the matter, but rather as he would consult any other faction or interest group with influence to sway votes in the parliament.

"The point I am attempting to make is that evangelism in the post–Cold War era must not be one dimensional. It must take into account these national strongholds, national differences, and cultural differences. I exhort you evangelists and leaders to be astute in your evangelism and to tune in to realities that exist in the nations to which you would take your message, so that you do more than throw words into the wind."

A lengthy pause followed.

"I would like to sound one other word of caution before I finish," Raedenburg continued. "Perhaps this will seem to you out of the flow and context of what I have said previously, but I feel the urgency of this word of warning to you—to *us* as the Christians upon whose shoulders rests the responsibility of taking the gospel to the world of the twenty-first century.

"That world will be vastly different in many ways. The toppling of the Berlin Wall in 1989 and the other remarkable events of these recent years did much more than reunify a nation and close the fifty-year period of tension that we called the Cold War. In the euphoria of those events, I think many throughout the world have missed the deeper significance of what this time in the earth's history means. When American President Bush coined the phrase 'new world order,' he was speaking deeper truth than even he realized.

"Everything has changed. Old alliances have suddenly crumbled. New ones will spring up in their place. New Age and humanist thinkers and gurus and writers and speakers are putting their own gloss on world events and are swaying millions, both here in Germany and elsewhere.

"But be not deceived, my brothers and sisters. The world has changed; man's sinful heart has not. I firmly believe that we are living in the last days before the return of our Lord, and these changes are spoken of in the Bible as those preceding His coming. Great deceptions are ahead, and we must walk into the future with eyes wide open to the wiles of the enemy. Do not be lulled into the false assumption that enmity between nations has been eliminated. Nationalism and greed and lust for power have not been eradicated from the human heart.

"But new conquerors will use the weapons of the new world order rather than the guns and tanks of our predecessors.

"I am a German, and I love my land and my people. But still I see the danger signs of xenophobic vanity throughout my country. I fear no military rise, but I do fear political and economic superiority—not just in my own nation, but in all of yours as well. The new world order will be ruled no less than the old by the lust and greed and selfish ambition of men. But the specifics and pawns in the game will change. They will be less easy to see than invasions of tanks and explosions of bombs. We Christians must heed our Master's words, now more than ever—be watchful, be vigilant, be alert, be on guard!

"We can see that the new world order is but a prelude to an utter collapse of the earth's systems as has been long prophesied. The Lord has opened great doors of opportunity for us to take His

157

gospel and His life abroad unto the world. It is a period of unprecedented opportunity for spiritual harvest. Yet, as I said, we must not be deceived into false delusions that these doors will remain open forever.

"I would not presume to prophesy what the future holds. I merely sound the warning that the times are not as rosy as they seem. Christ's evangelists in this new era must be equipped more fully than their fellow evangelists of any previous age in history—equipped intellectually, equipped for spiritual battle, equipped with helping hands to meet the needs of people, equipped to voice the gospel message in fresh ways. Ours is no calling merely to stand on street corners preaching outmoded sermons to unconcerned passersby, satisfying our own need to feel important but doing little to impact those who hear us. Our calling is rather to take with transforming power the life of Christ to those in desperate need of it—astute and intellectually honed to stand on the cutting edge of today's world, compassionate and full of hearts that love—and to battle the cunning and evil resourcefulness of the enemy.

"We must equip ourselves to walk in *all* these ways. Without such depth of preparedness and vision and without an encompassing and discerning worldview, I fear we evangelists of Christ's church will be doing little more than talking among ourselves."

Raedenburg walked back to his chair among the row of dignitaries. The applause which followed, though slow at first, rose steadily as the listeners gradually sensed the dynamics of the message they had just heard.

Anthony Powers rose, went to the podium, mumbled a few words of bland praise, then closed the meeting with a prayer a bit too eloquent for the occasion.

PART 6

Out of the Past

33

August 7, 3:30 A.M.
Moscow

The darkened streets did not hint that dawn was less than two hours away.

Sounds were few, distant, muffled. The squeal of tires on pavement, the scream of a car's engine were amplified all out of proportion, as if they were the only sounds in the entire city.

Then silence once more—followed by the dull thudding of a cushioned footfall, pounding rapidly and rhythmically through the darkness.

Pursuer and prey—searching, hiding, chasing, eluding.

Sixteen hundred kilometers to the east, even as Klaus Drexler revolved in his mind the many factors that would propel him onto center stage of the world's affairs, another man ran for his life through the deserted predawn streets of the Russian capital. The futures of the two men were destined to intertwine in a way neither was yet aware.

They each knew of the other, though they had never spoken face to face. Within hours Drexler's bone-crushing lackey would be en route to Moscow to finish the job if the men now chasing him were unsuccessful. Galanov's snooping since the press conference a week ago had brought all this trouble down upon his head. All he thought about as he ran desperately through the deserted streets was to find cover before the gray of dawn began to show signs of life in the east and betrayed him.

He was older than Drexler, late 40s, though in the darkness it would have been difficult to tell. In his own way he had been equally powerful on his country's behalf for many years. His influence had been quiet, however, and out of the public eye, unlike Drexler, or even his own countryman, Drexler's clandestine ally, whose order had sent these neo-KGB agents after him. But whatever influence he had had, that was then, and now was now. The power he had once wielded suddenly seemed like the illusion of some dreaming fancy.

He was no bureaucrat. Though had he been he might have been safer at this moment. But he could never have taken that stifling life, and his own background had at least kept him trim and in shape, for which he was deeply grateful at this instant. The morning was about to break, and he was going to have to make a run for it, come what may. They'd been on his trail all night, and even using all the old hideouts and routes and gimmicks, he hadn't been able to shake them. Light would expose him, and he'd be finished. God—how he prayed his hideaway flat was still safe! If they'd uncovered that too—he was a dead man.

He took one last deep gulp of air, then stepped out of the alley and bolted across the wide stretch that was Vorovskovo Prospekt. With the gait of an aging marathoner well beyond the point of "the wall," he sprinted as best he could. The imported Nikes silenced his footfall.

That was some help at least, and the nearest streetlamp was a block away. Panting, he reached the opposite side, turned along the street, continued running half a block, then darted into another blackened alley, and instantly stooped down into a crouch.

Exhaustion from a night of intermittent running was overtaking him. He closed his eyes and tried to relax, sucking in huge draughts of air. But the oxygen didn't come fast enough to ease the pain in his chest or quiet his gasping lungs.

He listened intently, trying to hear over his own breathlessness. *Silence.* He closed his eyes in relief. Maybe he had eluded them at last. If only he could make it back to his place and sleep for an hour or two. Then he'd be able to think about what—

The screeching of tires suddenly ended his thoughts of safety. Curse them! They were still there!

He leaped up from his temporary hiding place, still out of breath, and ran into the depths of the darkened alleyway. Where it led he hadn't a clue, but he couldn't risk the open street again. They would spot him instantly.

Behind him the car grew louder, its engine racing. Brakes skidded. The tires squealed again, then headlights shone bright behind him, illuminating the alley in front of him.

How had they seen him in here? Sprinting with every ounce of fading energy, he felt his legs like lead.

The car roared toward him, the headlights scattering menacing spotlights, probing the darkness in search of their prey.

Shots exploded behind him.

Still he ran. His own pistol would do him no good. He'd run out of ammunition hours ago. Besides, there were probably four or five agents in the car.

More gunfire. A shattering series of sparks leaped off the stone building to his right, as the slug ricocheted off to the end of the alley. Another slammed into a window to his left. The sound of tinkling glass followed.

Without even realizing what he'd done, suddenly he found himself turning sharply, into a narrow courtyard between two tall tenement buildings. Whether there was a way out at the other end, he didn't know. But he couldn't go back.

Behind him the car suddenly slammed to a stop.

He heard cursing and angry shouts. Two doors opened, then slammed.

The echo of footsteps running in pursuit followed. Tires squealed, the car raced in reverse out of the alley.

He hesitated, listening.

A thin gray was about. Dawn was coming. But this poverty-stricken part of the city still slept.

He could hear the running steps, two men he thought. In the distance, the Mercedes tore through the streets. He could hear the occasional squeal of its tires. It was trying to cut him off at the other end.

He bolted again, wheezing in agony, chest heaving, calves tightening, arms nearly numb. His lungs stabbed with pain as he gulped for air that would not come, on—on—toward what seemed a futile attempt to escape.

But as long as he was seventy-five or a hundred meters ahead of his pursuers he would not give up.

Gradually his sleep-starved mind went numb. With dreamlike unreality, the buildings around him began to fade. The sounds of his own lungs and feet grew distant. The night's events seemed a phantasm. Visions and illusions and mirages rose before the eye of his mind.

Yet he knew he was still awake, still running.

Was this what happened before death? his hallucinating brain asked. Was his life passing before his eyes?

Lucid again, suddenly his mind and eyes were clear. He still had a chance! He could see the end of the narrow passageway now. It opened into another alley. There was no sound of the Mercedes. His pursuers had gained no ground. They were probably ex-bureaucrats.

After years as the hunter, suddenly he had become the hunted—the former top KGB operative, the man the chief depended on, all-powerful, all feared, ruthless and cunning—now *he* was at the mercy of a carful of vindictive bureaucrats of old. How quickly the tables turned! Now *they* were the new agents of so-called freedom.

Again his vision fuzzed. Images and faces and fragmentary glimpses of the past rose and fell in an illusory sequence of somnolent memories.

Still he ran . . .

34

He had wanted to be an agent since before he could remember.

He'd only been two when the war ended, born, his father had enjoyed telling him, just after the encirclement and destruction of the German armies besieging Stalingrad, as the mighty Russian army moved westward to liberate Rostov, Kharkov, and the Caucasus.

He remembered nothing of that time of course. His first definable memories were of fear—of hearing his parents talking about the American threat, about the need to protect the Motherland from invasion and attack.

That was later, after the war. He didn't know when exactly.

1948—1950 maybe. His father was a Party member, and such had been his boyhood dream during the 50s as well. As he had grown up into his teen years, talk at home and at school and in the news-papers was of the imperialist aggression of the United States in attempts to gain military dominance over his homeland through those countries bordering the Soviet Union. Crisis after crisis had required the sending of brave Russian soldiers to such places to secure their safety, and even—where the American threats were most severe—sending troops to help the innocent nations by oc-cupation. Only so could they have been saved from destruction by the cruel American bombs and vicious plundering GIs.

He remembered being told of U.S. and British attempts to rape and ransack Eastern Europe and how Stalin had saved those coun-tries. But he was old enough personally to remember Greece and the crisis in Egypt and the American-led revolts in Poland and Hungary in 1956, as well as growing anxieties in Asia and Latin America. There was no place, it seemed, that the Americans were not trying to take over.

He had only been seven when the first American spy plane had been shot down over the Baltic in 1950, and his memories of that incident were vague. But ten years later, when the American U-2 was downed, he had been a scrappy seventeen year old and ready to go to war like many of his fellow soldiers and comrades. And he had rejoiced the following year with the explosion in Siberia of the largest atomic bomb ever made by mankind.

But it had taken the missile crisis in Cuba to set the course of his future. How they hated Kennedy! But when Khrushchev had backed down from the confrontation after the revolution in Cuba, they had come to despise him too for being soft and indecisive. His ouster in 1964 had almost been welcome.

It was the day of the Cuban crisis that he had decided what path to follow, and his desire to be an agent had never abated. It would be a way to channel his love of his country into practical protection of it against the hated enemy who would destroy it. If the U.S. continued to arm itself and build bombs and make threats and send subverting forces behind the Iron Curtain to work mischief, kill, undermine, and destroy—then as an agent for the mighty Soviet Union, he would counter it at every turn.

He had joined the KGB in the mid-60s, the moment he had

been released from the army, the passion of his hatred toward the American President Kennedy never slacking, even after the assassination. His father had risen steadily in the Communist party and was then a local section chief. The connection had done him no harm, for he found promotions regular, and gradually rose within the ranks of the Committee for State Security.

Still the rampant spread of democracy and capitalism instilled both fear and hatred in the hearts of loyal Communists like him. The United States was taking over dozens of countries—Japan, Korea, Mexico, Indonesia, Israel, the new nations of Africa—and installing puppet governments they had the audacity to call "free." Everywhere they were bent on world domination, pouring billions of dollars into so-called foreign aid in attempts to seduce nations to ally themselves against the Soviet Union.

As he rose in the KGB, how thankful he was for being able to play such a vital role in protecting the world against aggression. The Committee was huge—with more employees in Moscow alone than the combined numbers of the American CIA and FBI worldwide—and he remained a staunch believer in its protective and potent role. During the Cold War years, paralleling his own rise in the secret organization, the KGB extended its reach into nearly every aspect of Soviet society—protecting the country's vast borders and many leaders, assembling dossiers on foreigners as well as its own people, from journalists to high officials, and carrying out the world's largest espionage operation from wherever it could—out of Soviet embassies, through businesses, and by using undercover agents as tourists and travelers and athletes. He himself had been fortunate to get out in the field early in his career rather than be stuck in the tangled web of bureaucracy. It had been an exciting life. He had traveled. He had seen much of the world. He had even been to America, witnessing the degradation of its materialism firsthand.

The job had had its unpleasant side. Hauling old men off to the gulag, beating screaming wives until they divulged the whereabouts of their husbands' secret papers, bribing little children with candy to betray their schoolmates' parents—such requirements demanded an allegiance to the State that was unquestioning. And a ruthlessness. You had to close your eyes to feelings. Emotions in the Cold War Soviet Union didn't exist. They taught you that in training and reinforced it at every opportunity. The screams did not matter. Do not listen to them. They count for nothing. They were not the screams of anguish of a heart being ripped from a countryman's breast. They were not screams of pain at all, only the sounds of those who didn't understand, didn't see the necessity. Didn't see that they were *protecting* the people by making the State supreme.

He had first killed at twenty-six. It had not been easy, but he had prepared himself for it. There were no emotions. You did not look into their eyes. Close your own for a moment afterward if you have to. But do not let their eyes find yours. They will lie to you about life—and death—and meaning. You must not let that happen. Killing was a necessary corollary to the protection of your people. They taught you that too.

And he had killed again, with steely resolve and unflustered determination. And beaten—and spied. He had lied, tricked, double-crossed, and browbeaten—and by thirty-five was known as one of the KGB's best and most ruthless.

His skills became so widely known in the intelligence community that many an attempt was made to recruit and lure him to the other side, most notably by the British. He had even been given a two-year sabbatical from his duties, had moved to England, and had given them completely to believe that they had turned him. Thereafter he had made several forays back into the Soviet Union, ostensibly on the business of the British MI6 as a double agent, a ruse he continued for many years, even to the point of feeding London information of apparent intelligence value.

It was all an eleborately conceived charade, of course, contrived in Moscow and plotted out in intricate detail. He had taken delight in the maneuvering and posturing and secrecy with the British and their stuffy ways, stringing them along, chuckling to himself at their seriousness and pomposity. It had been like taking candy from a baby!

But even the double agent operations with the British had not been his first love, if *love* it could be called. Hatred would more accurately describe his feelings toward the Jews and ridiculous fundamentalist believers. Where the intense antipathy had come from, he didn't know. Probably from his mother—forever praying and angering his father, who always said that that kind of thing had no place in the modern Soviet Union.

As he had grown and moved up in his career, no group of irritants had been more stealthy, underhanded, crafty, insidious, subtle, and outright treasonous and subversive.

Something about the Christians had always enraged him more than the rest. They had seemed more determined than anyone else to thwart and resist and destroy the Communist system—meeting in secret, praying for its overthrow, distributing their Bibles and literature, smuggling in material and supplies, and smuggling out known outlaws. As a group, they had been more obstreperous and antagonistic than any other.

He had at first taken a special delight in rooting them out, spying on their leaders, breaking up their prayer meetings, sending their ringleaders to Siberia.

It never stopped them, of course. They were a determined lot! As committed to their cause as he was his, he would say that much for them.

That had been impressed upon him most graphically that night he had led the raid on their Bible factory in the small town outside Moscow. It had been the dead of night. He and his men had broken in without giving a hint of their approach and had thus discovered the lawbreakers in the very midst of their treachery. He hadn't believed it at first. Children, teenagers, women, and men spread out at tables or on the floor, each hand-copying different sections of a single Bible that had been cut apart into its separate books. In questioning them he learned that their laborious work went on every night.

A search of the rest of the house and attic uncovered a dozen completed Bibles, hand stitched together, representing several months' work. Everything had been confiscated—the whole Bibles, the portions being worked on, and the printed original—and promptly burned. But he had never forgotten the lesson of that night— how tenacious and hard-working those people could be. And henceforth he kept a keen eye about for any sign of other hidden book and Bible factories, especially those involving typewriters. One of the worst had been an old crippled man with a broken-down typewriter who had apparently spent every waking minute for years typing out carbon-copies of Bible-teaching books, which he gave to others to bind and circulate all over Russia. Galanov hadn't had the heart to send the old traitor to prison. He was probably seventy-five already, so what difference did it make? But he smashed the typewriter to bits right in front of his tear-filled eyes and kept up surveillance on the place thereafter.

Yes, they were a determined lot!

He had become known as the Believers' Worst Enemy—a nickname he had learned of after intercepting a hastily scrawled note just before a raid on a prayer meeting—who knew more of their ways, more of their secret hideouts, and more of their routines than anyone else in the KGB. Whenever there was a major assignment involving underground believers, it was turned over to him.

When Bolotnikov had risen to head the security organization eight years ago, Galanov had not had difficulty ingratiating himself and rising still further, for the new top man was also known for his loathing of Christians. His nemesis, a high-up Christian leader by the name of Rostovchev, had eluded Bolotnikov for years, and he was consumed with a passionate vendetta to put him away permanently.

When and why the change had come—who could tell? Whereas the Christians had always enraged him, slowly they began to unnerve him.

It might have begun early in his career, though the incident had only recently come back to him, the memory sowing seeds of doubt he had ignored back then. It had been one of his first such raids. His superior had burst into the room, with Galanov and a half dozen others following on his heels.

"What are you doing?" his superior had demanded. From the singing that continued even after their interruption, they knew very well what was going on.

One man answered in a quiet, peaceful voice. "We are worshiping God."

"There is no God. You will have to stop immediately," said the KGB man.

"We believe there is, and we are worshiping Him," replied the man.

"You cannot!"

"Why?"

"Because it is against the law. We have been sent with orders that it must be stopped immediately."

"But we are *not* breaking the law," replied the man, still speaking very politely. "Comrade Lenin himself said that citizens of our country have the right and freedom to worship God."

The KGB leader was at a momentary loss for anything to say. The Christian man had gone on. "Comrade Lenin said that every citizen of our country has the full right to exercise his belief in religious worship, or not to believe, as he chooses."

Then he had begun to quote from the Soviet constitution, where the very words did in fact state that every citizen had the right to fulfill his religious beliefs. "All we're doing, comrade," the man had concluded, "is exercising the right the founder of our country and our Soviet constitution provide. We are harming no one. We simply believe in God and are worshiping Him. What have we done wrong?"

He waited for a reply from the leader of the KGB raiding party.

But the agent could not refute what had been said. All he could do was fall back on the old argument. "None of what you say matters," he had replied. "You are violating the laws of our country!"

He had grabbed the gentle Christian viciously by the arm, yanked him outside the house, and proceeded to beat him as if he had been a punching bag. The man never uttered a peep of protest, and three minutes later the raiding party had gone leaving the man motionless in the snow, his face unrecognizable.

If his doubts had began that far back, he hadn't known it. Before long he was conducting raids himself, hardening himself to the reality that in truth it was *not* against Soviet law to worship the God of one's choice.

Perhaps doubts began to creep in that time he had gone to the prison, accepting an invitation from the warden to see what befell the cursed believers after he had brought them to his domain. There he had watched, silently trying to keep his stomach under control, as the prison guard had shown him tortures too horrible to imagine—red-hot pokers, razor-sharp knives, merciless beatings. He was shown specially designed pipes into various cells, through which starving rats could be released. Prisoners chosen for such torment could not sleep but had to constantly defend themselves against the disease-infected rodents, or else be literally eaten. Many and gruesome were the cruelties devised by the warden, whose eyes gleamed with pride in displaying his ingenuity.

Mostly the doubts had come when he began to make the mistake of looking into their eyes. Then he knew why they said never to do so. He found hesitation creeping in, doubt—lethal to one in his position.

Something was in those eyes that all his years of KGB training and experience had not prepared him to see.

It had probably begun during that madcap dash across Poland and into the DDR when Rostovchev had eluded him and Bolotnikov. It wasn't that he had actually found any pangs of conscience, yet the long, furious drive had given him time to think. The idiocy of their efforts to capture one man had come to his mind a time or two. He tried to tell himself that *Der Prophet* was a vital connection, a ringleader, one of the worst men in the country and that no effort to capture or kill him could be spared.

But when he had seen Rostovchev face to face in that field, that's when he had first made the fatal mistake of looking into his eyes! It had unhinged him momentarily. When he came to himself, he was enraged.

He'd found the eyes of the Christians he persecuted more difficult to avoid than ever after that night. He'd kept it to himself and worked doubly hard to root them out, angered all the more by their seeming capacity to twist his stomach in knots. And he had to admit, when the orders began coming down after Gorbachev came to power to ease the harassment and persecutions of Christians, inside he felt a sense of relief. He'd be content to have nothing more to do with them.

Rostovchev's eyes had begun it! He never should have let himself get drawn into the banter with him. He should have thrown him into the car and been off. Then that idiotic farmer would not have had the chance to get in the way and louse the whole thing up!

That hadn't helped either. Getting knocked to the ground by the bumbling fool, then *Der Prophet's* getting away in the darkness. Then accidentally shooting the girl who was running off with him— the whole night had ended in a dismal failure.

He was glad he hadn't seen the *girl's* eyes. In the state he'd been in he doubted if he'd have been able to take it. But the memory of her back had not been easy to erase from his mind—running, running—the explosion from his pistol—the sound of her scream— then the thud of her fall. . .

It had replayed itself in his mind over and over a thousand times since! What was he turning into? He had killed before. A KGB agent feeling pangs of remorse, even guilt? It was not supposed to happen. They were enemies of the State. They had to be— Suddenly his feet gave way beneath him as he stumbled over a piece of broken cement. He crashed to the ground—just like the girl he had killed. Suddenly he was wide awake and alert again, his dreamlike recollections vanishing instantly.

35

Where he was, he wasn't even sure.

He'd been running steadily, judging from the panting of his lungs and the sweat pouring from his face and shirt. How he'd summoned the energy to keep it up he couldn't imagine.

He struggled to one knee. He'd fallen hard on the pavement. There was a shooting pain coming from both hands where he'd tried to break the fall. His left knee was bleeding, though he didn't discover it for some time.

He listened.

No footsteps followed. There was no sign of the Mercedes.

Even in his relief at having eluded his pursuers, he could not help berating them. *Stupid bureaucrats!* he thought. *They are no match for the real KGB!* But their bullets were just as real. Desyatovsky had to know he was onto him and was scared. It seemed *everybody* was after him!

He rose, painfully, and took stock of his surroundings. There was barely more light now than when he remembered dashing through that narrow place between the buildings. How much time had elapsed—five, ten minutes at the most. He didn't immediately recognize where he was. He was alone, and that was good. And he knew the general vicinity.

He couldn't risk going home. He hadn't been there in days. They'd have had it surrounded the moment his name was put on the list. He wasn't far from the flat he used as a hideaway. *No one* knew of its whereabouts! Not even Bolotnikov. He wondered how *he* was making out in this present purge. No doubt landing on his feet. His type always did. He'd find some "position" in the new order of things. It was the second-level hatchet men—men like himself!—who were now in most danger.

The irony struck him again. *He* running for his life! But Russia had had a history of ironies, with constant switchings and realignments. In 1917, in one masterful stroke, Lenin had replaced the czarist bourgeoisie with the proletariat. Suddenly commoners ruled the Empire. Yet in time Lenin and Stalin and the Communist party had become a brand-new elite, squelching and oppressing those under them. What had *he* been all those years as a KGB agent but a member of an elite of sorts? And now, just as suddenly, it was gone. The Soviet Union was dead. Lenin was a disgrace. Communism was undone.

Topsy-turvy it went. The cultural revolution in China. The ups are down, the downs up. The haves are suddenly cast adrift. And now it was *his* turn. The elite KGB agent suddenly on the underside of the realignment. The hunter had become the hunted!

He had laughed when Lithuania's black berets had complained of not being able to get out after the Baltics declared their independence, appealing for the very human rights they had denied those under them. He was not laughing now. Now the new democratic regime had to toss the old bad guys to the wolves, and his reputation had always been as one of the KGB's worst. The very bureaucrats he had always disdained were now in power, and hunting him down.

Nowhere in Russia would be safe for him. Democracy, freedom—what did those words mean to people like him, caught in the web of old and new, trying to sort themselves out? This was the side of Russian "democracy" the outside world would never witness—the housecleaning. Every set of Russian leaders did it— Lenin purged himself of troublesome people *within* the party, as did Stalin, Brezhnev, all of them. The new democratic leaders were still Russians. A new gloss. But the old rules still applied. They always would. Russia was Russia, there was no getting around it.

173

He had to get out!

He'd never be free here. He had to escape to the West. No matter how many democratic freedoms were given to the Russian people themselves, *he* would never be free. Those freedoms were meant for some, but not for the bad guys of the old regime. It would be death to remain behind. His only hope was escape—and to find a new life.

As soon as he got out of this immediate fix, he had to get back on track with his investigation, though it would be difficult given his outlaw status. He still had plenty of contacts and friends. He'd have to conduct the investigation deep underground.

He had to find out what was going on with Desyatovsky and the German! He could smell it. He knew it was big. Hopefully big enough to deal his way out of the country. He'd been an agent too long to back away from something this significant, even if his life depended on it—which at this moment, he had the clear feeling it *did*.

He was a fool. But he had to play out this hand—and *then* get out of Russia.

36

On the fugitive walked.

KGB agent, persecutor of God's people—suddenly alone, adrift—all his former reference points of life gone—with no friends, no place to turn but the remaining pride in his own strength.

Visions again encroached his consciousness—people he had herded into waiting prison vans, beatings, screams, women out of whose hands he had brutally torn Bibles, a man he had knocked into unconsciousness for kneeling down to pray for him.

Pray for *him*! How could anyone pray for *him*? He hated them all! He had killed—he had spit on them and flogged them and imprisoned them for even mentioning the name of their so-called

Savior. They praying for him!

The thing was logically absurd.

Their eyes were always filled with that—that look he could never describe. He could still recall the man's words as he knelt down, "O loving Father, in the name of Jesus Your Son I ask You to forgive this man, and by Your love to draw him one day to—"

There had been no more. The butt of his rifle had smashed cruelly against the side of the man's head the next instant, and he had crumbled to the floor without uttering another sound.

He had never been able to forget the words. God, how he had tried! But they had been indelibly burned into some deep place in his heart.

Love, forgive—what could the man have meant? How did those words bear relation to him? And the man's eyes—as he had gazed upon him before closing them to utter those words. Never would he forget the man's eyes.

Suddenly he sensed a presence in front of him.

Panic seized him. They had known his whereabouts all along!

Quickly he spun around and began dashing the opposite direction.

Then he remembered he had been followed. He stopped and turned back. Still no sound disturbed the gray morning air. He was filled with a terrible dread, a feeling that he was not alone.

An inner compulsion filled him. He could not disobey. Slowly he began walking again, inching toward whatever was in front of him.

The dread engulfed him. Had he finally gone over the edge into lunacy? It happened in his line of work. Had exhaustion taken over and scrambled his brain so that he could no longer distinguish fantasy from reality?

Still there was no sound—no footsteps, no car. Only the unknown something ahead of him.

Something seemed to tell him to stop. He stood—motionless, silent—waiting.

Dread and expectancy mingled throughout his being.

Suddenly a voice spoke from the darkness ahead—or at least he heard a voice. Whether it was audible he did not know. He only knew he *heard* it.

"Why do you tyrannize My people?"

175

He was filled with terror. The voice was deep, clear, and commanding.

This is the end, he thought. He was either hallucinating or had finally gone completely mad. Yet the voice had spoken with an authority that could not be ignored, and he found himself answering it timidly.

"But who—what—are you?" he said. To his own ears, his voice sounded small, feeble, faint. "Have you come to arrest me—kill me?"

He gazed forward, seeing nothing.

"I come to bring you life."

"But—who sent you?" he squeaked.

"I am the Sender, the Giver of life."

"I do not—but who—"

"I am the *Lord,*" came the answer, full of mingled severity, compassion, and energy. The power of the voice was not in its volume but in its quality, which commanded attention—and obedience. "Now go. From this day forward, you shall serve Me and spread My life among men."

Suddenly the presence was gone. Silence and the gray dawn were his only companions. Galanov stood alone on the deserted street.

Instantly his brain cleared, and he recognized his surroundings. His step gradually became more steady. He took two or three deep breaths, then quickened his pace.

A clarity of focus and a renewed sense of hopefulness infused his consciousness. He did not pause to reflect upon whether the sensations were directly connected to the extraordinary experience he had just had. He merely flowed with the feelings rising up within him. He would sort out the implications later.

In spite of his sleeplessness and exhaustion, he found himself filled with a great sense of energy and well-being, and quickly he strode the remaining ten blocks to his flat. He encountered no one and scarcely bothered to make sure he was not being followed. Somehow he knew he would be safe now. His step seemed lighter with every stride.

Out of habit rather than fear he took all the usual precautions, entered the alley two blocks away, sat to rest in its darkness for five minutes, then climbed the nearby fire escape by which he entered the building beside him. It was never locked. He knew its long corridor even in the dark, and the only light burning was a dim 15-watt bulb at the far end. Reaching it, he descended three flights of stairs, opened the door into the storage basement. Only now did he pull out his tiny flashlight. It was pitch black. Stealthily he traversed the basement hallway the end of which had been broken in to connect by a dirt tunnel only about five feet high to the basement of the building across the street. Stooping, he hurried through the passageway, and within another two or three minutes was safely into the next building.

Up several more flights of stairs, out an open window, another fire escape, across the roof and over to the roof of his own building with a short leap of four or five feet. Down the fire escape, into the building, down the stairs, and at last he was nearing his hideaway—two rooms he'd procured years ago in a rundown tenement building that had been used for storage longer than anybody could remember. It still said so on the door, though he possessed the only key to the lock. The outer room he still kept full of boxes and crates and discarded equipment, just in case. The inner room was just large enough for a bed, a chair, a desk, and a commode.

He unlocked the door, breathing a long sigh of relief at last, and again flipped on his penlight. Everything was undisturbed. He made his way through the cartons and refuse and into his inner lair.

Without turning on the light, he collapsed across his bed. The weak springs under the mattress had barely ceased their groaning, when the sound of a human voice in the room made him choke in terror.

"It is good to see you again at last, Herr Andrassy Galanov," said a man less than five feet away. "I have been sent for you."

37

Bludayev Desyatovsky was not a pensive man but rather a pragmatist. Leave philosophy to the Chinese. Leave technology to the Japanese or Germans. Leave bluster to the Americans. The one thing the Russian understood better than them all was power—raw power.

That's why he would come out on top in the end. That was the one thing the fool Drexler did not grasp. The Germans had always taken Russians for granted, had thought they could have their way with them. But not now—not *this* Russian. New times were ahead. A new world order indeed. One that *he*, not the soft-spoken American president, would dictate!

In his early 60s, Desyatovsky was the oldest of the principal players in the drama he was helping to write. He had waited many years, been a good soldier, and come up slowly through the Khrushchev, Brezhnev, Gorbachev, and Yeltsin eras, awaiting his opportunity. Now it had come.

As he sat reflecting at his desk, slowly sipping the vodka in his hand, the bulk of his massive frame sank into his chair. His eyes gazed forward, not with the probing fire of vision but with a contented pride in at last having reached nearly the apex of power. He would not philosophize about it, he would just move forward into it.

Again he raised the glass to his full, fleshy lips. Above them, wide-set eyes peered out from between a high forehead and folds of ample cheek skin. Thinning hair, nearly all gray, was hidden during the day by his military hat. But now, in the privacy of his late-night solitude, his German counterpart would have been shocked to see how old the man appeared. Old and in not very good shape, for Desyatovsky's thick frame had acquired a good deal of flab over the past ten years—also skillfully kept hidden by his military uniform. But in public and on the phone, where he conducted much of his business these days, the general still exerted a powerful will that did not depend upon his deteriorating physique.

Desyatovsky threw back his head and emptied the small crystal glass. He walked to his file cabinet, unlocked it, flipped through masses of folders, pulling out a stiff cardboard packet, itself sealed by a miniature padlock and marked in bright red "TOP SECRET: For the Eyes of General Desyatovsky Only." True, he reflected, neither the padlock nor the warning would keep anyone who really wanted inside from slicing it with a sharp knife. But it would keep prying secretarial eyes from getting too curious. If he was ousted or his office broken into—well, it would be all over by then anyway. By the time they got to the file, he had already determined to make a quick exit by the Boris Pugo route. And if he was greeted by Pugo on a cloud someplace bemoaning their mutual failures, then anyone could have the packet who wanted it!

The Defense Minister of the Sovereign State of Russia closed the file drawer and walked, packet in hand, to his desk, where he opened the third drawer down and pulled out a small box, locked by combination. With deft motions his fingers spun the tiny dial to the right, then left, then right again. Flipping open the top, he extracted a tiny brass key, by which he then opened the Top Secret envelope. Replacing key and box, and closing the drawer to his desk, Desyatovsky opened the file and pulled out several manila folders. They were marked: "Military," "Industry/Business," "Foreign Leaders," "Political/Moscow," "Political/Republics," "Media," "Transportation," "Finance."

Inside each, on the folder itself, was printed a single telephone number.

This was what Yanayev, Kryuchkov, Baklanov, Starodubtsev, and Tizyakov had never grasped. The sprawling Soviet empire had changed dramatically since 1984 and Gorbachev's ascension. The strings to pull were more complicated now. The people were more aware. Those who had failed hadn't taken into account all the necessary factors, hadn't struck decisively, boldly, and quickly, hadn't seized control of enough sectors. And of course they hadn't taken into account Boris Yeltsin and the massive public and international support he had behind him.

He wouldn't make the same mistakes. He would have *all* the elements solidly in place.

It was all in the files, he thought with satisfaction. Years of work, hundreds of favors, and great patience. Luckily he'd seen the handwriting on the wall years ago. He'd disassociated himself from the party early in the reorganizing struggle in the 80s. He'd known the futility of wedding himself to the past like the apparatchiks and defeated party stalwarts who had failed in 1991. His was a new movement, new in the mold of Bolsky and Kozyrev and Eduard Shevardnadze, but going far beyond *glasnost* and *perestroika,* going further into the future than either Gorbachev or Yeltsin or any of their own breed of rising stars could ever hope to have taken the republics. He would make of the sovereign state of Russia the foundation of the new order that Drexler liked to call the Eurasian Alliance—strong, dazzling, prosperous, energetic, and without peer on the global scene. The Revolution of 1917 was dead, Communism was dead, the Common Market was dead, the Warsaw Pact and NATO were dead. Many of his colleagues would have had a difficult time admitting it, but capitalism had endured as the victor.

But like Communism, *American* capitalism was dead too! *Both* sides had lost the Cold War. The new community of nations and peoples would emerge from the ashes. No longer weighed down by the excess baggage of the other Soviet republics, Russia would stand tall among those of the new Eurasian community, with new might, and a loud voice to proclaim the future—and he, Bludayev Desyatovsky, neither Communist nor American capitalist, but a new breed of leader for the new era of mankind—he would lead the way into the twenty-first century!

He thumbed through the single folder without a title. This was where it would begin—and the key was timing. Circumstances had to be just right. All the men together if possible—an accident, a limousine, the train, some mad terrorist. The perfect situation had fallen into his lap with the so-called summit. The man in this file had plenty of experience in disguising his work. He trusted him completely, more than the fellow the German had told him about. If the whole plan unraveled, he'd given him instructions to see to his *own* untimely end too. He didn't want to be around to face the music if something went wrong. He'd already paid the man the fee for his own head, just in case.

His thoughts flitted again to Pugo. He winced and shook the thought from his brain. Nothing would go wrong—nothing *could* go wrong. He had seen to everything. That's what all the other files were about.

He set down the stack, took out one marked "Communication," and eased back into his chair, his feet propped on the edge of his desk. This is where he had to make sure there were no slip-ups. Radio, television, newspaper—they all had to tell the same story, and simultaneously. He had the individuals who could do it. They were people in high places—people whose friendships he had been cultivating for years. None of them knew the whole story, not yet. They didn't need to. Each just had to do his own part. The military, that had been more difficult, he thought, setting down the file and lifting another from the stack. A few key individuals here were all the way in, full members and cooperators in the plan—colonels mostly. Only two other generals besides himself. Most of the generals were of the old guard and out of touch with the men. The colonels, that's where the true power lay, with the colonels. They could take the officers with them. That's why years ago he had begun concentrating his efforts of the substratas within the military machine, the rising stars who had yet to make their mark. The generals of '91 had been out of touch with the reality of the new Soviet military. The army had not come with them. But they would come with *him*, because he had the men the soldiers would trust and listen to. Likewise he had recruited a bevy of sergeants from every republic, every city, every battalion, every regiment. As the colonels would bring along the officer corp, they each had a sergeant or two under them who would bring along the ranks of common soldiers. There would be no disintegration of the lines of command this time.

It was a foolproof plan, he thought with a smile, setting the military file down again and picking up that marked "Political/Republics." Here too, he was confident. He had to have simultaneous support from the leadership of every one of the republics, at all levels—city mayors, republic leaders, politicians. Flipping through the pages he scanned the dozens of names, files, reports that had been accumulated for him. Budapest had raised some troubling questions—Donetsk was now OK—Riga and the Latvians—*Hmm,* he thought, *it could go without them.* A few holes might exist. He would have to see about those. But by and large, things seemed in place. He removed the letter from the Hungarian in the "Foreign Leaders" file, reflecting again on the irony of the times.

"Industry"—worker unrest and the union strike were already in progress.

One by one, Desyatovsky went through each file in the packet, making notes, jotting down names, thinking through last-minute arrangements, and rethinking every phase of this grand strategy for the thirteen-dozenth time.

Nothing could be left to chance!

When he had satisfied himself of what arrangements still lay before him two hours later, a list of some twenty-three contacts to be made was in his hand.

It would not do for it to be seen. Carefully he folded the paper and put it in his pocket. Then he replaced all the folders in the thick pouch, folded over its top lid, snapped on the padlock, and replaced it in the file cabinet.

He walked to his office couch and lay down. It had been a long day. He would catch a few hours' sleep, then perhaps go out at about 7:00 for some breakfast.

Still in his uniform, Desyatovsky was asleep within ten minutes. He did not awaken until the light of morning was streaming into his office. He rose, stretched, did his best to make himself presentable, then left to find something to eat.

38

August 7
Moscow

As the Defense Minister exited his office, the drab gray stone building was coming to life. In an outer office his own secretary sat at her desk, and a half-dozen or so assistants and mid-level bureaucrats had begun busying themselves with the morning's duties.

The wary eye of a woman in her early forties followed his

moves closely as he strode across the floor. He cast her a quick glance as he passed, catching her eyes with his but allowing no hint of intimacy to pass his lips, only a brief smile. She saw, and her heart thumped quickly for the next several beats. The emotions, however, were confused. A week ago such a look from Bludayev would have melted her heart. Today it brought anger and uncertainty. What was she to do? Pretend she had never heard? Hope she had misconstrued the words? Warn Yuri and tell him to undo what he had done? But they would only find out, and then perhaps even worse would come of it. If only there were somebody to talk to, somebody who could help!

By the time Marta Repninka reached her cold lonely flat that evening, she was no nearer a resolution to her emotional quandary than she had been that morning. She put down her things and walked toward the small kitchen of the one bedroom apartment, pausing for a glance in the small oval mirror that hung on the wall. Taking a hard look at what she saw, she unconsciously attempted to deal with several stray strands of her graying black hair.

But then suddenly she turned away in disgust, tears forming in her eyes. What could he have ever seen in that face! She was a fool for believing his charming lies! She was aging, plain, and too plump even for a Russian woman. Yet he had made her believe she was beautiful. It had felt so good! She would give anything not to have found out what he *really* thought of her. But it was too late now. She could never go back, and now she was more miserable than she had ever been before.

Curse him! How she would love to drive a knife into that huge, strong chest of his . . . *if* she thought she could get away with it. But she wasn't quite ready to die herself yet, and she could not betray Yuri.

She opened the single unpainted cupboard in the room and scanned the meager contents. Half a loaf of dry bread, a few canned vegetables—not much to make a meal. There was some cheese in the small icebox. She hadn't had any meat for a month. From the cupboard she took a half-opened bottle and glass.

She made her way out of the kitchen and flopped down in the only piece of comfortable furniture she owned, a threadbare, black, moderately stuffed chair. She wasn't hungry anyway. Perhaps the vodka would help her forget the misery. She opened the bottle, poured the glass full to the brim, and drank half the contents with one long swallow.

Marta Repnincka had worked all her adult life in various menial positions at two dozen different posts in and around the Kremlin. She had never married, never been noticed, and never allowed herself to hope for anything better in life.

The changes that had begun with Secretary Gorbachev had brought them hope at first. She and some of the other women of her level had occasionally been given parcels of food for special occasions and coupons allowing them to buy new clothes, even shoes, before the general public. But for most of Russia she knew the "changes" and "better times" spoken of by the Secretary in his speeches about *perestroika* lay somewhere in the future, and the promises became thinner and less tangible as the country's economy continued to decline.

She had been one of the fortunate ones. As the once-invincible Motherland had crumbled from within, fate had shown its light upon her, and suddenly she found herself working as a clerk and filing assistant in the new Russian Defense Minister's office, as one of several assistants to his personal secretary. Her pay had only increased moderately. Still she lived in the same dingy flat. Still she could neither obtain nor afford meat except rarely. But hope had sprung up within her breast that better times might perhaps lie ahead.

About the same time her brother, Yuri, who lived down in Kiev, had been promoted at the factory where he worked, and she had rejoiced along with his wife and son and daughter. They were the only family Marta Pavlovna had, and though seven hundred kilometers separated them, she never lost hope that perhaps one day she would be able to find a position in Kiev and join them there.

How the Minister had learned of her brother she had never stopped to ask herself, nor why he would be interested in either of them. But almost from the first day when he began to show subtle interest in her—smiling when he passed, paying her a compliment on her dress or her work—he also began casually inquiring about her brother in Kiev.

Now she could see—ah, what cruelty there was in hindsight!—that she should have been more cautious, asked herself questions, asked herself why she had been given the job in the Defense Ministry in the first place. But she had been blinded by his blandishments. She was a thick, slow-witted moron, nothing more! He had seduced her mind and emotions—and she had succumbed. He had used her—and was now preparing to throw her out like a discarded piece of trash.

What pleasure there had been in his attentions! She had forgotten her age, forgotten her graying hair, forgotten her sinking jowls and hips. He made her feel young again with the simplest of phrases, with a wink or a smile or a kind word. And steadily, without even knowing it, she revealed more and more of herself to the Minister—the hopes she harbored about bettering her life, and especially about going to Kiev to live near her brother. He was interested, and she willingly confided in him.

It had all culminated in that wildly joyous day six months ago when he had actually invited her to lunch—discreetly and privately. Her heart had raced all morning in anticipation, and she even dared to whisper his first name under her breath—Bludayev. What sensations the mere word caused to rise up within her!

"I need your help, Marta Pavlovna Repninka," the Defense Minister had said sincerely. She remembered the words as if it had been yesterday. How her head had spun at the thought that the great man needed *her.*

Anything, Bludayev, my darling! she had said in her mind. But the words that came from her lips had been more modest. "How may I serve you, Defense Minister?"

"It is a highly secretive matter," Desyatovsky had replied. "No one may ever know of this conversation."

She had nodded her assent eagerly and listened as he had promised many things fantastically beyond her dreams, *if* she would help him, and could guarantee her brother's help as well, for he needed a man he could trust in Kiev. It was the most sensitive and top secret matter of national security, even survival. There were forces, he said, attempting even now to gain control of the government. As Defense Minister, he must stop them. But to do so he needed their help. Could he trust her? If his efforts were successful, her brother's family would be well rewarded and she could expect a promotion and move to Kiev.

What would she not have done for the man who now filled her every waking thought? She contacted her brother immediately, and a time and place was set up for him to meet with the Defense Minister's man there. Yuri began to assemble what he needed, and the countdown began toward the initial target date of the first of August.

Meanwhile in Moscow, Marta took more care in readying herself for the office every day, bought some cheap fragrances to bolster the effect, and tried to eat less when she came home at night. She even began to entertain fanciful daydreams about *not* moving to Kiev after all. She knew Bludayev was married. But to a lonely woman in love, what does reality matter when there are castles in the air to build! She would find ways to please him, and soon he would forget his wife altogether!

In dreamlike ecstacy she had flitted and fumbled through the routines of her job day after day, living for the chance moments when the Minister would walk by, or else—most wonderful of all!—give her some assignment to handle *personally*.

Until yesterday . . .

As quickly as her Pushkinesque fairy tale world had arisen, it crumbled beneath her feet like a dissolving mirage.

Foolish heart of a smitten woman, she had yielded to the awful yet irresistable urge to listen to her phantom lover in private. In the solitude of an office temporarily vacated by others, including her own boss, the Minister's secretary, and seeing the red light on the secretary's desk that indicated the Minister was engaged in conversation in his office, she had stolen closer and picked up the phone line he was on. With trembling heart she had listened, entranced by the mere sound of Desyatovsky's voice. And once the horrifying realization broke through that he was talking about *her*, she was too mesmerized by mingled fear and agony to be capable of removing the receiver from her ear.

"—yes, as soon as possible," Desyatovsky was saying. "I don't want there to be any possibility of his being linked to the blast. An investigation could lead straight back to his sister and my office."

"What is your preference?" asked the voice at the other end of the line, sounding impersonal and cold.

"That is your business," the Defense Minister had snapped. "However you people take care of these things these days—an explosion in his car, some hoodlums after work. I don't even care if it's a bullet in his head. I just want to make sure it's done."

"And the family?"

"Be creative."

"Will they all be eliminated?"

"Look, when Drexler told me to use you, he said you were the best. I don't want to have to spell out every—"

"Say no more. It will be done," came the quick reply. "You also mentioned a woman."

"I will see to her."

"You have people?"

"I have ways. What do you think I am, a fool?" A brief pause, then Desyatovsky had broken into a quiet and cruel laugh. "I may even take care of this one myself. Ha, ha, ha! I actually think the old hag is in love with me! Ha, ha! A good one, wouldn't you say— what's your name again?"

"My name is none of your concern. All you have to remember is that if *you* slip up, my boss may order me to put a Scottish broadsword through *your* heart."

"Ah yes, that sounds exactly like what my melodramatic friend Herr Drexler would say. Ha, ha! But you had better tell him to watch his *own* step! In the meantime, I'll make sure the woman never says anything to anyone again—you do the same to her brother. I've given you all the information you need. I'll expect you to be in Kiev tomorrow."

With the ashen expression of looking death in the face, Marta replaced the receiver and hastened to another corner of the room where she would not be noticed. It was a good thing the day was almost over. She was trembling from head to foot in the cold panic of suffocating dread. In stunned shock she somehow managed to finish the day and stumble home, alternating between disbelief and terror. She had scarcely slept but could not think clearly what to do.

Today, as the man's evil words replayed themselves in her brain for the two hundredth time and the horrifying realization sank in that she had been but a pawn in his cruel game—whatever it was— and that she had never meant anything to him, a silent rage had gradually filled her, giving way to a defeating sense of her own inbecilic blindness.

Her own life hardly mattered now. But she had to save Yuri and his family. She would call him tonight—immediately, and warn him. But what was she to do about that despicable, hateful man she

187

had thought she loved? What could he have been up to that he was willing to kill to achieve it? How dearly she would love to see him undone, to see him toppled from his high and mighty throne! She may have been an idiot, but she was not such a fool that she could not find a way to turn the tables on him.

She looked up. It was dark already. How long had she been sitting here brooding? She looked down at the vodka bottle in her hand. It was empty. She had unconsciously drunk half a bottle. It had hardly phased her.

She tried to stand, but her knees gave way and she collapsed into the chair. Before she could even think again about telephoning her brother or gaining her revenge against Desyatovsky, her head dropped back and the snoring in her throat began almost the next moment.

She remained sound asleep until sometime after 3:00 A.M., when she stumbled to her bed.

39

August 7, 10:46 A.M.
Moscow

It was admittedly a rotten way to make a living. But he had been in the intelligence business long enough to let many of his scruples go by the boards. And one of the first lessons they had taught him in training back in Langley, Virginia, was that the quickest way to a man's secrets is through a woman.

Dan Davidson liked women fine. Even respected them, though he wasn't married himself. But they were emotional creatures. And often talkative—if you could find the right pressure points. It was a weakness he had exploited dozens of times already and would dozens more before he was either captured, killed, or put out to pasture.

And with the Cold War over, he thought, the latter seemed the more likely scenario. He was surprised they hadn't yanked him back to the States already. A lot of his old colleagues throughout the Eastern Bloc—or what they *used* to call the Eastern Bloc! Would he *ever* get used to the changes?—had been shipped home and were now sitting behind desks or carrying out other trivial assignments. But he'd been fortunate. Two or three years of change wasn't that long, he supposed, and Washington still needed to know what was going on behind the scenes, even though the Kremlin and the White House were the best of buddies.

So he supposed he would keep trying to find women who would talk, keep oiling the machinery of the apparatus he had managed to develop over the years, and hope that every once in a while something turned up that would justify his staying here to his superiors. He'd quit before he'd sit behind a desk eight hours a day! Even though the excitement of the old days had gone out with the toppling of the Berlin Wall, being here was a long sight better than being relegated to the home front.

Ah, but memories of the old days, dangerous as they were, still tugged at him sometimes. Yugoslavia and the coining of his nickname—the chase in Leningrad—his underground flight from Kiev to Prague in '79 when he'd got wind of the Afghanistan invasion—what times they'd been!

Of course, he'd come close to buying the farm that time on the Adriatic, if not from the gunfire then certainly from the cold. But he'd lived to tell about it. And done some important work for his country besides. If he'd made it to Prague two days sooner and got word through, he might have saved the Carter presidency! But there had been some notable successes as well. And he had saved Ronald Reagan's skin a time or two, though the old coot never knew it. Iran-contra. Now there was a fiasco! If it hadn't been for his quick legwork and several hefty payoffs in the right places, George Bush would never have become president.

Yeah, he'd made a difference to his country—not as a Democrat or a Republican or anything else. Just an American. A loyal, hardworking one. And that's what he'd keep being—a loyal American.

Davidson gulped the lukewarm coffee in his mug, grimaced at the taste, and looked at the two papers on his desk. Something was there, he thought, if he could just *see* it. What was all this point-

189

ing to? It had the definite aroma of importance—of something big. Or was he just fantasizing—pretending subterfuge and plot and secretive maneuverings where there were none? Was he nothing but a worn-out agent, living in the past, hoping in vain for the old thrill of the espionage game in the new world order where there was none? Was he—death to a CIA agent!—getting senile and losing his perspective?

Still—there *did* seem to be something going on. He'd been in this country long enough to recognize the signs. Freedom and democracy notwithstanding, Russians were Russians, and they had their peculiar ways of doing things. He could spot a ruse when he saw one—in *any* language.

That's why he had to get information from the inside. If he could just find someone to talk. Low-level people always knew something, and usually more than they realized.

But finding either a man *or* a woman's weakness was harder these days. It used to be you could coax someone into betraying his own mother. Promises of freedom in the West, an automobile, furs, even food for a commoner—they had all worked wonders ten years ago when such things were priceless commodities in the Soviet Union. Dangle the right carrot under the nose, and you had them.

But now it was all upside down. Travel restrictions were nearly gone. The standard of living showed hints of improvement. Democracy in the Commonwealth was a good thing, but it made his job of extracting information more difficult. There weren't many carrots left. Although with the economy so miserable, food could still sometimes do the trick.

There was always money. Which was why he had told his superiors recently that they were going to have to cough up more dough for him to have at his disposal if they expected the ongoing flow of information. Every person had his weak spot, which he had to discover. More important, every woman had *her* weak spot. That was often more subtle and difficult to find. But once you found a woman's soft underbelly, if you aimed your arrow true—you had her!

Again he scanned the sheets before him, then drained off the remainder of his mug.

It was time to call Yaschak. A little weasel if ever there was one, but a useful fellow if you paid his price. An agent needed a stool pigeon in every town where he hoped to make good, and in Moscow, Yaschak was his.

No scruples, only rubles was Yaschak's little jingle—about the only clever English he knew. It certainly was highly descriptive of the parasite's character. And he knew people of all kinds, in high and low places.

He picked up the phone.

On second thought, he said to himself, he'd better handle this personally. Quickly he set down the receiver, grabbed his lightweight jacket, and headed toward the door.

40

August 7, 12:23 P.M.
Moscow

"Yaschak, you little skunk!" said Davidson in colloquial Russian, but with a lightness in his tone so that the other took no offense.

"Anyone else call me that, Dan," replied the little man in a high-pitched voice, "they be dead before morning."

"But you know I treat you well, do you not? Eh, Yaschak?"

"One day you may go too far."

"I doubt that," laughed Davidson. "I know your kind, and you have no more intention of cutting off the easy money I bring you than you have of cutting off your own hand."

Yaschak eyed him beadily, betraying no emotion. He was the sort of man who made a living by being able to conceal his true motives. Dressed in a tasteless black suit, with white shirt frayed and dirty around the neck, Yaschak's low-level bureaucratic position at the Kremlin was of less than inconsequential significance. Yet everyone knew him, for he made a habit of hanging around where important people gathered. His hearing was preternaturally keen and, when combined with his wit and shrewd ability to read people far better than they gave him credit for, Yaschak was a fountain of information. No one was particularly fond of his ingratiating manner, but most put up with him as little more than a petty annoyance. His oily black hair, yellowed teeth, and persistent odor that stood out even in Russia, where deodorant was not high on the list of sought after imports, all created a not inaccurate impression of unrefined sloppiness and crudity. But as obnoxious as Yaschak was, Davidson had dealt with worse. And he had proved himself dozens of times. Whatever you needed, he could usually get. In a pinch, Davidson may even have admitted to liking him a little.

"I may be onto something, Yaschak," Davidson went on. "I need to get inside the Defense Ministry."

"You—personally?"

"No, not *me*. I need a contact, a pair of eyes. If not someone I can trust, at least someone who can be bought, someone who has a gripe, someone who's angry at his or her boss. I need information, and I'm not particular about how I get it."

"Defense Ministry—that's high up stuff. It cost you, Danny."

"Useful goods always do. You know anyone?"

"I might," replied Yaschak with a sly grin.

"You always do, eh, Yaschak?"

"I have my contacts in the city and through the Kremlin."

"In all the new republics too?"

"I work on that."

"And in the gutters?"

"Careful, Danny. You don't want to spite the hand that feeds you is. That is, I believe, one of your sayings."

"So—do you know someone who might help me?"

"I might. I will snoop around."

"A woman?"

"Perhaps. They work best for our purposes. Men in high places overlook or ignore them. They resent it. Emotions rise, makes them eager to talk."

"You are a cunning rascal, Yaschak!"

"If she in proper place, woman makes best informant. Most of time they do not realize they have revealed information to damage their man. So it safe too—they don't know what they have done."

"You know someone in the Russian Defense Ministry?"

"I know people who know people. There is someone I have in mind. Why all questions, Danny? I never disappoint you before. You tell me what you want, I deliver. Have patience, Danny."

"I might not have a great deal of time."

"What is up? Come on, Danny, you can tell Yaschak."

"Tell you! Not on your life. I pay for what you tell *me*! If I told you half what I know, you'd take it elsewhere, bargain for a few extra rubles, and sell me down the Moskva River!"

"Not me."

"I just got wind of something very peculiar in a communique my people intercepted between Russian Defense and Budapest—seemed to be from the mayor of that city to someone in the Kremlin. Very cryptic. I just want another angle on it."

"I see what I can dig up."

"You find me a dissatisfied woman in Defense, set up a meet, and you'll have earned your pay. And remember, Yaschak, not a word about my involvement, as always."

"I remember. Rule number one, just like you taught me."

"Don't forget it."

PART 7

Past Meets Future

41

At the strange voice speaking in German out of the blackness in his room, Galanov's heart lept into his throat. Even KGB agents could be frightened when their guards were down.

"Who's there?" cried Galanov, leaping forward off the bed with a start.

"One who comes in God's name," answered the voice. "You need have no fear."

"May I turn on the light," asked Galanov, recovering himself, "so that I may at least see who has succeeded in getting the drop on me? I presume you have a gun on me."

"You may turn on the light," the voice answered.

He pulled the string where it hung down in the middle of the room. Though it was a mere 40-watt bulb, the room seemed to explode into light. A stranger sat calmly watching him from his own chair.

"But—but—I've never seen—who *are* you?" said the agent in surprise, the tiredness of his sleepless night and strange experience coming back to him. He still could not disassociate the stranger from the men who had been chasing him.

"I am a friend."

"But—but how did you get here? No one knows of this location!"

"I have many friends. There are people who want to help you."

"Help me! Bah, who could want to help me? You don't even have a gun! What makes you think you can sit there and tell me— *how* did you get in here? I demand to know!"

Now that he had begun to realize his danger was not so great as he had suspected and seeing that he was not really held captive at all, that no weapon was trained on him, Galanov began to bluster. Fatigue had frayed his nerves and brought anger near the surface.

His unwelcome guest continued to calmly stare at him, with a serious but kind look on his face, tinged with an undefined sadness and pain. He said nothing.

"I tell you, I will bodily throw you out of here if I don't get some answers from you—and soon!" exclaimed Galanov, growing enraged. "If you are going to take me in, then be about your business. Though without a gun, you wouldn't have a chance. I'll kill *you* if you try!"

"I have not come to take you in."

"What have you come for then?"

"Sit down, Herr Galanov."

Galanov hesitated, glaring at the man. The serenity of his expression finally began to calm him. At length he ceased his fuming and sat down on the edge of his bed. The stranger eyed him steadily.

"I am a friend. I have been sent for you."

"Sent? By whom?"

"By One who is your friend."

"I have no friends! I have not made friends in my line of work. Who could want me but those who want me bound for Siberia?"

"You *do* have friends. I am one of them, and so is the one who sent me."

"Who sent you, man? Stop playing games with me!"

The stranger gazed into Galanov's face without answering. He was silent a long while, until the Russian settled into a quieter state. At length he spoke.

"Look into my eyes, and tell me what you see."

As absurd as it sounded, the agent found himself powerless to disobey.

"I see—what should I see? I see a man's face! A stranger—who are you?"

"Look carefully, Herr Galanov. Is there nothing more you see?"

Slowly Galanov felt himself weakening. Even in the dim light of his dingy flat, he found the same spell coming over him that he had noticed many times before.

All at once he remembered the terrifying voice he had heard in the street. The same sense of dread suddenly came over him.

"Were you—was that you back there—in the street?" he asked, confused.

"I have been here waiting in your room for three hours," replied the man.

"Then how did you come—and—and your voice—I recognize your voice. If it was not you back there, in the street—then why I—"

"Look into my eyes, Herr Galanov," said the man again.

A lengthy silence ensued.

"I—I *do* know you, don't I?" faltered Galanov. "It's not only your voice. I—I know those eyes—I *have* seen you before."

The stranger gazed at him.

Slowly across Galanov's face spread a look, first of recognition, then doubt, then recognition again. He seemed to be questioning himself, reliving an old memory, perhaps painful. A wince squinted his eyes, but only for the briefest of instants. He seemed trying to maintain his self-control, but gradually the recognition gave way to a sense of knowing, and with it came pain and grief so profound and intense as to be completely foreign to him.

"You—you're—" he began, but could not bring himself to say it. At last he looked away.

"Say it, Herr Galanov. Who am I?"

"You're—you're the man in the field—the man who attacked me—that morning outside Berlin."

"That is correct, Herr Galanov. It was my daughter you shot in the back, as *Der Prophet* was making his escape."

42

All his former KGB instincts of self-preservation, unfeeling nerves of steel, emotionless carelessness toward any other human being suddenly evaporated. At the shocking words, thirty years of training was gone in an instant.

At the words *It was my daughter you shot,* something broke inside KGB agent and loyal Communist Andrassy Papovich Galanov. The man who had for years resisted emotions—who had, in fact, denied their very existence—suddenly felt vulnerable.

He swallowed hard, trying to still whatever it was that was attempting to rise in his throat. His eyes scanned the room. Try as he might, he could not keep them from returning to the awful presence sitting across from him in the chair. A simple farmer, was this man. And he—*he* had been one of the most powerful men in the empire! Why then did he feel intimidated? Why was he— dare he admit it!—why was he—afraid to look at this man?

He blinked his eyes—then again. Blast them, why were they watering! He must be about to sneeze.

Involuntarily he glanced up. The man was still gazing at him full in the face.

"If that is true—then—why are you here?" he said hesitantly. "Have you come to kill me?"

"In a manner of speaking" he said with a hint of a smile. "But not in the way you think."

"Why then—if what you say is true, and you are who you say?"

"I told you before—to help you."

"Help me—how?"

"To help you escape. Word came to us that you were in danger."

"Why should you care? Bah! I hardly know whether to believe you. This is preposterous!"

"I care because I have not ceased to pray for you since that fateful day. I have prayed for you daily, Herr Galanov, prayed that our paths might cross again some day and that I might look you in the eye and express my forgiveness to you."

The words might as well have been in a foreign tongue. The Russian sat stunned. The German's meaning did not seem to register at first. Slowly the meaning dawned. As it did, he remembered the other incident he had recalled when running down the alley, the other man who had prayed for him, whom he had knocked unconscious for his trouble.

"Forgive—" Galanov repeated incredulously. "But—I do not understand."

"We received word that you were in danger, that you were attempting to get out of your country. I had been praying, and I saw my opportunity to help you, to get you out through *Das Netzwerk*, the very network of believers you sought with such vehemence to destroy. I prayed and I fasted on your behalf. And then our Lord said to me in my spirit, 'Go to this man. Go to him in Moscow. My hand is upon him. I will touch him and will speak to him Myself. But you must be there personally. You must tell him of forgiveness. You must tell him that the new life he seeks will not come from asylum in the West, but from giving his heart to Me. You must tell him that I have chosen him, in spite of the blackness of his sin, to carry word of My life forth.'

"And so, Herr Galanov, that is why I am here—to speak forgiveness to you, *my* forgiveness and the forgiveness of Almighty God, your Father, the maker of heaven and earth. For it is *He* who has recently spoken to you. But He has instructed me to tell you that it was *His* voice that came to you. And you must now heed His word."

The words he had heard in the deserted street suddenly exploded in his brain. *I come to bring you life—I am the Lord—you shall serve Me.* In benumbed silence Galanov sat motionless, staring distantly into regions no other human could penetrate.

"But—but *how* can what you tell me be true?" he said at last, his voice barely above a whisper. The fight from his spirit was gone.

"The ways of God are beyond what our reasoning and intellect can grasp," replied the German. "I am a simple man, Herr Galanov. You are perhaps more educated than me. I cannot provide you satisfactory arguments for why a Communist and atheist should suddenly believe in the Christian faith. The passing on of life is no mere intellectual exercise, but a birthing that takes place in the spirit of man. I come telling you, not of the Christian religion, but of a *Man* who brought God's life to earth, who died for our sin, through whom we can be forgiven, and whose spirit can dwell with us and give us a permanent relationship with God, our Father and His Father. That man is Jesus Christ. And His *life* He now offers you."

Again a long silence followed.

"But—why *you*? How could you be the one telling me of such things? You should hate me."

The German's mouth hinted at the trace of a thin smile, revealing his own prayerful struggle over the same question.

"I have no answer for you," he answered softly. "Our Lord spoke of laying down our lives for one another. Through my own personal agony, I came to recognize that I had been chosen to share an intimate form of mingled love and pain with my Father—a sacrifice known but to a few: giving the life of a child, in love, for the salvation of many. He gave His Son that the world might know of His love. He allowed me to give my daughter, that *you* might know His love."

He paused, thoughtfully, smiling again with a look that revealed depths unspoken of both anguish and victory.

Never in all the years of his life had Galanov heard such words. As he stared vacantly ahead, within the space of but a few minutes his mind replayed fragmentary images of hundreds of scenes from his past. In poignant internal agony, the horrifying wickedness of what he had been slowly revealed itself to the newly awakening conciousness of his spirit. Faces rose and fell—words—shouts—screams—sickening cruelties. His own voice stood out from the rest. Even as he heard himself from years before, in the very sound of his own voice he could detect the stubborn denial of truth that had always been in front of him. How blind he had been—how foolish not to have seen all along! Mingled with the rest were flashes of light and the words he had heard an hour before in the deserted alley. Pervading the memories was the life-changing and dreadful import of this thing his brain could not fathom—being forgiven by the father of the girl he had murdered eight years earlier!

Round and round rang the words—*so too He has caused me to love you.*

Slowly the *how* and *why* he had desperately sought only a moment earlier faded into a blur of emptiness. From within him, as of a rising inner spring of being, giving way gradually to the gathering waters of rushing new life, the hardened KGB agent found words of repentance and surrender escaping his lips, words he had never uttered, words whose meaning he scarcely recognized. The miracle of the second birth swept over him and, unconsciously falling to his knees and bending his tear-filled face to the floor, he yielded himself in abandonment to it.

The German, placing a tender hand on the Russian's heaving shoulder, knelt at his side.

For the next thirty minutes, both men prayed—weeping freely.

43

August 7, midday
Moscow

Six hours had passed.

The man who had brought such an unexpected thunderbolt into the life of Andrassy Galanov sat calmly on the floor of the filthy, deserted hallway, on guard so that his new brother could get some desperately needed sleep. Before he had left him, Galanov had said, "But I still do not know your name." "I have it!" he had exclaimed the next instant, "I shall call you *Der Deutscher Prophet,* now that we have driven our Russian *Prophet* out of the land."

His visitor shook his head. "You may call me 'The German,' if you like," he said. "But please, nothing more."

About the time agent Davidson was meeting with his information broker, Galanov reappeared in the corridor. The German rose and greeted him with a smile. "I hope you have slept well," he said.

"Like a baby," replied the Russian. "So soundly, in fact, that for a moment after I awoke it all seemed like a dream. I half expected to open this door and find no one here."

The German smiled again, placing a tender arm around Galanov's shoulder. "Many things will be new for you. But I have the feeling you will grow rapidly."

"Grow?"

"As I said—a great deal to learn. I will explain as much to you as our time together permits. But first, I need to get you something to eat."

"I am sorry I have nothing to offer," apologized Galanov. "It would seem that you are *my* guest, but I do not spend enough time here to keep food on hand."

"Think nothing of it. Now that you are awake, I will go and buy some bread, or whatever I can find. While I am gone—" he added, searching with his hands in the pocket of his jacket "—take this."

He pulled out a small pamphlet and handed it to him. "Do you remember what I said about Jesus being the Man who brought us the Father's life? This is His story, His biography. I'm sorry it's in German. I will get you a full Testament in Russian as soon as I can. But for now, I hope your German will get you by. I marked several passages for you to read while I was sitting out here. Look it over, and we can talk more as soon as I get back."

Galanov took the small book with almost a reverent touch, and even as he turned and went back into his small room, his eyes were scanning the first several pages of the gospel.

44

The remainder of the afternoon, after the German's return, the two men spent in the depths of the most unusual dialogue either had ever experienced. Upon the German steadily grew a sense of extreme urgency, both with respect to Galanov's safety, and concerning a host of spiritual principles necessary to build into him quickly. He was such a receptive and humble listener, absorbing all that he heard, that he could almost visibly see the effect that eight years of intercession had wrought. To compare the hungry Russian to a spiritual sponge would have understated his eagerness. The German could not keep himself from thinking of Acts 9:18-21 with a humble astonishment that God was allowing him to be part of such a remarkable conversion.

"Look—look what I found," Galanov said excitedly, glancing up with book in one hand and pen in the other, "here is where *Der Prophet* got his name."

The German glanced down at the verses Galanov had noted, then smiled. "And I suppose the same thing could be said of your Russian prophet that Jesus said of Himself—no honor in his own land."

The painful memory shot across Galanov's face but was soon gone.

It was late in the day when the subject turned to the circumstances of the Russian's plight.

"We've got to get you out of here," said the German at length. "The Father's investment in you is too great for us to treat it carelessly."

"I can't leave Moscow yet. This—this trail I have been on is something I must see through to the end."

"The whole concept of *Das Netzwerk* is speed and stealth," replied the German. "You should know that better than anyone."

Galanov smiled a wry smile. So much had changed in such a short time that the reminder of his past brought still again a host of conflicting memories and emotions.

"You escaped your pursuers last night. But it is only a matter of time before they discover this location as well. The people I am associated with are good, but if we can locate you, they can too."

"How *did* you find me?" asked Galanov. "I still cannot understand how you could possibly have located my hideaway."

"I don't think you have any idea how widespread the Network is."

"Even now—after the easing of restrictions and all the religious freedoms that have come to my country? Surely you haven't had to help people escape in years?"

"Yes, things have changed, and our work has changed too. It has been probably three years, I think, since I was personally involved in an escape such as—" he hesitated, but only briefly "— such as the one that brought us into contact together. But such change is not overnight nor always complete. People were still shot and killed a short time ago. Many pastors and Christian teachers remain in prison or exile. Our people were alerted, and safe-houses were in full operation during the Czechoslovakian freedom train. There were many dangers during those days of first openings, with even stiffer resistance from some quarters. Many lost their lives, including some of the Network's people."

"But—*now?* Democracy has come. Look at me—I am living proof that the persecutors of old are in disfavor."

"Times have changed politically, yes. The age-old struggle between good and evil, however, between God's people and the enemy, the Prince of this world, continues."

"The enemy—you mean the Communist state? How can that be? Communism is dead in Russia."

The German laughed, but his mirth contained no rancor, only tender love at the other man's ignorance. "God's people have *another* enemy, Andrassy," he replied, "an enemy in the spirit realm who has to be fought in ways and with weapons that even many of His people are unaware of. But there will be time for me to tell you about that later. In any case, the bonds between God's body of believers *has* remained intact for a variety of reasons. What was a pipeline for getting people out and smuggling Bibles *in* has become a distribution network for great new volumes of Christian literature. Now we pass people along in reverse order, bringing leaders and preachers and teachers *into* our countries to help train us."

"Are *you* now its leader, since you were successful in getting *Das Prophet*—past me and into West Berlin safely?"

The other man laughed. "No, Andrassy. I am by no means its leader! I am merely one among hundreds, probably thousands."

"You did not organize this attempt to—to locate me?"

"Far from it! As I told you, I was praying for you and received a strong urging from the Lord to find you and help you. But I had never been to Moscow before. I speak no Russian. Had you not spoken such fluent German, I do not know what we would have done! As always, God makes provision even in our deficiencies."

"So how do you come to be here?"

"I let my need to locate you be known, and the Network did the rest. I found my way to Moscow, where I was warmly taken in by the believers here. They had heard of you and were very skeptical when I told them of my plan. But they agreed to help."

Galanov was silent, contemplating again the enormity of his past sin.

"You know," he said at length, "there was a young fellow following in my footsteps. It's been so long ago I had all but forgotten about him. But suddenly his face comes back to my mind. He was young, enthusiastic, and was assigned to inflict terror upon Christians in our country. By the time he was twenty, he was actually leading many of the attacks, and I even had secret fears that one day he would take over *my* job."

"I take it from your words that he did not."

"No, his flame in the agency, though strong, was short-lived."

"What became of him?"

"He defected," replied Galanov. "Jumped from a naval ship off British Columbia."

"Did you hear from him?"

"Not directly. There were reports that he had become a Christian. His name was hated everywhere in the Committee. Word of his treachery even reached the Kremlin, and there were reprisals against some of my superiors for their carelessness in the matter."

Again Galanov fell to reflecting.

"What we heard was that he was sending messages back into Russia from Canada—messages to the Christian underground, to the very people he had once persecuted. By radio communication smuggled in, even the book he wrote in the U.S. was said to contain specific words of apology to those whom he had injured, even to relatives of those killed in his raids."

He paused, then looked with great sincerity into the German's face.

"Perhaps you might be able to arrange for me to meet some of those whom I persecuted," he said, "some of these people you have told me about?"

"Many of them would be too afraid to risk letting you see them."

"But how else can I tell them? How can I say how sorry—how can I possibly begin to make up for what I have done?"

"I fear they would not trust your change of heart."

"But I *must* speak to them. I could never write a book like Sergei Kourdakov. I must go to them face to face and try to say what is now inside me. What if *you* told them?"

"That might help with some, but others would think I had been taken in too. To Moscovites, I am a foreigner. They did not know me before two days ago."

"What has become of Rostovchev? He would speak on my behalf."

"He is no longer even in Europe."

"Where is he?"

"Even I do not know that. Somewhere in the United States."

"What does he do?"

"Andrassy, I do not know. He has been given a job, a new identity I suppose. I have heard that he is working with others to alert people of the perilous times that await the world. But beyond that I know no specifics. Perhaps he and your former associate have run across one another."

"I'm afraid that is impossible," said Galanov sadly.

"Why."

"Because our people got to Kourdakov a little more than a year after he jumped ship."

"Prison?"

"No, they arranged a suicide."

The small room was silent a long time. It was the Russian who spoke first.

"Will you try?" he said.

"Try what?"

"To arrange for me to meet some of your Christian friends

in the city?"

"Your friends now too, Andrassy. My brothers and sisters—and yours. Yes, of course I will try. I only wanted to caution you about the possible response. But it is the least I can do for *my* new brother."

He extended his hand. Nothing could take away the pain of having lost his daughter. But the smile on his face evidenced that she had not given her life in vain.

45

August 8, 5:27 P.M.
Moscow

Marta Repninka pulled her black shawl down more tightly against her ears. It was too hot a day to have her head covered like this, but she would rather sweat than let her face be seen.

Inside she was trembling. From all she had been taught about American spies, she was taking her life in danger to speak with one. But the friend of the office clerk who had come to see her a few hours ago during midday meal had assured her this man would be different.

"The CIA are our friends now," he said. "You can trust Dan. And if you help him," the little man had added with a yellow-toothed grin, "he can make it worth your while."

Maybe so, thought Marta. But she was still nervous. What if some friend of Bludayev's or someone from the office saw her?

She glanced out from behind the black wool that covered half her face. There he was! Walking toward her, with the newspaper under his arm, just like the little man Yaschak had said he would be. For a fleeting moment, Marta considered turning the other way. Maybe she had misunderstood the phone call. Perhaps she should go to Bludayev himself, tell him what she had heard, and ask what he had meant by the awful words. Surely his intent could not be so black as it seemed!

Even as the thoughts flitted through her brain, she knew she was deluding herself. Besides it was too late—the man had spotted her and was now making straight for her.

Her confused mind continued to race in a thousand directions until the very moment the American's voice broke through. "Miss Repninka, I am the man I believe you are waiting to see," he said in flawless Russian.

Startled, she looked up. There he was, right next to her! Though he wore no smile, he didn't look altogether as fearsome as the ogre she half expected.

"Shall we walk?" he said. Marta obeyed, and fell in slowly beside him.

"I understand you might be able to help me obtain information?" he said after some moments.

"Perhaps," she replied in a timorous voice.

"You are privy to the Defense Minister's plans?"

"What plans?"

"I was led to believe you knew what he—"

"I know nothing," she interrupted defensively. "Only that my life is in danger," she added.

"But you are in a position perhaps to learn more."

"I do not know. It is possible."

"If I can assure your safety, you might be able to gain access to what he is planning, certain information—perhaps from his files?"

"I do not know what it is you want."

"I will make that clear to you. Do you have access?"

"I have heard him talk about something he says is very secretive."

"And what is it, do you know?"

She hesitated.

"What is it you want, Miss Repninka?" asked Davidson. "If it is money, I can arrange it—a new home in the West, that too would be possible."

"No," she said, shaking her head and putting an edge of wool to her eye to dab at a tear. "I only want a position in Kiev, to be near my brother's family. And you must keep them safe too—if I help you."

"It can be arranged, and security for you all."

She breathed in deeply, trying to control the many emotions. Then she remembered the sense of betrayal she had felt last night, and anger once again rose up within her.

"I will get you what you want," she said. "But you must tell me what to do."

They continued walking, while the American relayed to the Russian woman the gist of the communique he had received from Belgrade.

"I don't know what it is we are looking for, Miss Repninka. I will have to rely on you to see what you can learn. It is very possibly linked to what you heard. But I will need hard facts."

"If I do find out something?"

"I will arrange either to telephone you or see you in person every evening, but you will not be able to contact me. I will be watching you, to make sure no harm comes, and to be ready if you discover something for me."

She nodded, seemingly satisfied. She glanced down at the ground, sighed again, then looked up. She was surprised to find herself again alone.

The man had disappeared.

46

August 8, 7:10 P.M.
Moscow

The basement was alive with expectation.

Not every face wore a smile. Indeed the expectancy in the air was split between a subdued climate of resentment and anger and an open-minded curiosity. This was a moment none of those gathered had ever anticipated—the opportunity to meet face-to-face with one of their chief antagonists and persecutors from the past two decades.

Not all were pleased. Some voiced open hostility to the notion. Others counseled restraint. Still others seemed positively and enthusiastically inclined, eager to do as their Master had instructed in the matter of enemies. But no one was indifferent to the proceedings.

The room where they gathered had at one time been hidden from the house above by a trapdoor covering the descending stairway. But *glasnost* had changed many things, including the need to hide religious gatherings, and in time the once life-protecting folding floor had been joyously removed as a relic to a time now gone, hopefully never to return. The basement, however, remained one of the largest rooms available to this fellowship of Moscow believers, and continued to be the site of weekly gatherings. Some forty or forty-five were now present, with more continuing to arrive. The number was expected to reach about seventy or eighty.

The meeting had been hastily convened since Galanov and his German mentor had discussed it the day before, and about fifteen minutes later the two men—both strangers of face but neither by reputation—entered the room, led by their Muscovite contact of the Network. A hubbub of whispered clamor whizzed about the room in all directions, followed almost immediately by a settling of quiet. All eyes rested upon the newcomers.

The Russian who led them immediately took to the front.

"My friends," he said, "in truth, I know as little as the rest of you about what we are to hear tonight. I only come to introduce to you my new friend from Germany, whom I met but three days ago myself. But I can attest to the fact that he is our brother, and he and I have enjoyed great fellowship in the name of our Saviour. He came to me yesterday afternoon with a story so incredible I could not believe it myself at first. But I believe *him,* so I agreed to spread the word among you to come tonight, and then to translate his words into Russian for you. So now I give you our German brother and comrade in the service of our Lord. I will let him tell you why he has asked you to come."

He stood to one side, while the German rose to his feet and took a place beside him.

"My brothers and sisters, I come to you as a relative stranger, yet not as a stranger, but as one of you in the communion of the saints. I come first bearing greetings from your brothers and sisters of Germany and Poland, through which I have come through the Network to you.

"Second, I come with a story to tell you which some of you may find difficult to believe." He proceded to relate how he had met Galanov—and what had transpired in the past two days. He explained why Galanov was being hunted in his own country. When he revealed the conversion of the Believers' Worst Enemy, a ripple of astonishment went through the room.

"Why should we believe what you say?" asked a large, gruff workingman about midway back in the gathering. His was a hardened face, toughened by years of backbreaking labor in the Soviet system, and he could be excused his apprehension on the same ground as his spiritual predecessor the apostle Thomas; if there was one thing he had learned in this society, it was that it was best to put your trust only in things you could see with your eyes and touch with your hands. "I do not say we should do the man any harm. But I for one see no call to welcome him when he has done so much harm to so many of our people."

"In answer, my brother, I will let Herr Galanov speak for himself. When he has spoken, you judge whether you should believe what I say."

The German resumed his seat. Slowly Galanov rose to face his countrymen. In their eyes were more questions than love.

47

It was several long moments before the KGB agent could find his voice. The man who had bullied and cowed thousands over the course of his cruel career now stood intimidated by less than one hundred commoners—awed by their very silence, knowing full well what was in their minds and knowing that if some of them hated him, their hatred was justified.

When at last he did speak, those in back strained to hear, for it was a quiet voice, suddenly chastened over the course of the previous thirty-six hours.

"I dare call you neither friends nor brothers," Galanov began softly. "All I can call you is my comrades, for if nothing else we share the same Russian blood of our Motherland. Yet even the word *comrade* has suddenly become a cold reminder of a time so quickly vanished yet already so distant in the past, a time when we pretended that all Russians were comrades in the Communist cause together."

He paused, reminiscing painfully. "But a pretense it was," he continued, "as you have long known much better than I.

"Hauntings from my past grew more frequent and tormenting. Then the new governmental systems began to look down on those of us who had given our unquestioning allegiance to the old leaders. Suddenly the KGB was itself suspect. And then, a mere three weeks ago, what should I discover but that there was a price on my head.

"And then—two nights ago, they nearly had me. I—"

He stopped, recalling the vivid vision he had seen after falling, and the voice he had heard.

"—I somehow reached my quarters safely. It was only a matter of time, I thought, before they would discover my whereabouts. I walked into my darkened room, fell upon my bed, only to discover this man waiting for me."

He gestured toward the German.

"How or why he had come there, I had not an idea, but I was frightened out of my wits. All my former KGB fight was gone. I was but one man on the run. I thought he was there to arrest me—or kill me on the spot.

"But his purpose was altogether different, as he has told you. When he began to tell me, I scarcely understood a word he said, though I have spoken German all my life. I was so consumed by guilt for what I had done, for the people I had tormented and— God forgive me!—even killed. Yet this man—this man spoke to me of forgiveness and of a Father who *loved* me!

"As he spoke, slowly began to dawn in my consciousness a recognition, somehow I had *known* this man. And gradually as my recognition grew, so did another bitter memory—a memory—"

He looked away, rubbing at his eyes, now full of tears.

"Do you hear me? I *knew* the very man who had come to find me—I knew him. Eight years ago, when I was stalking your beloved Prophet, this man who brought me to you tonight—he threw himself in front of my loaded gun—and in so doing saved the life of your Prophet—only to find several minutes later—forgive my cruel deed—only to find his own daughter—O God—his own daughter killed—by the bullet from *my* gun!"

It was all he could do to get the words out. He collapsed into a nearby chair and wept, as the roomful of stunned Muscovite Christians looked on in prayerful silence.

The German was the first out of his chair. He approached Galanov, said nothing but merely laid his hand reassuringly on his shoulder. Gradually one or two others came forward to join him. Within two or three minutes, Galanov was surrounded by ten or fifteen, and the small group prayed, some audibly, some silently, for their new brother.

This went on for some thirty minutes. As gradually they began to step back, some stood nearby while others resumed their seats. Then the large, doubting Russian miner, his hands and face still blackened from his day in the coal pits, lumbered forward to where Galanov still sat.

The miner extended his muscular hand. "If a German brother can believe you, I don't see how a fellow Russian can do any less. I'd be pleased to call you my brother, Galanov, and extend you my hand of welcome."

48

The next two days were ones of unexpected pleasure for both Galanov and his German friend. Welcomed wholeheartedly into the fellowship of Moscow believers, they found themselves shunted around to meet many more Christians in other fellowships. Both were well provided for in food and lodging, and Galanov did not once return to his own quarters.

Both men told their stories to different groups of believers, and they had numerous opportunities to sit in on prayer and teaching meetings in various corners of what had once been a vast underground congregation of several thousand, and was now growing daily.

On his part, Galanov received a crash course in the basics of his new faith, and it struck root the deeper that the teaching came from countrymen he had once disdained, and indeed many of whose meetings he had persecuted, and yet to whom he now found himself indebted. The tables had indeed been reversed, and he was the first to acknowledge it.

Wherever they went they were warmly received, for word about the two men spread throughout the fabric of the fellowship quickly. Skepticism and anger were always in supply also, though in diminishing quantities, and usually a few words either from the German or their Russian host, a pastor by the name of Karl Medvedev, set the stage for Galanov to tell his new friends his story.

One day, after they had left a meeting and were waiting for an afternoon's fellowship in another part of the city to begin, an inrush of despair overwhelmed Galanov. He cried out again to be crushed and his misery and remorse ended once and for all.

"But do you not want to see my daughter again, and tell her how sorry you are?" asked his German friend tenderly.

"Of course, nothing could delight my heart more!"

"Then take heart. You shall see her."

"Let me end my life now, that I might go to her immediately!"

"Ah, my friend," said the German, following well in the footsteps of his predecessor Barnabas—whose name, *son of encouragement*, he was living out—"but would she not receive your gift of forgiveness with far more rejoicing if you brought with you a hundred more? Or perhaps a thousand—or still more! Brothers and sisters for whom her death opened the way into the kingdom?"

Galanov could hardly take in the magnitude of the question. The German continued, speaking words of life and hope.

"Do you not see, my brother," he said gently, "that unless you offer this opportunity the Father is giving you back into *His* hands, then my daughter will have died in vain?"

"My heart leaps at the very thought." The Russian sighed. "Do you mean it might be possible for me to present your daughter with a gift that will cause her to *rejoice* upon seeing me?"

"Not only will she rejoice, she will throw her arms around you in the gladness of unbounded delight, greeting you not as her adversary but as her brother, not as one who *took* her life but as one who allowed your mutual Father to *give* His life to thousands. She will look upon her death as the greatest and most blessed sacrifice she could make for her Savior, following His own pathway.

"In fact, it is possible that the purpose for which my daughter was given life in the first place was that she might pour out that life, to give true life to you.

"It is a principle of the kingdom that life comes only through death. The Master said that unless a grain of wheat falls to the ground and dies, it remains alone. But when it pours out its being, its very life-blood, new life results.

"My daughter was a single seed," the German continued, "a grain of wheat—*one* life. But in her falling, new life is springing forth, and people are already hearing the good news of God's recreative power of forgiveness—through your mouth—that they never would have heard from my own daughter. Today you are speaking to believers. But the day will come when I believe your voice will carry into the unbelieving world, like the great traveling apostle of old in whose footsteps I believe you are destined to follow. Don't you see? God is already at work, preparing the ground to bring forth the hundredfold grain out of your life, because my daughter poured out hers."

"But—but how can that be? It is too incredible!"

"God's ways are not man's. The laws of God's kingdom work upside down and in reverse from the laws of man's kingdom."

Galanov was silent. He had many things to ponder.

49

August 10
Moscow

That evening, as he was concluding his talk at what was to be their final such gathering, Galanov returned to the theme that was so heavy on his mind.

"And so, my friends," he was saying, "I am struggling to believe what my brother tells me, though it is foreign to my former ways of thinking. I am grappling to accept forgiveness. My brother is living his forgiveness by his every word and deed, and through him I am coming to understand the Father's heart toward me.

"And thus, I would ask you, my brothers and sisters of who I have no right to make any request, I beg your forgiveness as well. How my heart agonizes—how bitter is my repentance. All I can humbly ask is for compassion toward one who knows he is a sinner."

He stopped, struggling with his composure.

"How could I have a purpose in His kingdom? Of what possible use could I be? I do not know. I know only this—that I will dedicate the remainder of my life, however long or short that may be, to spreading the life and love and forgiving power of God, that the young child shall not have poured out her life on that lonely field in vain.

"I shall tell the world of her and of her father. How those who took seriously the words of their Savior, how they gave their lives for Him and prayed diligently for their hated enemy. I shall tell the world their story, that through them many may believe, as have I, that Jesus Christ is God's Son, and that He came from heaven to redeem His Father's children."

He paused again, this time deep in thought. When he went on, his voice was serious.

"I know it is taking a tremendous presumption upon myself to speak to you about the meaning of the Scriptures. You all know so much more than I. But since I was first given a New Testament in my own language just two days ago, I have been reading it in every spare moment. I wanted to shout to the world that in spite of my sorrow, I had at last found the peace that all men long for. I wanted to go to my former KGB associates, even to the leaders of our country, and tell them of my great discovery. I cared nothing for my own safety any longer. I only wanted to share this new life!

"This man—this very man—" Galanov gestured toward his German friend "—trusted in God's Word enough to obey its command to 'Love your enemies.' Even in the face of the bitterest loss a man can face, even as his daughter's blood was soaking into the dirt, he lifted his voice to heaven to pray—for me, her murderer! God, the anguish of heart that causes—"

He turned away, stifling sobs.

"Jesus also said," he went on, "—and I must read it, I cannot remember the words exactly—"

He fumbled for a moment with his Testament, then walked over to where the German sat in the front row and whispered to him, "I can't remember where it is—the verse about rejoicing in persecution."

The German smiled, took his Testament, and quickly located the passage for him in Matthew.

"Here it is," Galanov said. " 'Blessed are those who are persecuted because of righteousness, for theirs is the kingdom of heaven. Blessed are you when you are persecuted because of me. Rejoice and be glad, because great is your reward in heaven.'

"If I am to believe the truth of that passage, then I must believe that even now, at this moment, the daughter of my friend here, my sister whose life I took, is rejoicing, as Jesus said she would. I must believe that she is blessed and glad, and that great is her reward in heaven. What else can these words mean?

"For the rest of my life I will look forward to that day when I shall see her, to tell her, 'My dead little sister, here are the ones to whom your spirit gave life. Welcome them home with rejoicing.' And I hope one day to look her in the eye, and speak to her of the forgiveness I have found, and then embrace her in my arms, and—"

He struggled through his weeping to continue.

"—embrace her, and say, 'I love you, my sister. Forgive me— thank you for giving your life—that I might know—the Father.' "

50

August 10, 9:07 P.M.
Moscow

"It is time for me to go home," said the German after the meeting had broken up and they were alone. "And I must get you out of here too. You are in more and more danger every day."

"Do you think that concerns me now?" said Galanov.

"It did a few days ago."

"Everything has changed since then. My life means nothing to me—now that I truly have *life*."

"But it means even more to me and to our Father! We must not squander what He has given us. Your responsibility is great to steward this marvelous and priceless gift. You must not be so careless as to throw it away."

"Perhaps you are right. Yet for so long I have harassed and tormented these people. It seems the least I can do is spend time among them, making up for the past in the small ways."

"But the more people you meet and the more you tell your story, the more likely it will be that those who are after you will get wind of your activities. I am surprised they have not found you already. Your own government, the British secret service, perhaps even my new government and officials in Warsaw—you were a blight to freedom in all these places, and men like you are being arrested daily."

"I do not fear arrest now."

"That may be true. Yet would you unnecessarily bring danger to your new brothers and sisters? We cannot tell what may be the repercussions. And what of the many to whom God may send you to tell of His Son? You cannot do the work that He is, I believe, giving you if you are behind bars or in Siberia."

"You make many good points, my friend. I had not considered the wider implications of my plight. There are now so many more things to think of."

"Which is why I urgently feel it is time we made our way west. I have been discussing the details today with Medvedev and most everything is in place."

Galanov pondered his friend's words carefully.

"Yes—yes, I see that you are probably right. As much as I might want to remain among the believers of my homeland, to do so may in the long run cut short the task God has given me."

"Exactly. We must get you out of danger and to freedom—in the West."

"I place myself in your hands then, my friend."

"And we will both place ourselves in the hands of our brothers and sisters of *Das Christliche Netzwerk.*

"They will help me, do you think? They will trust me? We will not have time to tell every contact our story."

"They will help us. Every one need not know your identity—I should say, your *former* identity. Andrassy Galanov is dead. He exists no longer."

"As you wish," consented Galanov. "When do you want to leave?"

"As soon as possible."

"Tonight? I must return to my hideout to gather some items."

"It is not so urgent we cannot get a few hours sleep first. What about family, friends, your other home?"

"Spies have no family," replied Galanov in a wistful tone. "My parents are both dead. Whatever other family I once had is distant. My only friends were in the KGB. My home itself is part of my past life. I'm certain it is being watched, and I have no need to return there. My car, furniture, clothes—I will have no more need of them. I took my money out of the bank long ago when tensions began. I will need nothing else."

"I'm sure that is wise; you give no appearance, should your enemies get wind of your whereabouts, of clearing out. Go back to your hideout tonight. I would like to leave very early in the morning—*very* early, so we are well out of Moscow before daybreak. The man who drove me most of the way from Smolensk is expecting us to contact him soon. We will get word to him immediately. He will drive east to the same place he dropped me off, and there will pick us up for the return trip."

"I will be ready."

51

August 11, 12:41 A.M.
Moscow

Andrassy Galanov lay on the bed in his hideaway staring up at the ceiling. It was after midnight. He was already supposed to have been back to meet the German where they would get a few hours' sleep before their flight west from Moscow.

Right here, such a short time ago, his life had been turned upside down. It was as if God had reached down and forcibly yanked him from one life and shoved him into another. Suddenly his surroundings seemed foreign, all the reminders of his many years as a KGB agent remote and insignificant.

He looked at the dilapidated chair in which his friend had been sitting waiting for him.

How terrified he had been when he had heard him speak out of the darkness!

And that other voice—out of the bright light—that had preceded the German's visit.

Now as he lay pondering and reflecting, both on his past and his unknown future, the words came back into his mind with a resonant clarity beyond what he had heard in the street.

"I am the Lord . . . From this day forward, you shall serve Me."

And then the German's words of what God had spoken to him: "My hand is upon this man," and what the German himself had said: "How mightily our Father will be able to use your life if you place it in His hands."

Where would it all lead? Where was his future? He was preparing to leave this place, this piece of his home, perhaps forever.

He slipped off of the bed and onto his knees.

God, he prayed, *everything is new. There is much that I do not know. Teach me, show me—help me be the man You want me to be. Show me what to do—what path to walk.*

Something had been nagging his mind since this morning. Now in the night quiet of his flat, kneeling by his bed praying, stronger grew the sense that he had indeed been sniffing the edge of a scheme of major import when he'd seen the political leaders of the two countries together. Maybe he was not to walk away from that.

What could it mean—all the clues, the gut instinct that told him something was in the wind? He was an agent and always had been.

Suddenly he was preparing to leave that past life behind. And yet—was he supposed to do something—*before* he left? He realized that that question had been gnawing at him all day.

Is there something that I should do, God? he whispered.

The unmistakable answer came—yes, one last assignment to be completed. But what it was, he was not sure. It definitely had to do with the two leaders.

Suddenly a wild, incredible idea struck him.

What could be the harm? With the Cold War over, hostilities and dangers were a thing of the past. And he could not trust any of his *own* people or sources anymore. He was, as they used to say, out in the cold. And he couldn't find out what was going on by himself. Solo flights didn't get you very far in this business. He needed help.

The Americans could have no reason to harm him now. He would get in touch with his old CIA nemesis. Maybe *he* had got wind of something. It was time he became friends with his old adversary of the CIA anyway.

He'd do it—he'd get in touch with Blue Doc!

In the darkness of early morning a few hours later, a soft knock came on the door. Galanov knew it was his German friend, come to retrieve him for their flight from Moscow.

He let him in.

"I'm afraid I can't leave yet," he said bluntly after closing the door. "I hope you can understand."

"Is—is something wrong? You're not going back on—"

"No, no, my friend," laughed Galanov. "Nothing like that. My faith is secure. You don't think I could have a week like this one without being forever changed, do you? No, it's about something I had stumbled onto just before you came. My gut tells me I must pursue it."

"You are sure? Every day you stay here the danger grows."

"You are right. I do not make this decision lightly. I have prayed, and still it comes back to me that I must see this through. I sense that it is important perhaps to the people of God as well as to my country."

"If you believe the Lord would have you stay, then you must stay."

"I want you to go ahead with your plans to return to Germany."

"I cannot go without you."

"You must. You are in danger too, the longer you remain with me."

"But it was for you that I came."

"And your mission was accomplished. I insist that you go ahead. I will be more free to do what I have to do, knowing that you are safe."

His German friend thought for a few moments, then nodded in assent.

"Good," replied Galanov. "I will follow you as soon as I am able. Leave instructions with Karl Medvedev of what I am to do when I am ready to leave. I hope it will not be more than a few days."

"I will pray for you night and day, my brother."

"And Godspeed to you as you return home. I will look forward to joining you."

They parted with an embrace.

PART 8

What Is Evangelism?

52

August 13, 7:15 P.M.
Berlin

On the fifth day of the conference Jackson and Jacob went out to enjoy an American-style dinner of steak and baked potato at one of the international restaurants not far from the hotel.

"You going tonight?" Jacob asked as they ate their dinner.

"I suppose, though I'm starting to reach the saturation point."

"Me too. Pretty eclectic group that's going to be there, from what I understand."

"What about you? You going?" asked Jackson.

"I imagine—actually, I have to."

"Why's that?"

"Tony approached me about two hours ago and asked me to be on the panel."

"Hey, great!" exclaimed Jackson. "And you said you would?"

"I have no idea why, but before I knew it, I was nodding my head."

An hour later Jackson entered the hall alone and found a seat as near the front as he could. With his father suddenly in the limelight, his interest in the proceedings had been piqued anew.

A couple minutes after 7:00 the panelists walked to the platform from a side door and took their chairs behind a large rectangular table, all of them facing the audience. Powers strode to the microphone.

"I'm not going to take any more time with introductions than I have to," he said. "We want to get right into the discussion. So let me tell you briefly about each panelist."

Powers turned so that he was looking at the panelists and yet still able to glance around and address the audience, and started down the table.

227

"On my far left," he began, "please welcome Trevor MacVey who works with Pilgrim Institute. Then we have a man for whom no introduction is necessary other than his first name—Brother Adam."

Before Powers could continue, his voice was drowned by applause for the man whose name had for nearly twenty years been synonymous with bold and daring evangelistic methods behind the Iron Curtain. There could scarcely have been a more universally respected man at the conference.

"Beside Brother Adam," Powers went on at last, "is seated Mr. Hamilton Jaeger, President of Evangelical Unity, Unlimited, then we have Miss Carmine Bell, representing Christian Women for Political Responsibility, Frank Dalryple of Reach Out With the Gospel, author and end-times authority Carson Mitchell, Father Ford Sherman of the Ecumentical Council for Global Accountability, and finally, to my right, another man requiring no introduction, Mr. Jacob Michaels."

Again Powers paused, while the audience recognized the entire assemblage of dignitaries.

"Now I realize that eight persons is a good many for a panel discussion. But we wanted to insure that there would be plenty of ideas to fuel a lively discussion, and to represent concerns and points of view as broadly as possible. So, with that, I'm going to turn to our distinguished panel, and simply ask the question we've all come here to consider: 'What *is* evangelism?' "

A pause ensued, with some shifting and glancing about, at the end of which Frank Dalryple, clearly the youngest member of the group, broke the silence.

"We might as well jump right into the middle of this," he said. "Where we might differ with one another is in method, but there can't be any doubt about what evangelism *is*. It's obviously taking the gospel to the world, testifying to the unsaved about the salvation of the blood of Jesus. I think what we ought to discuss are the various methods and approaches to getting people saved, rather than arguing the semantics of a definition. The Word cautions us against overmuch empty talk of this kind."

"Don't lump *me* in with your definition," interjected Carmine Bell in a tone that didn't particularly hide her disdain. "You're naive, Mr. Dalryple, if you actually think that all of us, much less all those listening out there, believe in your narrow, fundamentalist view of evangelism."

"How can you say that?" asked a stunned Dalryple in true astonishment. "The Word is very clear—"

"The Word," repeated Miss Bell. "People like you base everything on a literal interpretation of your favorite passages, which you overspiritualize. It would probably surprise you to know that all the rest of us believe in the Bible too but view its contents and injunctions far differently than you do."

"So what is evangelism, by your view, Miss Bell?" asked Powers, trying to keep the discussion on course.

"It is many things," she answered, more calmly. "To try to narrow it to the confines of what some might consider evangelism per se would be difficult. I see it as much more than a one-time experience of salvation, or whatever you call it. For me it has to do with the entire worldview that we proponents of the Christian faith present to the world. I personally happen to believe in living that worldview out in the context of a political and social framework."

"So you do not advocate *personal* evangelism?" asked Powers.

"Let's just say I do not feel such to be my calling," she answered. "It strikes me as the height of presumption to walk up to someone with the blunt question, 'Are you saved?' To me, that is not evangelism, but self-righteous judging—something Jesus warned against strongly. What the founding fathers of the U.S. did has impacted the world on behalf of the Christian faith, if you ask me, far more than all the tracts and so-called witnessing tools that have been printed in the last two centuries."

"There is only one flaw in your theory, Miss Bell," said Brother Adam. At his words, both Mitchell and Bell eased back into their seats to allow him to continue. His voice was calm, and the hint of a smile played upon his lips. An inaudible hush settled upon the auditorium in expectation. Though he was scheduled to address the general session the next day, the conference had not yet heard from him.

"It is just this," Brother Adam continued. "Whether you believe in 'personal evangelism' or not, I can tell you that personal salvation *does* exist."

Scattered applause and several *Amens!* erupted throughout the hall, but silence was quickly restored.

"Look at me," he went on. "What do you see?"

He paused briefly then continued. "What you are looking at is a man who would have been dead years ago had it not been for a personal salvation experience! I am sitting here precisely because the Lord Jesus Christ touched my heart by the power of new birth and began a lifelong process of transformation within me. I was born again. And lest you think it too old-fashioned to speak of such things, we might do well to look at the third chapter of John's gospel. And it was Jesus Himself—not the fundamentalists or the charismatics or the revivalist preachers in England—who coined the term *born again*. He said that without being born again there could be no life."

This time the applause and amens were even more pronounced.

"I would not dispute your thesis that evangelism can be seen in a wider context that encompasses social and political aspects of life. But evangelism *must* be personal, because being born again cannot be done corporately. Jesus addressed not the crowds or the Sanhedrin when He talked about salvation, but one man—*one* man alone, where he confronted him with his need to be born of the Spirit. Read about it in John three—that is where we find our model for evangelism. The model is our Lord Himself, as He led Nicodemus into a personal salvation encounter with the Lord of Life by the Spirit of God."

Brother Adam stopped and leaned back. The applause that followed gave audible evidence, if any further was needed, of the large fundamentalist faction present.

"Where do you, then, place the larger picture?" asked Father Sherman. "It seems to me that most discussions on evangelism ignore the word *nations* in the Great Commiss—"

"I beg to differ," interrupted Carson Mitchell. "I do not think evangelicals have ignored it at all. We view evangelism as a charge to go to all the nations of the world for the purpose of calling *individual* men and women in those nations to repentance. Interpreting the word *nations* in the Great Commission to mean we're supposed to make governments live according to the three-thousand-year-old pattern of Moses while ignoring the saving work of the Holy Spirit is beyond comprehension! Evangelism is *clearly* about personal salvation—as Brother Adam said."

"All I was attempting to address," went on Father Sherman, unruffled, "was to find out how Brother Adam *does* view such things as political and social action for the Christian, such things as global accountability for what we—Christians included—are doing to our planet, which is the chief emphasis of my organization. I would like you to clarify how you view the larger picture."

Brother Adam smiled cordially, then thought for a moment before responding. "I have no intrinsic quarrel with the national or global perspective. I'm all for clean air, I'm in favor of reducing the ozone we have put into the atmosphere, and I'm certainly in favor of governments operating according to biblical principles.

"However, as I read the New Testament, I do not see those issues as the primary area of responsibility placed by Jesus upon His followers. How is reducing the ozone layer or overturning a certain Supreme Court decision going to translate into winning souls for the kingdom of God?"

"In terms of evangelism, then, you see no urgency for Christians to be involved in the larger political and social issues?" asked Sherman.

"I take exception with your use of the word *larger.* What issue could be 'larger' than eternal life? I consider any man or woman's salvation the largest of all issues in the universe."

"That is *your* view, Brother Adam," interjected Miss Bell, "but *not* one shared by all who consider themselves Christians."

"Well, I share his view!" voiced Dalryple.

"As do I!" chimed in Mitchell.

"But you do not believe in doing good in the world?" persisted Miss Bell.

"Wherever in my words did you hear that?" asked Brother Adam in surprise.

Before she could reply, Frank Dalryple piped up. "Goodness will not get a single soul into heaven. Our righteousness is as filthy rags."

"That pious jargon has nothing to do with anything!" shot back Bell.

"Might I respond to the matter of goodness?" asked Trevor MacVey of the Pilgrim Institute. His tone was not commanding, yet because it was a new voice in the discussion, all heads turned to him and gave him the floor.

"Goodness," he went on, "seems almost as misunderstood a concept in Christian circles as Father Sherman's word *nations*. To the fundamentalist right, goodness has incredibly become almost a nefarious term, equated with unspirituality and even going to hell, as Mr. Dalryple has reminded us. They are quick to point out that there is no salvation in goodness, almost with the implication that goodness is the opposite of spirituality. I've never understood that. It's an unbelievable twisting of the word—*goodness*—to imply almost its exact opposite."

He paused and took a breath. There not being much to argue with, no one commented immediately, and he went on.

"But it strikes me that as grievous an error is made on the opposite side, what we might call the liberal Christian left, where goodness is made the end-all of the gospel. Upon good deeds in government and social betterment and kindness to all mankind is hung the whole basis for spirituality. And that is simply too heavy a burden for goodness to carry alone.

"It's all about balance. And in the life of Jesus we find the ultimate, the perfect balance. He went about the countryside doing good among men and women. But He rarely did good and then just walked away. He usually used the incident to speak to deeper issues—*spiritual* issues, not social or political or global action issues. He did good, then He taught the spiritual implications of what He had done.

"Evangelism, therefore, as I see it, encompasses more than merely doing good and more than the salvation experience itself. If Jesus is our example, then evangelism must encompass the whole of life, as He sought to give it to His disciples. Teaching, training, showing by example—He did all these things all the time. It's inculcating a godly value system into men, which is then lived out in the practical, daily routine of life."

"I couldn't agree more," said Carson Mitchell. "Discipleship is very important. However, knowing that the rapture could happen any moment places an urgency upon us to get people saved as quickly as possible, and—not to be crass about it—to worry about discipleship later. Get the horses into the corral and the gate closed, so to speak, and then set about breaking them and teaching them good manners."

"You have no idea how ridiculous and arrogant that sounds!"

huffed Carmine Bell. "I'm embarrassed that people have to hear that kind of self-important gibberish. It makes our job of representing ourselves as intelligent, articulate, and broad-minded Christians impossible when you fundamentalists are spouting off preposterous hogwash like that!"

"Perhaps we might hear from one of the panelists who has not yet entered the discussion—Mr. Jaeger?"

Hamilton Jaeger was only too happy to oblige.

"I have been awaiting an opportunity," he said with glowing smile and a countenance of confidence, "to examine the question of evangelism from yet another perspective—one which I think is perhaps the most important."

He paused, and now that he had their attention, the others were willing to listen.

"I am speaking of that set forth by our Savior Himself in John, the seventeenth chapter, in which He prayed for unity among His followers. Whatever else may be encompassed in the subject we call evangelism, the very fact that Jesus prayed for unity among His followers certainly places the imperative upon us to work toward that unity in all ways possible."

As Jaeger spoke, Jacob Michaels could not help reflecting on the irony of listening to Hamilton spout on about unity.

If only they knew him as well as I do, he could not help thinking. *Hamilton, you've got the word right, but I don't think you know the most basic thing about John 17 or what Jesus' words in John 13:35 really mean. It's all organizational for you, isn't it, Hamilton? Building your empire in the name of unity?*

Jacob's thoughts trailed distantly away, and by the time he woke to the present, it was not Jaeger's voice he heard but that of the Catholic priest.

". . . warms my heart," Father Sherman was saying, "to hear an evangelical such as yourself, Mr. Jaeger, speaking of unity in a broader context than your own enclave of like-minded traditionalists. Unity is one of the visions to which I have dedicated myself, which is why I agreed to head up the Ecumenical Council, especially in that our chief concern was going to be the issues facing the global community in the twenty-first century . . ."

Jacob could not keep his mind focused on the blur of words that seemed to have less and less of a bearing on evangelism.

Vaguely he heard Carson Mitchell objecting to talk about the next century in light of Jesus' imminent return, with here and there a tangential attempt by Frank Dalryple to spiritualize someone else's point. When he suddenly became conscious of the flow of words, it was as Powers was turning to him.

"It looks like our time will be up shortly," Powers was saying. "I wondered—uh, Jacob, would you like to offer some comments? We haven't heard from you yet."

Most of the heads turned in Jacob's direction. A lengthy pause followed.

"Well, all of you probably know," he said after forty or fifty seconds, "that I've made evangelism the business of my life. I've headed an organization called Evangelize the World. I've spoken, written, and conducted training seminars on evangelism. I've led more altar calls than I can remember and witnessed thousands of tearful salvation prayers."

He paused, thinking, and the second silence went on nearly as long as the first.

"But being at this conference has been sobering and humbling. As has sitting here listening to this panel discussion. I've been stimulated. My thoughts have been challenged. But I realize just how little I know about evangelism and how much I've taken for granted. I've heard some things in the last hour that, to be honest with you, I've never so much as considered before. Some points I agree with, some I disagree with—but I have a great deal to think and pray further about.

"To answer your question, Tony—no, I don't really want to offer any comments. For the first time in my life, I have to admit that I don't know what evangelism is. All I can say is that I will continue to ask God to show me."

The unexpected abruptness of Jacob's final words took the other speakers off guard, and no one was inclined to add anything. After a few closing pleasantries, therefore, and a final prayer, Powers dismissed the assembly for the night.

53

Jackson rose from his seat, and while the rest of the crowd slowly made its way toward the rear exits of the hall, he jostled toward the front, trying not to lose sight of his father. Most of the panelists were standing near the front, chatting among themselves, and with a growing circle of listeners who were, like Jackson, making their way forward to ask questions or otherwise continue the discussion along the lines of their own personal interest. Jacob, however, had already turned and was walking away from the podium and toward the exit by which he had entered with the others. Jackson hurried after him.

He caught him just as he reached the door. Jacob turned. There were unspoken thoughts and emotions written all over his face. The short speech he had made had obviously but scratched the surface of his thoughts. When he turned, Jackson found himself momentarily taken aback by the depth of questioning he read in the eyes of his father.

"You—you said just—what needed to be said," faltered Jackson.

Jacob returned a wan smile, as if to say, "Thanks, but don't bother—nothing can cheer me up."

"Are you OK?" asked Jackson with concern.

"What do you think?" Jacob sighed. "You heard all that—it's confusing, all of us supposedly brothers and sisters, with such vastly different perspectives, at each others' throats—no, I'm not OK. I don't know what to make of it."

Jackson studied his father's face for a few moments as Jacob stared distantly at the spectacle being played out in the neighborhood of the podium. A clamor of voices and questions and minidissertations could still be heard. At least Frank Dalryple and Carmine Bell were on opposite sides of the gathering, both engaged in discussions with people who had come up to them, though Frank's high and forceful voice was easy to discern above the rest, as were his phrases and exclamations. Every once in a while Jackson thought he detected an annoyed glance in his direction from Miss Bell, even as she continued on with her own conversation. In the center of it all stood an ebullient Hamilton Jaeger, engaging in mutual congratulatory praise with Father Sherman and others who were clustered around them. Jaeger appeared to be taking notes on a sheet of paper, even in the midst of the bustle.

"Look," said Jacob, as if reading Jackson's thoughts, "there's Hamilton no doubt taking names and addresses, always adding to his stockpile of potential individuals and organizations he can draw into his web, all in the name of unity just like when he was with me. What do I do, Jackson? Interfere, tell those people what they're getting themselves into? Let them know he's going to fleece them and manipulate them with smooth talk? Do I expose his schemes or let well enough alone?"

"Do you know that's what he's doing?"

"Not to prove. But I've heard some things about EU—enough to know what he's up to. Remember, I've known Hamilton closely longer than just about anyone in the world. I know how his mind works."

"Maybe you should do something."

"No, it's out of my hands. It's not my business anymore to interfere, but seeing his conniving hands at work, along with everything else—sharing the podium with him, for heaven's sake!—it all just adds to my quandary. What is evangelism? Good grief, you're asking me!"

As they were talking, Trevor MacVey approached, heading toward the door. No one seemed particularly eager to question or talk with him further, and he had opted, like Jacob, to make his exit.

Jacob saw him coming and extended his hand. "I appreciated your comments, MacVey," he said, giving him a firm handshake. "I don't know about anybody else, but you gave me some things to think about I haven't considered before."

"Thank you," returned MacVey. "And your comments were some of the most straightforward and honest I've ever heard."

"I'd like you to meet my—this is Jackson Maxwell, my associate and friend," said Jacob.

The two young men shook hands. "Good to meet you, Maxwell."

"Likewise. I appreciated what you had to say also."

"Maybe we could get together sometime this week," said Jacob to MacVey. "I'd like to talk with you further about some of what you said."

"I'd enjoy that. Let me know—I'm here in the hotel."

MacVey exited, and still Jackson and Jacob stood watching the emptying hall.

"Come on," Jacob said at length, turning back toward the door through which MacVey had just exited, "let's get out of here."

"You feel like doing something?" asked Jackson as the sounds of the hall behind them snapped into silence with the shutting of the door.

"What did you have in mind?" asked Jacob as they began making their way along the carpeted corridor.

Jackson shrugged. "I don't know—go out for a walk, have some strudel, go see the Brandenburg Gate. It's all lit up at night. It might be interesting."

"That sounds good," replied Jacob. "You're on."

54

August 13, 9:13 P.M.
Berlin

They emerged from the taxi into the pleasantly warm night air. A hundred meters away the column of the Brandenburg Gate rose awesomely before them, the most recognizable symbol throughout the world of the newly united German nation.

As they walked about the expansive, open area, they observed the diversity of people who, like themselves, were wandering about. It was a few minutes after nine, yet from the crowd it might have seemed noon—tourists, families, many Americans, along with a wide mixture of foreigners, all sprinkled together with Berlin's indigenous crop of eccentric and bizarre street-walkers—mostly young, colored hair, or no hair, shredded trousers, leather jackets and black boots adorned with metal, rebellion in the eyes, the smell of alcohol in the clothes, with voices of loud, get-out-of-my-way

237

anger filling the air now and then with outbursts of defiance and disdain for order and decency. Everyone with a cause or a message seemed to be here roaming the streets, attempting to attract followers, some carrying placards boasting frightening slogans of the past. In the distance, at the end of the sidewalk they saw one such youth suddenly stop, loosen his pants, and relieve himself in the landscaped shrubbery. A clean-dressed man who had been following several steps behind with his daughter quickly turned her away and hurried out into the street to avoid him. Loud, mocking laughter erupted, even as the lawless mocker was buttoning up his pants, and he continued to throw profane, contemptuous insults after the poor man and girl. Jacob turned from the scene with sickening disgust, and Jackson followed him down a side street away from the thick of the crowd.

Neither spoke for some time. It was quieter here, though well enough lit, and they continued slowly.

"When I was here before," Jackson began at length, "you can't believe how different it was."

"How so?" asked Jacob.

"Empty, silent, cold," answered Jackson. "I walked over from Checkpoint Charlie to just about here, to the Brandenburg Gate. It was in the East. There were some huge, broad streets but empty —no pedestrians, no cars, no shoppers, no tourists. There weren't even any stores or souvenir shops. It was bleak, almost like being in a silent movie. It was eerie. There were still buildings bombed out and desolate from the war. It was the eighties, but they sat there as if the bombs had just fallen. Then in the middle of it—was the huge Brandenburg Gate and all the other landmarks, like the Reichstag building, that happened to fall on the eastern side when they built the wall, standing there like silent mausoleums and sentinals to a time long past. It was—almost a feeling of death. Especially in that just a mile or two away in the West—well, you've seen it this week—full of life and people and activity and energy and wealth. What contrast! Now all of a sudden, it is here too— the people and activity and liveliness. It's a remarkable change."

As they made their way around a large quiet block, they continued to discuss Jackson's previous experience. In ten minutes they again found themselves approaching the square where they had begun. Voices and the noises of cars and horns told them they were almost back to the center of the hubbub. On they walked, past booths and street vendors, tourists, taxis, buses, stands full of pornography and other literature, magic acts and jugglers and musicians and activists handing out pamphlets and preaching at anyone who chanced to look their way. Religious street preachers were represented along with any of another dozen causes, including several Christians passing out tracts in both English and German.

As Jacob observed everything around him, his thoughts went back to all that Jackson had said to him on the plane about Germany as well as what Heinrich and Marla had recounted about their country and its people. How could this vibrant, new, energetic country have so much and yet be so lost? Here they were at the very heart of Berlin, the city at the center of Europe, at the very core of what would soon be a united Europe. Across town they were participating in the most prestigious gathering of Christian evangelists ever assembled. And yet, Jacob wondered, did a single one of these people walking by even know it? *How are we impacting them? We are over there in our hotel—here they are wandering about the streets. How separate are the two worlds? Who are we talking to, if not to these people?*

They continued along the avenue called Unter den Linden, after the lime trees that lined the thoroughfare. This was the centrum, where Germany shone its brightest before the 1930s. A few of the hotels and cafes from the past still stood, but without the glamour of sixty years earlier. In the distance, black now, rose the building where was until recently located the headquarters for the *Stasi*, the notorious East German secret police force—*Staatssicherheitsdienst*—almost a modern version of the SS. Behind its walls were kept files on more than two million men and women of the West. Probably no two countries, save the United States and the USSR, conducted so heavy an espionage program upon one another as had the two Germanys. One in five East Germans was said to have been an informer. The Stasi saw and heard everything.

Over and over in Jacob's mind, snatches of the evening panel replayed itself. Was it fair to indict the conference because the people walking the streets in this sprawling urban colossus were not standing up and taking notice? Probably not. After all, the gathering had been designed to express ideas so that they could get out into further corners of the world; its purpose had not been to organize a citywide witnessing rally.

But by the same token, he could not help wondering what an observer would have thought, watching and listening to tonight's discussion. Would he have been compelled, drawn, convicted by the vital and energetic gospel? Hardly. He would instead have been bickering and debating over differences of ideas—rather sharp and heated at times. What difference would he have seen between the exchange of viewpoints at the Worldwide Hotel and the shouting matches on these same streets between the neo-Nazis presenting their diatribes against aliens, Jews, and Communists, and the leftists and their own banners and speeches *against* a modern-day revival of Nazism? What difference indeed—other than that perhaps the conference debate was a bit more dignified?

Jacob's thoughts drifted to the speech he was scheduled to make. Everything boiled down to the fundamental question of tonight's panel, "What *is* evangelism?"

The face and voice of the soft-spoken Trevor MacVey came into his mind. There was a guy who seemed above the argumentative fray. What he'd said made sense too—the importance of goodness and balance and following Jesus' example. "Teaching, training, showing by example," he had said. "Jesus did these things all the time." Other points he had made were new to Jacob, about giving to people values and a system of belief that could be lived out in the affairs of daily life. It was an approach to evangelism refreshingly different from that of witnessing and salvation prayers. He hoped he could get to know the young man better.

By now he and Jackson had turned around and walked back to the Gate area again, chatting sporadically on the surface, though each man was absorbed at deeper levels with his own thoughts.

"How about that strudel?" Jackson asked at length.

Jacob sighed. "You know, Jackson," he said, "I think I'd like to pass. Do you mind?"

"No, that's fine."

"I just need some more time alone, to think—maybe pray. Why don't you go on without me. I'll get a cab later and meet you back at the room."

"Sure."

"You don't mind?"

"No, of course not," said Jackson cheerily, walking off toward a row of black taxis.

Jacob walked on, under the huge Brandenburgertor, and on into what had been West Berlin. *I want to understand, Lord,* he silently prayed, unconscious now of the people around him. *I need to understand what evangelism truly is—at root. What do You mean it to be? How would You want us to spread the gospel?*

Again, as if in answer to his prayerful yearnings, the words of young MacVey returned to his consciousness: *In the life of Jesus we find the ultimate, the perfect balance. He went about the countryside. . . . He spoke to deep issues. . . . He did good. . . . Evangelism must encompass the whole of life as He sought to give it . . . a value system lived out in the practical, daily routine of life.*

Of course! Jacob thought. *That's where the answer must be—in the life of Jesus!*

With noticeable excitement, Jacob's step unconsciously quickened. It was suddenly clear. He would go to the New Testament, specifically to the four gospels. If there was an answer to the question of Anthony Powers's panel of this evening, that's where he would find it!

How did Jesus approach evangelism? Did He hand out tracts? Did He lead people in salvation prayers? Did He conduct seminars? How did *He*—the Master, our example, our Teacher—how did *He* evangelize?

How did You communicate what You had to give people, Lord?" he asked. *"What did You do? Did You talk to them, pray with them, give them a copy of the Old Testament in their own language? What did You tell Your disciples to do? What instructions did You give them for carrying it on after You were gone?*

His mind was racing now—images, stories, incidents from a lifetime of familiarity with the gospel accounts, fragments of teachings, the Scriptures he had noticed when reading in his room, the Sermon on the Mount, the many parables. And then there were the accounts in the gospels of demons and evil spirits. Jesus even had encounters with demonic forces, yet you never heard that kind of thing talked about today. What about healing and miracles?

"O God, what are You trying to show me?" Jacob asked. "Am I being naive to think we can model present-day evangelism by Your methods from back then? Show me the balance that MacVey talked about. Show me how it's to be lived out in our lives to accomplish Your purpose. Show me what evangelism is—show me how to take the life of Christ into the world."

He could wait no longer. Now that he knew where the answer was to be found, a sudden urgency filled him not to waste another moment. He hailed the first taxi that came into view. "Worldwide Hotel," was all he said. It was enough for the German driver, who immediately sped off through the busy night streets of Berlin.

When he walked into the room, he was glad to find Jackson still awake and reading. As Jackson looked up he could instantly see that something had changed in his father's face. But before he could say a word, Jacob spoke.

"I've just had an incredible idea!" he said. "How'd you like to get out of here for a while?"

"What, out of the hotel—go for another walk?"

"No!" Jacob laughed. "—out of Berlin! I've had enough of this conference for a while. We've got a few days to spare. What do you say—let's go find that guy Bietmann!"

"Whoa! That *is* unexpected!"

"How about it?"

"Uh—sure! I could take a break from all this easily enough."

"Great. Shall we leave in the morning?"

"Well, then I'm going to hit the hay. I'm tired!"

"You mind if I read a while?" Jacob asked, more serious now.

"Of course not."

"I'll go into the little alcove there—I won't need much light."

Five minutes later Jackson dove into his fluffy featherbed and buried his face in the oversized pillow. Jacob, meanwhile, sat down at the small desk in the adjoining alcove, blank piece of paper on the table, pen between his fingers. With trembling hand and eyes aglow with the intense light of eager anticipation, he opened his old but only moderately used Bible and flipped through the pages until he came to Matthew 1:1.

He did not climb into bed until well past 1:00 A.M. Even then, he could hardly quiet his racing brain and heart.

PART 9

A Different Vantage Point

55

August 11, 9:47 A.M.
Moscow

Dan Davidson sat down across the table from his old rival Andrassy Galanov.

"Times have indeed changed," said Blue Doc. "The CIA and KGB sitting together out in the open."

"Not so open," replied Galanov. "There is a price on my head."

"I had wind of that."

"Comrades have become enemies, and—well, here I am sitting across from *you.*"

"If not exactly as friends, at least I don't have the table bugged. Of course, maybe you have *me* bugged!"

Galanov laughed. "No bugs. But what signifies the change most of all is what we're trying to do—on the same side."

"One big, happy family," rejoined Davidson ironically. "Who'd have ever thought the Cold War would come to this!"

"Not exactly a happy family," said the Russian. "If what I'm onto indicates what I think."

"You haven't let go of the spy game altogether, eh?"

"I couldn't help myself," replied Galanov. "Besides, if I can get to the bottom of this, I may be able to deal myself out altogether."

"So—what's up? And why me?"

"No one else to turn to. The very nature of the thing puts us on the same side of the fence for a change."

"You think I can help?"

"I have nothing to lose. Two ex-spies are better than one."

"OK, I'm listening," said Blue Doc. "What have you got?"

"Only a hunch so far," answered the Russian. "What do you know about a fellow named Desyatovsky?"

"The Russian Minister of Defense?"

"That's him."

"Not much," replied Davidson, keeping his own counsel for the moment.

"If my instincts are worth anything, there's something big about to break loose, and it's got his name written all over it."

"Why don't you follow through?"

"Because he's turned up the heat on me. One false move and I'm dead. I need help if I'm going to penetrate his game."

Blue Doc was silent, considering carefully how much to confide in this agent who had been his rival for so many years. Several long moments passed, during which his experienced eyes tried to read the sincerity in Galanov's expression. At last, seemingly satisfied, he decided to reveal his own hand.

"It wouldn't surprise me if your hunches *were* correct," he said at length.

"Oh?" Galanov raised an eyebrow.

"Some information came my way recently that would seem to confirm your suspicions."

"What kind of information?"

"A peculiar communique—from outside of the country."

"And?"

"I've got someone on it," said Blue Doc.

"What did it say?"

"The meaning was unclear, though the undertones caught my eye. I hope to hear from my contact soon. I'll get in touch with you the moment I do. How can I reach you?"

"You can't," replied the former KGB agent. "I'm hot, I tell you. I'll contact you tomorrow." He rose, then paused. "You wouldn't hold out on me, would you, Davidson?"

"What do you mean?"

"You've got to play it straight with me on this one. Anything I come up with is yours, anything you get you share with me. We're in it together. My life may depend on it."

"Straight up, Andrassy. I still owe you for that time in Kiev when you let me get lost in the pandemonium after the shooting. That could have been my life. Now this could be yours. Honor among agents, you know. I don't forget favors of that magnitude."

"Thanks, Dan," said Galanov, shaking the American's hand.

56

The drive southeast of Berlin in their rented Volkswagen was a tonic for Jackson Maxwell and Jacob Michaels after the stifling atmosphere of Berlin and the conference. Even if they only managed to get out for a few hours, for the first time in days they were breathing genuine country air.

They passed quickly out of the city and into the farmland of what had only recently been known ironically as the German Democratic Republic, or DDR. Here and there they passed through a lightly forested section of the Brandenburg Forest—clumps of birch and pine crisscrossed with dirt roads and paths—but most of the land grew ripening expanses of grain. Most of the fields were golden in the sun, although the green leaves of potatoes and sugar beets were also occasionally visible. The tracts of growing crops were enormous, in contrast to the individually owned farms of the West, where variety and crop rotation were practiced. Though thousands of prior land-ownership claims were being sorted by the German government, records were difficult to verify and the process tedious. The collectives that had been operated by the Communist regime had to continue in operation as best as the Bonn and Berlin government could manage, while piecemeal portions of East German farmland gradually found their way back into the hands of families that had owned them, in some cases for centuries.

Once leaving the four-lane autobahn, they noticed a dramatic difference in the two-lane road from those they had driven near the Folenweiter farm in the West. Those had been spacious, well paved, with bright white and yellow striping and wide shoulders. Here the roads were narrow, pitted, and largely still made of cobblestones from decades earlier. Dodging potholes on the outdated and ruined roads made for a bumpy, winding ride, and passing oncoming traffic an adventure.

A great deal of road work was being done, however, with the reunified government in Berlin making every effort to bring the East up to par with the West as quickly as possible. In every city and village they passed through, construction equipment was at work, buildings were being both torn down and constructed, piles of dirt lay alongside huge ditches where foundations were being poured and new pipes being laid. All manner of construction! They had seen this throughout the eastern sector of Berlin as well, as if fifty years of dormancy now had to be made up for within one or two years.

"When I saw the East briefly before," said Jackson, "besides the roads, buildings, railroads, and streets being run-down, the people were run-down too—lethargic, listless, unsmiling. Now suddenly everything's alive. The people walk with German vigor again. They are smiling. It must be wonderful for them."

They noticed many differences in the structures of buildings— many large institutional buildings, enormous plain apartment houses, with few individual homes, all evidence of the communal nature of a society under Communism for fifty years. Yet still could be seen, even in the midst of continuing poor conditions, a pride in appearances, flower boxes bright with color in front of hopelessly run-down homes.

"Look," said Jackson, pointing to an elderly lady. "I never get used to some of their ways. Such an attention to order and neatness!"

The woman was carefully sweeping off the packed dirt walkway that bordered the fence in front of her home.

"It's not everywhere that you see people sweeping up *dirt*! But if there's no cement sidewalk, in Germany they'll keep the dirt neat and tidy!"

About ten-thirty, with Jacob in the passenger's seat trying to follow the map they had purchased and Jackson at the wheel, they arrived at the intersection of the road between Neu-Lubbenau and Beeskow.

"Which way?" asked Jackson, pulling to the side of the narrow road.

Still holding the map, half-unfolded, in front of him, Jacob replied, "To the left, as far as I can tell. It shouldn't be but another eight or ten miles."

"And what are we going to do, even if we manage to find the town?" said Jackson, voicing for the first time the flaw in their plan that neither had yet acknowledged. "With no address or phone number and only a sixteen-year-old letter it could be a dead end."

"Come on," said Jacob, putting down the map, "where's your faith—your sense of adventure? We'll find him! Remember Proverbs three, six—'In all your ways acknowledge Him, and He will direct your paths.' We'll find him." Without waiting for Jackson's reply, Jacob prayed, "Lord, we give You acknowledgment as being our Lord and Father. Now we ask You to direct our paths to find our brother Beitmann."

"Amen," added Jackson. "OK—to the left we go!" He thrust his foot down onto the accelerator, and off they jostled along the bumpy road.

About twenty minutes later they crept into the small village of Kehrigkburg, from which Bietmann's letter had been posted sixteen years earlier.

"Look for a phone booth," said Jackson, glancing about.

"All I see are run-down farmhouses," replied Jacob. "I can't imagine a village this small even having a public phone."

"You may be right," said Jackson as they made their way along the single street that seemed to be the village's only paved road. "Wait—there's a store up ahead!"

"Hardly much of a store."

"For East Germany, in a village of this size, I'd say we're lucky to have that. And it's next to the *Postamt*—we *are* in business!"

Jackson sped up slightly and pulled in front of the tiny market. A few men were standing around the door chatting. The Americans got out of the car, receiving the kind of stares reserved for strangers as they approached.

"Guten tag," said Jackson. "Wir suchen ein Herr Bietmann."

"Bietmann—Bietmann?" repeated a couple of the men, casting looks of recognition but noncommitment at one another. It was clear that they knew the name. In a village of this size, everyone would know each other. Their looks of questioning, however, seemed to indicate, "What could you possibly want with him?" Then followed several brisk exchanges between the men in colloquial *Platt-Deutsch* that was far too rapid for Jackson to understand a single word. He and Jacob stood silent and ignored.

Before their awkwardness could deepen much further, they heard a thickly accented voice, speaking in English. "Might I be of help to you?" They turned, and found the smiling face of a humbly dressed German Frau standing behind them.

"Yes, thank you," replied Jackson. "We are hoping to find a man by the name of Bietmann. Do you know him?"

"Of course," she replied. "Come, I will show you the way."

Without another word, she turned, hopped onto the bicycle beside her, and wheeled off down the road. Jackson hurried back to the car, followed by Jacob, while the German onlookers continued to stare.

They followed the woman to the outskirts of the village and into the countryside. At last she stopped. Jackson pulled alongside her with his window down.

"There is the house of the man you seek," she said, pointing to a large brick barn in the distance. A dirt road barely wide enough for a car wound through the fields toward it.

"Danke—vielen Danke!" said Jackson.

The woman nodded with a smile, then dug her feet against the pedals of her bicycle and continued on.

Reaching the farmhouse, Jackson turned off the ignition, then glanced at Jacob. "Well—here we are, I guess."

They got out and approached the door. Jacob knocked. A minute passed. At last the door was opened by a woman with a blank expression.

"Frau—Bietmann?" asked Jackson timidly.

"Ja, ich bin Grete Bietmann."

"Ist Herr Bietmann zu Hause?"

"Ja, er ist im Feld," she replied, pointing behind the house.

Now for the first time, they heard the sound of a tractor in the distance. They saw where her husband was busy plowing over the freshly harvested field of oats. They thanked her, then Jackson led the way around the side of the red-brick barn next to the house, and out across the newly overturned earth. Traipsing over the furrowed ground, they were noticed at length by the man in the tractor. He turned off his engine, and hopped down to meet them. He looked extremely tired, but nevertheless greeted the two strangers with a smile and the offer of a dirt-stained hand.

"Herr Bietmann?" said Jacob, so anxious that he now took the lead.

"Yes, I am Udo Bietmann," he replied in broken English, recognizing the men before him to be Americans.

Jacob reached out and took his hand with a smile. "I am so happy to meet you at last," he said, "I am—"

Before he could get the rest of the words out, the German interrupted, a dawn of light suddenly spreading over his face.

"But of course!" he cried. "I would know your face anywhere. You are Jacob Michaels!"

57

August 14
Kehrigkburg, Germany

Thirty minutes later the three men and Frau Bietmann were sitting around a humble kitchen table on four wooden chairs, drinking coffee and nibbling sweetbread snacks. Whether well off or not, no self-respecting German Hausfrau was without a supply of tasty treats to offer unexpected guests.

The discussion had been animated. They had reread Herr Bietmann's letter several times. When Jacob had withdrawn it from his pocket, Udo had half-cried, half broken out in disbelieving laughter. Frau Bietmann spoke not a word of English, but Udo's was proficient, and he and Jackson combined their skills.

It was indeed a joyous occasion, and the fellowship of newly discovered brotherhood was rich. It was with tears standing in his eyes that Jacob recounted his story. He told him of his own superficiality, about the faithfulness of his prayer warrior friend Bob Means, whom, he said, they all had to thank for this wonderful time together. His apology and request for forgiveness was moving, as was Bietmann's warm and sympathetic response.

After they had been together about an hour or hour and a half, Jacob said, "Well, I know you are busy with your harvest. It is probably time for us—"

He was rising from his chair as he spoke, but Frau Bietmann cut him off, understanding Jacob's intent well enough.

"Setzen Sei noch!" she said, reaching out a firm restraining arm and placing it on Jacob's. "Sie mussen mit uns Mitagessen!"

Jacob glanced at her with a hopeless expression of uncomprehension.

"My wife is absolutely right, Mr. Michaels," said Udo smiling, but trying to supress a yawn as he did. "If you are thinking of leaving, put the thought completely out of your mind. As my wife has said, first you must eat our midday meal with us. After that, we shall see. *Mal sehen*, as we say in my language. After waiting fifteen years, you do not expect me to let you go now so easily, do you?"

Jacob laughed. "I don't want to be a bother or annoyance. The fields don't wait. That much about farming I do know."

"You are right. But food of the spirit is far more important than grain. Besides, most of my harvest is in. My brothers saw to it when I was called away recently."

"You have brothers who are also farmers?" asked Jackson.

"Others of our fellowship," answered the German. "My spiritual brothers. We help one another. When I was forced away for a few days, they added my fields to their own. Almost all I have left is to plow the fields under." Again he yawned.

"I can see that you are tired," objected Jacob. "We mustn't take you—"

"Nonsense," interrupted the farmer. "I will not let you go so soon. There is much to be done, and I do not mean in the fields. I thought you had come to fulfill my request." He pointed to the letter still laying on the table.

"I did not want to be presumptuous," rejoined Jacob. "I didn't know if we would find you, much less if you still wanted us. I only knew I had to try to contact you."

"Everything has changed, of course, my friend. But we are still God's people who have the same need of spiritual nourishment as before. I would count it a joy undescribable to introduce you to the people of our fellowship."

"The honor would be mine," replied Jacob. "I am only sorry that it has waited so long."

"God's timing is never too slow. We have learned that lesson

252

in our corner of the world many times. Whenever I begin to get anxious about timing, I remember a saying. It is this: In God's economy, you cannot go too slow. You have come now; therefore this is the right time."

"Not a bad prescription to keep you from rash decisions," commented Jacob.

"Exactly. It's a truth with a thousand applications. God is never in a hurry. His purposes are always accomplished, but rarely overnight."

"Do you have any children?" Jackson asked.

Herr Bietmann was slow to answer. "No—no we do not," he answered and then seemed relieved when the conversation did not dwell on that topic further.

"What is it like now?" asked Jackson, unable to keep the inquisitive reporter within him down for long. "Now that freedom has come to the East, is it better than before?"

A long pause followed, during which Herr Bietmann was clearly deep in thought and reflection. At last he drew in a deep sigh. "I have often wondered what I would say to a Westerner if given the liberty to explain our situation in depth," he said.

"Now you have your chance," rejoined Jackson.

"Many of the things I would say are not what an American would expect," said Bietmann in German.

"All the better. I want to know what you really think. I want your perception, not the newspaper version."

There was again silence, then Bietmann plunged in.

"Everyone was excited at first," he said. "Excited is an understatement. Euphoric! Travel, visitation in the West, freedom to buy goods, the return of seized property—how wonderful it was! You cannot imagine how priceless freedom is unless you have been denied it beyond memory. Freedom of travel, freedom of speech, freedom of religion, freedom of the press, freedom of ownership— all we of the Eastern Bloc nations have not stopped rejoicing over these freedoms from the day the wall in Berlin fell on November 9, 1989."

"From the tone of your voice I sense a *but* coming," said Jackson when Bietmann paused.

Their host smiled.

"You're right. The *but* is this—the euphoria did not last for long. Immediately after reunification doubts and even regrets began to surface. For our brothers in the West, those doubts had mainly to do with the cost. Of course the Deutsche mark is the strongest currency in Europe, but reunification is causing hardship in Germany. The West has had to face new taxes, and the government has had to borrow—it is painful for our prosperous brothers."

"What about for you?"

"The pain for us is completely different. We received valuable German marks in exchange for our worthless Eastern currency. We were ecstatic. But in the end it was a blessing without substance. When the original supply was gone, there were no more marks. 'Which is better,' our people have asked over and over, 'to have money as we did under Communism, but little in the stores to buy, or to have stores full of Western goods, but no money to purchase even staples?' Such is the situation throughout most of the countries of the East."

"Why is there no money?"

"Because the economies of the East have virtually collapsed. In four decades of Communism everything deteriorated—housing, industry, transportation, the environment. Some of our railroad lines, date back to the late 1800s. After World War Two, the Soviets dismantled the best of East Germany's factories and shipped them to Russia. Then they raped the land. In some forests the leaves are gone by mid-summer. Sulfur from burning coal is in the air. The Elbe is filled with lead and pesticides.

"Capitalism and free enterprise sound good on paper, and we in the East have been eager for democracy. But in reality it has caused much misery. With free enterprise installed, stores and merchants were allowed to set their own prices. Suddenly everything cost ten and twenty times more than it had before. What had once been readily available was instantly out of reach. In Czechoslovakia it is far worse. It was the same in Russia when Yeltsin removed price controls in January of '92. Fresh fruit is far beyond the means of most people. Fuel is so expensive that people cannot afford to travel, even though now they are free to go where they will.

"And unemployment is an even deeper and more widespread difficulty. In some towns there is seventy to eighty percent unemployment. Virtually every factory in the DDR has closed. They could not begin to compete with the West. The average East

German worker produces only twenty-five percent of his West German counterpart."

"What about unemployment benefits? Did West Germany make no provision for this?"

"There have been payments. But they are meager. Along with the staggering expense of trying to rebuild East Germany, the new government in Berlin can't afford to bankrupt itself. And yet we are fortunate to have had a West Germany with which to reunite. For all the other Eastern countries the recovery will take much longer—perhaps two generations, not just a few years or decades. Yes, there is freedom, but the financial hardships are enormous. The DDR was the strongest of the Communist nations, yet we cannot begin to compete with the West. It is much worse in Russia, Czechoslovakia, Bulgaria."

Bietmann stopped, and Jackson translated for Jacob the gist of what he had said. They were silent a while, reflecting on the bleak outlook.

"Do you still call it *East Germany*?" asked Jackson.

"Officially this part of Germany is known as 'Die funf neuen Bundeslander'—"

"The five new federal states," said Jackson to Jacob.

"—but yes," Bietmann added, "the designation *Ostdeutschland* is still in common use."

Jacob spoke to Jackson. "It reminds me of what Eagleburger said about the Cold War."

"I didn't read it."

"It was something like, that for all its risks and uncertainties, that period was characterized by long-term predictable relationships among the great powers. Now there is the danger that the changes coming to the East are too tumultuous to be sustained."

"That seems to be just what Udo is saying," concluded Jackson as he turned to Beitmann and asked him to continue.

"Only a third of our population lives better today than before the wall came down," Beitmann went on. "I have even heard it said, 'I wish the wall was still there.' "

"You can't mean it!" exclaimed Jackson.

"The discouragement is so widespread that yes, some do feel that life was better before."

"But surely this is a small minority?"

"Of course."

"What about the church? How has it fared?"

"It is the same—mixed. There has always been a religious freedom here in the DDR, but it was accompanied by harassment and prejudice. We rejoice in the new tolerance, though many people are in such dire financial straits, they cannot even think about spiritual things."

"Do you know how Christians are faring elsewhere?"

"Generally God's people are flourishing. It was always true that the farther east you went, the more primitive conditions became. The church was allowed here; in Russia the true church was forced underground. In Czechoslovakia young people under the age of eighteen were forbidden to attend church, even though the church was technically legal. If they disobeyed, their higher education privileges were taken away. Similar conditions have existed here in the DDR."

"How do you see the outlook now? What is it like for your fellowship?"

"We have much to be thankful for," answered Bietmann. "God is good, and we are seeing many people respond to the Savior, now that there is no longer the fear of a sudden knock on the door. And too, we of this region are faring well economically. A decree in July of 1990 required that property confiscated by Communists after 1949 be returned to the rightful owners. Because many of the farms of this region, including ours, were ancestral holdings, we now have work. Our equipment is poor and money remains scarce, but we help one another. We can grow food to eat, and honest labor itself is healthy."

"But no national revival has come with freedom?"

"There is great spiritual activity, but I would not call it revival. In fact, the breakneck speed with which all of society is being transformed is bringing many undesirable things too. You cannot imagine the flood of pornographic books, magazines, and videos that have suddenly appeared. The curse of Western Europe's decadence overwhelmed the East overnight. Communist censorship had kept all such materials out."

"Why?"

"Because they saw it as a distraction from their socialistic goals. And in the wake of Communism's demise, a spiritual vacuum has suddenly appeared. The ideology that held all of society together is instantly gone. City fathers and government leaders and school officials are hungry to find substitutes with which to replace it. They are begging pastors and qualified laymen to come and teach Christianity and the Bible in the public schools."

"That is amazing!" exclaimed Jackson, turning to translate everything Bietmann had said to his father.

"But it is the cults who are primarily responding. They have been quick to move into that vacuum. So it is the Mormons and Jehovah's Witnesses who are providing most of this teaching, and the former Communists have no idea of the falsehoods involved. Everywhere you look, cults and other such groups are making inroads. To answer your question, there is a hunger in the East for spiritual things. But it is tempered with confusion."

"Is the persecution over?"

"Here in the DDR, yes. I have contacts in Czechoslovakia, however, who tell me that in some cases it is actually worse. Entrenched Communists continue to fight the changes that have taken place, sometimes taking their anger out on Christians, churches, and pastors. Those in power today—and this is true in all the Eastern countries—are reformed Communists. Their conversion and denial of the Party was opportunistic rather than idealistic. Much of the former bureaucracy and police force are still in power.

"Even donations and literature now flooding in from the West do not always reach those who need it the most. Large shipments of Christian literature and Bibles have gone into Prague and other big cities, only to be grabbed by church officials of the large denominations and sold for hugely inflated prices. We have received shipments too, for which we praise God. But usually the Westerners who donate materials show little concern for what happens to the contents of their boxes after they drop them off."

"Yet you say things are going well in your own fellowship?"

"Yes. We are blessed to have the cloud of angst lifted from being a Christian. We have meetings several evenings a week now, relishing, I suppose, the exuberance of freedom. I will begin spreading the word through the village immediately that you will be with us tonight." This last sentence he spoke to Jacob in English.

Jacob glanced at Jackson, then said to Bietmann, "We would be honored—but, we—well, it's a couple hours back to the hotel in Berlin. I don't think we want to be too late—"

"Hotel!" he exclaimed. "Nonsense! You stay tonight with us—perhaps several nights."

"But the conference?"

"You yourself said that you had grown weary of it. You do not have to speak for several evenings. That gives you some time to spend with us. You will be our guest. You will meet many brothers and sisters."

The two glanced at one another again, then shrugged and let their large smiles speak their acceptance.

58

August 14, 7:18 P.M.
Kehrigkburg

That evening Jackson and Jacob were treated like royalty, participating in fellowship richer than either had experienced for some time. During the afternoon they had walked about the premises and had carried on a lively discussion with Bietmann's wife, Greta, with Jackson again acting as translator, while the farmer took a much needed nap.

After *Abendbrot,* they piled into the farmer's small car and drove two or three kilometers to the large home where the fellowship met. The instant they walked in, both Americans knew they were in the midst of something refreshing.

"Udo!" came several voices at once. Within seconds they were surrounded by handskaking, hugging, shoulder-slapping greetings followed by many introductions and words of welcome and a steady torrent of well-wishing in German and here and there a voice in broken English. Among the many new friends they met was the lady who had shown them the way that morning, whose smile was particularly warm.

In the midst of the proceedings, Jackson noticed one of the men take their host aside and apparently ask a question of him. A grave expression came over Bietmann's face, and Jackson could make out but a little of the German of his soft-spoken reply, ". . . God is faithful . . . much to pray about . . . crucial time . . ."

The other man again spoke. Bietmann nodded. "Perhaps soon" were the only words Jackson thought he understood before Greta took his arm to introduce him to another friend.

Most of those present were dressed in simple farming garb. A few wore beards, caps, hats, and dresses indicating their Mennonite connections, though they mixed with the others freely. Afterward Bietmann explained that Catholics, Baptists, Lutherans, and a couple of Adventists were included in the fellowship, along with ten or twelve new believers who acknowledged no affiliation whatsoever.

"We are a mixed-up group of believers in Jesus," he had said. "Without a name, with no ties to any church, where all are welcome—whether they believe or not!"

"You include nonbelievers too?" asked Jacob, taken aback but intrigued.

"Oh, of course!" replied Bietmann. "Why else do you think there is such spontaneous enthusiasm? Every time we come together there are new people, friends, neighbors. The excitement of sharing our faith is infectious. The people you meet are praying all the day long for their acquaintances whom they hope to bring to our fellowship. When we come together there is joy in seeing these prayers answered every week—every day!"

"Do you visit other fellowships?"

"I do not travel a great deal," replied Bietmann, "but occasionally business requires my presence elsewhere. I can tell you that many men and women are coming to know our Savior personally."

After Bietmann had informally explained who his visitors were, singing broke out, bringing a worshipful calm to the room. As they sang, everyone found a seat, mostly on the floor.

There were no instruments or hymnbooks, and belying the joyous and even boisterous beginning, the songs were mostly older hymns, and many in a minor key. It took nothing from their power, however, for every voice raised itself in unison with the others, reminding Jackson of an ancient monastery choir. This was no light-hearted songfest of choruses, but deep-throated tones, somber, with intent regard to the words of worship, praise, and adoration. Visible on their faces were deeply etched lines of labor, hardship, and persecution through which their hard-won faith had been tested and verified under Communist oppression.

Both Jackson and Jacob found themselves moved deeply by the experience, though neither could have said exactly why. As Jackson glanced over at the man his father had come so far to see, now singing with his eyes closed, he could see that these people had paid dearly for their faith and that the exuberant enthusiasm they manifested was born of years of endurance, even suffering, that he himself had never known.

Beitmann was a quiet man of profound character. On sight, Jackson would have known that he had been a Christian many years. The maturity and wisdom with which he spoke and carried himself were clearly evident. He looked to be forty-eight or fifty years of age, though in the short time Jackson had been in the former Eastern sector, he had discovered that people looked older here, that despair told upon their countenances at a younger age. Bietmann was not the pastor of the fellowship. As far as Jackson could tell, they didn't even have a pastor. But he was clearly one of its acknowledged leaders.

As the singing ended Jackson looked up to see his father being thrust forward by Bietmann to the front of the room. There was not a sound from the twenty-five or thirty persons present as Jacob stood, awkward and embarrassed, trying to collect his thoughts.

"I am at a loss for words," he began, then paused while Bietmann translated. "When we left Berlin this morning in search of our new friend—" He gestured toward Bietmann. To his words the German added several of his own as he gestured toward himself, getting a great round of laughter from his friends.

"—we had no idea what would be the result," Jacob went on. "Frankly, I did not think I would have the opportunity to fulfill his request of so many years ago."

He paused when he spoke again, his voice was soft, somewhat shaky. "I have to tell you," he continued, "that after being with hundreds of my fellow Christians from the West, your fellowship is so energizing that I shall not soon forget it. I find myself wondering what you could possibly learn from the likes of *me*. Herr Bietmann may have written me years ago, hoping I could bring you words of encouragement and teaching. But I would have had none to give you then—and now I realize how much *you* have to teach *me* about living by faith."

He stopped again. He seemed to be struggling with deep emotion.

"As ironic as it now seems," he went on, "I am supposed to address a gathering of Christian leaders on the subject of evangelism. Yet here, where you are doing it—making it a real and daily pattern of life—I find myself at a loss for words to say. I simply want to ask—for your prayers. At this moment, I need *your* encouragement more than—"

He stopped and turned away, unable to speak. In an instant, Beitmann was at his side.

He spoke to Jacob, then motioned to several of the other men to join him. As they came, he and Jacob sank to their knees and within moments Jacob was surrounded by strong voices of prayer in a language he did not understand, while they laid their hardworking yet gentle hands upon his shoulders and legs. Around the room, the rest of the men and women joined in prayer for him whom they viewed as a great man of God, who had humbled himself and confessed his need in their midst.

59

"I told you it could be any day," Blue Doc said to his old KGB rival.

"I did not expect anything so soon," said Galanov.

"Can you meet?"

"Where?"

"You're the one who's hot. Tell me, and I'll be there. You won't believe what I have to show you."

"All right then—let me think," said the Russian. He gave the CIA man instructions. "I'll be there in half an hour."

Blue Doc hung up the phone with a click.

He looked again at the incredible file in his hand that had been delivered to him an hour ago. How the woman had managed it, and how she had got it into Yaschak's hands, he didn't know. He didn't need to know! He had it, that was all that mattered. His mind was reeling, and he still wondered if it was the right thing to show it to the Russian. But he owed Galanov. And he had given his word.

Thirty minutes later the two agents sat huddled under the sheltering shadow of a little-used bridge over one of the small tributaries of the Moskva River. What they had to discuss could not be heard by inquisitive ears without bringing danger upon them both.

"Was my hunch about Desyatovsky correct?" asked Galanov.

"A jackpot," replied Davidson, "if you want to call a plot to completely overturn the governments of all the Soviet republics and bring the Commonwealth back under a single power source a jackpot."

"What!"

"It's all here—a plan to wrest control from the hands of the republics and straight into the hands of our friend Bludayev Desyatovsky."

"I can hardly believe it! Do you mean—another coup attempt? It would never work."

"He's got every angle covered. It could be nothing less than that. Have a look for yourself."

Davidson opened the file that was in his hand, stooped down to one knee, and spread out several smaller files on the ground before Galanov.

The Russian looked through one set of papers, scanning them then moving to another, with deepening concern etched across the lines of his face. When he at last spoke, his tone reflected the severity of the situation.

"That's exactly what it looks like," he said. "Everything has changed so much since '91 and the breakup of the Union, I can't see how he could pull it off. Yet this has none of the earmarks of the coup de farce of that year. Why, he's got every segment of society tied into this thing, besides top leaders in all of the republics."

"You think Desyatovsky's the mastermind?"

"Who else? You got these things from his department, didn't you?"

Blue Doc nodded. "But look at this other file," he said.

Galanov took the additional sheets from the CIA agent's hand and read quickly. A long whistle followed. "This is as big as I'd imagined—"

"I take it you're not surprised?" said Blue Doc.

"I suspected it when I saw them together a week and a half ago."

"I knew there must be some good reason to let you in on this thing." The CIA man grinned.

"This guy is a leader in the German parliament."

"So," said Blue Doc, "what's Drexler's game?"

"Don't know exactly. He's a powerful man, head of the SPD party, opposition leader of the Bundestag, second to Kolter in power."

"And you've seen him with Desyatovsky recently?"

Galanov nodded. "After the summit on the third."

"The aid package, of course," exclaimed Blue Doc. You think that has anything to do with all this?"

"I don't know. But they were up to something—I could smell it. That's what aroused my suspicions. I've been trying to find out what ever since. But then things started getting hot. I'm sure they're onto me."

Now it was Blue Doc's turn to whistle. "Maybe you should say, now that they know you're onto them."

"How did you get these files anyway?" asked Galanov. "I used to be high up in the KGB, but I would never have dreamed of getting my hands onto anything this explosive. We've got enough to bring the whole thing down around their ears."

"Stole them."

"*You* stole them? From Desyatovsky's office?"

"Not exactly. I had help."

"You Americans always were more clever than we gave you credit for!"

"The help I had was pure Russian." Blue Doc laughed. "In this business, success depends on who you know and what kind of information they can buy."

"On the other hand," mused Galanov, "once you find yourself out in the cold without friends, it's over."

"Maybe you can use this to bargain your way out."

"It's got to be handled with care—and quickly. Especially given my present status here, there's nobody in my country I'd trust enough."

"Kolter and the U.S. State Department seem the likely people to deliver the files to," said Blue Doc. "They'll know what to do. We've got to get the information out of Moscow and to Berlin and Washington."

"Don't you have a CIA hot line? Call your superiors," suggested Galanov.

Blue Doc thought a moment, many factors running through his mind. Just when he'd thought all the tension in the world was over, here he was with dynamite in his hands and not sure what to do with it!

Finally he spoke. "You're the one who needs to blow the whistle."

"Why? You could get word back to your country faster than I could do a thing."

"If it comes from us, they'll be able to claim the U.S. is trying to resume Cold War hostilities. With the media contacts they have in their pocket, they could bury anything that originated with the CIA, and the world would probably believe them. It's got to come from your end."

"Hmm—I see what you mean." Galanov perused one of the files again. "You're right—with Alekdanyov on his team, there wouldn't be much *anyone* could do."

"Listen, we'll go back to my office and make a set of copies. You take these. In case you get fouled up along the way I'll have another set."

"Why don't you give them the information immediately and tell them to sit on it until I can expose it?"

"Once the State Department got wind of it, they would be up in arms. It wouldn't stay quiet an hour. Washington doesn't have any idea of the contempt with which the United States is viewed in the rest of the world. No, it's a judgment call, and I'm going to sit on it—for a few days at least."

"Then I must get out of Russia with this. But be ready. They're looking for me as it is. If I'm found, I've had it."

"You want me to get you out? I've got ways."

"No. I have that covered."

"How? I thought all your contacts had gone dry."

"Never mind. The less you know, the better."

"I'll take your word for it."

"Once we get two sets, we have to go our own separate ways. We can't take any chance of being caught together. I'm not even going to go back to my place. Time is too critical. I'll be out of Moscow before midnight."

"I won't act until I know you have or aren't going to be able to."

"If you see the coup starting to go down, forget about me. It probably means that they've got me or I'm lying dead someplace."

"OK," said Blue Doc. "But I'm going to give you the name of my contact in Washington." He took out a scrap of paper and wrote down a name and telephone number. "Take this. If you get into trouble you can't get out of, call this number. The instant you tell them that code word written there, they'll listen. It'll be my insurance too, if something happens to me here. I want to make sure *one* of us gets to Washington or Berlin."

Galanov nodded. Blue Doc replaced the papers in their appropriate files. Both men returned to Davidson's office at the American embassy, and after the files had been duplicated, they parted with handshakes and serious expressions.

Each was fully aware of the irony of how much trust he had suddenly placed in his longtime adversary.

60

The following morning, Jackson awoke with faint strains of *Weiss wie der Schnee* filtering through his consciousness and the entrancing faces of the Mennonite singers before his mind's eye.

In mid-morning, therefore, leaving Jacob and their host engaged in earnest conversation, Jackson found himself bicycling toward the Mennonite farm of the Moeller's some four kilometers distant, according to the directions Udo's wife had given him. He wanted to find what it was on these people's faces that had struck such a distinctive chord in his heart.

The farm, it had been explained to him, was a cooperative effort involving four families who had been allowed to retain their ownership of the land as long as the State received its share, because of the efficiency of their output. Officials even came periodically, ostensibly to inspect the premises, but in reality to glean information from the simple Mennonite farmers whose methods obviously worked far better than those of the Communist regime.

As he approached, he heard machinery at work in the fields. Two combines chewed away in a field of grain, and several tractors pulling wagons sped to and fro. Another large John Deere plowed a completed field beyond. Adjacent to the house stood an enormous storage barn.

Not wanting to get in the way, Jackson rode to the house, leaned the bicycle against a tree, and knocked on the door. Several moments later, a stout woman answered, dressed in a traditional Mennonite pale blue dress, with a white cotton apron over it, and a small cap upon tightly gathered hair. Jackson was spared the awkwardness of trying to explain himself when the woman recognized him from the night before.

"Come in . . . please, Herr Maxwell," she said in German, opening the door wide.

Jackson followed her inside, now noting her rolled up sleeves and the flour on her hands. "I'm sorry," he said, "I did not mean to interrupt. I simply wanted to see your farm."

"No interruption," she rejoined. "Come," she added, "we are preparing the midday meal for the men. You may join us—please, it is no interruption."

He followed and found himself in a huge kitchen where six or eight women, all dressed identically, worked on different phases of food preparation. One had her hands in dark brown bread dough, another stood at a large pot of boiling water, one sat on a three-legged stool snapping beans and tossing them into a bowl at her feet, one scrubbed a table, while three elderly women sat in a circle around an immense pot on the floor, into which they tossed chunks of peeled potatoes that fell from their hands so fast that the motions were almost invisible, as were the deft movements of the knives they so skillfully wielded. At his entrance, every head turned toward him.

The woman who had met him at the door rapidly explained who Jackson was, following which smiles of recognition dawned about the room. The next instant he was battered by a barrage of welcomes.

"Thank you," he said, embarrassed at being the center of such a fuss.

Most of the women appeared to be in their 40s or 50s, although one of the potato-peelers must have been more than eighty, judging from the lines of her wrinkled skin. Abruptly, a side door opened, and in scampered a young boy and girl, probably aged seven or eight.

"Papa says to bring more twine for the bailer," shouted the boy.

"And a fresh jug of water," added the girl.

One of the women nodded and left the room.

"Anna, would you show Herr Maxwell about the farm?" said the woman who had met Jackson at the door. Jackson turned, wondering to whom she was speaking. As he did, he saw a young lady who looked to be in her early twenties emerging from what appeared to be a pantry. He recognized her, as well as most of the women in the room, from the choir.

"Yes, Mama," said the girl, setting three jars onto the counter. "But I am not finished with the soup."

"I will watch it. Herr Maxwell is our guest and deserves more attention than the vegetables."

"Yes, Mama," said the girl.

"You will join us for dinner?" asked the girl's mother, speaking again to Jackson.

"I—I don't want to interfere with—"

"The men will scold us if we let you visit with us without staying to see them," she replied. "Anna, bring Herr Maxwell back for dinner, and do not let him leave before then!"

"Yes, Mama," said the girl, with the hint of a smile.

"Where did the two little ones go?" asked Jackson once they were outside.

"My little cousins are probably back in the field by now," said Anna.

"There are more children?"

"Oh yes. Six small ones between the four families."

"I only see one house," said Jackson, glancing about. "Does everyone live here?"

Anna laughed lightly. It was a soft, musical laugh. "There are twenty-eight of us altogether," she said. "That would be a houseful!"

"It is a big farmhouse," said Jackson.

"Not that big, I'm afraid. My uncle and his family live here. He has the two you just saw, two sons near my age, and his mother is still alive as well, one of the women cutting up potatoes. The other three houses are across the land about a kilometer away in different directions."

"Where do you live?" asked Jackson.

"On the other side of that little wood there," replied Anna, pointing.

"And you all come here to work every day?"

"Not every day, but most—especially in the summer when there is so much to be done. My father and uncles and cousins work in the fields, and the women work in the house. Though," she

268

added, looking down at the ground, then glancing back up with a smile, "I must admit I love to get my hands dirty and feel my arms ache and work so hard that my body sweats."

She paused, looking at Jackson, who was momentarily taken aback by her sudden forthrightness.

"What does an American think of a German girl who says such things?" she asked. "Is it unbecoming?"

"No, it's wonderful!" laughed Jackson. "What else should a farm girl say?"

"Do American girls enjoy such work?"

"None that I have ever met," Jackson replied, laughing again. "Even where I grew up, in a farming community, I can't recall ever hearing any of the girls say she enjoyed hard, sweaty work."

"Oh, I do enjoy it! It makes me feel close to the earth, the way God made us to be. I don't want soft hands and flabby arms. I want to be strong, as strong as God made me, and able to do any task He gives me."

"So you get to work in the fields?"

"On most days during the harvest. Papa likes it when I help him, but this morning Mama wanted me in the house."

"Do you always do just what they say?"

"Of course, they are my parents—but here we are at the storage barn. I will show you inside. You will meet my two brothers."

Thirty minutes later when they emerged from the barn, Jackson's brain was full. But it was not the storage bins nor the machinery nor the pace of the harvest that struck root in his consciousness. Rather he found himself full of the people, their relationships, the harmony between them—and especially with Anna.

He had met her brothers, several cousins of varied ages, and two uncles. All of their faces bore the same peaceful countenance that he had seen in the women in the kitchen, and which he now realized was the feature that drew him to Anna. They spoke to one another, in the midst of the demands of heavy work, with respect and courtesy. No one seemed frantic, yet the pace was steady, even rapid, and it was clear that, though it still lacked much of the modernization enjoyed by his friends Marla and Heinrich, this farm was efficient and prosperous by East German standards.

At first glance he had taken Anna for little more than a teenager, perhaps twenty-one at the most. She had a transparency that showed unconcern for what he might think, and a willingness to show who and what she was without pretension. She did not seem old enough to have achieved that form of "maturity" that guards the inner chambers of the soul, letting out only those portions deemed appropriate for public view.

Jackson's astonishment was great, therefore, to learn that Anna was twenty-eight, a mere three and a half years younger than he was. He found himself looking at her with disbelief, his eyes trying to assimilate the fact that this person whom he had thought almost a child was in fact nearly his own age. As they had continued walking about the other farm buildings and out among the fields, talking as they went—through it all he had begun to observe qualities in Anna's face and voice and carriage that confirmed not merely her age, but a subtle maturity and depth of character that he had not noticed previously.

The lines around her eyes and mouth spoke of experience beyond mere youth. The pale blueness of her eyes—under abundant light blonde hair adorned, like her mother's, with a small white scarf—looked upon her surroundings with a wisdom and love that could only have been ingrained by years. And as she explained this and that to Jackson, the flashes of light from the depths of the blueness revealed beyond words how dearly she loved this place, her family, and how content she was with the life God had appointed for her.

What Jackson had taken for youthful naivete, he now began to perceive, was an innocent maturity. She was too busy with the daily work of the farm and too eager to serve her parents and the community family to expend energy worrying about what she ought to do, think, or be. She was brimming with life; therefore she *lived.*

By the time they were walking back toward the farmhouse for midday dinner, Jackson had begun to regard the young German Mennonite woman at his side with a sense of awe. In her expression and demeanor he detected reservoirs of unspoken wisdom, which he doubted even she knew she possessed.

He could not help wanting to explore more deeply that storehouse of the innermost essence of the young lady's being.

61

Jackson had not planned to spend the entire day at the Mennonite farm, but he could not refuse the invitation to accompany Anna to the home of her aunt after dinner. She had been ill for several days, Anna explained, and she was taking her a basket of soup and bread. It was a walk of about a kilometer and a half.

They were now on their way back and had grown comfortable enough together that they were talking freely. The flow of conversation had gone in a number of directions.

"But do you never feel," Jackson was asking, "I don't know—hemmed in by your circumstances, like you want to *do* something more—go, travel, see things—make a life for yourself?"

"Naturally we in the East have felt confined for many years. We are happy to now be free."

"I didn't mean as a country—you personally—living here with your parents, working day after day."

"What is so unusual about it?" asked Anna.

"In my country is it *very* unusual."

"Why?"

"Because young people are anxious to get on their own, to make lives for themselves, to be independent of their parents."

"I cannot think of anything I would want less than that. Why would I want to cut myself off from everything that is good, from what has given me life? Why would I want to be independent from a mother and father who love me and want only the best for me?"

"So that you could discover what is best for you on your own."

"But I trust my father entirely. I do not care to seek anything on my own, as you say. I trust my father, and I trust God to work for my best through my father."

"But have you no wish to marry someday, to have a family of your own?"

"Perhaps—yes, of course. But I am not anxious about that. I trust God for the future as well as the present, and in the meantime, I do what He gives me to do and am thankful."

"But it seems that you would want to be with people of your own age, out where you can experience things and meet people.

271

Here you are only around your own family."

"And you would have me be out in the world?" asked Anna innocently.

"I only want to know what you think," replied Jackson. "I have not often encountered such contentment. I am curious to know where it comes from."

Anna was thoughtful. "Let me see if I understand your question. Is it that you think I ought to be out in the world to expose myself to a broader view of life?"

"Something like that."

Anna smiled. "Forgive me if I sound critical, but why should I do the very opposite from what the Bible says?"

"How do you mean?"

"We are told to *not* be as the world and to *separate* ourselves from it. Yet you wonder why I do not go out into it."

"I hadn't thought of it that way."

"We have had to think of it like that. Perhaps we Christians of the East have been more fortunate than you realize. For us, separation from the world has been a necessity. Now that we are free politically, I see no benefit to be gained by forsaking obedience to the Bible. I am happy. I am loved by my family and my heavenly Father. Why should I want to mix with a world that does not know its Maker? If the Father has plans for my future, I need not concern myself with them—He will open the doors that He desires for me."

"A family of your own, a home—how will God be able to do such things for you if you remain here all your life?"

"You think it would be difficult for Him?"

"It seems we have to allow God opportunities."

"My, what a small God you must believe in." Anna laughed. "Must He depend on *your* efforts to accomplish *His* will?"

"How do you think He accomplishes things, then," asked Jackson, "if we do nothing?"

"Did I say we were to do nothing?" she asked, a slight crease appearing on her forehead. "I didn't mean to."

"Perhaps you didn't. What *do* you think is your part then?"

"To trust Him to do *everything*."

"Isn't that the same as your doing nothing?"

"Oh no! You think trusting God is nothing?"

"Now you're putting words in *my* mouth!" Jackson laughed. Anna joined him in light-hearted laughter.

"I am sorry," she said sincerely. "I did not mean to do that."

"No—of course trust is important. But it is not *doing* anything tangible. Trust takes place in the mind, the heart."

Anna was thoughtful. "I would say that what takes place in our mind and heart is the most important thing of all. That is where we form our *attitude* toward God. Is He truly our Father who takes care of our every need? Or do we merely see Him as a co-laborer, like my uncle and father, working side-by-side in a field? If He is a co-laborer, then we must do our share of the work. If He is a loving Father, then we must trust Him so much that we do not interfere or get in the way."

"But what do you see as your part, once you have settled that God is to be trusted?"

Again Anna thought a minute before answering. "To do what He puts before me to do," she said finally. "If I trust Him, then I trust that what comes to me is sent from Him. Therefore, I can do it wholeheartedly, knowing that God is accomplishing His perfect will in my life."

"And when there is something new He wants for you, He will put it before you without your seeking it?"

"Of course. Trusting Him enables Him to have His way. If I attempt to take matters into my own hands, I only take the best possibilities *out* of His. How could I not be content to wait for Him?"

"Is there no time when you might need to go out and seek a new direction?"

"Of course. But God would make it clear. Then I would obey because the direction had come from Him. Yet it would be death to originate ideas and plans on my own, because of something I wanted for *myself*."

They fell silent. At last Jackson spoke.

"You mustn't think, Anna," he said, "that my questions mean I do not agree with you. In fact, I find you mirroring beliefs I have, things I have struggled with. I only wanted to know what you thought and why. I suppose a writer is always trying to prove all sides of a question. I hope you don't take offense."

"How could I take offense?" Anna smiled. "I knew that you

wanted to know what I thought but were not arguing with me. It is good to talk about these things. Sometimes I try with my brothers or my cousins. But they do not always understand."

"Have your parents taught you these things?"

"Much of it comes from my father. He is a wise man. Much of it has come from my own mind and heart. God always stirs up my mind and imagination, and I often talk to Him about what is inside me."

"What *do* you want, Anna Moeller?" asked Jackson after another pause.

Anna glanced about the fields through which they were walking, then smiled.

"I think more than anything I want to *be*," she replied.

"Be—what?"

"Be the kind of lady that makes God smile. I want to be a daughter that trusts Him and loves Him and acts and thinks the way He wants me to."

"Is there nothing you want *for yourself?*"

"I can think of nothing I could even want that is not summed up in wanting to be fully and completely His daughter. That is not only enough—it is *everything!*"

They were nearly back to the house. Jackson stopped. Anna paused too and looked up at him.

"Have I said something wrong?" she asked.

"Oh no," answered Jackson earnestly. "But I have not often heard such words."

"You asked what I wanted. If one is a Christian, what else is there? Do you have a different heart's desire, Jackson?"

"No. I want very much the same thing. I want to be a certain kind of man. I want my life to reflect the character of Jesus. In a different way that is what you said, isn't it?"

"Exactly. Why do you look at me so funny then?"

"Because I have not found many people—even Christians— with whom I do share that part of my deepest self. It suddenly struck me as strange that that chord would be touched by a girl from East Germany I did not even know yesterday."

"Perhaps it is strange," she replied. "Yet is it not just the kind of unexpected thing our Father is often doing?"

Jackson nodded.

274

Just then a voice sounded from the door of the house. "Anna!" called her mother, "your father wants you in the field."

"Yes, Mama," she repied. "I will be there in a moment." She turned back toward Jackson.

"I must go to my father," she said. "Will you visit us again?"

"I don't know," replied Jackson. "We have no firm plans, but I would like to."

"Please—know that you are welcome."

"Good-bye, Anna."

She smiled broadly, blue eyes flashing, then spun around and ran toward the house. It was a smile Jackson would carry with him forever.

PART 10

Which Direction Destiny?

62

Bludayev Desyatovsky walked among the remaining staff of underlings who had not yet gone home for the evening with a tall stride of confidence. He hardly took the slightest note of his pawn and former confidante Marta Repninka. In truth, for the last three days she had trembled at the very sight of him, and clung to the shadows of the office in hopes that he would not detect the look of terror in her eyes.

She had done the horrible deed. Within her breast pulsated, along with the fierce anger against the two-faced beast, a nearly uncontrollable feeling of dread that he should take one look at her and know everything. If she could just make it through today, she would never have to come back to this place! The American had promised safety. By tomorrow at this time she would—well, she didn't know where she would be. But she wouldn't be *here*!

Marta need not have worried. The mind of the Defense Minister of the Republic of Russia was a thousand miles away, and he walked into his office with a smug grin of satisfaction and then closed the door behind him.

It had been one of those days when, contrary to the usual saying, everything had gone *right*. He could hardly believe it. Events were falling perfectly into his lap.

He had had three interviews today, all of which not only boosted the likelihood of his success but actually impelled circumstances toward the very end he desired by the force of their own momentum. He would have to do little to prod events toward the inevitable outcome. He would simply push the first domino, to borrow that ridiculous analogy from the paranoid Americans, and—the rest would happen!

The very cosmos itself seemed lining itself up with his destiny, as that blow-hard Drexler was always saying. It was all bilge water, of course, though he would never say so to Drexler's face. It was what the affluent Germans and the rest who had nothing to do but gaze at stars and crystals wanted to hear. Desyatovsky knew his own countrymen, and to them the whole thing was hocus-pocus. But he would go along with it if that's what it took.

The earthquake in Azerbaijan—they could not have scripted a more fortuitous prelude! Everything would flow naturally from that. And the recent accident at the Kuybyshev nuclear plant. It wasn't a fiftieth as serious as Chernobyl and actually had little industrial significance. But it had made worldwide headlines, and the people were edgy.

A jittery populace was the perfect backdrop. And with Yeltsin and Shevardnadze and the presidents of three of the largest of the other republics scheduled to visit the reactor site in Russia and travel together down to Kirovabad—it was perfect! The first "Commonwealth crisis," they were calling it. An opportunity to demonstrate unity between the republics. They would all be gone at the most critical time. He had allayed Donetsk's last minute reservations in Budapest. Nearly all the holes of previous concern had been plugged. If two or three of the smaller republics proved obstinate, the momentum of events would pull them along. All he had to do was wait.

Eight phone calls was all it would take.

The union strike had been already set in motion, thanks to his sweet-talking the old woman. By the time anyone knew anything he would have assembled about him a committee that was in touch with leaders of all eight vital groups—intrinsic links to power—in each of the republics. The takeover would be so quick and thorough that there would be no possibility of failure. He would step in, and his committee would take command in all the capitals. No one would even use the dreaded "C" word.

A sudden and shocking state of emergency, he would call it when he went on nationwide television to announce the tragic accident that had claimed the lives of several of the Commonwealth leaders. He had gathered around him leaders in every sphere, "dedicated to preserving the democratic principles of independence set in motion by the beloved former leaders."

He might even use the "C" word, to assure the people that there would be *no* disruption of order, that no *coup* would be possible, and that everything would continue in each republic as before. He would tell them that he had already spoken with the American president and other world leaders, assuring them that everything in the Commonwealth of Independent States was stable, that they need have no fear of unrest, violence, civil strife, or the disruption of democratization and independence.

His mind soared. It was actually going to happen!

He poured himself a glass of vodka and sat down at his desk, reflecting on the events of the day.

He'd met that morning with television giant Valeri Alekdanyov. To use the term "media mogul" about a Russian would have seemed inconceivable just a decade ago. But now Valeri was as close to a Soviet version of his hero, Ted Turner, as could be imagined. He had been Desyatovsky's friend for years, and they had hashed over the plan for months. *Valeri is as thirsty for power as I am,* he thought with a smile. He would give him total control over the media. Alekdanyov would control the news flow both in and out of the Soviet Commonwealth and would put just the right spin on the impact of that flow. In exchange, Alekdanyov would give him what *he* wanted.

Desyatovsky opened the television cabinet in his room and shoved the videotape he had received just two hours earlier into the VCR. In the silence of his own office he watched Valeri's production once again.

Genius, that's what it was. Positive genius! Valeri was every bit the media master he claimed he was—and had an ego to match. There it was, the news broadcast prepared *before* the fact, ready to be played nationwide and "intercepted" by the CNN wires to be shot instantly around the world. There *he* was, Bludayev Desyatovsky, confident, in command, at the helm of the Commonwealth by the request of Yeltsin and other republic presidents during their absence. Granted, the requests were implied and the absences forced. But Alekdanyov had put the package together with such skill that not a speck of his adroit splicing was visible, and not a word of the speeches would be questioned for a moment. Especially with the accompanying interviews from leaders throughout society giving overt support and encouragement to the temporary "consolidation" of power, as it was called. Parliamentary leaders in all the republics had been interviewed, and all sang praises of the new acting president of the Commonwealth, Bludayev Desyatovsky.

He couldn't imagine how Valeri had come up with all those interviews. A good number from people he didn't even know were in on the scheme. Had he patched them together? Were they pure fakery? Could splicing tapes really make something out of nothing? He had asked, but Alekdanyov had only smiled and replied, "My friend, it is not wise to ask too many questions. If I tell you everything, *my* power is gone."

He was a sly one. The point was, in any case, that the tape was so utterly flawless that they would question nothing. Especially when follow-up interviews with influential leaders would confirm everything. Let CNN's Shaw interview them himself, the outcome would be the same—unanimous support for the new president of the Soviet Commonwealth and chairman of the Committee for the Preservation of the Commonwealth.

Desyatovsky laid aside the videotape and inserted a copy of the interview he had taped today, which Alekdanyov would splice in with the other, adding pertinent bits of current news and details when the time came. He watched himself addressing the world, a serious expression on his face, recounting events that had not even happened yet, the change that had been requested, in fact, and set in motion by Boris and Eduard and the other republic presidents.

It was good. Even he had to admit it. If he didn't know better, he would have believed it all himself!

The moment of crisis was nearly upon them. In less than a week the whole world would be watching these two videos as if they had emerged from the events themselves. He had been wise to bring Alekdanyov in so early. The man could take the country whenever he wanted with his media genius.

The second interview had been with General Fydor Shaposhnikov. He had arrived at the General's office about 2:00. He had had a long relationship with the former chairman of the Soviet General Staff and first acting Defense Minister for the Belorussian Republic. The native Kievian, however, had resigned that post in favor of taking up quarters again in the Kremlin, where he had been for six months, acting as liaison and chief military attache between the separate military agencies of the Commonwealth. He had been selected to coordinate military affairs between the fifteen republics and was especially close to subordinate leaders in his native Belorussia, as well as in Uzbekistan and Kazakhstan—all three of whose presidents would be with Yeltsin and the others. Those three republics, along with Russia, represented an overwhelming majority of the population. If Estonia or Turkmenistan or Tadzhikistan with their one or two percent didn't come along, who would care? The four major republics would be enough, and Shaposhnikov would make sure their military leaders fell into step. It was only too bad the Ukraine had withdrawn from the Commonwealth.

Having climbed the ladder slowly during the Gorbachev era, Shaposhnikov was the perfect military ally, thought Desyatovsky with satisfaction. He had never been a hard-liner, so when the change had come after the '91 coup, he was groomed and ready to step in as a moderate, one of what the American Kremlin-watchers called a "new breed" of Soviet leader. No one knew Fydor's secret motives and ambitions like his old friend Bludayev Desyatovsky, and he had been an intrinsic part of the plan almost from the beginning.

Shaposhnikov's preparations were just as effective and widespread as Alekdanyov's. He had every conceivable military scenario and anti-scenario and counter-scenario covered, from generals down to lieutenants—and with the officers leading the way, the conscript soldiers would follow.

Fydor wasn't the only one behind him. He had at least two dozen very high-ranking leaders committed to the cause as well, some frustrated, dissenting old-liners had never gone along with the reforms, and some aggressive new blood—all of whom were willing to put aside Communist-verses-democracy disparities to participate together in a new world order—actually a new *Soviet* order in which they would have power and prestige once again. The plan was genius.

The Defense Minister of Russia mentally ran through the military details once more. Granted, communicating to all the subordinate positions at the precise moment of the coup would be tricky, though vital. Then there was the apportioning of power later—again, not without its potential hazards. And he had to keep the newspapers behind them, though Alekdanyov should be able to insure that. Nothing of this magnitude was without its intricacies—and risks.

There were other key members of his plan—the *inside putsch,* as he called it. There was Günder Haslack of the European Community Bank and chairman of the World Banking Cartel headquartered in The Hague with a center of operations in Geneva. He would swing European financial leaders in their favor. They had Carter McPherson in New York and Hawasaki Nakasone in Tokyo as hands-on liaisons to keep Wall Street and the Nikkei Index from tumultuous swings. Both would participate in "live" interviews, saying that all was calm and no major fluctuations in the markets were anticipated. Business was proceeding normally, they would say, and even seemed buoyed by the news. Those interviews were already in the video editing room. They would be ready within twenty-four hours to be inserted into world news telecasts the moment word came from Desyatovsky.

Valentin Gorbunovyev came into his mind, chairman of the Committee for Democratization and Information—a loosely assembled body linking the fourteen republics in a joint vision of the future. It was designed to keep leaders of the former Soviet provinces in touch with one another. His communiques to the republics had already been prepared as well, ready to set each parliament not merely at ease but to swing them solidly behind the new Kremlin leadership with pledges that the new President Desyatovsky was firmly committed to the continuing independence and autonomy of the provinces. The temporary need to consolidate, it would be explained, was merely a strengthening maneuver to accelerate the democratization process.

Desyatovsky was, in fact, the documents said, planning a visit to each of the republics to reassure them of his support. First he would focus his attentions on Russia, the Ukraine, Uzbekistan, and Kazakhstan, whose presidents had so tragically been taken from them. He would speak personally at the funerals, of course, and preside over the smooth transition of leadership. What was *not* said was that he had already hand-selected their successors.

Throughout the days of crisis, every assurance would be made—in speeches, on television, through the print media, in meetings with foreign leaders—that Desyatovsky was progressive and would speed the move toward independence, Westernization, and a market economy. They had actually spoken with Vadim Petrikov, president of Moldavia, Anatoli Dzasokhov, president of Belorussia, and Yevgeny Baramertnykh, president of Kirghizia. It was risky bringing so many high level leaders into the plan. But without risk, there could be no high rewards. And all three, his informants had told him, were disgruntled about the course of events over the last two years. True, their constituencies were small. But with four republic presidents dead and three more lending their eager support, he would not fear dissension from the others. The miracle would be if none of them caused a leak.

Union leader Marktov Bobrikov would have all he needed for explosive unrest once the sabotage at the factory in Kiev led to a widespread worker walkout. Tensions were already so high after recent food shortages that Bobrikov assured him that within thirty-six hours, the entire labor force in the Ukraine would be at a standstill. The Defense Minister's stepping in would, under the circumstances of that republic's suddenly incapacitated leadership, be absolutely justified. Which reminded him, he still had to take care of the woman and her brother. He should never have used anyone so close. It was a sloppy mistake—but containable.

He had just left his third meeting a short while ago, with Commonwealth Minister of Transportation Nursultan Khasbulacheck and Euro-Asian industrialist Max Harmin. Their three-way summit had not been secretive, for distribution of goods and foodstuffs had been one of their most severe problems for decades. Harmin's commitment to bring American, French, and Japanese technology and know-how to bear on the problem and to assist in the implementation of the sweeping reforms that were necessary—the discussion had been well documented. No one had a hint, however, of the larger magnitude of plans the three had made once the doors closed behind them.

He ran down the list of principal players, recalling the years of preparation, the moles and circumstances set in place long before, and then the waiting for events to line up, watching the rise and fall of men like Gorbachev, watching—waiting—knitting together the fabric of the master plan from the grass roots to the mountaintops.

He would make Russia great again, he thought with satisfaction, leaning his head back and emptying the last of the clear liquid from the glass. He would keep his people from starving. He would give them hope and purpose. The masses would love him for it!

He walked to the file cabinet across the room. He pulled the key from his pocket, inserted one into the top drawer of the oak cabinet, and slid out the deep drawer to its full extension, reaching without concentration about two-thirds of the way back where the locked cardboard packet of secret files was kept.

His hand fell only upon the top of standard manila folders.

Suddenly a cold dread swept over the huge man, and his face went pale.

The file was gone!

63

Frantically, with sweat already beading on his clammy white forehead, Desyatovsky flew through the files again, fingers trembling.

It was impossible—but the thing was gone!

With the cabinet drawer still hanging open and a few files strewn on the floor from his panicked search, Desyatovsky spun around and ran to the door, striding in horror into his outer office, struggling desperately to conceal the ghastly sickness that was sweeping over him.

A quick glance revealed the entire staff gone for the evening, except his own faithful secretary. A hasty questioning assured him that she knew nothing. She had been with him too long and was not nearly clever enough to lie her way out of something of this magnitude.

Ignoring her questions of alarm over his anxiety, he retreated to his office, closing the door behind him. Breathing heavily and feeling the thick shirt getting wet under his arms, he sat down heavily at his desk, staring straight ahead in stupified silence.

How was this possible? How could anyone have infiltrated his office?

And—what to do now!

With the file missing, suddenly everything changed! If the plan hadn't been unraveled by now, it would be soon. It all depended on who had found the file—and how astute he or she was to understand what he had stumbled into.

If they didn't act with lightning speed and decisive force, all the years of planning would be down the sink—and *he* would be chipping salt out of some cave in Siberia! Democracy hadn't changed everything.

He paced around his desk, as if movement were the only escape from the terrible feeling of the walls closing in around him.

How could it have happened? he asked himself again.

But that question didn't matter anymore! Who cared *how* it had been pulled off? Someone had penetrated the inner sanctum of his private files. It was too late to change that.

The question that mattered now was *who.*

Again he sat down at his desk, fiddling with his tie and loosening the top button of his nearly drenched shirt.

Who would have the know-how—the expertise—the daring? Who would stand to gain from such a—

Suddenly his large palm slammed down onto the wood desk with a violent force of anger and instant realization.

"Of course!" he exclaimed. "How could I have been such a fool?"

It was clear. Why else had the misbegot been following him? He should have put more men on him immediately! Only the KGB could have got in and out so cleanly!

The blundering fools almost had him four nights ago! How could they have possibly lost his trail?

There was only one thing to do. The former agent *had* to be found and the file recovered. Whatever it took—whoever got in the way!

He picked up the phone, his shaking but purposeful fingers attacking the dial with venom.

"Bolotnikov," he said after a moment, "it is time you became involved in this thing at a more personal level. Whatever you have attempted thus far has not been enough. A serious compromise has occurred. A file crucial to the plan has been stolen. Galanov must be found and silenced—immediately!"

The silence that followed lasted only three or four seconds.

"Of course it's him!" exploded the Defense Minister.

Bolotnikov again spoke.

"That may be," said Desyatovsky, calming. "But best people or not, they haven't done the job. He's got to be put away, and I mean immediately. You're the only one I can trust at the moment, and the job must be done without delay."

He listened at the receiver to several more questions.

". . . good, that sounds like the lead to follow—good! Yes, personally . . . Look, do I have to spell it out for you, Leonid? This is it, the final gambit—checkmate! Silence him, snuff him out, put a slug through his head! If you want to move up in the new regime as we talked about, get that file."

He hung up with vexation and annoyance, then sat back in his chair. Bolotnikov was a frightening man. If he didn't have a complete dossier on him, Desyatovsky would have worried that *he'd* take over. But he was the only kind of man to have on this assignment—ruthless and without scruples.

He had to make one more call. He dreaded it. This one would be much more difficult.

64

August 16, 5:24 P.M.
Berlin

Klaus Drexler put down the briefing paper on the aid package and walked with slow but purposeful steps toward the window of his office, then drew in a deep breath and slowly exhaled.

The situation had nearly reached critical mass, he thought. Action would be required soon—very soon. As the paper delivered to him just hours ago by special courier from the Chancellor's office made clear, Kolter was making his move. He was going ahead with his bold strategem that had begun when he had called the Bundestag back to town to act without delay. Now he had requested them to vote immediately on the package.

But Drexler was ready. He had been lining up the necessary factors for a long time now, including Gerhardt Woeniger's support. He would take the fight to the floor, would use the opportunity to knock Kolter off his high horse with a vote of no confidence, and step into the leadership void himself.

At last the moment had arrived!

The aid package would be easy to defeat on its own merits, reflected Drexler. Germany had already provided far more than it could reasonably afford in credits to the former Soviet Union. On top of DM250 billion spent on former East Germany's reconstruction, the massive aid package proposed by Kolter would bankrupt Berlin's treasury. And it would only prop up a grossly inefficient and scattered and confused Soviet industry that hadn't a clue as to how a free market economy really worked. Money through a sieve is all it would be, throwing millions at the C.I.S. as an expensive reward for finally admitting that Communism couldn't work.

Let the Americans give away their dollars to revamp Soviet industry, to establish free market reforms, to establish a Commonwealth stock exchange, and to bring foreign industry and investment into the Soviet republics. They were dragging their feet, but they would do it—as long as Germany didn't step in and do it for them! Germany had to reserve her own efforts so that—once the Soviet Commonwealth and the other Eastern Bloc countries were humming along smoothly to the tune of profitable capitalism—she would be powerfully poised to guide the new Eastern alliance into the twenty-first century.

The time was right, the forces aligned—he *would* win the battle, and within a week or two, *he* would be the new Chancellor of Germany!

Truly the karma of a foreordained role in global affairs was his! All that remained were a few final pieces. The alliance with the Soviet Commonwealth was the hinge, as was making sure the industrial/military syndicate in both countries was cemented together.

Kolter was strong, yes. But he had been in power more than a decade now, and was vulnerable for that reason alone, if for no other. It was the Thatcher syndrome. No matter how great a politician's achievements, there was a limit to how long he could ride the favorable crest of approval.

That limit had been reached! And he, Klaus Drexler, was prepared to step forward.

In his eye burned the deep fire of self-appointed destiny, a futuristic vision, far-reaching and cunning. Almost since the moment Mikhail Gorbachev had succeeded Chernenko and began making noises of *glasnost* and *perestroika* seven or eight years ago, Klaus Drexler, then barely into his second term in the Bundestag, had seen the handwriting on the wall. He had begun even then garnering support among businessmen and in the intellectual community, making himself agreeable to his fellow politicians, and most important, taking frequent trips to the Soviet Union to spy out the land, as it were, assessing strengths and weaknesses, keeping an eye peeled for the next generation of up-and-coming Soviet leaders. He had known even back then that Boris Yeltsin would be a force to be reckoned with. But he did not suit Drexler's purposes—too independent, too forceful, too much bluster and not enough craft. Both Yeltsin and Gorbachev were skilled politicians, but without the vision to truly affect the future. Neither could hope to lead with him into the twenty-first century.

So he had continued his search, eventually in the late 80s being drawn into relationship with the crafty Desyatovsky, discovering many mutual unspoken and beneficial goals. They had learned a great deal from the Moscow Eight—what mistakes to avoid, and the necessity for full and instantaneous coordination of *all* elements.

All the while, Drexler was fashioning his own image and reputation to dovetail into his perception of the German leader of the future—a renaissance man for a new era, subtly capitalizing on past dreams and future hopes. He was foremost among a new generation of astute and savvy, highly popular German politicians, with appeal to those who had conveniently forgotten (or never known firsthand) the events of the '30s and '40s. Packaging his speeches in New Age rhetoric, his dedication to Germany's rise again was viewed mostly in economic terms. In Drexler's vision, the power of the future was neither information nor industry, as many claimed, but simple money. Technology, business, industrial modernization and competitiveness, productivity, communications—it all began with cash reserves in the world's banks. The country with the most solid currency, the highest asset-to-liability ratio, and the lowest national debt, would lead others into the future. In all these respects, to Klaus Drexler Germany stood at the forefront of the nations of the world.

The moment George Bush began talking about a new world order, Drexler had seen visionary implications far beyond what anyone else in the West could possibly see. He had seen the economic possibilities east of ten degrees longitude, and the sight had dazzled him with its brilliance. He was content to let Bush and Gorbachev and Kolter and Yeltsin and Santierre and Major bask in the limelight for now. They had moved everything in just the right direction. But now the new era had come, and his cue to step onto center stage was at hand!

He was interrupted from his reverie by the ringing of his phone behind him.

65

"Drexler," said the voice on the other end, "Desyatovsky. Is the line secure?"

"Of course, this line is for our ears only."

"Good, because what I have to say is—"

Desyatovsky faltered.

"What is it?"

"The jig is up," he finally managed.

"What?"

"My entire file on the coup and the alliance has been stolen."

"Why, you idiot!" exclaimed Drexler. "How could you let such a thing happen?"

"It happened," rejoined Desyatovsky testily, not appreciative of Drexler's condescension. "How he broke in I don't know, but the file will be retrieved."

"You know who stole it?"

"A former KGB agent. We're onto him."

"How can you be sure?"

"We are taking precautions to plug other possible security holes as well."

"My man Claymore is in Moscow. I will send him to assist in cleaning this thing up."

"I have my own people," replied Desyatovsky. "We need no help. We will handle it."

"The way you let the file be stolen out from under your nose! I want Claymore there. If security problems exist, he will see to them quickly and efficiently."

"I resent your implication!" shot back Desyatovsky.

"If you have objections, then I will put you at the top of Claymore's list while he's in Moscow. I *will* have him contact you. Do you understand?"

Gradually the two would-be world leaders calmed down.

"You know what this means," said Desyatovsky finally.

"We must act without delay."

"I will take steps the minute we are off the phone."

"Steps—which are?"

"The first domino. I will make my phone calls. The union strike will be instigated. All is in place to trigger the worker revolt. Then everything else will begin to happen."

"Are Yeltsin and the republic presidents still meeting at the earthquake and reactor sites?"

"This weekend. By the middle of next week, I will control the Soviet Commonwealth. Just make sure you are ready to move on *your* end."

"Don't worry, my Siberian friend. The German will make sure everything goes as planned, *without* anyone breaking into my office."

Desyatovsky breathed a deep sigh of relief to have the phone call over. Still sweating, he poured himself another vodka.

In Berlin, a cool, confident, and eager Klaus Drexler stood still for a moment behind his desk. His calculating mind spun through the upcoming scenario for the hundredth time, pausing only long enough to think what a fool the big Russian bear was.

If only I could do this without the rest of them, he thought. Alas, given the scope of his dream, he couldn't do it without help.

It was too bad they couldn't all be as competent as Germans!

66

August 16, 8:13 P.M.
Moscow

If there was a uniquely Russian look and physique, Leonid Bolotnikov carried it. Large, calculating, and cunning, he was committed to one cause and only one—his own.

As former head of the KGB, he now had to walk a treacherous tightrope between the past and the future. He had to fit in with the new "system" and pretend to go along, without compromising his long-range, personal agenda. So far he had been reasonably successful. No one knew what he *really* thought of Gorbachev and

293

Yeltsin and all the other reformers. His time would come.

But times were about to change. That is why he had committed himself to Desyatovsky's plan. Bludayev Desyatovsky was a reasonably competent bureaucrat, and he had vision. Bolotnikov had to give him that much. Vision *and* contacts. Desyatovsky had the position and contacts and prestige to pull this thing off. If he didn't and the whole thing went down the toilet—well, Bolotnikov was a survivor and had been around long enough to know how to cover his tracks pretty well. He'd do his part, but if the coup unraveled, he'd land on his feet one way or another—and continue to move up. For Leonid Bolotnikov was a man with his own vision. Some would call it a lust. That lust was for nothing short of power. And no one who knew him would make the mistake of thinking he had yet reached the apex of his political career.

He walked down the deserted street, his footsteps echoing sharply against the vacant buildings. *What a sleazy section of town,* he thought. But if his lead proved correct it was the perfect place for a hideout. It's what *he* would have done under the circumstances. He had taught his subordinate well. Now here he was trying to root out the very man he had handpicked—and with whom he had rounded up all kinds of creeps back in the old days. How things changed. Now the shoe was suddenly on the other foot. The fortunes of peace as well as war. Why couldn't Galanov see that the future lay with them instead of trying to undermine . . .

His thoughts trailed away indistinctly. It wasn't as if Galanov had had much choice. After all Bolotnikov himself had turned him in to boost his own standing with the new powers of the Commonwealth. He hadn't let Desyatovsky in on that tidbit of information but instead had played the innocent bystander. That was the only way to move up in this part of the world, making sure you always knew more than your colleagues—friends and foes alike!—gave you credit for.

Bolotnikov grinned. Actually, if he was in Galanov's shoes, stealing the file would be exactly what he'd have done too. Yes, his protege was in some ways still his protege. He was almost proud of him.

Of course that changed nothing, he thought, as he entered the run-down building of the address he'd scribbled on a piece of paper. Proud of him or not, he still had to kill him.

Down the hall he walked, now and then hearing a squeal of a rat in some distant part of the building. He used the flashlight he carried only intermittently, in case anyone was about. But he doubted that he needed to worry, the place seemed deserted. A slight breeze came through the dark corridor from the broken windows at each end. Pieces of broken plaster lay about the floor, fallen from the ceiling who could tell how many months ago. The place probably hadn't been cleaned in five years!

Around a corner, then up two flights of stairs, peering in the darkness for labels on the doors. It was not quite as filthy here, and a few signs of life were apparent. *A few tenants must still live in this flea trap,* he thought.

When he reached the third floor, he stopped, then began to tiptoe more quietly. Galanov's secret room should be right down this corridor, if his snitch had told him the truth. As hard as he'd pummeled him, he had little reason to doubt it.

Quite a nice touch, he thought, still half-congratulating the man he was on his way to kill. Two completely separate living quarters, only a mile from each other. *How ingenious of you, Andrassy! And you even kept it from me, your boss.*

Again Bolotnikov smiled, then reached into his pocket and pulled out his high-tech automatic pistol.

As he tiptoed, gun drawn, his face told the entire story of his character. The eyes squinting against the darkness would have been black even in broad daylight, reflecting the color of his heart. The broad chest and muscular biceps had not been won with niceties.

Through his mind revolved the incident eight years ago when he and Galanov had let that no good Rostovchev slip through their fingers. That couldn't help reminding him of all the time he'd spent trying to get his hands on the spiritual leader.

He arrived at the door, eyes wide, flashlight off, gun ready.

He stopped. Then with a swift punishing blow, the door shattered under his foot. The sound exploded down the dimly lit hallway, but even as it crashed to the floor, Bolotnikov charged inside.

As the sound died away, he looked around at the room. Why it was nothing but a storage room! Boxes and crates and cleaning supplies.

Slowly he stepped over boxes, including the mess he had made of the door which lay in four pieces splintered on the floor. He made his way to the far darkened end. A curtain hung down. He pulled it aside with his left hand, gun posied again, and peered behind it.

All was black. Still holding the gun in his right hand, with his left he flipped on his flashlight. The next instant it was off again, but he had had long enough to see that it was empty. He flipped on the light again, located the string hanging down from a single bulb on the ceiling. He reached up, and pulled on the light.

He glanced around, taking in the small room, which was just as Galanov had left it. Slowly he put his gun away. The look, the feel, even the smell said that this room had been deserted for at least twenty-four or thirty-six hours.

This was Galanov all right. He recognized some of the clothes, the style, the—he even thought he could faintly smell his old colleague. And now it was just the two of them, he in person, the ghostly shell of Galanov's departed spirit, engaged in a battle for supremacy. He *would* find something here that would betray his old protege and the one man who stood between him and the next rung on the ladder. He *must* find something that would deliver Galanov into his hands.

He searched for twenty minutes, turning over every corner, every shred of clothing, every scrap of paper.

At last his eyes fell upon what looked like a small pamphlet, partially obscured by a shirt on top of it. Why hadn't he noticed it before? He grabbed it up with interest. It was the only thing written he had found in the whole place and thus potentially a clue.

It was not large enough for a book, had paper covers and only twenty or thirty pages in length. Hurriedly he flipped through it. The script was noticeably German. He tried to make something of it, but his German was too scanty. It appeared to be some kind of religious tract or pamphlet. Across the top of the title page were the words, *Das Evangelium mach Narkus.*

"Why German?" mused Bolotnikov. "And why a religious document?"

Flipping through it somewhat idly, suddenly Bolotnikov's eyes fell upon several lines that had been underlined. His mind snapped back to attention. He squinted in the thin light, bringing the pamphlet closer to his eyes, trying to make something of the words that came just shortly after the large 6 to the side of the text. *"Aber*

296

Jesus sagte zu ihnen: 'Ein Prophet wird uberall geachtet, nur nicht in seiner Heimat, bei seinen Verwandten und in seiner Familie.' "

What was it all about? puzzled Bolotnikov. What was so important here that it had been underlined?

He looked at the passage again.

Suddenly the word jumped at him off the page. That was a word whose German meaning he understood well enough! *Prophet!*

His mind flashed back to that day he had been thinking of as he walked down the hallway—that day so long ago when he had finally got the drop on Rostovchev, only to see him slip through his fingers. That's what they had called him—*Der Prophet!*

A *German* appellation!

Galanov had been sent after Rostovchev too, all the way to the outskirts of Berlin, and likewise had failed. Was this booklet some bizarre reminder he kept for himself all this time of his failure?

No. Bolotnikov doubted that. He had a feeling—a hunch—a gut instinct that something here was bigger than he'd imagined. Something . . .

Hastily he grabbed up the booklet again. There were a few other underlined passages too. He saw them now as he hurriedly scanned through the pages. Here was one that seemed to be marked with the numbers 8:34, whatever that meant: *". . . Dann rief Jesus die ganze Menschenmenge hinzu und sagte: 'Wer mit mir kommen will, der darf nicht mehr an sich selbst denken. Er muss sein Kreuz auf sich nehmen und mir auf meinem Weg folgen. Denn wer sein Leben retten will, wird er verlieren. Aber wer sein Leben für mich und für das Evangelium verliert, wird es retten.' "*

He read the words over and over, trying to make sense of them from the little German he knew.

". . . anyone . . . come after me . . . deny . . . follow . . . lose life . . . for me . . ."

He stopped, thinking again.

Suddenly his brain was seared with a lightning bolt of realization!

Of course! The fool had gone off the deep end—he had become one of them! The persecutor had been seduced by his prey! The fool Galanov had become a Christian!

Bolotnikov threw his head back and roared with laughter. The idiocy of it was ironic—beautiful. The stress of finding himself out in the cold had fried the idiot's brain! "Ha, ha, ha!" he laughed. It was altogether too comical.

All at once he stopped. His head jerked down, glancing at the pamphlet again. But it could not tell him the answer to the question which had suddenly slammed into his brain. Suddenly he remembered why he had come, that Galanov had the files.

His job was to find him. And suddenly he knew how. It all had to do with that ridiculous Rostovchev and his band of Christians scattered throughout Europe.

That was it! Galanov was trying to escape through what they had called *Das Christliche Netzwerk*!

The next instant the KGB chief stormed out of the small room as loudly as he had come, his hard boots crashing through the debris he had made upon his entry.

Those people worked fast. There wasn't a moment to lose!

67

August 16, 9:34 P.M.
Moscow

Bolotnikov blew into his own office with nearly as much fury as he had Galanov's flat an hour earlier. He ran to his cabinet, threw it open, pulled out the second sliding drawer nearly crashing it to the floor, and flipped back through the old "Closed" files.

Here it is, he thought. Everything he'd accumulated through the years on the Christian network, including the files of his predecessor. Twenty-five years of names, places, contacts, spies, moles—all the way back to the days of Nikiforov and Kourdakov, the executions at the Elizovo baptism ceremony, and Sergei's defection in 1971. It was all here!

How much in the file was still valid, he had no way of knowing. And in spite of all their research and informants and KGB efforts, they never had got all the way to the bottom of the vast interconnecting matrix of Christians, especially the escape network. They knew some of the connections, but certainly not all of them, a few of the hand-off points, but not nearly enough to form a continuous thread of how the people worked and what they did. But he'd kept a few of his people working on it secretly even after Gorbachev eased religious restrictions—just in case. They had filled in a few more of the gaps, gathered a few more names.

The border crossings were clearly the most crucial points, and upon those he had had his people concentrate their efforts in the last few years. Galanov was probably making for the West, and the most direct route would be through Poland to Germany. But there were dozens of other directions he could go—north through Scandinavia, south—Turkey, the Mediterranean, even perhaps into the Middle East—who could tell what he was going to do with those documents! But if he was indeed in the hands of the Christians, their main escape network had always been due west.

If he was wrong—well, he couldn't cover the whole world! That was a chance he had to take. He began digging through the old records.

He turned to the file marked "Polish Border Crossings." He hoped Galanov was still in Russia. That was the one good thing about his being in the hands of the Christians. Though they wasted no time, they tended to be overly careful and took many precautions. He might be able to intercept them this side of the border!

He grabbed a map of the northwest and spread it out on the table before him. There were three crossings where they were likely to make their break. His finger traced over the border on his map southward from Kaliningrad to L'vov. The Christians, according to the files—at least KGB sources in the past thought as much—used the borders at Brest and Przemysl, but also had ways past the border where the roads had been closed at Grodno and south of Kaunas. The road was open at Brest. He discounted the northernmost and southernmost spots. Galanov would be urging speed and therefore would take the most direct route possible.

Bolotnikov would therefore concentrate on the two crossing points, fortunately near one another, at Grodno and Brest. Meanwhile, he would take steps to shut the entire border down.

He grabbed his telephone and called the Defense Minister.

68

Marta Repninka had no intention of returning to the office. She only wanted to get as far away from Moscow as she could.

When the man Davidson had told her where to go and what to do, she had packed and was ready for the train to Kiev an hour later. She had waited in her place all the rest of the day, hiding, fearful, counting every minute until time to go.

He was supposed to be outside for her at 10:00 and would take her to the station for the overnight ride south to Kiev. An associate of his would meet her, he said, and take her to her brother's. She would be reunited with her family and safely out of Desyatovsky's reach by noon the next day.

Finally she could stand the waiting no longer. At quarter till ten, Marta took one final wistful look around her small apartment, then turned off the lights and headed down the flight of stairs with her two bags. She would wait the last minutes on the street, just in case the American happened to be early. She didn't want to miss him.

The man his associates knew only as Claymore didn't like working for two people at once. Drexler had always been good to him, though annoyingly uppity. But this Russian fellow Drexler had instructed him to get in touch with—he wasn't so sure about him.

He had warned Drexler on the phone that he was stretching their previously agreeable business relationship to the limit on this. The German had promised to make it all worth his while when it was over. And after all, Claymore reflected, that was supposed to be the name of the game. Anyway, if something went wrong, he could always dust off both the German and the Russian. No extra charge.

The big Russian had said to do it on the street. "There can be no ties to my office, not even to her apartment. Make it look like the work of street violence, imported from the United States. A by-product of democracy. I'll make sure it's reported that way to the press."

Politicians were such a peculiar breed, thought Claymore, pouring himself another cup of coffee in the car where he sat. It would be dark soon. So much the better, though he was anxious to have it over with. He'd been sitting here most of the day. Was she never going to leave that apartment?

All at once he saw the lights go out. Perhaps she was just going to bed. But he'd better be ready, just in case.

He set down the coffee cup on the dash, and reached down to retrieve the implement of his wicked trade.

Blue Doc had had growing reservations about his decision all day. Things were not always black and white in this business, and this was one of the murkiest he'd faced.

Not that he doubted Andrassy's motives, or even his ability to get through. But he wasn't used to sitting around and doing nothing, waiting for somebody *else* to do a job he ought to be doing. The only thing he'd had to occupy himself with today was making the final arrangements with his people in Kiev for the woman and her family down there. It was all taken care of, including a place for her to stay for the first month. Now all he had to do was get her safely out of Moscow.

He probably should have put her on an earlier train, he thought, or made arrangements with a special CIA courier. But he didn't want to risk her being seen in broad daylight. If the thing was as serious as he thought, there was no telling what the fellow Desyatovsky might try. The overnight train would be quiet, safe, and he would see her personally on board himself, with a few hundred extra rubles in her pocket. She would be deliriously happy, and it would be the lowest price in history to unravel an international coup.

He rounded the corner three blocks from Marta's run-down apartment building, the headbeams from his car the only light or movement disturbing the silent dusk of the evening. Driving slowly, he saw a car door open suddenly a block ahead of him. Instinctively, he hit the brakes and extinguished the lights. He must not be seen picking her up. The diplomatic plates of his car would be too easily recognizable.

He sat in the middle of the street. It was a tall, thin man who emerged from the driver's side of the car. Another tenant, Doc thought. He would wait until he was safely inside whatever building he lived in. In fact, there was Marta in the distance, standing alone with her two suitcases waiting for him.

Wait, what was in the fellow's hands?

It couldn't—he had been watching too many old spy pictures—these were times—no one—not now!

No—it *was* a rifle!

All the years of training and experience in his brain suddenly scrambled into disarrayed confusion. By instinct his right foot sought the accelerator to send the car screaming forward, even as his right hand flew inside his coat after his gun. But the recent conditioning of his brain stopped him. Low profile—everything is low profile these days—so had said every order and communique for the past two years. *No incidents—don't provoke so much as a sneeze—let this democratic revolution work itself out without our help.* Hadn't a briefing from Langley said those very words less than four months ago?

But counter-democracy was in the air, threatening everything. Wasn't it his business to protect American interests? Marta had stood up for democracy. Didn't she deserve his help and protection?

The conflicting thoughts battling for supremacy bounced through his mind in less than two seconds. But that was all the hesitation it took for the unknown enemy to lock onto his prey.

Even as Blue Doc finally loosened his foot and jammed it to the floor, his eyes beheld with sickening horror the man stooping, laying the deadly weapon across the top of his car, and taking aim. Doc's car had not lurched more than twenty feet toward him before the explosive crack of a single shot shattered the night air, drowning out the squeal of his tires. As if in slow motion, Doc saw the poor woman's body slump to the pavement in a red pool of her own blood.

As used to all this as he had once been, in the recent years of the thaw Blue Doc's humanity had slowly begun to re-emerge, and with awful revulsion he gagged at the sight. Accelerating, his hand drew out the pistol he had not used for three or four years. He would use it now! He would kill the evil scum who had shot that innocent woman!

The blast of another shot brought him to his senses, shattering the plate glass of his windshield.

Doc slammed on the brakes. His car careened sideways and to a stop. More rifle fire crashed through the metal sides of his car. In a second Doc was outside, kneeling on the street behind the protection of the open door.

Blindly he reached his hand above the hood and returned several shots in the direction of the murderer. He would have no chance against an automatic rifle unless one of his shots happened to get lucky.

Again, rifle fire exploded. Inches away from his ear, the rearview mirror exploded, the glass shattering against him. Doc fell to the ground, protecting his face. When the echo had again faded, he rose to one knee, then vainly tried to return the fire again.

It was useless. The only sound to meet his ears in return was the screeching of tires receding in the distance.

69

August 16, 19:39 P.M.
Moscow

It was late. He should be in bed by now.

But these were perilous times. He had spent many entire nights in this office of late. There would probably not be much sleep tonight. Fear and anxiety would no doubt keep him on edge until those files were back in his own hands.

The ringing of his phone startled him. He grabbed at it hastily.

"I was assured there would be no unexpected hitches," said a voice he didn't recognize at first.

"What do you mean?" asked Desyatovsky.

"Someone else was there," said the man.

303

"Where?"

"At the woman's apartment, you idiot!" snapped the man. Now he knew him—it was the fool Drexler had insisted on using.

"And?"

"I got out of there, but I don't like being seen. It's a messy complication."

"A witness?"

"No. I wasn't seen."

"The woman?"

"The job is done. You need not worry about her."

"And the other person—what makes you think—"

"Because I was fired at, that's why!" interrupted Claymore.

Desyatovsky thought for a moment. Who else could have stumbled into the middle of this scenario?

"Were you followed?" he asked after a moment.

"What kind of fool do you take me for? Of course I wasn't followed!"

"Then how could—"

"How it happened is your business to figure out!" snapped the angry hit man.

"Did you get a look at him?"

"I was too busy dodging his bullets to look at him!"

"The car?"

"Russian make—different license."

"Polish, German?"

"No. I can't be sure. He was racing toward me before I fired at him. But I think they were embassy plates."

"Whose?"

"Can't be positive—probably American."

"Hmm," mumbled Desyatovsky, his mind spinning rapidly. "All right—lay low. I'll take care of it."

"You had better, my Russian friend—for your *own* sake!"

70

August 16, 11:13 P.M.
Moscow

When the Defense Minister's phone rang again a short while later, he was still deep in thought. He was glad, however, for at least the hint of positive news.

"I think we've got him," said Bolotnikov. "Can you do what is required to close down the Polish border?"

"All of it?"

"Of course!"

Desyatovsky thought for a moment. "That will involve the Lithuanians, Belorussians, and Ukrainians and could be somewhat ticklish before we make our move."

Bolotnikov swore. Just three years ago, as KGB chief he could have shut *every* border down within an hour. Now they were at the mercy of a handful of ridiculous independent republics! Fortunately, that was soon to change.

"At least we could call for enforced checkpoints," he suggested.

Desyatovsky hesitated. Every move they made could imperil the coup.

"Here's what we'll do," he said after a moment. "I'll shut the Russian border down in the north. And General Shaposhnikov will shut down the Polish border in the south. The Lithuanian border isn't long. We'll have to hope for the best. I don't want to stir up the Lithuanians. The problem is going to be the Belorussian border. That's his most direct route. You say there are two most likely spots?"

"Grodno and Brest," replied Bolotnikov.

"Both in Belorussia—hmm—no, we just can't take the chance of stirring something up there."

"Can you put it in my hands?" asked Bolotnikov.

"Do you still have people?"

"If you put it in my hands, I will do what needs to be done."

Desyatovsky hesitated only a moment. He had come too far to turn back now. "If you fail," he said seriously, "you must understand, I would disavow any knowledge of your actions."

"I understand," replied the former KGB chief.

"Then we are clear on the fact that you are not acting under my direct orders?"

"Clear."

"Then do what you have to do. The Belorussian border is in your hands."

"I will intercept the traitor and have the file back in your hands before the Belorussians have any idea I have been there."

A slight pause followed.

"We have one other—uh, problem," said Desyatovsky.

"I'm listening," replied Bolotnikov.

"It appears the CIA may somehow have stumbled into this thing."

"Where—here in town?"

"Yes."

"I know them all. Do you want me—"

"No," interrupted Desyatovsky, thinking through the myriad of options even as he spoke. "I'll take care of it. We *must* get that file! You get on to the border and after Galanov."

Bolotnikov hung up the phone. He thought a minute. Then he picked it up again.

"Order my chopper!" he barked.

Then gathering up the files with everything they had in the Minsk, Kiev, L'vov areas, and everything they had on the Christians of eastern Poland, he stormed from the room, grabbing coat, hat, and gun.

He needed nothing else. This was not a complicated mission. The tiny slug in his weapon was all he *really* needed.

71

Dan Davidson, alias "Blue Doc," had received his nickname through a frightening escape on the Yugoslavian coast of the Adriatic. It had been his first run-in with the KGB, and the method by which he'd managed to escape with his life had labeled him with his sobriquet for the rest of his undercover career.

He chuckled morosely at the thought. That's when there were countries called Yugoslavia and the Soviet Union!

He'd been driving all night, trying to make some sense out of what had happened hours ago, trying to figure out whether to cut his conscience some slack over the woman's death or whether to chastise himself for letting it happen. Thus far he had not arrived at a solid conclusion.

He'd been lucky last night, just like he had been on the Adriatic. But you never knew if next time fate would fall with you or against you. They said times had eased. It probably was true, in spite of the incident outside the woman's apartment. But now more than ever, he had no reason to trust the KGB a hair's breadth.

Thoughts of the old Communist security agency sent his mind once more in the direction of his new ally.

Galanov was different. He didn't know why exactly, but he believed him, and certainly the files didn't lie. Something had to be done and his own sources told him Galanov had been on the "new KGB's" hit list. So that, if nothing else, that put them on the same side. But the "new KGB" was technically the U.S.'s friend, which would make their enemy, the old-style Galanov, still his adversary.

Good grief! He couldn't keep straight all the alliances in this ridiculous changing world order! Sometimes he wished they could just go back to the good guys and bad guys of the Cold War. At least you knew where you stood.

In any event, he didn't trust the new people any more than he had the old. And whether Galanov was on the level hardly mattered. They both had the files in their hands. If Galanov in fact did get through and blew the whistle on the coup, fine. But he wasn't going to wait around to find out. He probably should have been on the phone to the president personally within minutes of seeing what was in those papers. It had gnawed at him all day yesterday, and had kept him awake the whole night. It had cost an innocent woman her life, the woman to whom they owed everything!

What to make of all that religious stuff Galanov had said to him, Blue Doc hadn't an idea. It didn't speak particularly well for Galanov's mental and emotional state. Which was one more reason, besides last night's incident, that now four days after they'd parted, Davidson had decided he couldn't sit on what he'd uncovered any longer. His life could be in danger now, as well as Galanov's.

True, the whistle ought to be blown from inside the Soviet Commonwealth rather than by the U.S. for maximum believability. But he realized that was not his decision to make. This was too big, potentially too explosive for him to make such a decision alone. Let the Joint Chiefs and the president and the National Security Council decide whether to swoop down in high-profile fashion or wait and let Galanov play out his hand.

He continued driving through the early morning Moscow streets toward the embassy, the stolen files beside him on the seat. He had been chastising himself for not making copies instantly and replacing the files in Desyatovsky's office. But there hadn't been time, and it would have only complicated everything with Yaschak and the woman. To try to replace them now was out of the question. He only hoped it wasn't too late, that he hadn't yet discovered them missing. He would FAX them to Washington, then follow it up with an immediate phone call.

Six blocks from the embassy, suddenly the blare of a police siren sounded behind him. He pulled over. Glancing in his rear-view mirror, he saw the policeman remain where he was at the wheel. From the other side of the automobile, a man got out and approached him. The long trenchcoat, hat, and facial expression left no doubt—he was KGB. Blue Doc had been around long enough to spot them in an instant, whether of the new *or* the old regime.

"Mr. Davidson," said the man in attempted English. "Would you please come with me?"

"I'm sorry," replied Doc, thinking that they just didn't make spies like they used to, "I'm afraid I won't be able to. I'm attached to the American embassy. I have my diplomatic papers right here." He started to reach inside his coat, but the man reached through the car window and grabbed his arm.

"Please, Mr. Davidson," he said, sternly this time. "My boss would like to see you—now."

"I don't want to see your boss."

"I'm afraid I really must insist." With the words, the barrel of a gun through his jacket exposed itself, and then protruded into his side.

"Well, I suppose I could spare *some* time," rejoined Blue Doc, trying to be humorous. "By the way, do you still answer to my old friend Bolotnikov, or did he not fare too well in the recent purge?"

"Comrade Bolotnikov has been called out of town suddenly," the man replied stiffly. "I have been ordered to deliver you to the Defense Minister, General Desyatovsky."

Blue Doc climbed out of the car.

"And Mr. Davidson," the agent added, "bring along the files on the seat there beside you."

PART 11

Das Christliche Netzwerk

72

The evening was calm and warm. From the stone fire pit came the smells that only a German-style barbeque could produce, as the smoke went straight up through the metal grating which held two or three dozen round, spicy sausages. No breath of wind disturbed the air.

Scattered about in groups of three to six were some thirty men and women, with probably an additional dozen youngsters scampering about the nearby field. A more classic "German" gathering could not have been imagined—about half the men held bottles of stout beer in their hands, another half fidgeted at the ground with their walking sticks. Most were attired in cotton workshirts above and either short lederhosen or knee breeches below. The women wore white blouses and bright fitted jumpers. Everyone of both sexes was talking and laughing freely, enjoying to the full this opportunity to fellowship in the time-honored tradition of the land.

Their three days with Udo and Grete Bietmann had been rich beyond measure. Jackson had visited Anna again, and now he and Jacob were saying their farewells to their new friends. When Jacob asked what they could do to repay the many kindnesses, Bietmann had replied, "How can you ask such a thing? It is *we* who thank *you* for caring enough to come to us!"

"Please," rejoined Jacob "I insist. It would make me happy to be able to do something."

"As I told you, times have been so severe for these dear people," Bietmann said after a moment's thought. "I know how much they would appreciate a dinner—grilled sausages and franks over an open fire. Even such simple pleasures as we once took for granted many have not been able to enjoy for more than a year."

"Consider it done!" exclaimed Jacob. "What will we need?"

"Meat, rolls, and beer. Greta will make the potato salad."

"Beer!" laughed Jacob. "What about my evangelical sensibilities?" he added with a wink toward Jackson.

"This is Germany," said Jackson. "We mustn't offend our hosts. The taboos here are altogether different."

"I'll adapt," said Jacob. "Just don't broadcast it back at the convention!"

Jacob has thus purchased all the necessary goods, and the plan met with instant approval and enthusiasm from everyone.

"Das Fleisch is gleich fertig!" called out a voice from near the fire, signaling the meat's near readiness. After a hearty prayer of thanksgiving, Greta began filling plates with her legendary *Kartoffelsalat,* as the round spicy pork instantly disappeared from the grill.

"These aren't exactly like hot dogs," commented Jacob after a bite of meat dabbed in the hot, dark mustard.

"Once you've had one of these, no American hot dog is the same," replied Jackson.

"But I still don't quite understand how to eat it," said Jacob. "The rolls aren't shaped right."

"The sausages aren't supposed to go *in* the rolls," Jackson laughed and glanced toward Anna, who was at his side. "The meat stands alone, with the mustard. The hunks of bread are just to cool off your mouth."

"Exactly," she said with a smile.

"We are all indebted to you forever, Jacob Michaels!" called out one man, raising his bottle of beer in cheerful toast.

"We haven't had such a celebration since reunification," added another.

"A toast!" called out Udo. "We must toast our guest."

"Here, here!"

"I shall offer it," said a large farmer by the name of Heiko.

Everyone fell silent. Heiko spoke out clearly in German as Udo translated: "To Jacob Michaels and Jackson Maxwell, unexpected but welcome guests of our fellowship. Our love and our thoughts and our prayers will follow them wherever they go. We wish them the fullness of God's blessings, and may they return speedily to us again!"

A great cheer and applause went around the group.

"Now they will want to hear from you," said Udo to Jacob.

"But surely they are tired of me," objected Jacob. "They have already heard me so much."

"They have toasted you, now you must reply. They will never grow weary of what you have to say to them. You are unlike any of the others who have been here in the past two years. These people sense a difference in you. You have not come with a plan to start your own ministry. You have simply come to share who you are, and to us such simple honesty of motive is like spring water to our parched spirits."

Jacob looked around to all those who were turned in his direction, some finished, some still munching on meat or rolls, while an occasional pop or sizzle came from the few remaining pieces of meat lying unclaimed on the grill.

"I have told you already," he began, "what a special time it had been here with you. I feel the recipient of blessing, which is why words like those of my brother Heiko's ring strange in my ears. This has been an important time for me—a time of growth, of prayer, and of attempting to hear the Lord's voice in and among and from you. All of you, and Kehrigkburg itself, will always hold a special place in my heart. I hope that you will let me know in what ways I might be able to help you in the future. I have seen firsthand the work of living and spreading the gospel that you are carrying out, and I desire to be part of it. I came to Germany—"

He hesitated slightly, seeing Greta coming from the farmhouse. She walked to her husband and whispered something in his ear. The look on his face was serious.

"I came," continued Jacob, "to attend a conference on evangelism, and yet I have learned more among you—both from observing your fellowship and from the things the Lord has been showing me—than in all my years—"

Again he stopped. Greta had turned and was now walking back to the house. Udo strode forward toward Jacob.

"Excuse me, my friend," he said. "Something has come up which requires our immediate attention—and prayer."

"Of course," said Jacob, standing aside.

"My brothers and sisters," said Bietmann speaking in German, "a call of great consequence has just come to the house. My wife is at this moment in touch with our new friends in Moscow that I told you about." Jackson listened carefully to try to understand every word. "Herr Karl Medvedev has called to inform us that our new brother, whom I told you about and who we have been praying for, is now on his way to us."

A noticeable rustling of whispered comments and exclamations swept through his friends.

"Though I have barely recovered from the fatigue since my return a few days ago, he says that our friend's danger is great. I firmly believe God's hand is upon this man, whatever he has been in the past. I must go to him personally—and bring him the rest of the way myself. I want you to see the transforming and miraculous power of God for which our dear Herga gave her life."

"Let someone else go, Udo," urged Heiko. "I am not working and have time—"

"Thank you, my friend," said Bietmann. "However, this is something I believe must fall to me. The Lord has uniquely chosen my family—my wife and myself and our daughter—as the vessels through which He has poured His spirit upon the heart of His former persecutor. It is my destiny also to lay down my life for this man—a destiny whose path I must follow."

73

An hour and a half later, after a time of concentrated prayer in the field around the fire, Jackson and Jacob sat with Udo and Greta Beitmann, listening to one of the most remarkable stories of heartbreak, prayer, and victory they had ever heard.

Jackson turned to Jacob, once Udo had completed the remarkable tale and said, "This may need to be an article one day." He glanced over at Greta, weeping silent tears of fresh pain mingled with the joy of God's goodness to them. "People need to hear about the evangelism of sacrifice."

Jacob sighed with deep thoughtfulness. "Greater love has no man than this," he said, "than he lay down his life for his friends. I was just reading that last night as I finished John's gospel again."

Jackson nodded.

In one accord, the four joined hands and began praying, in mingled German and English, for the safety and future of their newborn brother in Christ who, even at that moment, though they knew not where he was, was being guided by the new life that was in him. Even as they prayed, an extraordinary idea began gradually to steal into Jackson's brain, discounted at first as mere fancy, but then confirmed as something deeper by Udo's next words.

"You know," he said, opening his eyes and glancing toward the two Americans, "something has just occurred to me as we were praying."

Both men waited, with looks of question on their faces.

"You really are interested in what I have been telling you?" he asked.

"Yes, of course—I've never heard anything like it," answered Jacob.

"You want to learn more?"

They nodded.

"Do you truly think you may write what I have told you someday, Jackson?"

"It's hard to say for certain," replied Jackson. "But I *am* a writer, and this is a special story. Yes, I *do* think people would be blessed to hear it."

"And you truly want, as you said earlier, to help us in what God has given us to do?" asked Bietmann, turning again toward Jacob.

"Of course."

"Then why don't the two of you come with me?" said the German finally.

"To Russia!" exclaimed his two guests, almost in unison.

"To the Polish border at least. Medvedev says we should reach the border just about the same time as their people.

Father and son looked at one another in astonishment.

"Wow, that *is* some incredible idea!" said Jacob with a wide-eyed sigh.

Jackson was silent. The thought had already occurred to him as he'd been praying.

"I would love to," Jacob went on. "But with the conference, I just don't see how I could. I'm feeling rather negligent already. I need to get back to Berlin, as reluctant as a part of me is to say it."

"You are right," said Udo. "It was thoughtless of me to put such a question before you when you have prior commitments to honor. You, Jackson," he added, turning in Jackson's direction, "you do not have to speak at the conference. What about you?"

"I am supposed to be covering it, writing about it. That's why I was sent to Berlin, after all." From his tone, it was abundantly clear that he had little enthusiasm remaining for his original assignment.

"This is ten times the story you'd get in Berlin," said Jacob. "If your editor doesn't understand the importance, send him to me. I'll straighten him around!"

Jackson laughed at the thought of Jacob squaring off with McClanahan.

A moment or two of silence followed.

At length Jackson simply nodded his head, as a grin spread across his face. "I think perhaps it's exactly what I'm supposed to do," he said.

"Sehr gut!" exclaimed Bietmann.

"When do we leave?" said Jackson, his excitement mounting.

"If we're going to get there in time," answered the German, "we'll have to leave tonight—at the soonest possible moment."

Jackson's first thought was of Anna. He had hoped to see her once again before they left. Now it would be impossible.

74

August 13-15
Western Belorussia

Andrassy Galanov wasn't accustomed to stopping to pray every time he turned around. Not everyone he'd met did so. But this fellow did.

It had been an education, meeting a new Christian every several hours as he'd been handed from one to the other across northwestern Russia, then into Belorussia, from Moscow to Smolensk to Minsk to Baranovici. He'd traveled in automobiles, in carts, on motorcycles, and in a boat along the Dnieper between Orsa and Mogilov. Most of the connections, however, had been made on foot, in woods and on obscure trails, at some of the most out of the way places imaginable.

There had been prayers and words of spiritual greeting at every juncture, mostly between the men and women of the network. Mostly he'd felt like an observer. With some there had been no conversation beyond absolute essentials. Others had been quite talkative, speaking positively of the changes that had taken place. The silent ones seemed still to live in the fear of the KGB. None, he realized, had any idea who he was.

"Come, my friend," his present guide said, interrupting his reverie, "we are nearly to the river where I will leave you. We must pray that we make it before daylight, otherwise our contact will return home and you will have to spend twelve hours in the woods until evening."

With the words, the slender, talkative man stopped, got to his knees, and prayed similar words to those he had just spoken to Galanov. Then he said, "We must hurry. We still have three kilometers ahead of us."

Galanov was a strong man but already tired. And after they reached the border, he still had to get across Poland. *That should be easier,* he thought. The KGB's access wasn't quite as free there these days from what he understood.

How could he have ever known what was in store for him when

319

he left Moscow with Karl? No wonder they'd never been able to lay hands on the network! Rostovchev had set everything up not only with painstaking brilliance, but even here and there with a stroke of flair and fun, almost daring the KGB to its face.

After hours of furtive hiding, they made one contact in a bakery right next to the police station, and at the very time when several policemen were gathered about. Who but a confident humorist could have dreamed up such a scheme!

He gathered, of course, that every job the network did went differently, that different people and routes and handoff patterns were used, and that no one knew much. Each merely did his own particular assignment, conveyed prior to every job by word of mouth. Sometimes telephones were used but always in code, giving rise to very odd-sounding conversations indeed.

Two hours later, they emerged from a clearing and his guide stopped. The half moon gave enough light for him to see the shimmering of a river in front of them.

"It is still dark and we have arrived," said his guide. "Here is the boat." Tied to a tree was a tiny skiff with a single paddle.

"Get in, then make your way to the middle of river," he said. "The current is not swift but you must paddle steadily. There—" he pointed downstream "—you can see a tall tree standing alone."

Galanov nodded.

"It is one-half kilometer downriver. At that tree you will be met by another brother, who will take you to his home in the town of Mosty, where you will have a few hours' sleep. Godspeed, my friend."

With that, the slender, praying man disappeared into the woods.

Galanov untied the boat. That was the way the Network went. They disappeared with as few words as they appeared. It was not a way to make lasting friends, he thought.

He gave the boat a shove with one foot, then leaped inside, and in a few moments was silently moving slowly downstream, wielding his oar as best he could toward the tree in the distance.

75

August 18, 10:42 A.M.
Moscow

Under most circumstances Blue Doc was a reasonably even-tempered man. But this was not a reasonable circumstance, and he was furious.

He stormed across the small room for the fifteenth time, letting fly a small wooden stool, which crashed up against the wall.

He had been in confinement now for more than twenty-four hours. He was cold. He was going stir-crazy, but most of all he was angry. How dare these Ruskies pull an old Cold War maneuver like this! Someone would pay when he got out! He would pull every diplomatic string he had up his sleeve, even if it meant going right to the top.

Going to the top. He didn't even know what that might mean by now. The thought sobered him. It was probably too late to stop the coup. They'd taken the files, his gun, even his ID, then had thrown him in this makeshift jail cell, where he'd been under locked house arrest ever since.

At least he wasn't hungry. They were feeding him, he'd say that much for his captors. And there had been not so much as a hint of violence. They had just immobilized him.

He recalled his brief interview with Desyatovsky. It hadn't amounted to much, only an interrogation: How had he got the files, who had helped him, who else knew—that kind of thing. He hadn't revealed anything, and though he could tell the General was nervous inside, he'd kept his cool.

"Well, at least I have the files back, Mr. Davidson," he had said at length. "But I do want to assure you, that whatever you may *think* you deduced from what you saw here, it is not what you may have surmised. We have different methods of operation in the Commonwealth of Independent States. Your Western minds are not able to grasp our ways. So in the interest of continued cooperation between our two nations, I would ask you to put the contents of these files out of your mind."

Yeah, yeah, sure! thought Blue Doc, but only nodding in acknowledgment.

Then they had hauled him off to this dump.

His only other visitor had been a KGB interrogator, probably a lackey of Bolotnikov's, a real throwback to the old days. He hadn't been too subtle. He made no attempt even to mask his anger. He'd come in threateningly and had demanded to know who else was in on it with him. He'd never said Galanov's name, but it was clear he knew. Doc had been intentionally vague and had implied that he'd already passed the information along to the powers in Washington.

He just wished he hadn't been lying!

It was a sure bet now that he wasn't going to have a chance to talk to anybody in the CIA or the State Department or the Pentagon until these guys had done whatever they planned to do.

He hoped Galanov was out of the country by now. Not merely to make public the plot but so that he'd be released from this sleazy place.

76

August 16, 10:03 P.M.
Western Poland

"It was perhaps selfish of me to ask you to join me," said Udo Bietmann.

"Are you kidding?" replied Jackson. "What an adventure! I wouldn't miss it."

"Even having to leave without seeing young Anna again?" asked Bietmann.

"Was it that obvious?" asked Jackson.

"She is a special young lady. Knowing you now as I do, I am not surprised."

The night was by now black as the two sped along the narrow, two-lane road heading east. They had crossed the Polish border about thirty minutes earlier, and in Beitmann's compact European-version Ford with the extra gas tank one of their number had installed for just such occasions, they would be able to drive easily to their Warsaw contact where they would refuel and find out if any further instructions had come. Bietmann hoped to be through Warsaw and on toward Bialystok well in advance of morning, but much would depend upon conditions as they drove through the night. Their destination at the Russian border lay some 550 kilometers ahead of them.

"Yes, I would have liked to see her again," admitted Jackson. "But this is the sort of opportunity that does not often come to one in my position."

"You mustn't be cavalier about what we have before us," rejoined Bietmann. "It is a mistake Westerners often make about Christian work in this part of the world."

"I'm sorry. I didn't mean to take it lightly," said Jackson. "I am curious, though. What did you mean?"

Bietmann thought seriously for a minute, then chuckled lightly. "It is perhaps a word that sounds what we call *komisch* coming from my lips, ja?"

"You mean *cavalier?*"

Bietmann laughed again. "I learned that word especially for this context," he said. "It was so difficult for me to understand the peculiar air I noticed when Christians from the West began filtering into East Germany a few years ago that I tried to find a word to describe it. So, as poor as my English is, it is one word I do know."

Now Jackson laughed. "Tell me, what was it you noticed?"

Again Bietmann fell silent, staring ahead through the darkness as the car bounded along the road.

"First let me tell you about two men. The first is our friend Franz Schmidt, a West German with relatives in the East. He has long been permitted to travel somewhat freely and has been visiting our fellowship and others like it for years, smuggling things to us that we have been unable to get. Bibles and literature sometimes, but more often items of a practical nature—a guitar or harmonica, a tape player, food, German books, perhaps fabric for the women, a new pair of boots for one of the men. Even a box of fresh fruit could bring tears. Franz has been a lifeline to keep us sometimes from despair.

"The second man I would tell you about is Jacob Michaels. Do you remember what he said at the barbeque, just a few hours ago?"

Jackson thought back. "Generally—yes," he answered.

"While he was with us," Bietmann went on, "he shared humbly about his own need. To hear such confessions ministered more greatly to my people than you can realize. But what he said tonight was that he desired to be part of our fellowship, that he wanted to help, that he had been touched."

He paused, reflecting.

"Do you understand, Jackson, how special it is for my people to hear such words? No," he went on, "you probably cannot understand it. Those are not words they are accustomed to hearing from Westerners. That *we* have touched someone from the West—that someone of Jacob Michaels's stature wants to remain in touch with *us,* and to help *us!*"

He drove a while in silence.

"These two men," he continued at length, "are unusual. Since the wall came down and especially since reunification, we have had many, many Christian visitors from the West. I do not know how, but they have found out about our fellowship and other churches and fellowships like ours. Some have even sought *me* out—by name. How they know of me, I have no idea. The isolation we felt for so long, and out of which I wrote to Jacob—that isolation no longer is present. There has been great contact with Christians from America. And do you know why they come?"

Jackson shook his head.

"They do not come to listen or pray. They do not want to know what we are thinking or feeling. They do not come to know us by first name, and when they leave they do not say the kinds of things Jacob said about helping us and wanting to be part of our lives."

"What then?" asked Jackson. "Why do they come?"

"They all come to start their own works, as they call them," replied Bietmann. "They come to us because they think we can provide a local base for their church or a ministry of what they so proudly call a *work* of God. I must apologize if I sound critical.

But they do not see us as fellow brothers and sisters. Their only desire is to expand their own organizations. If we will join them and let them affix their label upon us, then great is their enthusiasm. Then money will come, and people will come, and literature will come, and 'missionaries' from the United States will come to 'spread the gospel' in the East. But if we say, 'God *is* at work here and we too are seeking to spread the gospel. We do not want to become part of your organization, but we do have needs that perhaps—' we cannot even finish our explanation before they are gone to find some other place to erect their buildings and put up their signs to proclaim the *work* that has their organizational name attached to it."

"Does your friend Schmidt still come?" asked Jackson.

"Yes, bless him! And still bringing needful items and still without any program to press upon us. His love has been demonstrated through the years, and he continues to show it in practical ways."

"But there is no one else like him—even now?"

"I tell you the truth, Jackson. I have been visited personally by twenty-one American Christians or groups of Christians since reunification. You and Jacob were the twenty-second."

"Wow. That must keep Greta busy! Did they all stay with you?"

"Jackson, don't you hear what I am telling you? None of them stayed with us! You are the first. There have been no fellowship meetings such as we enjoyed with you, no barbeques. Not a single one of them knows of the Network or of the expansiveness of the links between the Christians and fellowships in the East. They came, they talked at us, and they left, as oblivious to our situation as when they came."

"But I don't understand—where did they stay—what did you do with them?"

"They stayed in hotels in Berlin. They drove out in rented cars, dressed in suits. They came with packaged speeches informing us of all the benefits of joining their organizations. They expected our people to rejoice as if the liberators had come. They came—and some even had the condescension to say it to our faces—to spy out the land for the Lord, as if now, at long last, God's work could proceed in these forsaken parts of the world, now that *they* had come.

"With some the arrogance was so thick I did not introduce

them to a single one of our number. I took their leaflets and told them we would not be interested. Others were genuine in their hearts' desires, and we enjoyed fellowship with some of these. But without fail, every one eventually came round to pulling out his agenda and asking us if we wanted the exciting opportunity to join them in their groundbreaking work of spreading the gospel. 'Can we establish our Baptist work or our this or our that ministry?' What we need are people to help and support us and our ministries, in the schools and workplace, to train our new young pastors. However, none, until you and Jacob, spoke the kind of words Jacob spoke tonight. Especially now, with *so* many of our people out of work and in desperate straits, the words of these well-dressed people with their talk of spying out the land fall on deaf ears. Your bringing meat and beer and treating us to a great feast went further to strengthen the bonds of brotherhood than anything any of the other twenty-one visitors ever thought of doing."

"Did none of them offer to help you, to bring you things you might need?"

"Well, there have been many more Bibles and literature available than in the past. We have always been able to get Bibles here in Germany without a great deal of difficulty. But in Poland and Russia and some of the other places it is opening up. So in a way I misspoke when I said they have offered nothing. Yet even that is often impersonal. As I told you, in some of the larger cities those materials either get to the black market or make enormous profits for officals rather than feeding hungry hearts. The Americans bring their loads of literature and Bibles almost, I think, for the sake of how it makes them look at home rather than for the lives that could be changed."

"Do you honestly think that is true?"

"You see it in their eyes. Some visitors come with boxes of Testaments and books. We take what they give with thankful hearts. We are appreciative. But in their faces you can see the pride, as visibly as if they said the words, 'Look at what *we* brought you! Aren't you grateful?' It used to be the same way with some of the Bible smugglers back in the old days—especially the teams who would come in for a two-week 'holiday' to take literature behind the Iron Curtain. They cared nothing about us as individuals with real needs. They only wanted to feed their own egos by being able to tell people about their 'experiences' out on the front lines smuggling Bibles for the Lord. Our friend Schmidt, Brother Adam, men who risked their very lives to *help* us, not just pad their list of spiritual credits—they were few and far between."

Bietmann drove on, passing not a single car for more than five minutes.

"All this is why I told you not to be *cavalier*," he said at length. "So many of your countrymen come here with a subtle spiritual superciliousness that does not dignify them or endear them to Christians in the East. You strike me as a young man of deeper substance than that. I have enjoyed your presence these last three days. I want you to see what we are more clearly than most of your countrymen have."

"I appreciate your talking to me so candidly."

"We are on a serious business. It could be dangerous. Quite frankly, when we were praying earlier I felt an impulse that I might need you on this mission. It was no accident that you and Jacob were at our house when the summons came. I hope that impulse is indeed the prompting of the Spirit."

"There are few accidents either of timing or circumstances for God's people," replied Jackson. "I too believe this has been set up by the Lord." Even as he said the words he thought back to the similar words Anna had said to him when speaking of trust.

"If the next couple of days are anything like what they *could* be, I will need a strong prayer warrior by my side. That was my chief reason for asking you to be here."

"I will do my best."

"Pray that the enemy's power will be bound, Jackson. There is a new order in the world, to be sure, but the power of evil is undiminished. Men out for their own gain still play for keeps."

Jackson was sober. "This man we are going to help—besides what you told us earlier, is he an important man in the government?"

"No," reflected Udo, "not in the government, no more than any ex-KGB agent running for his life. No man is more important eternally than any other. Yet this man's conversion was dynamic, and I believe his testimony will carry wide and far. We have to get him out, Jackson. There are forces who would silence him. But I believe God's hand is upon him to spread the gospel."

"Why did he not come with you when you were in Moscow

just days ago?"

"As I told you, he was a KGB agent. His conversion was sudden and unexpected. It reminded me of the events of Acts nine, and it was a privilege to be a small part of it. So suddenly did the change come upon him that he was not able to instantly leave his old life. He did not confide totally in me, but he said he had to tie up some ends. He was onto something political that he had to resolve. Believe me, I know the danger he was in even in Moscow, and I did my best to get him to come with me. But he said that there were plots afoot and that he had to follow up."

"Sounds dangerous."

"The man spent his whole life as a spy, Jackson. It is a far different world from what you and I know."

"Do you know why there was difficulty getting him out?"

"No details. It was an emergency message, and they are usually scant on specifics."

"Why you? Are you Mr. Big?"

Bietmann laughed. "Hardly. But I have been involved in the network for a long time. And because of my proximity to Berlin, I suppose, I have been rather in a prominent position, like the Western focal point as Der Prophet was its Moscow link. He was the start of the line, I was the end, so to speak."

"Der Prophet?"

"A long story. I'll tell you about him, perhaps, on our way *back* through Poland—that is *if* we get back. In any event, no, I'm not Mr. Big, but I am one of the key members of the network on this end."

Bietmann paused, thinking. "You need to understand what a dreadful persecutor and Saul this man was," he went on. "His conversion was one of the most remarkable things I have ever witnessed. But there are others among the believing fellowships that may not be so ready to accept an old enemy. With him now in difficulty, it is doubly important that I be there with him. He may need an advocate even among believers, if we get him safely out of Russia."

"His own personal Barnabas," mused Jackson. "This is certainly more intriguing than the speeches I was hearing in Berlin!"

"You ought to get some sleep," said Bietmann. "It's after midnight, and I may need you to help me drive later."

77

It wasn't the most deluxe of accommodations.

Andrassy Galanov had slept in some of the finest hotels in Moscow, Kiev, Prague, Bucharest, and Belgrade. Even in Paris and London. A pile of straw and hay didn't exactly compare to silk sheets and luxurious featherbeds.

But at least the barn's roof seemed intact. And the straw was dry. After the night hours he'd spent getting here from Mosty, he wasn't about to complain. The sun was just coming up, and its orange rays splintered through the boards on the barn's eastern wall. Even that wouldn't keep him awake. He lay down in a soft pile of straw, leaned his back against a still-bundled bale, and closed his eyes.

They'd come down through Volkovysk by car. They were not big towns and would not be watched, his guide said, especially not these days. There had been a border crossing, he'd said, at one time between Volovysk and Bialystok in Poland. But the fence had been erected and the road torn up for about seven kilometers on the Russian side. Those last seven kilometers they had walked. And now, within sight of the border fence, he would spend the night in this old barn, owned by the Christian brother who was supposed to know how to get him across the border, over the fence, and into Poland.

How, he didn't know. But if there was one thing he'd learned, it was to trust these people. They knew what they were doing. And they prayed a great deal. Too much was at stake for them not to pray, as they were teaching him, without ceasing.

His guide had a cousin on the other side, in Poland. Because of their relation, they had been allowed to maintain contact with one another, more contact in fact than the authorities on either side knew of or would have approved.

The huge tract of land had been in the Polish family for generations, and had been farmed by their great-grandfather and grandfather prior to the Second World War when the entire region was part of Poland. As Russia encroached ever further westward between 1940 and 1945, however, a portion of the land fell under Soviet domination. The result was that when the borders of the Soviet Union were redrawn after the war to include its areas of conquest, Poland lost more of its land than Estonia, Latvia, Lithuania, Romania, or Czechoslovakia. The family farm was split right down the middle. And Galanov's present guide, though a Pole by birth, heritage, and blood, found himself raised in the Belorussia province of the Union of Soviet Socialist Republics. His father's portion of the land was confiscated by the state and made part of the Soviet communal system, though the family was allowed to live on it and work a small segment of what had once been their ancestors' fields.

Somehow the brothers, fathers of the two present cousins, had contrived to keep up communication across the border, a development aided by the fact that this section of the Polish/Russian border was not as closely patroled as others. As teenagers the boys had rigged up a makeshift telegraph between their own homes by the use of underground wires. Though men of the soil by day, both had something of a flair for gadgetry, as well as the dramatic, and thus by night they continued to fiddle with contraptions and expand their modes of communication to the point that, though they could not visit in person, they could talk with one another nearly at will.

Their mutual delight being to outwit the system that had destroyed their farm, they eventually designed a means to cut a hole about half a meter in diameter through the border fence, while bypassing the electrical signal that would have tripped the alarm at the guardhouse three kilometers away. All it had taken was an hour during which the electricity was shut down for maintainance. The hole was cut, new electrical connections soldered in place, and the removed piece was put back in place. Because some transplanted wild shrubbery that grew freely in the region, the woodsy portion of fence was never inspected carefully.

The immediate effect was that the cousins were now able to visit one another and plan additional relatively innocent shenanigans. In time, however, as their faith deepened and they became more involved in underground Christian activities, dozens of believers fleeing the Soviet Union had made their way through the homes of these two Polish cousins living on either side of the border. Galanov was their first visitor in two years.

"Why do you not simply cross at the border?" the man had asked him. "They hardly check papers these days. If I want to see my cousin, I just drive around. I could take you into Poland by car."

"They would check *my* papers." Galanov laughed. "Unfortunately, they are looking for me, probably at every border crossing between the Black Sea and Finland."

"What did you do?" asked the man in some surprise. "Are you a criminal?"

Again Galanov laughed. "The less you know, the better, my friend. No, I am no criminal. At least not against the Soviet state," he added pensively, thinking sadly again of the crimes against God's people that were on his shoulders. "No, if I am to get out, I will have to do it in secret. I am sorry to have to put you through all this."

"Please, do not apologize! You cannot imagine how dull life has been. I have scarcely slept since receiving word that you were coming to us. I do not know why your escape is so important, but my cousin and I will do all we can to help you. Until this fence is torn down and I am reunited with my family and we can once again farm this land that is *ours,* I will dedicate myself to the work of freedom."

"I cannot thank you enough."

"I do not care if it is called the Independent State of Belorussia or if it is a union or a Commonwealth or if Gorbachev or Yeltsin or the president of Belorussia is in power. This land is *Polish* ground, and I will always be a Pole. I will never forget that they stole it from us, whatever talk of so-called *independence* they now make so freely. They are still a nation of robbers and murderers, and making it a Commonwealth of Independent States changes nothing. They are still descendents of Stalin, whose soldiers killed my grandfather."

"I am sorry," said Galanov.

"It is a time long past," said the farmer. "I carry no bitterness. But you can see why my cousin and I take freedom seriously. Being Christians means nothing to us unless we can give tangible help to others. And this is the way He has given us to do it. Here we are," he said, opening the rickety door and leading his guest inside.

"What now?" asked Galanov.

"You'll sleep in the barn today. My wife will bring you dinner at dusk. Get as much sleep as you can. At midnight you will make your escape into Poland."

78

August 17, 6:09 P.M.
Brest, Belorussia

"I thought you had him!" exploded the Russian Defense Minister into the telephone.

"I *will* retrieve your files. It will just take a little longer than I had anticipated."

"Your last words to me were that if we closed down as much of the border as possible, you would intercept the traitor. Now I've involved Shaposnikov. We picked up the CIA man and have him on ice—"

"Did he talk?" interrupted Bolotnikov.

"He's blustering, trying to make us believe he did. But he couldn't have. He still had the file, and there's been no whisper out of Washington. If he'd talked, their lines would be buzzing.

"If he had the file, then perhaps Galanov is a red herring."

"No, you idiot!" yelled Desyatovsky. "Davidson had a *duplicate* file. He and Galanov must be together on it. You *must* locate Galanov without delay!"

"My leads at Brest were all dry. Nothing is coming through here. I have memorized every route used from here to the Lithuanian border. I'm leaving momentarily and will personally inspect every known possibility. I have some of the best people tracking down every Christian we have in our files to personally interrogate them. If something is afoot through the old network, my people will discover it."

"Time is critical."

"I will be in the air momentarily. We will work all night."

"I tell you, there is not a moment to lose. The accident for the presidents en route to Kirovabad from the reactor site at Kuybyshev is all set. It's in motion, I tell you. We're *all* dead if you don't get to Galanov! Alekdanyov is set to roll the interviews. I've been in touch with Gorbunovyev, and I've spoken by phone with Petrikov, Dzasokhov, and Baramertnykh. The second round of factory explosions began last night. Bobrikov called a general strike on nationwide television two hours ago. Khasbulachek is going to seize control of the rail lines tonight. The dominos are falling!"

"What about Germany?"

"You leave Germany and that featherhead Drexler to me! He'll do what he has to do. I'm going to call him immediately and tell him he'd better make his move or be left behind."

"You can count on me to do my part."

"Words, Leonid! I want results. You put that file in my hands before sunrise, or I'll send you down the river with the rest of them!"

Bolotnikov winced as he heard the phone being slammed down at the other end of the line. Shaking off the residual effects of being dressed down by his superior, he left the office and ran back toward his waiting helicopter.

79

"So your imprisonment was not because of your faith?" Jackson asked the man who had been their host for the last three hours.

"I was considered a dissident," he answered. "It was before Solidarity made strikes popular. Lech Walesa became president. I, however, years earlier was imprisoned, beaten, and eventually released to live out my days in quiet retirement. It's what comes, I suppose, of trying to change the system before the time is right."

"How long were you in prison?" asked Bietmann.

"Seven years."

"But Palacki wasn't a union or labor leader."

"No, only a pastor. But he was more outspoken on matters of religious intolerance than the rest of us who were speaking against other things. Moscow and its Warsaw puppets hated him."

"You met him in prison?"

"He had already been there six years when I arrived—a pitiful sight. I remember thinking to myself with horror, *What if the same fate awaits me?* I thought I would rather die than go through what that man had obviously endured. He was covered with purple splotches from the beatings, lumps upon his head, and scabs of dried blood on his lips. It was nauseating to look at the poor man."

Jackson and Udo Bietmann had arrived at the home of Kochow Rydz a little after 2:00 in the afternoon Warsaw time. They had napped and were now conversing with their host as his wife prepared supper for them. They would try to sleep again before receiving their instructions from Rydz as to their nighttime rendezvous with their final contact, his friend and network brother, Waclau Chmielnicki, whose farm was adjacent to the Russian border about forty-three kilometers to the east.

"How did you meet Palacki?" asked Bietmann.

"We were in adjoining cells," replied Rydz. "But that hardly mattered. Everyone in the prison knew Dieder. Even in prison he was on a mission, and eventually he managed to speak to every man there."

"Mission?" repeated Jackson.

"His faith. How seriously he took the Lord's command to spread the gospel! Even though he received more beatings every time they caught him talking about God, he never stopped."

"How did he survive?"

"One look into that man's eyes and you could tell something burned inside him unlike other men. I recognized it the first day. In spite of the bruises and scars and obvious malnutrition, in his eyes glowed life, and even in the midst of that horrible place—a love. You knew he loved you with one look from his eyes."

"And you became a believer there?" asked Beitmann.

"I don't think any man could witness the sufferings of a man like Dieder Palacki and see the love in his heart and not be changed by it. I couldn't. After only two or three conversations with him, yes, I gave my heart to the Father. I wanted the life I saw in him, and he willingly shared it with me. He *joyfully* shared it with me. When I opened my eyes after he prayed with me for the first time, he was weeping and a broad smile covered his bruised face. There was a good chance we would both be beaten for what we had done, yet he wept for joy."

Both listeners were silent for a moment. Then Jackson asked, "Were you?"

"What?"

"Beaten for it?"

Rydz smiled. "Yes. That same day and many other days. We prayed together every chance we had. More often than not we were beaten or sent to solitary confinement afterward. I could not have endured it for a month had not Dieder set a constant example of faith before me. No man could ask for a more loving and faithful and suffering mentor than God blessed me with. How many times I heard him pray for his tormentors!"

"And you were there another seven years?" asked Bietmann.

"Altogether, yes—seven."

Bietmann chuckled. "I thought it was difficult for me. I was imprisoned three times, and the total was only about two and a half years."

"You never told me that," exclaimed Jackson, turning toward

the man he thought he had known so well.

"In this part of the world, Jackson," smiled Udo, "we do not make so much of our badges of honor as you Americans like to. Suffering has come to us all for our faith." Bietmann turned toward Rydz. "Was Palacki still there after you left?" he asked.

"He had been out for two or three years by then," replied Kochow. "He had been in prison a total of fifteen years. By the time he got out, though weak in body, the man had become a saint. I was not surprised in the least to discover after my release that he had begun fellowships and underground churches all over Poland, Bulgaria, Romania, even in Russia. Everywhere I went, I found people exactly like me, who credited Palacki's love and faith and forgiving heart with their own salvation. How many spiritual sons and daughters that man has throughout the Eastern countries—it must number in the many thousands!"

"It's a pretty amazing story," reflected Jackson. "But then this whole trip has been one amazing story after another."

"We're not through yet," said Beitmann. "Hopefully before this night is over, you will meet a man with one of the most moving salvation experiences you will ever hear about."

"Who is this man?" asked Rydz.

"I hope to be able to introduce you to him as well," said Bietmann. "Truly, our Father makes no distinction between men when He sovereignly chooses who will carry His work into the world."

80

Andrassy slept well. As well as he'd ever slept between silk sheets. The day passed quickly. Cold dinner off a wooden plate could not have tasted better with candles and linen and silver. He slept again in the evening. Before he knew it, a hand on his shoulder roused him.

"The time has come," said the voice of the Belorussian Pole.

They crept out of the barn. His guide carried a pocket flashlight. They walked some distance across a field and through some trees.

They stopped. His guide signaled three short flashes. A moment later, two brief flickers of light shone from amid the trees. He flashed an answering signal of two flashes.

"That is my cousin," he said. "He is ready. The coast is clear on his end."

"Is it always the same?" asked Galanov, surprised at the seeming simplicity of the exchange.

"No, we always contrive a different signal and go at different times of the night. We used to use elaborate systems of camouflaging our movements. But it is different now. The dangers of the past do not exist as they once did."

"I hope you are right."

"Let us go."

They moved toward the fence, walking in the darkness through a lightly wooded field of sward and shrubbery.

Suddenly the whirring blades of a huge helicopter thundered menacingly through the night.

A giant spotlight roamed and scanned the ground. It took but two or three seconds to find them, and it zeroed in. The two stood emblazoned in a wide beam of light from which it was impossible to escape.

The helicopter hovered, sending hurricane winds down upon their heads. A voice spoke over its loudspeaker. "Do not move!

337

You are well covered, and ground patrols have you surrounded. Any attempt to flee will be met with machine-gun fire."

As if to punctuate the seriousness of the speaker's intent, the air split apart the next instant with a deafening round of fire. A volley of bullets slammed into the ground about ten feet from were they stood.

Galanov made no attempt to run. It would be futile. He knew the man in the helicopter meant business.

It was a voice he knew only too well.

PART 12

Climax of the Quest

81

August 18, 10:45 A.M.
Berlin

A knock came on the door. Jacob rose and answered it. In the hall stood Anthony Powers.

"I heard you were back in town," he said, shaking Michaels's hand, "but I didn't see you all day yesterday. I thought I'd better check and see if everything was OK."

"Sure, Tony," answered Jacob, "couldn't be better. Would you like to come in?"

"Only for a minute."

"Well, tonight's the big night, Jacob," said Powers, doing his best to draw Michaels into conversation.

Jacob nodded unenthusiastically.

"Come on, this is the climax of the week. I hate to say it, Jacob, old man, but this sharing of the podium tonight between Bob MacPatrick and Dieder Palacki might even upstage your address tomorrow."

"I'm hardly worried about that," said Jacob. "I don't even know what I'm going to say anyway."

"Your speech isn't written yet?" Powers was incredulous.

"I've had two or three sets of notes on paper. But they've all wound up in the garbage can."

"Come on, Jacob. You can't leave me hanging like this! You'd better get your head on before you take the podium."

"Don't worry, Tony. Look," he said, gesturing toward the desk where an open Bible and several sheets of paper lay spread out, "I'm hard at work on it."

"It might do you some good to hear these guys tonight. I tell you, Jacob, I haven't believed half the things I've heard about you in the last year. But seeing you wander around with your expression full of who knows what makes me wonder if you aren't slipping a bit. Take care of yourself."

"I'll watch it."

"It's not too late for me to bring in someone else as a substitute for you tomorrow if you're not up to it. Hamilton Jaeger has mentioned that he's available at a moment's notice."

Jacob smiled. He wasn't surprised. "I'll let you know, Tony," he said.

"OK, see you tonight, then."

"Perhaps."

"You'd be welcome to share the platform with the rest of us."

"Not a chance. If I attend, I'll be in the back somewhere. I don't want to pretend that I'm more important than the next guy."

"But, Jacob, some of us are, you know—in positions where we must occasionally assert our leadership gifts. The flocks need shepherds."

"Speak for yourself, Tony. All I want to do is figure out how to live as God's man—as God's *child,* I should say. But *not* as God's leader and spokesman. So thanks all the same, but I don't want to be on the platform with you. We'll see about tomorrow. I'll let you know."

"All right, pal. Watch yourself. I don't want it to get out that you backslid while at *my* conference. Bad for my reputation, you know!"

He laughed, and Jacob closed the door behind him.

The visit had been indicative of the mood of the conference for Jacob since his return from Kehrigkburg the night before last. He had scarcely attended a single session but had spent most of the time in his room with his New Testament, especially the gospels.

He glanced down at the pages opened in the middle of Luke where he had been reading and jotting down notes before Powers's visit.

He lay down on the bed and closed his eyes. He tried to pray, as he had so many times already this week, but with frustrating results.

"God, help me break through the impasse!" he implored. "Speak to me, Lord. Tell me what You want me to say. Please, Father, shed light on the words of Your Son. Give me perspective. I don't want to misread what I am seeing."

He fell silent, though the prayers continued for some time. At length he left the room and went out into the late morning streets of Berlin. He might as well try again.

He had wandered out of the hotel several times since returning from Bietmann's, in search of the woman and her baby. They had occupied his mind almost exclusively, blocking out even thoughts of the conference and what he was to say in his speech. It had been with difficulty that he had focused his mind on the study he was engaged in with his Bible. An inner compulsion had risen within him once back in the city, to make another attempt to give himself to the poor, needy, young soul. Though he was new to recognizing the Spirit's impulses as such, Jacob could feel life growing and expanding inside him. Like the unfolding of a tender flower, his eyes and ears were suddenly atuned to new regions of the pulsating life around him, feeling the heartbeat of people's hopes and yearnings, looking into their faces and being stung with a new kind of love, unlike any he had known before, sensing hurt and loneliness and fear.

What stirred him as he walked along the crowded, noisy sidewalk, teeming with life and need, was utterly foreign to the isolated, glitzy atmosphere of the hotel and conference. His soul desired more. He wanted to touch, to taste, to listen, to talk, to love—to interact with real life!

In the center of his mind's eye had burned the image of the lady and her child, her lonely eyes, the baby's sad silence—and his total incapacity to *give,* to transmit life and hope and love to her.

All he had given was money.

It was what she had been asking for. But surely the life within him was worth far more than thirty-some German marks. How could he give that to her—the life and love of God? The question burned on his heart. He had no more answers now than when he had first seen her. But the first step was to find her again. He had been praying to that end for more than a day now.

For two hours Jacob walked, noticing only the endless string of faces, praying as he passed them. Gradually they seemed to become more than nameless strangers. Into each face he looked, even if only for a second or two, asking, *God, do You reside there? Where are You, Father, in this dear one's life?*

Just as quickly, his eyes fell upon another, now the bewildered

343

face of a small child, now the preoccupied look of a businessman talking to his colleague or secretary, then the blank stare of one of a thousand street-walkers or beggars or would-be revolutionaries.

Lord, Jesus, he thought, *what would* You *do if* You *were walking this street right now? Would* You *walk by them praying? Would* You *stop and preach of* Your *Father? Would* You *work a miracle?*

Then the thought struck him, *But* You *are walking the street, aren't* You, *Lord?* You *are walking beside me—inside me—with me.* You *are here! So what would* You *do—what would* You *have me do? If I am* Your *representative now,* Your *hands,* Your *feet,* Your *eyes,* Your *mouth,* Your *ears, how do I take the life that is inside me—*Your *life!—among these people?*

Ahead was a souvenir and magazine kiosk in the middle of the wide walkway. An assortment of postcards were displayed on a wire rack to one side, half with photographs of Berlin, the other with lewd and suggestive pictures. Behind the counter two or three dozen different magazine covers shouted their indecency and erotic wantonness to all the world. A man dressed in an expensive blue suit stood in conversation with the owner of the stand, a fat, balding, man with a dirty shirt and a pathetic-looking grin of lecherous and coarse intent shining out of his hollow eyes. He had been holding a magazine up for his customer to see, and now with a quick movement opened it to just the right page, where fell down a three-page fold-out, which he brandished luridly before the man's eager, lustful eyes.

Jacob could understand not a word either man spoke. He didn't need to. The tones of foulmouthed obscenities required no translation, nor the satyric glow in each man's eyes.

He cast his eyes to the ground and walked quickly by. The kiosk man, not wanting his wares ignored, threw out a crude invitation, flashing the shameless picture in Jacob's direction. The man in the suit half-turned, then stepped into Jacob's path, placing his hand to the side of his mouth and making some equally suggestive comment, as if, in confidence from one man of the world to another, the fellow wasn't really as bad as he seemed and that he could give a man a little happiness. His words were followed by a wink and a knowing glance.

Jacob looked into his face. It was only for a second, but it was enough. His eyes suddenly swam in tears, and he hurried on.

He did not even hear the annoyed kiosk man shouting after him.

Where he went next, Jacob never knew. Even with a map he could not have retraced his steps. When he came to himself, he was a great distance from the center of traffic and tourism and activity. He was near a small park with two or three old statues and a few benches. Paper and litter were strewn about. The few people in the vicinity were hurrying elsewhere. He sat down on an empty bench and cradled his head in his hands. Through his brain flew thoughts of the conference and his conversation with Powers. Tonight was the night MacPatrick would deliver his stirring speech on how they were going to join together to save the world by the year 2000.

Oh, my self-satisfied brothers, his heart cried out, *you are so caught up in your programs that you can't feel the heartbeat of the real world!*

A passage from the little devotional book he had been reading came back into his mind. He remembered he had stuck the booklet in his pocket before leaving the hotel. He pulled it out and flipped through the pages to locate the passage. He read it again, as he had this morning.

What a breeding nest of cares and pains is the human heart! Surely it needs refuge! How the world needs a Saviour to whom anyone might go, at any moment. *Come unto me, all that labor and are heavy laden, and I will give you rest.*

Did ever a man really say such words? Such words they are! It is rest we want. *Rest*—such peace of mind as we had when we were children. Do not waste time asking how He can give it. Ask Him to forgive you and make you clean and set things right. If He will not do it, then He is not the Saviour of men and was wrongly named Jesus.

Come then at the call of the Maker, the Healer, the Giver of repentance and light, the Friend of sinners, all you on whom lies the weight of sin. Heartily He loves you! Call to mind how He forgave men's sins, thus lifting from their hearts the crushing load that paralyzed them—the repentant woman who wept sore-hearted from very love, the publicans who knew they were despised because they were despicable. In Him they sought and found shelter. He received them, and the life within them rose up, and the light shone. They heard and believed and obeyed His words. And of all words that ever were spoken, were there ever any gentler, tenderer, humbler, lovelier than these? *Come unto me all you that labor and are heavy-laden, and I will give you rest. Take my yoke upon you, and learn of me; for I am meek and lowly in heart: and you shall find rest for your souls. For my yoke is easy, and my burden is light.*

Long before he had finished reading the words again, Jacob's eyes were nearly blinded by the tears streaming down his face. With the words of the old writer in his ears, mingling with distorted images from the conference, and with his mind's eye filled with the face of the woman he had not found and the sickening voices of the two men at the kiosk, the heart of Jacob Michaels filled with the general suffering of the universal human soul.

The book fell from his hands. On a lonely bench, unseen by any other, the man who had once been hailed as a great evangelist quietly wept for the world he did not know how to reach.

82

August 18, 11:47 A.M.
Berlin

"Gerhardt—how are you?"

"Sehr gut, Herr Chancellor," replied Woeniger.

"Please, Gerhardt," said Kolter, "why so formal among old friends? Allies *and* friends, am I not right, Gerhardt?"

"Yes—yes, of course, Hans," replied Woeniger, trying to swallow his nervousness. He had hoped not to have to speak to the Chancellor again personally. But at least he had telephoned and not summoned him again to his office.

"The time has come, Gerhardt," Kolter went on, "for us again to put that friendship to the test and to demonstrate to the world, as we have to our own nation, that we are dedicated to the future.

Do you not agree?"

"Certainly, Hans."

"The debate has nearly run its course, Gerhardt. I am planning to call for a vote on the aid package this afternoon. It will no doubt be tight. Our friend Herr Drexler has succeeded in being highly persuasive among some of our colleagues. It could be that the Greens and FDP will vote with him. Have you heard anything to that effect, Gerhardt?" queried the Chancellor.

"Only that what you say is correct," replied Woeniger. "Klaus has been very active." His tone was guarded.

"The international community is with us in this," rejoined Kolter. "The others, I am certain, will see their required course of action in the end. The mandate upon the German government to take the leading role in helping the new Soviet Commonwealth is clear. I do not think we have anything to worry about."

"I am sure you are right."

"Still, I was uncomfortable with what I heard from the floor this morning. Though Drexler himself cleverly remained silent, it was clear where the arguments against me had originated."

Woeniger did not reply.

"In any case," Kolter went on, "though it would tarnish my standing somewhat if he does take the FDP and Greens with him, the CSDU/CDU coalition will carry the vote."

"I see what you mean," said Woeniger, sidestepping Kolter's primary point. "A strong victory would speak a firmer assurance of our position."

"Yes, but we will take what *we* can get, won't we, Gerhardt?" replied Kolter, deliberately emphasizing the word *we*.

"A victory is a victory," answered Woeniger.

"Good—good! I wanted to make sure we were still together on this," said the Chancellor. "But I'm sure you have things to do before we reconvene, so I'll let you go. By the way, Gerhardt, how are your wife and girls?"

"Very well, sir."

"Good! I'm so glad to hear it. I'll see you in session, Gerhardt."

Woeniger hung up the phone. He was sweating freely.

83

"What's the idea of calling me here, Claymore? I gave you this number only for an emergency."

"This may qualify."

"What's happened?" asked Drexler.

"It's all hitting the fan."

"Don't worry—it's controllable."

"I'm not so sure. Your Russian friend is flying loose."

"Desyatovsky?"

"Yes. This place is a powder keg. I'm coming back for payment and to get out of the way before this plan of yours comes down on my head!"

"Wait!" exclaimed Drexler, thinking rapidly.

Claymore, however, was in no mood for patience. "Wait for what?" he rejoined. "Another day or two and the military is in control here. By then the borders may be closed. I tell you, the Commonwealth is about to unravel, and it's going to get ugly. Half the republics are on the verge of anarchy."

"Relax—relax," Drexler chuckled at the man's anxiety. "That's all part of the script. Believe me, it's all under control. Desyatovsky has people pulling the strings everywhere—the military included. And even if they do close the borders and fighting breaks out between the republics here and there, you have no need to worry. As long as you're with me, Desyatovsky will protect you."

"Hah! The man's a Russian!"

"We can trust him."

"I trust no one!"

"I tell you, everything's under control."

"And I tell you, this country's about to explode! Do you know the fellow Bolotnikov?"

"Heard of him," replied Drexler. "He's in on it with us, from what I understand."

"He's a loose wire too."

"Then follow him. If he gets dangerous, kill him. Desyatovsky would never link it to us."

"Easier said than done. *I'm* not willing to tangle with that man. Besides, I lost track of him. He took off after someone."

"Ah, yes," reflected Drexler, "the agent with the file. Is *he* still on the loose? I was assured the hole would be quickly plugged!"

"Who knows!" spat back Claymore icily. "Bolotnikov's still not returned to Moscow."

"Then pick up his trail and get on it. The fellow he's after *must* be stopped dead."

"Find someone else."

"There is no one else. Neither is there time to fool around. You get to Bolotnikov's prey ahead of him, snuff him, and retrieve what he's carrying, and I'll triple your payoff."

The phone was silent. Now it was Claymore who had gone pensive.

"You've got yourself a deal," he said after a couple of moments.

"Good. The next time I hear from you, I expect you to be calling from here in Germany to tell me you have the file."

Drexler hung up the phone. Slowly a smile spread across his lips. If the fool Claymore *could* get to the traitor before Bolotnikov, he would then have the ultimate weapon to use against Desyatovsky in the future—proof that he had orchestrated the whole thing. It would make the Russian dolt his puppet forever. The file's being stolen from Desyatovsky's office might turn out to be the best thing that could have happened!

The smile faded. However, in one thing Claymore had been right—his concern over the volatility in the Commonwealth once the dominos started to fall. There was always the possibility that Desyatovsky, like Gorbachev before him, would not be able to control events once he opened the door to change. The next forty-eight hours would tell the whole story and determine the course of the world's future. Even if Russia and the other republics *did* unravel, he still had to insure his own destiny.

It was time to make his move against Kolter. He would do so this very day.

He walked from his office and down the long corridor. The vote was imminent. He needed to talk once more to Keil Weisskopf, leader of the Greens, and the FDP's Otto Greim. He would play his final cards with each man and insure his desired result with a bit of unexpected coercion.

84

Jackson Maxwell and Udo Bietmann had arrived two hours after midnight the night before at the Chmielnicki farm just over the Polish border from the former Soviet Union. An earlier rendezvous had been planned, but at the last moment a call had informed them that strange movements and the sound of a helicopter had been detected on the Soviet side of the border. They were asked to delay their leaving a few hours. They had heard nothing more of the state of affairs.

Waclau had quickly filled them in on the situation.

"They were captured just on the other side of the fence," he told them. "We were so close—and then suddenly the helicopter was there, and I could do nothing."

Jackson and Bietmann looked at one another in alarm.

"I cannot imagine how they knew precisely where we would be," continued Chmielnicki.

"Were they hurt?" asked Bietmann. "Have they been taken back to Moscow?"

"Nobody was hurt, and no, they are still in the area," replied Waclau in mingled Polish and German. "Luckily they did not know I was hiding in the trees. Otherwise their spotlight could have found me too. I have no doubt the man in the helicopter would not have hesitated to use his machine gun."

"They did not see you?"

"I crouched down and watched. The helicopter landed. A large man got out, carrying a gun. They loaded my cousin, Jahn, and your man into a car, then drove off. But they did not go far. I was able to follow the light and sound of the helicopter. After they were gone, I sneaked through the fence and pursued the direction they went. It was less than three kilometers, to an old abandoned guardhouse where the road used to go through. The helicopter set down there. I have had someone watching it ever since. It seems that they are still holding them in one of the detention rooms—all the old border crossings had facilities for prisoners. The helicopter flew away after a while, but the cars remained."

"And now?" asked Bietmann.

"How long they will hold them I do not know. They could transfer them back to Moscow at any moment."

"Is there a way across the border by the old road?" asked Bietmann.

"No," replied Chmielnicki. "The road used to go through, but was divided by a high fence with deep concrete footings and treacherous barbed wire along the top. They keep it well lit. And especially now that they have prisoners there, it is heavily manned."

"And where you went through?"

"An opening we made years ago that bypasses their circuitry."

"What's the distance?"

"Approximately three kilometers."

"Wooded or open plain?"

"Both. There are many trees nearby and dense shrubbery, which we make sure stays healthy and growing freely. Still, it is a wonder they have not discovered the opening. Perhaps it seems so desolate that they do not think to search it. We have been blessed with safety through the years."

"Well, I suppose what we must do first is pray," suggested Bietmann.

"We already have the word spreading out to the Christians of the neighborhood," said Chmielnicki.

"In the middle of the night?"

"You are here, are you not? When it comes to God's work, there are no off-hours, either for the laborers such as yourself or for those who pray."

"You are right," smiled Bietmann. "Are there others we can use to help us?"

"Four or five I can count on."

"Good."

"One of them is standing watch even now. Come," said Chmielnicki, turning from where they had been standing with a vantage point toward the border, "let us go inside. My wife will make us something warm to drink. We will pray and talk about what is to be done. Then the two of you must sleep."

That had been some fourteen hours earlier. Jackson and Bietmann had slept, and now, sitting in the Chmielnicki farmhouse with a half-dozen Polish Christians, they discussed one final time the plan that had been formulated that morning. It was not without a good many risks, but Bietmann had insisted that risks fall primarily upon him, and Jackson had offered to take his own share of the danger. Waclau had to remain where he was, Udo had said. There could be no risk of his capture without jeopardizing the future of the escape network, should it be needed again. Likewise, he had insisted, the rest of the local Polish fellowship had to remain behind the scenes where their risk of apprehension would be small. They would all assist in creating the diversion. But Bietmann himself would drive the primary target vehicle.

"They could blow the car up with one explosive missile from the helicopter," objected one of the Poles.

"That is a chance I shall have to take," replied Udo. "I do not think they will, however. They will try to take us alive."

"When they stop you, what is to keep them from killing you?"

"They may do that. But I will be on Polish soil, and I doubt they will want to risk an incident. Second, I believe I will be able to convince them that I am merely an innocent German on a sightseeing trip who got too close to the Soviet border."

The men around the table fell silent, thinking through the many details that would have to work with precision if their plan was to succeed.

"Now remember," said Bietmann at length, "the car I need must have a powerful engine, preferably a Mercedes, and *not* an automatic transmission. It must have loud gears. Will you be able to locate such an automobile?"

"We shall find one."

"And soon. We must be ready to act the moment the helicopter returns."

"If the man in the helicopter does not return to the guard-house?"

"We must hope he will. The helicopter is vital to our success."

"The car you request will be here within an hour."

"Good. Make sure your watchman informs us the instant there is a hint of the chopper. Once it lands, we will have to act speedily. His intent will probably be to transfer the prisoners immediately."

85

August 18, 5:07 P.M.
Berlin

The atmosphere in the German parliament throughout the afternoon of discussion and debate had been tense. But even that did not indicate the momentous course of events that was about to be precipitated.

By day's end the 650-plus Bundestag members were tired of the arguments, tired of this unwelcome interruption of their summer's recess, and ready to vote and return to their homes. Most were inwardly annoyed at Kolter's calling of the special session but had gone along with it in view of the seriousness of the issue at hand.

The vote had at length been called for and was now proceeding. After a few predictable remarks that no one in the huge hall paid much attention to, Chancellor Hans Kolter, speaking on behalf of the CDU, cast all of that party's 211 votes for the proposed aid package.

Klaus Drexler rose next, and with a smile a bit too smug in Kolter's view, in light of his certain defeat, cast the 197 votes of the RDP against the measure, without so much as a sentence spoken besides. Keil Weisskopf of the Greens rose, spoke of the merits of the bill and the need for the nations of the West to lend their resources to upgrade the standard of living in the newly freed countries of the former Soviet Union. Certain reservations, however, had come to his mind about the bill recently, he said, which was why he had felt compelled to modify his party's previous inclinations. He was therefore voting *nein* on the measure, in hopes that a more comprehensive package would emerge in the near future.

He sat down amid noisy surprise. Kolter was clearly shocked by the sudden reversal. He tried to relax, however. The loss of 51 votes would not hurt him. But he would talk sternly to Weisskopf later.

Next came Alex Mieklin of the DHP, whose 63 *ja* votes quickly put Kolter's coalition back in a comfortable lead. But as soon as the Chancellor began to breathe somewhat easier, he was stunned by another defection—the 33 *nein* votes of the FDP's Otto Greim, whose brief speech of explanation resembled Weisskopf's too much to be coincidental. Kolter grew furious at the turn of events. He hardly heard the *ja* ballots of the CSP's 27 votes.

Kolter now had 301 votes. And though the CSDU's 87 would sufficiently bury the opposition, that Drexler had managed to amass 281 votes and take two of the minor parties with him was infuriating. There would be recriminations, he would see to that!

Slowly Gerhardt Woeniger rose to his feet. As the largest of the five smaller parties in the Bundestag, how many times had he relished the role of being the last to cast the votes of the CSDU. The CDU/CSDU/DHP coalition had survived for ten years as a result of his loyalty. He and Kolter had lost a few battles, but he had remained loyal all those years. Usually two or three of the other minority parties sided with them. But now suddenly an unsettling shift seemed occurring in the Kolter coalition. Only he, Gerhardt Woeniger, knew how titanic that shift truly was.

He felt himself perspiring uncomfortably. But he had made up his mind some days ago. His course was set. He wasn't going to look back now.

All eyes rested upon him. Gerhardt Woeniger, for better or worse, was suddenly the man with the fate of Germany's future in the new world order resting upon his shoulders. Not Kolter's, not Drexler's—his.

"My colleagues and friends," he began softly, trying desperately to mask his nervousness, "this matter before us today is one of far wider import than merely monetary aid to the Soviet republics. Were economics the sole issue, our decision would be relatively simple. However, what we face, whether we are fully aware of it or not, is a decision that will set us on a course for relationship with these new sovereign states to the east."

As he spoke, Woeniger's confidence grew. Kolter found himself listening in rapt attention, hardly recognizing the longtime friend he had taken for granted in the past.

"A destiny rises before us," Woeniger went on, "that supersedes this present moment—a *German* destiny. The questions we must ask ourselves, we of the newly reunited German nation, must focus intently on where *we* are going and what role we will play in the new realignments of the European community. Do we sacrifice our own assets, our own strengths, at this critical time when we are already stretched to our limits? Or do we perhaps take a long-range view, saying no today in order that a strong Germany of the future can offer more leadership and assistance in the future? These are questions it behooves us to consider as—"

If he had not already begun to divine the extent of the defection against him by the resolute timbre of Woeniger's voice and the steadfast avoidance of his eyes as he spoke, the single word *no* of the last sentence surely alerted Hans Kolter to the danger. For a moment his brain ceased to comprehend the meaning of the sounds flowing from his former friend's lips. And when he came to himself, it was only to hear the staggering words "—for all of which reasons, my party, the CSDU, has decided to cast the entirety of our ballots against the measure before us."

Woeniger sat down. Immediate shouts, along with astonished gasps broke out all over the floor, while two dozen MPs raced for the doors. The unexpected defeat of the Chancellor would make international headlines within the hour!

Kolter sat ashen and stunned. He sought Woeniger's face amid the pandemonium. But Gerhardt knew what he had done, and he would not gaze upon the victim of his treason.

Suddenly Drexler was on his feet, calling in a loud voice to be heard. "Meine Damen und Herren!" he cried. "Please—remain in your seats yet a moment more!"

Gradually he was able to restore order sufficiently to be heard.

"In spite of anxiousness to leave Berlin, I must yet ask you to remain another day," he said, still speaking loudly. "This recent vote indicates but the last in a series of disturbing fractures in the Kolter coalition, demonstrating the inability of our Chancellor to effectively govern this body. I am therefore calling upon the Bundestag to render a vote of no-confidence, so that the coalition I will be forming will be free to form a new majority in this body. I call upon you to render your decision tomorrow afternoon. At that time each of the parties will finalize this referendum upon who is to lead Germany forward in the years ahead!"

Again pandemonium broke loose, and this time did not diminish until the hall was empty an hour later.

86

August 18, 8:07 P.M. (7:07 German time)
Polish/Belorussian Border

"The car is in place!" said a triumphant voice in Polish as the young man entered the house.

The men gathered around Waclau Chmielnicki's table turned their eyes upon the newcomer.

"They saw it from the guardhouse on the other side?"

"Perhaps. I do not know. I backed up slowly, by degrees, while they were occupied elsewhere. By the time I sneaked off to the woods, the car sat only fifty meters from the fence."

"Excellent! But they did not see you?"

"I made sure of that. I slipped away when the two men had returned to the guardhouse for a moment."

"Probably to report the presence of the automobile," laughed one of the men.

"If not," remarked Bietmann, whose rusty Polish was quickly returning, "be sure they will take note of it before long. Exactly as we wish. And still there is no sign of the helicopter?" he asked the man who had just returned.

"None," the man said, shaking his head. "When I left the car, I ran to the wood and rejoined Raul and young Leeka where they were watching north of the old road. Raul said all was still quiet and that there had been no change."

There was a thoughtful moment.

"And the key?" asked Bietmann at length.

"In the ignition. No one will bother the automobile."

"Anything special I should know?"

"It's a standard Mercedes. Pull it down into first gear and it should make all the noise you want."

"How did you come by it?"

"Please, my friend," the man grinned, revealing a smile only half full of teeth. "Do not ask questions. I am a mechanic with many contacts. I borrowed it from an acquaintance who will never know."

The other Poles laughed. This was clearly not the first time their comrade's ingenuity had been used on behalf of the Network.

Bietmann nodded with a smile, joining in the fun. But when he spoke again, it was to return to the serious business at hand.

"Timing is key," he said. "We must act instantly. If they get them away from the guardhouse, everything is lost."

"Young Leeka is the fastest boy in our fellowship. He is but eleven, but he will cover the three kilometers in ten minutes."

"Ten minutes here . . . another fifteen for us to return to the site—I fear that is too long."

"For him to run to Raul's farm, and then for us to wait for Raul's wife to drive here would take much longer. Through the woods is the quickest way."

"Bicycle?" suggested someone.

"Through the woods, no bike could keep pace with Leeka's swift little legs," answered Chmielnicki.

"Hmm . . ." mused Bietmann, considering the possibilities. "Perhaps we ought not to wait. We could assemble now, where the two are standing guard. Everything would be ready the moment the chopper sets back down."

"But the only way through the fence is here, three kilometers south," objected Waclau. "Most of the rescue team must be on the Soviet side."

"Of course! How could I forget?"

"Why do we not split up now?" suggested one of the men. "Those of us going over could get through and wait in the thick shrubbery at the edge off the plain. We would only be about half a kilometer from the guardhouse. The rest of you move around and join Raul. We will await your signal, and then make our move."

"What signal?" asked Bietmann.

"A grenade. Why else have we been collecting them all day but to set off?" the man asked with a grin.

Udo and Waclau looked at one another with expressions of assent.

"The explosives are all ready?" asked Biemann.

"World War Two surplus," answered Chmielnicki with a hopeful sigh mingled with a shade of doubt. "But they *are* gathered."

"And the guns?"

"Rusty and only about half with bullets in the chambers, but we do have the three pistols we will need."

"Good. Then perhaps we should split up and get to our respective posts."

Chmielnicki and one of the others handed three of their number the old revolvers, along with several grenades and masks to cover their faces. In the meantime, Bietmann and the others were gathering up the explosives they would carry to the site on the Polish side of the border, north of the old road where the Mercedes waited.

"Remember," said Beitmann, "no grenades must get close to the helicopter. It *must* remain undamaged."

"We want no injuries," reminded Waclau. "Only loud distraction and confusion. Do not hit the guards."

"If you three on the inside can take out any of their cars without hurting anyone," said Udo, "do so. But you must not hesitate long. Get to the back of the guardhouse quickly and back to the protection of the trees. Hopefully it will be dark by then. Do not begin making your way back southward along the border until you see that chopper in the air and after me. You *must* stay hidden until he is gone." He looked intently at the three men carrying the guns.

"He would spot you even in the dark in an instant from the air if you make a run for it prematurely. You must delay until he is well across the border."

The men nodded.

"Then, shall we go?" said Bietmann.

He shook hands with the three men who would now make their way through the fence. "Godspeed to you," he said. "I will not see you again. Thank you for everything."

"And you, Waclau," he added, turning to Chmielnicki, "I pray I shall rejoin you either in Krynk, or perhaps walking in that directtion if he disables the car. Or," he added, "if he kills me, get word to Jackson and get the two of them safely to Berlin."

The Pole nodded with a smile. "God will be with you, my friend. We have prayed for the success of this enterprise and for protection. I *will* see you at the rendezvous point."

"Well, Jackson," said Bietmann, shaking his young friend's hand and looking deeply into his eyes. "I hope you do not have to wait long for the rest of us."

With those words, he turned and left the house with the four who carried the bulk of the grenades and other outdated explosives. The three others left and made their way toward the fence.

Chmielnicki and Jackson looked at one another, then sat down to begin their wait.

87

Jacob Michaels's afternoon had been uneventful. He had not found the lady.

He had been in and out all day, and it was around 6:00 when he entered the Worldwide Hotel for the last time. He went straight to his room, ordered dinner from room service, and took a cold shower, hoping it would invigorate his sagging spirits.

Here he was in a hotel filled with hundreds of Christian

brothers and sisters, yet he felt alone, as if he were on a desert island.

He missed Jackson. He hoped it was going well with him and Udo Bietmann. He paused long enough to utter a few words of prayer for their safety.

Slowly he ate his dinner, reflecting on the conference.

Evangelism, evangelism, evangelism! The very word rang through his brain.

What was it? What else could it be but telling, communicating, transmitting the *life* of the gospel to others? Yet the one means by which Jesus said His people could do that most effectively was being ignored. At least so it seemed to Jacob. In the workshops and speeches they were discussing it, analyzing it, and conducting panel discussions about it.

God! thought Jacob. *What have we become, Lord, to be so caught up in the trappings of theory that we miss the practicality of Your words?*

Of course, Christians everywhere needed Bibles and literature. The gospel had to be articulated to a non-Christian world. The *message* was certainly vital. But was money really so crucial to the message's success? Raising money was much easier when you could point to huge things "happening." It was the classic fund-raising trap of Western evengelicalism. And it was easier to give money than to give yourself. It was a vicious cycle. Donors gave money rather than themselves. Then the money was spent on external programs so that there were visible results that would please the donors.

What is the point of our in-house discussions? Do we really think we're going to evangelize the world by throwing money at it?

Arriving at no meaningful conclusions, Jacob went downstairs for the highly anticipated evening session.

The plush room was already buzzing with enthusiasm when he walked in. The exchange had been hyped for several days. No one would miss it.

Try as he might, Jacob could not unobtrusively melt into the woodwork. Wherever he went, people attempted to catch his eye and shake his hand and offer a few words. Keeping up the surface banter as well as he could, he eased into one of the back rows, wanting to keep as much of the crowd as possible in front of him so as to see its reaction.

Anthony Powers was introducing Bob MacPatrick, amid applause from the audience and beaming smiles from MacPatrick.

Jacob listened with one ear, while the other resounded with the unsettled hesitations in his heart.

". . . this man whose ministry and impact . . . more for the cause of Christ through the media and . . ."

MacPatrick stood.

". . . thank you . . . thank you . . ." he was saying, though the welcoming ovation kept his words from being heard. He smiled, waving to the crowd as if to quiet his admirers.

Jacob found himself wondering if the five thousand clapped and raved when Peter introduced the Lord, prefacing it with a recounting of all the great things He had done? When the four thousand gathered, thought Jacob sardonically, did John say, "Jews, heathen, lepers, and Pharisees—I want you to give a warm welcome today to the man who has healed thousands and who has done more to make God's voice alive in our time than anyone since John the Baptist. Please join me in welcoming—we don't know his full name yet, but we call him—Jesus of Nazareth!"

Was it sacrilege to think such a thing? asked Jacob inwardy, almost shocked with himself. Yet what else was he to think of this public adulation, and the willingness with which his colleagues basked in the glow?

O God! he cried in his heart. *When did we forget the New Testament as our example? When did we forget to model our lives after You?*

Jacob again turned his attention toward the podium. The applause had died down. MacPatrick was silent, but still the large smile spread across his face.

"Ladies and gentlemen," he began, "you cannot know the joy it brings to my heart . . . position to further the gospel in such significant ways as . . . our organization . . . thanks to the support . . . millions of dollars . . ."

Is it really about money? thought Jacob. *Must evangelism always be reduced to fund-raising? Did Jesus get pledges from the folks in Nazareth before He left home?*

". . . would like to share with you my vision for evangelism," MacPatrick continued. ". . . vision I hope you will catch sight of . . . before 2000 . . . your own ministries and people . . . get them out there raising support . . . take them the challenge of winning the world for Christ . . . time is short, my friends . . . must use every means available . . . techniques in the workshop . . . friend and colleague Hamilton Jaeger . . . so desperately needed literature and Bibles and tracts . . . money to send out teams . . . beam television programs . . . proposal of Christian satellite . . . opportunities made possible by today's media advances . . . staggering possibilities . . ."

What would Jackson think of this? Jacob wondered. *Or Bob Means . . . or Elizabeth?* What he wouldn't give for ten minutes with his friend, his wife, and his son right now! Ten minutes to pray and get their perspective.

". . . proud of what we have done . . . the Lord has called us . . . preach the gospel to every creature . . . we are taking steps toward fulfilling that . . . all our ministries together . . . I believe before the year 2000 . . . we will be able to make the claim that indeed *every* creature has heard the gospel message . . . we will be able to look the Lord in the eye . . . hear His words, 'Well done, good and faithful servant' . . ."

Bob, thought Jacob incredulously, *don't you hear what you are saying? Listen to yourself! 'I am proud . . . We are taking steps . . . We will be able to make claim . . . We will be able to . . . We are working together to fulfill the Great Commission . . . it takes money . . . My vision . . . My vision.' Bob, listen to your own words. Where is God's hand in it? Where is there room for the Holy Spirit to convict people and draw them to Himself?*

". . . which is why I am so proud to be able . . . my own personal vision . . . such a fulfillment after all my years . . ."

Jacob could take no more. Perhaps this *was* the way God intended to redeem the world. Maybe *he* was the one out of step. Perhaps, as Tony had said that morning, he was slipping a few cogs.

All at once, he rose, and bumping a few knees, managed to make his way to the aisle. A few seconds later he was out the door into the corridor. A short walk more, and he was alone, breathing deeply in the night air.

88

By the time the panting young Leeka burst through the door of the Chmielnicki farmhouse, Jackson and Waclau had been listening to the sounds of explosions in the distance for four or five minutes. They had been praying for safety, both for their brothers and their enemies since the first grenade had sounded faintly in the air toward the north.

Bietmann's instincts had been correct about the helicopter. As soon as it touched down, a flurry of activity began. The man in the chopper jumped to the ground almost before the skids were on the pavement. A minute or two later, the men standing watch by the border fence were called inside the guardhouse.

Another minute the Poles waited. Then when the sprinting Leeka was about halfway to the house to report the landing of the helicopter, the first grenade was lobbed over the fence, exploding harmlessly some twenty meters north of the guardhouse.

It was followed by another, then another, until continuous explosions were ringing the place with smoke and fire. Two of the unoccupied outbuildings were hit and were now burning. The sudden chaos camouflaged the approach of the three armed Poles, who made their way stealthily toward the guardhouse from the south. Bietmann's comrades had intentionally concentrated all their fire to the north of the building, toward which all the guards had directed their attention.

Once inside the compound, the three saboteurs were able to take more accurate aim with the grenades they carried. Two cars were blown to bits, another outer building exploded into flames, and one of the rifle towers next to the fence was shattered and fell to the ground.

The pandemonium at last gave way to some attempt on the part of the Soviet guards to protect the chopper. Between the explosions of dozens of grenades, which worked to a higher percentage than any of the plotters had expected, rifle fire could be heard, though the guards still had no clear idea where the enemy was located.

The three insiders now donned their masks. A terrible grenade blast ripped through the back wall of the guardhouse, and even before the dust and smoke had settled, they rushed through the gaping hole, weapons poised.

"Where are the prisoners?" shouted one in the best Russian he could manage.

The single guard present, a boy of not more than twenty, threw one hand in the air and pointed with the other to a door. The man who had spoken continued to wave his pistol menacingly in the boy's face while one of the other three flew to the door, tore it open, and ran inside.

"Jahn . . . come quickly!" he cried in Polish to Chmielnicki's cousin.

In less than a minute after the liberating blast, the three Poles and two prisoners—one with a well wrinkled parcel under his arm which he had grabbed from a table on the way out—were sprinting away to the south of the guardhouse, while the young guard shook with terror. By the time the others arrived, the five had dived beneath bushes and low-lying shrubbery some seventy-five meters away. They all lay motionless, praying that the last phase of the grand delusion would keep them from detection.

Seeing their escape from his vantage point with Raul on the Polish side of the fence to the north, Bietmann now bade his brothers a hasty farewell and inched his way toward the waiting Mercedes for the final and most dangerous charade of the evening.

"Give me two minutes," he said. "If I am not behind the wheel by then, I will be close enough. Then blast the fence to smithereens, and run for your lives!"

"Godspeed to you, German brother," said Raul, embracing Bietmann.

"I will make noise enough for ten escapes," said Bietmann. "You all get home and to your families before they can mount a search. Bless you all, my brothers!" he added, then hurried off.

Meanwhile, Leeka had delivered his message and was enjoying a glass of milk and piece of bread at the hand of Chmielnicki's wife, while Jackson and Waclau made their way to the breached section of fence to receive cousin and Russian fugitive.

The blast which opened a gaping hole in the fence to the north of where Raul and the others stood was so loud it was heard clearly three kilometers south where Jackson and Waclau stood. It was still louder where the three rescuers and two prisoners still lay huddled in the brush. Raul had saved two or three sticks of dynamite for just such an occasion, and the TNT now accomplished its diversionary work. The explosion was sufficiently loud to rock the entire guardhouse compound, and instantly all attention refocused toward where the smoke and debris now flew into the air. Machine-gun fire pulverized the area, even as one of the commanders shouted above the fray, "After them—after them!"

As the echo from the blast died down and a lull followed the answering rifle fire, suddenly a new and unexpected sound rent the night air.

An automobile engine roared to life. After several loud idling vrooms, its driver ground it into gear. With a screeching of tires and throttle pressed to the floor, the high-powered Mercedes tore off away from the border fence into Poland.

"The car—you let them get through and to the car! You idiots!" screamed Bolotnikov in white fury. "To the chopper!" he yelled to one of the rifle-bearing guards, running toward the helicopter. "We'll cut him off before he's a kilometer away!"

Thirty seconds later the helicopter was in the air and zooming at a mere twenty meter's elevation over the border into Poland, its spotlight focused on the once traveled border road. The low-whirring blades whooshed past the five concealed bodies south of the guardhouse, bending the grass and brush of their shelter toward the earth in windy turbulence. Still they lay low in their sanctuary.

A minute longer they waited. Then finally—as the sound of the chopper receded in the distance and as every available guard from the compound raced through the blown-open gap in the fence to the north, and as their comrades, now scattered, made their way to their homes—the five rose, and with as much haste as they could summon, ran southward to the still undiscovered border crossing that had been so vital through the years.

Chmielnicki was there to welcome them. Quickly he greeted his cousin, gathered the weapons for safekeeping, replaced the patch of fence in the hole until Jahn was ready to return home, sent his three comrades back to their homes, and hurried his Russian brother to the waiting automobile that was already idling in readiness a few hundred meters away.

They ran toward it. Hastily he shoved the Russian into the backseat, closed the door, spoke a few words to the driver, punctuated with an affectionate pat on the back through the open window, then waved them off.

They drove away from the Chmielnicki farm, then westward on the road that would lead them through the woods and fields toward Wasilkow. It was not paved, but it was the shortest route to the highway. Several men were supposed to be stationed along the way to guide them at intersections of possible confusion, for the driver of the automobile had never been this way in his life.

After about five minutes, during which, though the darkness was deepening, the lights of the automobile remained off, the driver turned around and spoke to his passenger over his shoulder.

"I don't know if you can understand me, Mr Galanov," he said. "But my name is Jackson Maxwell."

89

While Jackson and his passenger bounded as fast as they were able over the fields, the speeding helicopter had caught the swiftly retreating Mercedes.

Boring in upon it with its beam bathing the road in light, the chopper raced past, ominously banking in a descending turn, and set down on the road a hundred and fifty meters in front of the car. Amid the windy whirling of the blades and the screeching of skidding tires, the Mercedes careened sideways to a stop as the former KGB chief leaped from the helicopter and ran forward with automatic rifle in hand.

"Out of the car!" he ordered.

With eyes wide open in astonished terror, Bietmann opened

the door and stepped out, hands on top of his head, crying in German, "Don't shoot—don't shoot!"

"What are you doing here?" barked Bolotnikov.

Bietmann's answer, still in German, professed ignorance both of the words and of any wrongdoing.

"What are you doing here?" repeated Bolotnikov, attempting to communicate in Polish this time.

"Tourist—German tourist," replied Bietmann in broken Polish dialect. It was sufficient for the Russian to understand.

"What were you doing back there?" he demanded, waving the rifle in Bietmann's face angrily.

"Want to see border—want to see Russia—please, no mean harm," stammered an apparently terrified Bietmann.

"Bah! You are lying!" he spat. "Where are the files?"

"I know not what—"

"Get out of the way, you fool!" yelled an incensed Bolotnikov. With the rifle he shoved Bietmann forcefully to the ground and stuck half his body unceremoniously into the vehicle. With rapid, almost panicky motions, he glanced about, felt under the seat, inside the glove box, then in the back. Then tearing the key from the ignition, he got out, ran to the rear of the car, and fumbling a moment, threw open the trunk and quickly scanned its contents. The entire car was empty.

He ran back to where the German was now struggling back to his feet. Kicking him viciously in the side, he knocked him again to the pavement. Bietmann groaned in pain.

"Where is the file?" he screamed. "Where is Galanov? Tell me, you lying cur, or I'll kill you!"

"Please," whimpered Bietman, covering his face in pathetic fear with his hands, "please—no hurt—only want to see Russian border—want to cause no trouble—" He began to cry.

"You are lying!" Bolotnikov retreated a step, looked down at the miserable heap of humanity cowering at his feet as if contemplating whether to let him live.

Suddenly he spun around, emptied several ear-shattering rounds from his gun into the car's tires, and even as the echo was resounding through the nearby countryside, ran back to the helicopter. Knowing he'd somehow allowed himself to be duped, he cursed, both at himself and at the traitor Galanov. He lifted the

367

chopper off the ground and banked it steeply in the direction of the border.

From a secluded vantage point on the Soviet side about five hundred meters from the battered guardhouse compound, a solitary figure sat in his German automobile, watching the proceedings with interest, attempting to piece together what had transpired. Seeing the helicopter's beam moving rapidly in his direction, he decided that either Bolotnikov had been succcessful in securing the missing documents or had been suckered into a wild goose chase.

In any event, the situation bore further watching. If indeed Bolotnikov *did* possess the file, there was little he could do. If not, then most likely his pursuit would lead him into Poland.

So much the better, he thought. Warsaw was halfway home, and he had had more than his fill of Moscow. He would watch further, and then if necessary pick up Galanov's trail again.

90

To the west and slightly south of the escape site, another car sat under covering of a wooded area. Its three occupants listened to the helicopter's giant blades swooshing through the night, and watched its searchlight rove about up and down the border fence, panning the area for any sign of the escapee.

They knew it was looking for them.

For twenty minutes they sat, mostly in silence. The Pole knew a scant amount of English, but communication was still mostly carried out by signs. After two or three passes up and down the border fence for several kilometers in both directions from the guardhouse, the sound of the helicopter suddenly came nearer, circling in wide arcs in every direction. Holding their breath, they heard it slash through the air overhead and whiz by, then off to the north.

"It safe now," said the Pole in the front seat next to Jackson. "You drive on—I show you."

Jackson obeyed, started up the engine, and crept from the wood and continued along the road where their guide had intercepted them a short time earlier. It was becoming increasingly difficult to see. But they would not turn on the headlights until further away from the helicopter's range. If Bolotnikov chanced to see them, he would be able to make up the distance with frightening speed.

Their route took them across several barren fields and through another wood, until the dirt road intersected another, crossing it at right angles.

Jackson stopped. "You go left," pointed the guide. "You go five kilometers—large empty barn. Stop there. Someone come to you."

Without further words he got out and was gone. Jackson watched him as he began the long walk back the way they had come.

As they drove, Jackson had an idea. "Sprechen Sie Deutsch?" he asked, glancing back into the backseat.

"Yes, I speak a little German," answered Galanov.

"Das ist gut!" said Jackson, relieved to at last find some means by which he could communicate with his passenger.

Ten minutes later Jackson stopped the car. Quickly he flashed on his headlights for a brief moment. Yes, there could be no mistaking it—there was the barn. He turned the lights off.

All was still. There seemed to be no one there to meet them.

"We're supposed to wait here," he said. "Shall we get out and stretch our legs?"

Galanov agreed.

By now it was too dark to see clearly. "I wish I had a flashlight," remarked Jackson. "I'd like to see inside the barn."

"No time for that, friend Maxwell," said a voice he recognized. Looking up, he saw two figures emerging from the barn. Even in the darkness he knew the form of Udo Bietmann.

"Udo!" he exclaimed, rushing forward. "Where did you come from?"

"Waclau and I have been waiting for you," replied Bietmann with a laugh. "We thought you'd never get here."

Galanov now approached from behind Jackson. "So, my German friend," he said, "I finally learn your name. You're called Udo!'

The two embraced. "It is good to see you again, my brother," said Bietmann.

"Likewise," rejoined Galanov. "I must say, you have resourceful persons in Das Netzwerk. I am no longer surprised that we were not able to follow you."

"Meet the man who is responsible for engineering your escape," said Udo, bringing Chmielnicki forward. "This man's cousin was your fellow captive."

Galanov and the Pole shook hands warmly.

"Indeed it was a masterpiece of deception," said Galanov. "But how did you manage to dupe one so clever as Leonid Bolotnikov?"

"No doubt because so many were praying," replied Bietmann. "I felt his boot in my side not long ago. He is not a man I will soon forget."

"Where is he now?"

"Unless I am mistaken, he is still circling about in the helicopter. But he will find no one. All our collaborators are safely home and in their beds."

"And you three must be off," said Chmielnicki to Bietmann.

"He will not give up easily," said Galanov.

"You are but three kilometers from the highway into Bialystok," said Waclau. "There you will rest and be fed by brother Rydz."

"We must not delay," said Galanov. He turned toward Bietmann. "You remember what I told you I was investigating?"

Bietmann nodded.

"It was far bigger than I thought. We must reach Berlin without delay."

"Then we will drive all night if need be," said Bietmann.

"All of our fellowship will continue praying," added Chmielnicki. "Now, Godspeed to you, all three!" He turned back toward the barn where his car was hidden.

"Go ahead, you drive, Jackson," said Bietmann, reaching for the door on the passenger side. "You got Andrassy safe this far."

Jackson and Galanov got in.

"Blessings, brother Waclau!" Udo called out toward the retreating Pole.

"How did you get here?" asked Jackson as soon as they were underway.

"Waclau was waiting nearby the minute Bolotnikov was back

in the air in the helicopter."

"Did he hurt you?"

"Not badly. He very easily could have killed me. Instead he took it out on the car."

"Did he destroy it?"

"No. But I hope that fellow who borrowed it knows where to come by a couple of new tires. When he realized I was the wrong man, he blew them to shreds!"

91

August 18, 8:42 P.M.
Berlin

Bob MacPatrick was at last winding down his speech, coming to the part of the evening for which most of the people had been waiting all week.

". . . I want to present to our beloved brothers and sisters in the church behind what we have called the Iron Curtain for the last fifty years, a check raised by faithful believers across America—money that we hope you will use joyfully and fruitfully in building up the body of believers and churches you have so faithfully maintained during these long hours of darkness under the shadow of Communism."

He glanced behind him and turned, smiling, back toward the audience. "Ladies and gentlemen," he went on, "I now want you to meet a man I know you are eager to hear, a man who has carried the standard of the cross bravely, as you know . . . imprisoned and tortured, he never gave in to those who would destroy his faith. And so now, Dieder . . . Dieder Palacki, won't you please come . . . accept this money on behalf of Christians behind the Iron Curtain everywhere. I have here a check for three million dollars—"

At the amount, sighs and gasps and a few low whistles could be heard, all of which gave way to a round of applause, with many *Praise the Lords* and *Hallelujahs*.

He turned, expecting Palacki to shake his outstretched hand. Instead Palacki remained seated until the clapping died down.

At last he rose, came forward, and took the check, shook MacPatrick's hand unaggressively, but still said nothing. Slightly unnerved, MacPatrick resumed his seat with the other dignitaries.

Palacki stood still, looking down at the lectern before him. He appeared not even to notice the applause.

The hall was silent. Still Palacki stared downward, while the delegates waited expectantly. He had no notes. It was several long uncomfortable moments before he spoke.

"It has been a curious several days," he began. "I have been listening with great interest to the many discussions and exhortations, all with the view of promoting the Christian faith in a region of the world where one might conclude people had never before heard the name Jesus of Nazareth. Indeed, if I were as an angel whose assignment was to report to our Father the state of His people on the earth, I would conclude that a large segment of the world's population had just been discovered and therefore had no Christian tradition whatsoever.

"I must admit that when the invitation came to address this gathering, I found myself seized by a certain trepidation. As you know, assemblies of Christians such as this have not been customary where I come from, and thus most of my work among Christians has been in groups of less than one hundred.

"In the end, however, I decided to join you, for pastors and Christians from the regions formerly behind the Iron Curtain are certainly excited about the new possibilities for evangelism in our nations too.

"But as I listened to talk of money and pamphlets, of missionaries being sent and books being shipped, of pastors coming to *help* and train us in spreading the gospel, of your gospel TV and radio stations and your gospel trains and gospel trucks full of gospel paraphernalia—your badges and tracts and stickers and music and happiness books with their razzle-dazzle Christianity—a knot has steadily risen in my stomach. I have spent much time in your countries. I have been in your churches and bookstores. I have witnessed with my own eyes the trappings of your so-called spiritual prosperity, which is really no prosperity at all but a hollow, empty shell. The good news of Jesus Christ is alive and vibrant and is fully capable of feeding the hearts of hungry men and women without the benefit of your lavish commercial efforts."

He stopped to wipe his forehead, which had begun to sweat. Not a sound was heard throughout the huge room.

"What do you think," he went on after a moment, "I and my brothers Wurmbrand and Popov and Duduman and Vins and others have been risking our lives for all these years? Each of us has been imprisoned, beaten, tortured, humiliated because of our preaching of Christ's gospel. For thirty years we have smuggled and traveled, taught, preached, gone hungry, yes, and even spoken and written to you in the West. Thousands upon thousands of our fellow Poles and Russians and Slavs and East Germans have laid their lives on the line for the sake of their faith and in order to share that faith with others. I tell you, my friends, God's church is alive and well in the areas you present as lost and in desperate need. It may be small, but it is thriving because in our corner of the world it costs everything to be a Christian.

"You continue to feed your mammoth religious systems, building yet bigger and bigger transmitting stations and more television stations and publishing more books—all in the name of proclaiming the gospel. But do you ever give of yourselves? Do you come help us? Have you suffered and starved with us? How much do you really care about the people you now so glibly claim you will 'save' for the kingdom?

"Come now! Did you seriously expect an outpouring of goodwill and gratefulness from those of us in the East for the grandiose plans you make for our people? Think again, my friends, those I would still call brothers and sisters in spite of your blindness. Consider the egotism of your presumption, and the worldliness of your method."

By now the auditorium was thick with the heaviness of shocked silence. No one dared move a muscle or so much as shift in his seat. But Palacki's diatribe was not over.

"How dare you fat, contented, rich Christians of the West," he went on bitterly, "come here now and think you can throw your money and technology at us poor unfortunates and suddenly 'save the world'?

"Where have you been all this time? We needed your help and prayers and support and Bibles when times were hard! But where were you? We have been beaten and imprisoned and killed for the gospel's sake. Where were you then—when it counted? We lived our faith behind the Iron Curtain, and now that it is down, how do you know we even want you to come?

"Go back from whence you came, and spend your evangelistic, self-gratifying mammon elsewhere!"

He stopped abruptly, glared at his listeners with red face and flaming eyes, and with decisive motion ripped the check he was holding into several pieces that floated to the floor.

He stomped off the platform, leaving his hearers gaping in stunned silence.

PART 13

The Making of Disciples

92

Early the next morning, Jacob Michaels was again walking the streets of Berlin. After last night's long walk and intense study of the twenty-eighth chapter of Matthew, he was more determined than ever to find the young lady and her baby.

He went back to the first place he had seen her. She was not there. He walked back and forth along Kürfurstendammstr., then along Achimsthalerstr. and finally two or three blocks down Augsburgstr., but nowhere did he catch so much as a glimpse of the figure that was now indelibly imprinted in his brain.

At length, about 10:00, walking dejectedly in the direction of the hotel, he suddenly thought he spotted her form up ahead of him. Immediately he broke into a run. With every step he became more and more convinced that it was indeed she. She carried a small baby in one arm.

Weaving his way awkwardly through the pedestrians along the crowded sidewalk, he finally caught up with her, laying a hand upon her shoulder from behind as he did. So overjoyed that he was laughing, Jacob momentarily forgot that he could not speak to her. At his touch, she jumped with fright, glanced at him with a look of fear, then started to run away.

"Please," he said, hastening to keep up with her, "please, I won't hurt you—I want to help you."

She hesitated, looking at him carefully. The fearful expression subsided, though the look of question remained. Slowly the light of knowing spread over her face as she recalled the man who had been kind to her before. Seeing that she knew him at last, Jacob reached a tender hand forward to touch the cheek of her child. The woman watched, motionless, with cautious question still upon her face, no doubt wondering if he was going to give her more money.

He smiled at the woman reassuringly, wishing he could speak to her. He'd been looking for her all this time, but now that he'd found her he realized that he didn't know what to do.

A thought came to him.

"Stay here," he said, trying to gesture to the woman in a way she would understand. "I'll be right back." He hoped she would not leave.

Quickly he ran into a shop nearby, asking the clerk and a customer if they spoke English. All he received were shakes of the head. Hurriedly he ran into the next shop.

"Do you speak English?" he asked again. No one did.

The sidewalk was full of people shopping, looking over the goods from the street vendors. In desperation, he called out loudly, "I need someone who speaks English—does anyone speak English?"

Several people turned their heads. Two or three offered him assistance. One young woman seemed to be about the same age as the other. "Would you help me?" he asked her. "I need to talk to a young German woman. Do you speak German?"

"Yes, I do," she answered in English with a German accent.

"Would you mind coming with me? It won't take long."

She agreed.

They approached the woman with the baby.

"Tell her that I would like to help her," Jacob said.

She spoke to the desolate-looking woman.

"Tell her that I would like to buy her something to eat, if she will let me."

The poor woman stared at the other woman, then responded with a question.

"She wants to know why. What do you want?"

"Tell her," Jacob began, then hesitated. "Tell her—that I'm a Christian and that—I found myself praying for her and her baby after I saw them. I honestly want to *do* something for them."

The two women talked back and forth a moment. Then the translator said to Jacob, "She says she will go with you because she is hungry and because you were kind to her before. But she still does not understand."

Jacob said, "Thank you very much for helping me."

"That is all? You will manage now?"

"I think so. May God bless you too, my dear."

With a minimum of difficulty, Jacob led the woman down the sidewalk. For lack of a better idea, he took her to the Worldwide Hotel. Walking into the lobby, he noticed the eyes of several fellow conferees upon them. He ignored their puzzled expressions and took her straight to the hotel's cafe. She looked around nervously but followed Michaels.

He led her to a table, where they sat down. When the waitress approached and spoke in German, the young woman seemed relieved and ordered. Recognizing Michaels, the waitress spoke to him in English, and he ordered himself a bowl of soup and bread for a light brunch. He asked the waitress to tell his young guest that he would return shortly, then rose from the table.

"Make sure she doesn't leave," he said. "I will be right back."

Jacob went to the lobby to have Gentz Raedenburg paged, telling the desk attendant to have one of the bellhops come to the cafe for him when Raedenburg arrived.

He returned and sat down across from the young woman just as their order arrived. They began to eat in silence, though by now Jacob had succeeded in drawing a few half-smiles from her. To his annoyance, the next face he saw was not the one he was waiting for.

"I heard you were here, Jacob," said Tony Powers seriously, sitting down beside Michaels.

Jacob looked up with an unabashed smile.

"What—is going on here?" asked Powers, his voice containing an edge of something more than mere concern.

"What do you mean, Tony?"

"You know well enough what I mean," retorted Powers, tilting his head toward the woman.

"I'm buying this young lady and her child some lunch."

Powers did not reply immediately, but sighed and shook his head with obvious significance. "You have been acting strangely, Jacob," he said. "Hardly participating in the conference—and now this. I have to tell you, there has been talk."

"What kind of talk?" rejoined Jacob with some irritation.

"I'm sure I don't have to spell it out to you, Jacob. People begin

379

to wonder when they see one of their number acting strangely—not along the lines of acceptable behavior for a Christian leader."

"Oh, for pete's sake, Tony! *Acceptable* behavior?"

"It's no laughing matter. You're a high profile member of this conference. And when you are seen in broad daylight with—with a—what can I say, Jacob—she is nothing but a common beggar."

"Tony!"

"It is true, Jacob. Even you could not deny it."

"I wouldn't stoop to denying it!"

"You would do well to stop and think about the consequences of your actions."

"Are you saying I should watch my reputation?" Jacob was incredulous.

"I am only saying that it looks improprietous, Jacob. What does someone like you have to do with this woman?"

"How dare you, Tony!" exclaimed Jacob. "I am glad she cannot understand us! Does her poverty make her less a human being? Should I pay less attention to her because she is not beautiful, because she dresses in rags? Please—would you be so kind as to excuse us? I would like to enjoy the rest of my meal with this dear, sweet mother."

Powers rose, adjusting his tie with noticeable agitation. "Do I take it that you still do not plan to address the conference tonight, Jacob?" he asked curtly.

"I don't know," answered Jacob, tightness in his tone. "Perhaps I should let Hamilton have it. The conference deserves him."

Powers nodded, then made an ungracious exit. As he was leaving, Raedenburg entered from the lobby.

"Ah, Mr. Powers," he said, "I believe you were looking for me."

The confused look on Powers's face did not last long. In a moment Jacob was out of his seat. "It was I who had you paged, Herr Raedenburg," he said, approaching with outstretched hand. The two had met several days earlier.

"Mr. Michaels—nice to see you again," said Raedenburg. "What may I do for you?"

"I hope you might be able to help me," answered Jacob. "I have a young German woman with me whom I found on the street. I've bought her lunch, but I'm completely incapable of communicating with her. Would you mind talking to her, telling her that I have been praying for her and wish for her to be filled with the love of God?"

Raedenburg smiled. "Of course I wouldn't mind," he said. "It would be an honor to communicate such a message."

They went back to the table and sat down. The woman looked up. A momentary flash of fear passed over her, as if Jacob had brought a policeman to take her away. But Raedenburg spoke tenderly to her, and she relaxed quickly. She replied to several of his questions. Before long she was speaking with some animation.

Raedenburg turned toward Jacob. "She is a sweet young girl," he said. "Half starved and desperately lonely, but underneath I believe is shining a light that perhaps might one day soon shine for our Savior. However did you find her? The hand of God must have been in it, for she is ripe and, I believe, even eager to discover new life in the kingdom."

"It is a long story," answered Jacob. "Did you get her name?"

"Rosa. Her daughter is Rita."

"How old are they?"

"Rosa is twenty-six, Rita just over a year."

"What is her situation—why is she on the streets?"

Raedenburg sighed. "She is one of the many casualties of the new Germany," he said. "She came from the East, hoping for a better life. She met a young man who promised to marry her. She became pregnant, he disappeared, and now she is homeless—without money, without family. Her parents are both dead. Unfortunately, in our cities such stories abound."

"In the cities of my country too," said Jacob. "Can anything be done for her?"

"I believe so. If you'll sit here a moment, I'll go make a phone call."

Jacob nodded.

The German churchman returned after only two or three minutes. "It's all arranged," he said smiling.

"What?" asked Jacob.

"I have someone coming for her." He glanced at his watch.

"I'm sorry," said Jacob. "I didn't mean to interrupt your day. You must be very busy."

"No, it's not that. I had hoped to meet with Chancellor Kolter

381

soon. You have heard about the trouble he's in?"

"Not really," replied Jacob. "I haven't paid much attention to anything lately."

"He suffered a devastating and unexpected defeat in the Bundestag last evening. A no-confidence referendum has been scheduled for this afternoon. He is beside himself."

"What does it mean?"

"A no-confidence vote means he would be ousted as Chancellor. A new coalition government would be formed. It hasn't happened since 1982 when Helmut Schmidt was ousted in the same way. The whole country has been in an uproar since the news broke last night."

They spoke a few more minutes, then Raedenburg turned to Rosa and again engaged her in conversation, this time more earnestly than before. After some time he turned again to Jacob.

"Our Father is indeed watching over this young lamb," he said. "I told her of Jesus' love for her. She is a dear one, Mr. Michaels—ah, but here is my friend now," he added, rising, and walking toward the door.

A stately woman in her mid-forties had entered. Raedenburg greeted her and explained the situation. They approached Rosa. The older woman immediately picked up young Rita and began murmuring words of love to her, while Raedenburg helped Rosa to her feet. The baby, the lost young mother, and the matronly lady left the hotel together.

"What will become of them?" asked Jacob.

"Both mother and daughter will be well taken care of."

"By that woman?"

"Yes. My friend Maria will help, as will others."

"What will she do?"

"Kiss them, wash them, give them some fresh clothes, feed them, and put them to bed tonight between clean sheets."

"And tomorrow?"

"Wake them with a smile and give them bread and milk."

"And after that?"

"By then Maria will have some idea what is to be done for them. She will not turn them out, and she will nourish both bodies and souls. Maria is one of a special breed of Christ's ministers, helping whom she can. She has a home for young women to which

382

she and three other sisters have dedicated their lives and the service of their hands."

"But surely they cannot help everyone in such a city."

"They do not try. They give themselves only to those whom the Lord specifically sends. Some they keep overnight. Others in whom they see a spiritual hunger and a desire to join them in ministry, they keep as long as necessary. I have a sense your Rosa may be with them a while."

"Are there many such places of refuge in Berlin?"

"Very few. Maria's ministry is unique. She not only feeds and clothes and wipes away the tears and stains of the world's hurts, but she also exposes all who sleep under her roof to Christ's message of salvation and new birth and hope. As I said, they do not tend to pour energy into those in whom is no correspondent spiritual hunger. They believe too strongly in the gospel message to dilute it with mere good works. Theirs is a ministry of good works *unto* salvation, which is no doubt why hundreds and hundreds of young women look to Maria as their spiritual mother."

Jacob absorbed everything with the keenest of interest.

"I am appreciative of what you have done," said Jacob sincerely. "After what I have just seen, my memories of this week will be happy ones."

93

August 19, 11:22 A.M.
Berlin

Back in his room, Jacob relaxed on his bed, feeling more at peace than he had in days. He had taken part in evangelism that actually affected the life of one young woman. And now at last he felt some focus beginning to dawn as a result of the Scriptures he had been studying.

For twenty or thirty minutes he lay in prayer and thankfulness, then went back to where he had left his Bible and notes the previous evening.

He did not have long to study, however.

Suddenly, the door swung open, almost crashing against the wall. Jacob glanced up from his chair, with a smile of contentment still on his face.

There stood Jackson. Two other men followed him into the room, one of whom Jacob recognized as Udo Bietmann. Jackson spoke immediately.

"We've got to find Gentz Raedenburg!" he exclaimed, without so much as a greeting. "And fast! Do you have any idea where he might be?"

"I, uh—" said Jacob. Jackson was too agitated even to allow him to finish.

"The guy at the desk said he had seen you two together this morning."

"Just half an hour ago," said Jacob.

"We have to find him!"

"Have you tried his room?"

"We came straight to you."

"I'll call him," said Jacob, going to the phone. "What's it all about, Jackson?"

Jackson hurriedly filled him in as Jacob waited to be connected.

"Gentz," he said after a moment, "Jacob Michaels again. We have to talk. Can you get over to my room—immediately?"

Jacob was full of more questions than was possible to answer quickly. "You've been driving all night?" he asked.

"Since ten o'clock last night, Polish time. What time is it here, anyway?" Jackson said, glancing down at his watch.

"Quarter till noon."

"So we gained an hour."

"Raedenburg just told me that there was a big explosion in the German parliament yesterday, and that the Chancellor may be ousted," Jacob said.

Jackson conveyed his statement in German to the others.

Galanov let out an exclamation. "The dominos have begun to fall in Germany!" he said.

"You must all be exhausted," said Jacob.

"We stopped once when we were all too sleepy to drive," Jackson explained, "and catnapped for a couple hours. If we hadn't, we might not have discovered the tail we had picked up."

"You were being followed?"

Jackson nodded. "And not by some impartial observer either. The first thing we knew we heard a shot, and one of our windows was blown out."

"What did you do?" exclaimed Jacob in alarm.

"We woke up and drove off in a hurry!"

"Who was it?"

"We never knew."

"Did he come after you?"

"Yeah, but we had one advantage he didn't know about."

"He probably did know," interrupted Bietmann. "You remember Andrassy said that the fellow was after him."

"Right," said Jackson. "Anyway, we had the advantage of having a shrewd ex-KGB man in our car." He chuckled at the thought.

"What happened? How did you shake the fellow loose?" asked Jacob.

"It's a long story," laughed Jackson. "It cost us about an hour, and then it took Andrassy *two* hours to tell us everything he'd done between the time we let him off and when we met up again. I still don't know exactly how he did it, but we never saw the guy again."

"I want to hear every detail," said Jacob, but even as he spoke the words, he was interrupted by a knock on the door. "Perhaps later," he added. "Come in, Gentz. I want to introduce you to three men, who are going to tell you the wildest story you've ever heard."

385

94

The scene was another underground parking garage, in Berlin this time rather than Bonn. The fact that it was broad daylight contributed to Drexler's infuriation nearly as much as the news he had just heard.

"How could you have let them give you the slip?" he exploded. "I pay you top mark to not make infantile mistakes!"

"Careful, my powerful friend," seethed Claymore. "I may have failed temporarily in my assignment. But I will not be insulted—by you or anyone!"

"Bah! What do I care for your sensitivities! How did it happen?"

"How do I know? I had them dead, even got a shot off. I may have even wounded one of them. But then suddenly, the trail went ice cold."

"*One* of them—how many were there?"

"Three."

Drexler was silent, wondering what the implications could be of there being two others in the car besides the ex-KGB agent.

"Whoever this guy is," added Claymore, "he is a pro. Once I played my hand, they split up—the car went one way, your fellow the other."

"On foot?" exclaimed Drexler.

Claymore nodded.

"And you let him elude you—I don't believe what I'm hearing!"

"Their route clearly indicates Berlin as the destination. Something will turn up here. I will find them. How much time is there?"

"Time—there is *no* time, you idiot! If that file surfaces before we silence him—"

His mind spun. "Never mind," he added. Then, almost to himself, "I'll have to make *sure* the vote goes through today." Another brief pause. "Listen, get back to Moscow," he said to

Claymore. "Get on the first plane and—"

"Are you crazy? I've been driving all night."

"Sleep on the plane."

"Tonight I sleep in a hotel. I make no moves until I'm paid."

"For what? You came to me empty-handed!"

"You forget, Herr Drexler, I know your face now. I killed for you in Moscow. I watched, I listened, I learned more of your little game than you gave me credit for. You pay me today, seventy-thousand D-marks—"

"Seventy thousand!"

"Forty for the hit, ten for the attempt, ten for expenses, and ten for the aggravation you have caused me. You pay me today, or you will be the next hit. If you want me back in Moscow, it will be half in advance—and not until tomorrow."

"Look, the thing's already happening in Moscow. If it unravels and Desyatovsky's found out, I can't take the chance he'll implicate me. I need you there so that at a moment's notice he can be taken out."

"How does that help you?"

"I've seen the file on his plan. It's all Commonwealth stuff, nothing to connect it to me."

"It will be a minimum of an additional seventy thousand to remove someone of Desyatovsky's stature, especially with the heat on."

"You are venom, Claymore!" spat Drexler. "But I will pay your price."

"One hundred thousand or I go nowhere," shot back Claymore. "Seventy for services rendered, thirty as down payment on the Russian."

"Agreed. Meet me back here in two hours. In the meantime I will do what I can to insure that your failure in the matter of the file does not change the outcome of the vote in the Bundestag. If it surfaces, chances are it will take so long to sift through the channels of whatever embassy or official he tries to show it to, it will be too late to hurt me and I will already be Chancellor."

"Two hours. You will have the money?"

"I will have it. Find me the file by then, and I will double the amount. And whatever you do, make arrangements to get to Moscow later today."

"Tomorrow, my friend—tomorrow. I go nowhere before then, for *any* amount of money!"

"Bah!" said Drexler, cursing. "For half the price I could get twice the cooperation!"

"There is only one Claymore. And if you insult him again, the next hit will not be against the Russian." The hit man grinned with malice, then turned and left the basement.

95

August 19, 1:36 P.M.
Berlin

The scene was the office of German Chancellor Hans Kolter.

It was an unlikely assembly. Now that they had gained an audience with one of the world's most powerful men, suddenly the anxiety of the past thirty-six hours seemed to give way to timidity.

"Well, Gentz," said Kolter, "what's this about? It's more than highly irregular. If it weren't for my regard for you, I would never have consented to such an interview." In spite of his overbearing tone, the Chancellor was noticeably agitated and somewhat distracted.

"I know this is a dreadful time for you, Hans," replied Raedenburg. "I was planning to come see you anyway about the crisis you're facing. Unfortunately, this is even more urgent."

"How can anything be more urgent?"

"I only ask you to hear them out."

"I had to cancel an extremely important—"

"Believe me, sir," interrupted Jackson, hardly realizing what he was doing, "this is more important than anything you could possibly have going on today. It's not only important—it's urgent. It may change everything."

Kolter was shocked by the interruption. But the ludicrousness

388

of the situation suddenly seemed to strike him. If he was going to lose his job, why not spend his last day in office listening to these kooks? Ready to enjoy a good joke, he finally sat down in the chair behind his large desk, and said, "All right, gentlemen. You have my attention. Let's hear this story."

The three looked at one another. Both Bietmann and Galanov nodded at Jackson.

"You do speak English, sir?" Jackson asked.

"Well enough," answered Kolter gruffly.

Jackson drew in a deep breath, then plunged in, telling first in brief what had brought Jacob and him to Berlin, how they had run into Bietmann, and how he had been drawn into the rescue of Galanov at the border.

"I see nothing that involves me in all that," interrupted Kolter impatiently. "It is fascinating, but tell it to the newspapers."

"Please, sir, it's *why* Mr. Galanov was fleeing Russia that involves you."

Kolter nodded skeptically, and Jackson went on.

"Mr. Galanov discovered a plan, sir, that is more widespread than any of us at first believed. Just hear us out, before you pass judgment.

"There is, even as we speak, another coup attempt in progress is the former Soviet Union."

"What? I don't believe it!" exclaimed Kolter.

"Surely you are aware that the presidents of four of the Commonwealth republics are gathered today at the nuclear reactor in Kuybyshev to inspect the damage. They are scheduled to leave tomorrow morning to travel together to Kirovabad in the Caucausus Mountains. We believe an attempt will be made en route to kill them all, thus triggering a massive takeover."

"Nothing of such a magnitude could ever succeed in this new day. It's all changed, haven't you heard?"

"Not everything, sir," said Bietmann calmly. "With all due respect to your position, men in high places still lust for power."

"They could never pull it off," replied a slightly flustered Kolter.

"It is already started," said Bietmann. "You are surely aware of the labor unrest and union strike that has been called."

"Isolated incidents."

"Not isolated, sir. All planned from *within* the Kremlin."

"It could never succeed," repeated Kolter. "That's been proved."

"Unlike the previous attempt," said Jackson, "every element of society has been included—leadership from all the provinces, from the military, from finance, from industry, *all* parts of the Soviet Commonwealth are involved, even a number of foreign leaders. There are documents, sir. Would you like to see them?"

"Yes, of course," said Kolter, beginning to pay more attention.

Galanov laid out the files on the Chancellor's desk. For several minutes Kolter studied them, then barked into his intercom. Three minutes later the door opened, and a man entered whom the Chancellor introduced as his top Russian linguist and intelligence analyst for Soviet affairs.

"Max," said Kolter, "what do you make of these?"

The other examined them for several minutes, flipping through and back and forth.

"If these documents are reliable, what I make of them is as explosive as Uranium 235. Are they reliable?"

Kolter glanced at Galanov.

"Stolen from Desyatovsky's personal file," answered the Russian in German.

Kolter gave a low whistle. "Have you had wind of anything of this magnitude brewing, Max?" Kolter asked.

"Not a whisper."

A silence pervaded the room. It was Galanov who broke it.

"That is not all," he said. Slowly he pulled out several additional sheets from an envelope he had kept back, waiting to see how the Chancellor would respond to the first half of the plot. Now it was time to fill him in on the rest. "Working with Desyatovsky has been a member of your own parliament, who plans to topple your government simultaneously with the coup in the Soviet republics."

"A coup here—a takeover? Impossible! We have no military to speak of, and the parliamentary system would never produce a coup." Even as he spoke, however, the eyes of the Chancellor's mind were opening to the scope of the events of the last twenty-four hours.

"This is a plan for whatever sort of takeover your system permits," replied the former KGB agent.

"There is only one man who could possibly—who would dare such a thing," said Kolter, sagging in his chair. Suddenly it was clear.

"Is his name Drexler?" asked Jackson.

Kolter nodded.

"Klaus Drexler, head of the RDP and my sternest opposition. Last evening he rallied three of the smaller parties of the Bundestag to vote down my aid package. It undid my coalition, and he has called for a no-confidence vote against me—today. I had no idea of the magnitude of his scheme. I've been on the phone all day trying to call in old debts and gather back my support. But Drexler seems to have every angle covered."

"Perhaps I do not understand all your ways in the West," Galanov said. "I have only been out of my own country a short time. But Drexler's plan is much larger than merely a desire to take your job, Herr Chancellor. If he gets away with it, it would amount to nothing less than a coup, by *any* name. Look at these."

He produced the three remaining sheets. Both the fellow called Max and the Chancellor stared at them intently.

"As you can see, Drexler and Desyatovsky are planning nothing short of a full scale military, financial, industrial, economic, and societal axis between Berlin and Moscow. Drexler intends to cast the lot of Germany's future with the East, eventually cutting off ties with the West. After the United States and Britain and France have poured billions into the rebuilding of the nations of the former Eastern Bloc, those nations would establish a new currency, new military and nuclear alliances, creating a completely restructured financial, industrial, and transportation foundation, and pulling out of the EEC and NATO."

"I never trusted Klaus," exclaimed Kolter at length, "but—this—this is too unbelievable! Where did you get these documents?"

"They came with the rest, from Desyatovsky's private file."

"If I may speak to the spiritual dimension, Hans," said Raedenburg, "from everything I have heard and seen in the last two hours, it is my conviction that our colleague Herr Drexler is a New Age Nazi. He has obviously succeeded very well in masking it from all of us. But it now seems obvious."

"I firmly believe that his sole goal is the supremacy of a new German state, with ties looking eastward," added Galanov.

"Do you realize what you are saying?" replied Kolter.

"Of course," said Raedenburg, "But thanks to these intrepid men, you ought to be able to stop him before any further damage is done."

Suddenly the Chancellor appeared to come to attention again. His active brain began to fill with thoughts of decisive action.

"Max," he said to his analyst, "get hold of Helmut, Wolfgang, and Ralf. Get them over here immediately. Then do whatever you have to do to get Yeltsin on the phone. Say anything you have to, just get me on a secure line with him. In the meantime, I'll phone the American president. But the instant you have Yeltsin, break in."

The others suddenly felt very much out of place.

"I'll have to gather all my facts and the people I can trust," Kolter was saying. "I'm going to have to have a foolproof strategy. Klaus has more behind him than I had any idea. He's probably in the parliament building right now rallying support for my downfall. Apparently he's already got to Woeniger, Weisskopf, and Greim."

"When is the vote scheduled, Hans?" asked Raedenburg.

"Debate is this afternoon. The vote will probably be later. The session might last into the evening."

He rose and warmly shook each man's hand.

"I cannot thank you enough for what you have done," he said. "It took courage. And now, it appears, I have my work cut out for me!"

96

August 19, 4:07 P.M.
Berlin

Once again Jacob found himself walking, only this time the peacefulness of the wooded areas and small lakes and grassy expanses of the huge Tiergarten offered a relaxing diversion from the streets where he had spent so much time recently. He and Jackson had driven the couple of miles here and had been walking in the park for the past hour.

Tonight's address was drawing near. He knew that after their morning interaction, Tony would fill the speaking slot with Hamilton Jaeger.

Yet all afternoon things had been coming into focus for him with a clarity he'd never known—everything he'd heard, the events in which he'd been involved, his questions and frustrations, and all the study he'd done in his Bible. Now he was glad to be away from the city where he could put everything together.

As he and Jackson walked, a growing sense came over him that more was going on inside his heart and brain than *mere* thoughts. The feeling stole through him that the Lord was truly *speaking* to him, giving him something to be communicated to His people.

For so long now the question, "What is evangelism?" had plagued him. Suddenly the fog was clearing. There were the faces of Udo Bietmann and Andrassy Galanov and young Rosa and Rita and Gentz Raedenburg and the people he had met in Kehrigkburg—they all were staring at him with bright, radiant smiles. While he and his colleagues had been trying to figure out the intellectual components of evangelism, the answer had been right beside him all along! In Udo Bietmann's remarkable interaction with a Russian KGB agent—in the tugging within his own heart caused by the hope-starved eyes of a German beggar and her hungry daughter—in the ministry of a woman by the name of Maria—in the poor but hospitable and loving fellowship of East German believers—and most of all, in the gospel accounts of the life of Jesus—where the evangelism of involvement in people's lives was the Lord's most visible message of all.

Relationships. What else could evangelism be? What else did Jesus' life signify?

Yet if he was going to communicate anything of lasting substance and value to his fellow Christians tonight, he had to give them more than that. Jacob turned to his son.

"You know, Jackson," he said, "I need to go back to the hotel. Do you mind if I have the next three hours to myself?"

"Not at all," replied Jackson. "What's up?"

"I think I'm at last ready for the Lord to show me what He wants me to say tonight."

"Finalize your notes, huh?"

"More accurately, spend some final time in prayer. And then, yes, I suppose I'll jot down a few main points. But I think I know what He's been trying to show me all this time."

"Good. This will be the first talk of the conference I'll look forward to!"

"You'll pray for me between now and then?"

"Of course," replied Jackson. "I do every time I think of you."

"And tonight—while you're sitting there?"

"Every second."

97

The hall was full.

Anthony Powers was winding down his opening remarks. He had made a game but transparently face-saving effort to explain Dieder Palacki's bombshell of the previous night. Now he had begun to introduce Hamilton Jaeger as a last-minute substitute for Jacob Michaels, who had been, he said, unavoidably called away.

About halfway through the introduction, Jacob entered from the side room and took a seat beside Jaeger. An immediate buzzing of anticipation spread through the room at seeing Michaels. Powers did not see his arrival and continued with his introduction. Jaeger sat stone-faced. He did not appreciate Jacob's raining on his parade.

At length Powers noted the rising reaction of the crowd and seemed to apprehend its cause. He glanced behind him, saw Michaels, and said:

"Why—it seems as if Jacob Michaels is with us after all! Give me a moment, ladies and gentlemen—"

"What is this, Jacob?" he whispered curtly.

"I said I'd let you know, Tony," Jacob answered in a low pleasant tone. "Now I'm telling you, I'm here as scheduled."

"It's too late! Can't you see I'm already introducing Hamilton?"

"I'm sorry, Tony," replied Jacob sincerely. "I honestly had no intention of doing it like this. But I *do* plan to speak this evening. For the first time in my life I have something to say."

Jacob rose, leaving the conference director no alternative.

Powers returned to the lectern with Jacob at his side. "It seems there has been *another* change in plans!" he said with a wide, enthusiastic smile. "So without further words, I give you—Jacob Michaels after all!"

Jacob stood a long while after the applause had died down. When at last he opened his mouth to speak, it was in a quiet voice. Never, thought Jackson as he listened from the fourth row, had a man sounded *less* like an evangelist or a preacher.

"I've been hesitant, almost terrified of this moment for the past month," he began at length, "because so much has changed in my life in the last year. Everything in my life was shaken to the very foundation. Yet at the same time, my eyes are seeing things with a clarity I have never known before.

"I've given my life to what evangelicals *call* evangelism. I've headed an organization whose avowed purpose has been to evangelize the world. I've preached evangelistic messages. I've watched thousands go through the process we call 'conversion.' Yet now in my mid-fifties, I find myself reevaluating it all and asking for the first time the very question we wrestled with on the panel a few days ago: 'What *is* evangelism?' My prayers and thoughts and Bible study time have taken on a whole new meaning. I'm having to start from the ground floor and rebuild a faith that I'd never thought through before. And I have to say, some of my realizations have surprised me."

He paused a moment.

"What I'm trying to tell you is that I don't profess to have ironclad answers. I've just been wondering about some important issues that I have never faced before.

"With us tonight, somewhere out among you—"

As Jacob spoke, he gestured widely about the room with his hand.

"—are two men. One of them I asked to address you tonight, but he declined. He has done more for the cause of evangelism, I would venture to say, this week than all of us here combined. With the willingness to make heavy sacrifice, he laid down his life for a new brother, who is the other man I mentioned. If I told you their story, and of the life that was in fact laid upon the altar for the salvation of our new brother, you probably would not believe me.

"I have never seen these two men embrace, but they love one another as I believe Jesus loved us when He gave Himself for us. They have laid their lives on the line, and the impact of their sacrifices will extend in wider and wider concentric circles of fruitfulness in the kingdom of God.

"If I, as their brother, who has been taught to expect such things, look at them and say, 'Behold how they love—their faith must come from the Source of life itself,' then imagine how the world will respond when it hears their story and witnesses their brotherhood."

Michaels stopped, this time long enough to take a sip of water from the glass on the podium.

"Please, you must understand," he went on, "that nothing I say is meant as an indictment, except against myself. I am struggling to come to terms with what my life has been to this point, and now what I hope it can be from this day forward. So for the rest of this evening, I'm going to tell you honestly how one particular man is trying to understand the reality of what the Great Commission means for him. That man happens to be me. It is my prayer that my search, and the perspectives I am trying to sort through, will help you apply the many things you have gleaned this week."

He took a deep breath, then plunged forward into a detailed explanation of the scriptural study that had absorbed such a great deal of his time during the past week.

"When I began to pray for a larger picture of evangelism, and then began to read through the gospels again from a fresh vantage point, what struck me first was the necessity of taking the entirety of Jesus' life as my example. That is something I had never done before. I had taken the bits and pieces that happened to fit in with my own personal agenda in life, but I had never looked at the *whole* of His life.

"Jesus was involved with people face-to-face, eye-to-eye, heart-to-heart. He didn't engage in what I might call 'distance-evangelism.' Have you ever noticed how much *touching* went on around Him? When I was reading in Mark a few days ago, suddenly it started to jump out at me everywhere I looked—Jesus touching people, touching eyes, touching tongues, touching ears, and people always trying to touch Him, even His robe. He spoke to large numbers, to be sure, but He always followed it up with intense, eye-to-eye teaching, often with His disciples.

"If you look at the gospels as a whole, the large group settings are in the minority. Most of the real life-changing is one-on-one, or close to it—the woman of Samaria, Nicodemus, the man in the tombs, the Syrophoenician woman, the hemorrhaging woman. Individuals. People that Jesus interacted with personally.

"Another astonishing thing I have learned is the geography

of evangelism—*where* does it take place?

"It takes place where the people are. Jesus went to them rather than waiting for them to come to wherever He happened to be. In other words, there weren't posters up all around Galilee announcing where Jesus was going to speak, or maps of the route He'd be taking through the region of Decapolis. He was constantly on the move, seeking people. There were no radio announcements, no flyers. He went to *find* the people!

"From the beginning, when Jesus was preparing for His first four-point sermon, Mark says, 'Jesus *went into Galilee,* proclaiming the gospel of God.' He *went,* he didn't wait.

"Jesus went about doing things—on both physical and spiritual planes. He met *physical* needs, such as hunger and sickness and blindness, and He confronted *spiritual* needs, such as sin and demons and forgiveness. He did it *all.* He helped, He cured, He fed, He clothed, He drove out demons, He forgave, He ministered to every human need. And all the while He taught and spoke and called men and women to repent and believe.

"If we are to follow the example of Jesus, our evangelism must be threefold—using each hand and our mouth.

"With one hand we must meet human needs. With that hand we feed, give water, soothe, comfort, minister kindess, build, share, clothe, offer aid, and relieve suffering. We collect food and blankets and money for the needy, operate rescue missions, hold the dying in our arms, work in hospitals, and devise ways to help the homeless.

"With the other hand, a hand imbued with the power and authority of the Holy Spirit, we must take authority on behalf of people who are held captive by the power of the enemy. Jesus spent a great amount of time using His authority to do battle against Satan in the lives of those He met—casting out spirits, healing, forgiving, and otherwise freeing people from the multitude of bondages they were in. Little understood though all this may be in our day, without it, our evangelism will be incomplete.

"Finally, as both hands are ministering in these ways, our mouths must speak—proclaiming, as Jesus did, the gospel message, telling men and women to repent and believe, and helping them to understand what that means.

"Such seems to me the threefold method of evangelism

398

demonstrated by Jesus—*doing good and meeting physical needs, freeing people from spiritual bondage and oppression by the authority of God,* and *teaching them about life in the kingdom.*

"It's well and good to say, 'Well, I'll be this hand, and you be that hand, and somebody else can be the mouth. I'll have a healing ministry, and you feed the homeless, and we'll let somebody else preach and teach the Word.' Certainly the truths of First Corinthians twelve and the different parts of the body are true. Yet Jesus was himself actively involved in *all three,* and such must remain our example. First Corinthians twelve is not a justification for incomplete evangelism.

"Two-hands-and-mouth evangelism—threefold evangelism. It's not the kind of thing you can do over a loudspeaker, through a television camera, through a book or tract or a musical recording. It's not the kind of thing that feeding a hungry man will accomplish either, if you leave the God-shaped void in his lonely, unrepentant heart empty—that is a void that no amount of food will ever fill. The lost of the world need *both* eternal and material sustenance. It's evangelism of the ultimate hands-on, eye-to-eye, heart-to-heart variety. It's how Jesus told the world in three short years about His Father. It's our example!"

98

The air in the Bundestag was charged with a current of energetic expectation.

The debate had not been as heated as expected.

Chancellor Hans Kolter had scarcely been seen. Reports were circulating through the Bundestag that he would address the assembly before the day was out, though Klaus Drexler was not worried. He had spent the entire day shoring up support and was supremely confident that when he went to bed, he would be the new Chancellor of Germany.

In the seeming absence, therefore, of a last-minute effort to save his crumbling coalition, the debate had been more perfunctory than necessary, and now the vote had been called for. Kolter, however was still not present, and out of deference for their Chancellor of so many years, the MPs awaited his arrival, though with growing annoyance at the lateness of the hour, before voting him out of office.

At long last Hans Kolter, Chancellor of the United Republic of Germany, strode into the hall. His step was as confident as ever, and in his eye was not the look of anticipated defeat. He walked confidently to the rostrum, and immediately took up a position from which to address his colleagues of the Bundestag.

"I apologize for my tardiness," Kolter began. "These are more momentous times than most of you realize, and I do not refer to the impending vote which you are awaiting to dismiss me from my post."

A low murmur swept through the parliament.

"Yes, I am more than aware of the plots and schemes against me which have run through this building. However, those of you who have already put your signatures on my obituary will, I'm afraid, have to wait yet a while longer. And some of you—" he glanced in the direction of Gerhardt Woeniger, and then toward Keil Weisskopf, "—who have been seduced into participating in this clandestine plot, will rue the day you allowed such treachery to poison old friendships and loyalties."

Woeniger could not return his gaze, but looked away with mortification.

"My afternoon has been spent attempting to avert nothing short of an international incident, indeed, an international crisis. I have been on the phone with the American president, the British prime minister, and President Yeltsin of Russia, about a matter, as I said, more momentous—"

He was interrupted in the midst of his discourse by a voice he knew only too well.

"Come, come, esteemed Chancellor," said Klaus Drexler, who had risen to his feet. "The defeat of your ill-advised aid package hardly qualifies as an international crisis, for which you need to begin telephoning all the leaders of—"

"I do not refer to the defeat of the bill!" boomed Kolter.

"Then what, pray tell, *do* you refer to?" asked Drexler. His tone dripped oily sarcasm.

"You know well enough, *esteemed* Herr Drexler!" shot back Kolter.

Still Drexler had no hint of just how thorough was Kolter's knowledge of the plan. Nothing in the Chancellor's words indicated to him the danger that lay ahead for him. He was beginning to grow angry at Kolter's bravado.

"Enough, enough!" he said, his voice now icy and demanding. "A vote has been called for. We have waited long enough. Your coalition has collapsed. We, your colleagues, judge you unfit to lead, and demand that you step aside, or else face an immediate vote of no-confidence."

"Hear, hear!" called out scattered voices from the RDP.

"Your reign has ended, Kolter—resign or be ousted!" said a loud voice.

"Do you hear them, sir?" said Drexler. "You can stall no longer with your tactics of magniloquence. The Kolter dynasty is over. Resign or be humiliated by a vote! The future lies with the coalition led by the RDP!"

Now cheers burst from Drexler's allies and Kolter's longtime political adversaries.

But even six hundred MPs could yet be silenced by Hans

Kolter's loud voice and towering presence.

"Silence!" reverberated his baritone through the great hall, accompanied by his hand slamming down onto the rostrum with angry finality. "You, Klaus Drexler, are a traitor! I call you what you are to your face. A traitor to this body and to your nation!"

As he spoke, he turned and strode angrily forward onto the floor where his colleagues sat. "I will resign when the membership of this body indeed deems me incapable of holding together a coalition. But not until the full truth is known!" he thundered.

"Truth!" spat Drexler. "Spare us your sermons!"

"I will preach no sermons, Herr Drexler," said Kolter, now standing face-to-face before his accuser, "but your colleagues will know the truth of your treason, if *you* do not resign immediately."

"Have you lost your senses? I have not the slightest intention of resigning! I shall be Chancellor by this time tomorrow."

Kolter did not reply. Instead, he calmly pulled from the inside pocket of his coat a single piece of paper and laid it face up on Drexler's desk. Drexler glanced down at it quickly.

"Now, perhaps," said Kolter in a low voice, "I might be able to convince you to have a few words with me in private?"

Drexler met his eyes with his own, squinted in narrow hatred, then nodded. Kolter led him out the nearest door. An immediate uproar of wonder burst through the parliament.

In the corridor, Kolter wasted no time.

"We know everything, Klaus," said the Chancellor. "We know the entire scope of the plan. All of the principals in the Soviet Commonwealth are being rounded up even as we speak. The leadership and military are in safe hands. President Yeltsin is on his way back to Moscow. The other presidents are likewise safe. And your friend Desyatovsky is under arrest and awaiting further orders from Yeltsin."

"What has all this to do with me?" said Drexler cooly. "Why should events in the Soviet Commonwealth concern me?"

"Come, Klaus, it's all over. The coup has failed. Desyatovsky has revealed everything and has sung an interesting tune regarding his chief accomplice."

"Why, that no good—"

"Please, such anger does not become you. Even without Desyatovsky's revealing all about your Claymore, the things you have done, both here and there—even without all that, Klaus, we have his complete file. He never recovered it. I understand your man was on it too, but he likewise failed."

"I have no idea what you are talking about," said Drexler, trying to regain his calm.

"Of course. But you see, the file, almost by a miracle, found its way to my office this very morning. Don't you see the irony of it? *Your* scheme found its way to *my* office!"

"Whatever Herr Desyatovsky might have been trying—"

"Oh, Klaus—Klaus! Do not continue the charade. Your Russian friend kept meticulous notes. He documented everything—every conversation, every phone call. Did you know that he recorded most of his talks with you? We have the transcriptions—word for word. Klaus, don't you understand? It's over. You have nothing left to do but resign."

Drexler's face was ashen. "Proof—I want to see proof!" was all he could say. His voice came in a gasp, barely above a whisper.

"You shall see it all," replied Kolter. "But in the meantime—" he pulled several more papers from his pocket, "—this should give you a fair idea that I am not bluffing."

Drexler grabbed them hastily. His face grew whiter still.

"What do you want me to do?" he whispered at last.

"For the good of the country, none of this will be made public. Mr. Yeltsin has agreed that such a course would be best for the sake of his Commonwealth also. Therefore, you will be allowed to resign your post in parliament with dignity, if you do so immediately, without explanation. If you do not, or if you delay, I cannot save you from the consequences."

Drexler sighed deeply, then looked into his Chancellor's face with resolve.

"My resignation shall be on your desk in the morning. You may make it public any way you see fit."

He turned and walked briskly down the corridor and out of the building.

Kolter watched him go, then not without a sense of sadness reentered the Bundestaghalle. When he came in alone, a renewed round of questions and exclamation resounded loudly through the room.

Kolter walked straight to the front of the hall to the rostrum, where he stood awaiting quiet. On his face was not a look of victory but of grief. His colleagues seemed to sense it. No more heckling came, even from the RDP side.

"My friends and colleagues," he said simply. "I ask you to postpone your referendum on your confidence in my coalition for at least twenty-four hours. Tomorrow, I request you, Gerhardt, and you, Keil, to see me in my office. Despite what you have done, I still consider you my friends. If the three of us are unable to hold our coalition together, then I will resign by this time tomorrow. All I ask for is twenty-four hours."

He paused, then continued, looking around to the entire assembly as he spoke. "Our colleague Klaus Drexler of the RDP has informed me of his intention to resign as Member of the German Bundestag, effective tomorrow."

Exclamations, and shocked questions, and excitement burst from the floor.

"Please," said Kolter. "I am nearly through. I trust this news may alter the position some of you may have on the no-confidence vote. In any case, you will have twenty-four hours to decide whether you want me to continue as your Chancellor or not. I would ask the president of the Bundestag to excuse my presence for the remainder of the session."

Without awaiting a reply, Kolter left the hall as quickly as he could, looking neither to the left or the right. He hated the black spot in his nation's past and loved his country for the democratic principles it now stood for too much to relish this victory over a man who had nearly succeeded in taking it down.

A roar of astonished disbelief followed him.

99

Back at the conference center, Jacob Michaels turned his focus in a new direction.

"It is time for us to look at how Jesus completed His public ministry. What were His final words to His disciples? And thus, what was His final injunction to us as well? Having lived His life and given His teachings and example, what single message did He leave us with?"

He paused briefly, then went on.

"It's one familiar to us all," he said. "We call it the Great Commission. It is a command He has given us, and therefore we do right to take it seriously. And upon it we have built much of present-day evangelism as we have come to know it."

From where he sat listening, Jackson Maxwell's heart swelled with mingled pride and awe. It was all he could do to keep the tears from spilling from his eyes in a flood. This man, whom no one else in the whole room knew as his father, had a short time ago been broken upon the altar of failure and humiliation. He had come to Berlin full of questions and unresolved quandaries of faith. Yet all the while the molten metal of his deepest being was being burned in the refining and purifying fires of the Father's foundry. Now suddenly the mettle of the man's character seemed to have coalesced and emerged, as from out of his mouth came humble words of piercing wisdom and truth. Even as Jacob spoke, the stature of his bearing seemed to increase, as with prophetic voice he gave forth from the deep and heretofore hidden reservoirs of his being. What anyone else in the room was thinking, Jackson did not care. His father's bold words were unmaking, remaking, and penetrating into him like no address he had even heard. As he listened, he recalled Bob Means's words about restoration of a year earlier. *Surely,* he said to himself, *the restoration of Jacob Michaels is nearly complete. Thank You, Lord, for Your amazing work of transformation. Use my father to accomplish Your purposes!*

Jacob continued speaking, oblivious to the reflections of his son.

"I've preached to hundreds of thousands. Millons of people have read my books and listened to my tapes. Yet I do not think that in almost thirty years of what we call public 'ministry' I've ever—in a personal, face-to-face way like Jesus did with Nicodemus—made a single disciple for my Lord. Can you imagine—"

Jacob stopped, and turned briefly away from the microphone, suddenly choked with emotion. The entire auditorium was still and silent, every eye beholding his inner struggle.

"—can you imagine," he repeated, his voice on the edge of cracking, "how that shames me? Can you imagine—what a hypocrite I feel—what a fool—how for all those years I deluded myself into thinking—"

Again he stopped. The tears flowed in earnest now.

He stood, waiting, but unable to speak. He pulled a handkerchief out of his pocket, wiped his eyes and nose, and struggled to pull in a breath to steady his emotions. Hundreds of watching eyes had never imagined a man of Jacob Michaels's stature weeping in public. Many themselves experienced the involuntary flow of tears. Others sat watching in astonishment or discomfort. A few were thinking that this was hardly the place for him to air his personal dirty laundry. But no one moved a muscle.

"Forgive me," Jacob said softly at last. "I didn't plan this. Sometimes these moments—just come over me without warning as I—"

He turned aside once more, but it only lasted a moment.

"What I have been attempting to convey," he went on, his voice soft, "is that it's all about making disciples. *That's* what Jesus told us to do. And I'm simply not sure how well we've been doing that—speaking for myself and the vantage point I represent.

"When I realized Jesus was commanding me to make disciples instead of preach, I faced a dilemma. It was this: I realized I didn't know *how*!

"I reflected long and hard on this. I grew troubled. Not only did I not know how to make disciples, I realized I didn't know what commands Jesus gave that the disciples were to obey.

"Of course I knew a few of them—but *all* of them! I knew He told men to repent and believe. I *thought* He had commanded us to preach the gospel but was now discovering maybe that wasn't as high a priority as I had assumed.

"So I took it as a challenge to find out what those commands were.

"Several nights ago, after walking in the streets of this city, I started through the four gospels again from the beginning, right here in this hotel. I read them with a fresh enthusiasm as I never had before.

"Simply put, I kept a tally sheet, a scorecard of the things Jesus told His followers to do. It was one of the most remarkable Bible studies I've ever done in my life. The results astounded me!

"Now I'm not claiming this to be authoritative. I went through the gospels with great haste. But for the purposes of *my* insight into Jesus' commands to me, I think that study is going to change my life and outlook on Scripture forever.

"I noticed, first of all, how much of Jesus' time He spent doing 'unspiritual' things. And His instructions were practical, not philosophical. He linked his principles with earthy, physical, gut-level realities of life.

"Jesus' instructions were down-to-earth. He said basic things about how we are to live: do good to your enemies, treat others kindly, visit those in prison, lend money when asked, show mercy, be kind, don't envy, speak graciously, give abundantly, rejoice in everything, feed the hungry, don't be pious, keep your mind pure, don't insult one another, don't judge, return good for evil, do to others what you would have them do to you. Neither is there an emphasis on *mere* practical goodness. Alongside 'feed the hungry' are commands to trust God, follow Jesus, and pray.

"The very familiarity of His words tends to obscure how astounding they are. If the Great Commission is centered here, then we have to completely reorient ourselves! What have we been doing all this time? Those have not been the traditional measures we have used to determine progress in the spiritual realm."

Jacob looked up from the page.

"I'm sure you all realize by now that you're not listening to an expert or a biblical scholar. Many of you may wonder why such a neophyte as I was asked to speak on the final night of a conference on evangelism. But *if* I know anything about evangelism now, it's certainly much more clear to me than it was a month ago. I think finally the words of the Great Commission of Matthew twenty-eight, nineteen and twenty are coming into focus for me. We are to make disciples, not converts. We are to teach people to listen carefully and to love God and to speak graciously and to give to the poor and to do good to their enemies and to live holy lives. *That's* what Jesus commanded us to do. We are to teach people to obey *everything* He commanded—by His word and by His example, including laying down their lives. Go into all the world and make disciples, teaching them to pray, to love, to be alert, to put others first, to be servants, to have faith, to be patient, to do good, to be humble, to be at peace with one another.

"That's how the Great Commission should be read. And we should close a reading of it with the words *and teaching them to lay down their lives, by laying down our* own *lives for them.*

"As much as I do not care for simplistic formulas or lists, I'm going to try to boil down everything I've said, as much for my own benefit as yours. This is not so that we can leave here with a seven or ten-point *program* guaranteed to make evangelism happen. But I think there are some general foundational principles that need to be infused into our efforts."

Jacob adjusted the paper on the podium and then read the following:

1. A verbalized articulation of our message. That entails all the principles of God's kingdom, especially *repentance* from sin and *belief* in the life Jesus brings.
2. A four way involvement with people:
   —*Going* where they are and where they live
   —*Personal,* close, intimate relationship
   —*Diverse involvement* with many types of people
   —*Spontaneous* settings giving rise to varied interaction
3. A threefold method of ministration:
   —Meeting *physical needs*
   —Bringing authority to bear against *spiritual bondages* of the enemy
   —*Explaining* and clarifying Jesus' teachings
4. Fulfilling the Great Commission of Matthew 28:18-20:
   —*Go* to the world.
   —*Make disciples* of men and women.
   —*Baptize* them.
   —*Teach them to obey* all the commands of Jesus.

"In closing, I just have to say that I don't think that much of what I've heard here in Berlin encompasses this full evangelism that is our calling. I've heard about many programs and ideas and opportunities, and there has been enthusiasm in abundance.

"But if we truly want to evangelize the world, it's going to happen when we start doing what Jesus did—getting involved in people's lives.

"I'm sorry to have to end on a negative note, but until we bring all these aspects into it, I'm afraid we will be merely beating the air, as Paul said, and talking largely to ourselves."

Jacob gathered up the few papers he had and walked away from the podium.

100

August 20, 10:45 A.M.
Berlin

Suitcases in hand, Jackson and Jacob made their way into the lobby of the Worldwide Hotel to check out. As eventful as their time in the German capital had been, they were looking forward to the drive west and the two days they had prior to their flight home. It would be good to walk the fields of the Folenweiter farm again, with no streets and noise and people around, and to let the calm of the countryside again wash over their spirits.

Hoping to slip out of the lobby and to their car unnoticed, Jacob's countenance sank momentarily when he heard his name called the moment they had turned from the checkout desk toward the door.

He turned, and immediately his face brightened. Toward him walked Trevor MacVey.

"I've been hoping to find you," he said shaking both their hands. "I went up to your room but found you had already left.

I'm glad I caught you."

"So am I," replied Michaels. "I had hoped to get together with you some time."

"I've got to tell you," said MacVey sincerely, "your talk last night was powerful. I commend you for having the courage to say what you did."

"If you could have seen my knees shaking," laughed Jacob, "you might not think it so courageous!"

"I mean it. You addressed some things that needed saying. I was proud of you, if it's not too presumptuous for me to say it."

"Thank you. I appreciate your kind words."

"What kind of response has there been?"

"Oh, I don't know. Mixed, I suppose. A few favorable comments here and there."

"From your—your *high-level* colleagues?"

Again Jacob chuckled. "No, not much response from any of them. From what I understand, Powers and MacPatrick had spent the whole morning trying to patch it up with Palacki by phone and trying to get him back here to accept the money and make amends."

"They probably want a good photo op," put in Jackson.

"I'm sure you're right," added Jacob. "A face-saving gesture so the outburst of the other night can be downplayed and written off to Palacki's temperamental nature."

"Have you seen Jaeger?"

"No. Hamilton's probably scurrying around signing up last-minute converts to his unity scheme."

Michaels sighed. "You know, somehow I have the feeling that nothing much will change. Most people will go home and continue doing exactly what they were doing before they came. The liberals will still try to feed the world's hungry without offering them eternal life. The conservatives will still talk about saving a billion souls by the year 2000 with money and high-tech evangelistic techniques. And the balance that you spoke of, MacVey, will still be as invisible as it has been for most of the past two thousand years."

"I hope you aren't discouraged, Mr. Michaels. I genuinely believe you may have set some things in motion here this week. Perhaps those who had the ears to hear and who will respond to your message may be few in number. Their responses may not be full of splash and noise, but you can take heart that there will be a profound impact from your words in time."

"I pray you are right."

"Listen, I know you are leaving. But I want to give you both my phone number. Get in touch with me in the States. I do want to spend some more time with you, both of you," he said, looking at Jackson, then back toward Jacob.

"I would like that," replied Jacob. "It would be a great honor for me."

MacVey wrote down his number on a piece of paper and handed it to Jacob.

They all shook hands again, then parted.

"I'm going to miss some of these people," said Jacob as they exited the lobby and headed for their car. "Udo and Gentz in particular. Whoever said there weren't spiritual men in Germany! Those are two of the most remarkable men I've ever met."

"I have the feeling we'll see them again," said Jackson.

"What about you—besides Anna, of course. I *know* you're going to think about her all the way home!"

Jackson smiled. "I developed quite an attachment to Andrassy too. He'll be hard to forget!"

"I'm certain we'll hear from all of them. I know I'd like to get both Bietmann and Galanov to the United States. Westerners need to hear the part of their story that *can* be told."

They had breakfasted with Raedenburg, Bietmann, and Galanov, and said their good-byes to their three new friends. Raedenburg had told them briefly of the political fallout from last evening's explosive session in the Bundestag. The last they had seen them, the three brothers in Christ—a West German, an East German, and a Russian—were walking off together. Raedenburg had plans, he said, and they were going to spend the day together, before driving out to Bietmann's home for supper and an evening with the people of his fellowship.

"Speaking of the part that *can't* be told, did you see the papers this morning?" Jackson asked.

"No, why?"

"Well, what was behind Drexler's resignation didn't come out of course, but the city's in an uproar anyway. Kolter's riding high."

"Was there any word about the Soviet side of the thing?" asked Jacob.

"I just scanned the first couple pages quickly. No, there wasn't much. It was all downplayed. The summit between the presidents cancelled, Yeltsin back in Moscow, I don't even think Desyatovsky's name was mentioned. I doubt anyone will ever know how close the Commonwealth came to blowing apart."

"What about your other friend—the guy in the helicopter?"

"Bolotnikov. Nope, no mention of him either. But Andrassy says we'll hear about him again."

"How so?"

"I don't know. He just says the guy has an uncanny knack for landing on his feet no matter how many are falling around him."

"Well, I hope *I* never see him."

They loaded their luggage into the car.

"You want to drive?" asked Jacob.

"I'm still bushed from that drive across Poland."

"You trust me behind the wheel?"

"You bet!"

101

August 23, 11:05 A.M.
Frankfurt

Jackson Maxwell and Jacob Michaels settled into their seats aboard the Lufthansa 747 flight for the return trip to Chicago.

This time, however, no thoughts of international intrigue, espionage, and mystery occupied Jackson's mind. He had had enough of the real thing! Now he had to try to figure out how to write about it—and the conference—without divulging politically sensitive information regarding which Chancellor Kolter had sworn them all to secrecy.

"How can I possibly tell the story," he asked his father,

"without actually telling it?"

"You'll come up with some creative way," replied Jacob. "Write about the conference. After all, that's why you were sent."

"Too boring—after all we went through *away* from the conference!"

"Does that evaluation cover *my* speech too?"

"I didn't say that." Jackson laughed.

"Write about the people you met. Andrassy, Udo and his wife, the fellowship, Trevor MacVey—Anna."

"I could hardly write about *her*," said Jackson. "My mind's too occupied with trying to figure out where she might fit into my life to make her a part of the story."

"That bad, huh?"

"The thing that's so unsettling is how different she is from any young woman I've ever met in the States. Surely you could see it—the calm, the peacefulness, the quiet demeanor, not a hint of the flirting games. Her simplicity struck me instantly—no perfume or makeup, no self-consciousness, no nervousness. She was just—I suppose, *real*."

"Why is that unsettling?"

"I don't know. Maybe that's the wrong word. What I mean is that I can't get her out of my mind. Somehow I sense that down deep we both shared a similar goal, the desire for no facades, for wanting to get right down into the bedrock of who we really were— not relating as a man and woman, but as two Christians, as brother and sister."

"I see nothing in that to be nervous about."

"It's not nervousness either. Let's just say I'm intrigued. I find myself wondering if the differences I see in Anna are because she is European, or because she was raised behind the Iron Curtain, or because she is a Mennonite. I've never known a Mennonite before. Even at home I've been aware that the agrarian lifestyle tends to produce a deeper reality in men and women, producers rather than consumers. Yet in Anna it seemed even more focused. What can I say—it was attractive, appealing."

"Perhaps it is because there is a spiritual bond, as you said, of shared heart motivation, that transcends those other differences. Maybe its not her setting at all—but just *her*, the person she is."

"If you're right, then it *is* unsettling."

"Why?" asked Jacob.

"Don't you see?" answered Jackson. "If there is that kind of a bond between us, then how can I not think about seeing her again?"

"Hmm," replied his father, with the hint of a smile. "I see what you mean."

"In any case, you can see why *she* can't be part of my article."

"I do indeed," said Jacob, smiling broadly now. "Who'd have thought it? We go to Berlin for an evangelism conference, and my son flies home heartsick! In love with a young Mennonite lady from East Germany!"

"Cut that out!" Jackson laughed. "Come on, you've got to help me decide what to focus on for my article. If I don't put together some notes and half an outline before we land, McClanahan will never send me on another assignment like this."

"OK, OK," said Jacob, "I'll try."

"All right," he said, "how about Maria's ministry in the streets of Berlin—say!" he added, not waiting for an answer, "you don't suppose we could do something like that with ETW in Chicago, do you?"

"Anything's possible."

"I'm going to talk to Bob about it! But on to your article—how about contrasting what used to be East and West Germany and the spiritual climate of each, the people we met?"

"Everything you say is good," said Jackson. "Every idea could be an article in itself. But I was supposed to cover the conference, not all those other things."

"The conference—there were two separate stories going on, weren't there—the conference and the political scenario. Yet how could you possibly write about the conference *without* mentioning the rest?"

"That's exactly it," said Jackson. "They are intrinsically inter-twined."

"Parallel stories, going along right beside each other."

"There's the angle for the story! Parallel but separate, like two train tracks. Linked, *both* part of the whole picture, impossible to separate—yet never intersecting! It's the perfect analogy of what happened to us."

"There's the writer coming to life," laughed Jacob. "But I'm not sure I follow. You'll have to explain."

"Don't you see—it's just like Christianity, the church, going along beside the world—*in* the world, but not impacting it. Two separate tracks that *should* be completely intertwined but go along side-by-side never meeting."

"What does that have to do with the conference?"

"Everything! Here we were involved in a political plot of global magnitude, but none of our fellow conferees, other than Raedenburg, will ever hear a thing about it. Galanov and Bietmann's story, too, is on a track separate from what most of them will ever give much attention to. It's a sad commentary about the impact of Christendom's efforts that the world remains so untouched. And likewise, we were involved in a huge worldwide evangelism conference of eternal significance, but the people walking by on the street outside the hotel had not the slightest idea. Coexistent but nonintersecting stories. Double oblivion, each side toward the other."

"There's too much," Jacob said at length.

"Too much what?"

"Too many ideas, too many people, too many parallel stories and tracks. Too much to fit into just one article. You'll have to tell McClanahan it can't be done."

"What's the solution then?"

"Simple—you'll have to write a book."